I0451357

Gatekeepers

by

Sam Ferguson

GATEKEEPERS

Text copyright © 2017 by Sam Ferguson
Illustration copyright © 2017 Dragon Scale Publishing
All Rights Reserved

Front cover art by Luciano Fleitas
ISBN:1943183414
ISBN-13:978-1-943183-41-8

CONTENTS

Other Books by Sam Ferguson

Other Books by Dragon Scale Publishing

Codex of Light by E.P. Stein

The Protector of Esparia by Lisa M. Wilson

Kingdom of Denall Series by Eric Buffington:
The Troven
Secrets at the Keep
The Changing

Tales of the NoWhere and NeverWhen by Jason Hauser
Wisp the Wayfinder
Puck the Pathwinder
Nobb the Nightbinder

Also available exclusively on the
Dragon Scale website:

Tharzule's Tome of Wishes by Malinda Smiley

Orcs and Elves by Bethan Owen

CHAPTER 1

Nobody ever expects their life to change so drastically, especially not on a plainly boring Tuesday in the beginning of April. The bad stuff is supposed to come on Mondays. Everyone knows that. The good things happen Friday, Saturday, and Sunday. But Tuesdays? Most people forget about Tuesday altogether. That's why so many people get days in the middle of the week mixed up. Not me. I always remember Tuesdays.

Tuesday is the day my life changed forever.

Right now I am sitting at a desk. There is a pen and a pad of paper in front of me. The detectives in their cheap off-the-rack suits have been gone for an hour or so. They want my story. They want to know how it all began and why I was picked up where I was today. I could tell them, but they wouldn't believe me. Who would ever believe that someone like me would ever do what I have done? Then again, I suppose it is usually the quiet people you have to watch out for.

I decide to take the pen in hand. I'm not sure what I am going to write. Should I put everything down on paper? All of it? Or should I trim it down so I don't make their bureaucratic supervisors' heads explode? If I tell them everything today, then their world will never be the same. I will transform their lives exactly like mine was altered.

Nothing will ever be the same again. In some ways it may be better, but it will be far worse in many more ways. This is not an easy decision to make. In my hand is a pen, and the words that come from that pen will decide a turning point in human history, for better, or worse.

Funny thing, today is Tuesday as well.

*****

It was a bright, warm Friday in June when I was released from county jail. I had spent the last eight months of my life in that cold, cement building. Eight months of sitting alone in a six by four cell. Could have been worse though. Had the prosecutor been able to prove anything, I would be moving to a higher security facility just outside of Dallas for the rest of my life. Seeing as how I am thirty-two years old, I would likely have been sitting there for several decades. Then again, it was Texas. They probably would have fast-tracked my butt toward the death penalty.

Good thing they couldn't prove my guilt.

The thing was, I did kill a man, or at least it was something *like* a man, but it wasn't the man they said it was, and it sure as heck wasn't murder. I've never been a violent person. Sure, I'll play first-person shooter games or squeal like a kid when I get a great cut-scene as my character on the latest fantasy RPG gets a sweet assassination, but in real life, not at all. I get nervous just making phone calls. I've been in a few scrapes, but only when I had to. Never started fights, and I tried to avoid them if at all possible. Getting jumped a few times in elementary school by a couple dozen kids will either turn you into a great brawler, or it will knock the violence out of you. I was more the latter. A well-timed joke, especially a self-deprecating one, can often end a fight before it's begun. Quick feet help too.

I know what you're thinking, what kind of elementary school did I go to to have such encounters? Well, I was poor growing up. Sometimes even a white kid can be a minority in some places. Other than that, I had a fairly nerdy appearance when I was younger. My first experience of being jumped by a group came in third grade. My first knife fight came in fourth grade. We moved around a lot though, so even when I won my fights, I still had to start all over as the new kid at some other forsaken dump where the teachers were frankly too tired to babysit us all the time. Shoot, I even had one teacher pay a kid to attack me once. I guess the going rate for beating up nerds was $15.

I guess that was why it was so ridiculous that I was here now. Collecting my personal items back from the county jail after being

2

accused of murder. The trial had been televised, given the nature of the circumstances. That had been enough to end my marriage. It's hard enough to go through an eight month ordeal like that yourself, but then to see your wife and kid mobbed by reporters... I couldn't blame her for leaving. It was the right thing to do. She moved back in with her parents and her two younger siblings. The apartment we had been renting was now being rented to someone else.

I was two states away, in Texas, signing for my cheap $20 watch I had bought from Target the day before coming down to this miserable state, and wondering what had happened to the $150 running shoes I had come in with.

"Sorry, sometimes things go missing," the fat cop said from behind the thick glass. He gave me one of those looks, you know the kind, a twisted smile that told me the "lost" shoes were likely on his feet right now and both of us knew there wasn't a dang thing I could do about it. "Sign here for your watch."

"My wallet?" I asked, trying to forget about the shoes.

The cop nodded and pulled a zip lock bag from a plastic basket nearby. "One wallet, black. Contents inside consist of a Utah driver's license, three dollars, a picture of a toddler..."

"My son," I said. It was enough that I had been here for months and lost my family over everything. I wasn't going to accept the term "toddler" from this judgmental prick.

"A picture of your son..." the cop said with a shrug.

That's better. I continued to sign the four different signature spots on the form and took my wallet and watch back.

"I'd give you your clothes, but they were in evidence for months with that blood all over them," the cop said. "I suppose you can have them if you want."

I had already had a pair of jeans and a t-shirt sent to me, so I shook my head.

"I still don't know why they didn't fry your sorry behind," the cop said with a sigh as he took the forms back. "I know you're guilty."

I glowered at the man. He had no idea what he was talking about.

I was escorted through a short series of halls and brought outside by a tall officer with a build much bigger than mine, and that was saying something, because I weighed in at a healthy two-hundred and seventy pounds. Sure, I always had a bit of fat around the edges, but I am built solid and thick. Wide shoulders, a 52 inch chest, and 19 inch biceps, and that was measuring before a good workout.

I had found out around thirteen that stopping fights was much easier if you looked like you could beat a bull with your bare fists. So, I have spent six days a week in the gym since my thirteenth birthday. I'll say this, it works better than jokes or trying to run away.

I remember one time I went to the gas station as a sixteen year old. I was in a pink rental car, my mustang had been in the shop. A group of Hispanics started approaching me with their baggy t-shirts and their blue bandanas tied around their heads and elbows and their boxers hanging out the back over their sagging jeans. Now don't get me wrong, I try not to judge people by appearance, but sometimes you just know. You get that thick feeling in your stomach, and they look at you with pure anger in their eyes. Of course, it didn't help that the knife fight in fourth grade was started by a couple of Hispanics that didn't like me. Anyway, I stepped out of the tiny little ford escort GT and all four of them stopped. I'm not sure what they had said before, but when I got out all I heard was "Ah, sheet, he's big man. Let's go." They turned and left just like that.

Like I said, the gym worked for me.

I suppose it might also have contributed to my current predicament though, looking back on it all. It's hard to present yourself as an innocent man caught up in the wrong circumstance at the wrong time when they have to give you a triple-x jumpsuit and use the big hand cuffs. I couldn't blame the jury for doubting as long as they did. I was just happy that enough of them came around to my side of it all.

Anyway, all this was to say that if the cop squeezing my arm made me feel small, then you have to understand he was humongous. He took me down to the bottom of the steps in front of the county jail house and let me go.

"Now stay outta trouble and don't come back, ya hear?" the giant cop said.

I nodded absently and rubbed the spot on my arm where he had been holding me. I looked out and saw only one car, a black town car with a tall man in a slick suit standing against it with his arms folded. Even on my best days, I wouldn't have any such car waiting for me. My bet is he was here for Slim, the "innocent" drug dealer I had met on the inside. Nice fellow, actually, if you can get over the squirmy feeling he puts in your stomach by talking to you. He was acquitted and scheduled to be released the same day. Funny that a drug dealer peddling meth to kids was being treated as if he did nothing, and was going to be driven away by a professional chauffer. On the other hand, I was going to be walking to the nearest bus station.

Susan had promised me that she would leave one of our joint cards open. I had exactly one thousand dollars to use however I saw fit.

I glanced back to the chauffer. His shoes were probably worth about that much. I shook my head and started walking down the sidewalk.

It wasn't long before a car pulled up alongside me. I glanced down, expecting it to be a reporter. The window hummed as it slid downward.

"The name is Hank," a man said as he reached into his pocket and pulled out a bent business card. "Wondering if you might be up for a chat?"

I didn't bother to take the card. I didn't even slow down. I just kept walking as the car rolled alongside. "You a reporter?" I asked. "I didn't kill him."

"Not a reporter, and I know you didn't."

"Lawyer then?" I had had three down-and-out lawyers try to convince me to hire them and sue the state for defamation of character. I'm no law expert, but even I saw the ridiculousness of such an idea.

"I'm a friend, just want to have a friendly chat. I've been looking for someone like you. I thought you might be able to use a job."

So it was another one of those, then. I had had several of those types of offers as well. Slim had offered me a "position" as a bouncer at some club. Another couple of guys, whose names I hadn't bothered to remember, offered me something similar. Unlike Slim, however, the other two had been moved to the state prison. "Not interested," I replied evenly.

"Well, take the card at least. Maybe you'll change your mind."

"Pretty sure I won't," I said.

"I know more about what happened than you might realize," Hank said.

"I doubt it." I kept walking, a little faster now. Hank tried to say something else, but I soon saw a sidewalk that turned away from the road. I turned. If Hank wanted to chat, he was going to have to get out

5

of his car now. As I had expected, the car drove off and I was once again left on my own.

I walked until I came to a park bench. It was about as empty and brown as the area around it, but it seemed as good a place as any to sit down and think about my next steps. As I did so, I found the current Dallas Morning News sitting there. In big, bold letters the words Joshua Mills Acquitted of Patricide! paraded across the top. I flipped the paper over. What did they know about it anyway? They hadn't been there.

That had been my first Terrible Tuesday, a term I would later come to use much more often.

When I was six, my parents had divorced. My father was one of *those* bad ones. He drank, he hit, he cheated on my mother. You name it, he did it. To the rest of the world he was a devout Mormon. I suppose he was nice enough at times. He left us on the side of the road shortly before my seventh birthday after a, shall we say, eventful, vacation. My mother and I had to make the trip back across seven states to reach our home in a small town in northwestern Montana. When we arrived, there was an eviction notice on the door. Apparently my father had gambled away the mortgage money as well. Growing up we moved around a lot. Good days would come when the alimony check came in. There weren't many of those. Still, we made it through. As any young boy in my shoes might, I had often fantasized about growing up, finding the deadbeat, and beating him to a bloody pulp.

I had never thought the first time we met would lead to his death.

We got in touch when I was in my late twenties. I hadn't thought about him for about ten years by that point, but he had apparently been trying to find me since my nineteenth birthday. Ironically, when he finally fished my phone number out of some PI willing to take his money, he said he was trying to make sure I had made the decision to serve as a missionary and became a good Mormon instead of following in his shoes. I'm still not sure if that was supposed to be a joke. In any case, I told him there were no hard feelings. Life is crazy for everyone. Lots of little boys lose parents, and many had it worse than I did. We chatted for maybe an hour and then I politely told him that it was a bit too late to try and start any sort of relationship. We didn't speak to each other much after that. A happy birthday here and there, but mostly just silence. Then there was the recent phone call. He said he urgently needed to see me. He said it was a matter of life or death.

The tremble in his voice was sincere. Something was very wrong. I knew he played a lot of games and tricks, but this sounded real. More than that, it *felt* real. Sometimes, even for people who don't deserve it, I try to go the extra mile to help out. That whole, treat people the way you would like them to treat you line is pretty hard-wired into my system. Now, I'd be lying if I said it was an entirely altruistic trip. Part of me moronically hoped that perhaps he had become a millionaire and was lying on his death bed ready to give me and my mom a nice fat check for all the crap he put us through. I know it isn't an honorable thought, but I had come a long way from the angry little boy who had fantasized about beating the man within an inch of his life.

So, I made the trip down by plane. I rented a car, and we met at a restaurant. I had learned from our first phone call that he was remarried and had seven children. Apparently he claimed he was even going back to church. I was not about to put myself in the middle of that, so I had suggested a great steak house I had heard about. Dinner was okay. The food was great, but the company was not. He was not the young, powerful man that used to shadow over me. He was a wrinkled little man who looked weaker than either of my grandfathers ever had. Then again, both of my grandfathers had been country boys, and always had a great deal of strength. My father, on the other hand, was a lifelong pencil-pushing schemer. His first weapon was charm. He saved his strength for the home.

We chatted in circles as I tried my best to enjoy my sixty-dollar buffalo rib-eye. God Bless Texas. The poor guy nearly died when I told the server that he would cover the bill, but he nodded slowly as his brown eyes glanced to my arms. I made sure to flex them just a bit for good measure.

We then left the restaurant and he stammered through a few sentences as we turned the corner and walked down a long alleyway. I thought perhaps he was trying to muster up the courage to apologize for the past. Maybe he felt he needed to do that before he died? I didn't know.

"Spit it out," I said finally.

"Do you remember our house in California?" he asked.

That was an abrupt change of subject. "Yeah, sure." I nodded.

We stopped in the middle of the alley and he glanced to both ends. "I should never have worked there."

That's it? You flew me down here to talk about work regrets? What are you playing at?

"Do you remember that job?" he asked. "I worked selling jet turbines. Do you remember?"

"Is this headed somewhere?" I asked. "I have a return flight in the morning. It's been fun and all, but I should get going."

He grabbed my arm and came in close, pleading with his eyes. "You have to listen. I don't know who else to trust. I stole engine plans while I was working there."

I pulled away. "I don't want anything to do with this," I said firmly. I was not about to get caught up in another one of his twisted schemes. I had already heard how he had tried to tack more than one hundred thousand dollars of back taxes onto my mother after the divorce. Now here he was, somehow trying to involve me with corporate espionage? I turned to walk away, but that's when everything went south.

Terrible Tuesday had begun.

A flash of silver light ripped through the air in the alley a few yards in front of me. The light widened, crackling and sizzling with electrical energy as bolts of lightning shot across the widening opening. A man stepped through. He wore a white mask over his face that looked like something a Persian Immortal would wear. At his side was a pair of long, curved swords.

"Oh, no, they found me! It's too late. Run!" I heard my sad excuse of a sperm-donor shout.

I turned just as another flash erupted on the other side. We were trapped in the alley. Through the second portal came something I wish I had never seen. It walked upright like a man, but its feet were covered in fur and tipped with claws. Its torso was wide and thick, with muscular arms held out to the side. The hands were almost human, but like the feet they too were covered in thick fur and long claws. Its head was the worst part. A long snout like a wolf's, filled with wickedly curved fangs. Its silver eyes penetrated my own and filled my body with fear. In an instant, I was frozen, paralyzed where I stood.

So was my father. He stood closest to the wolf-thing. His arms were up and his knees were bent, as if he had stopped half way through dropping down to beg for mercy. The wolf snarled with a voice that filled the alley and made the ground tremble. I'm not sure what caused my body to move, to break the spell the wolf had placed upon me. Maybe it was all the times I had been jumped growing up. Maybe it was simply the adrenaline pumping through my nearly three hundred pound body. Either way, I did the dumbest thing I could do. I ran toward the wolf.

With a shout I lunged at it football style as it moved for my father. I caught him with my right shoulder, instantly grabbing the wolf's sides with my hands and driving until I pushed through the portal. When I played ball in high school, my coach taught me to tackle hard, and to always keep driving with my legs to run the opposing player back. Muscle memory is a wonderful thing. My feet pounded the pavement, and they were still pumping in the air when we toppled over. We both fell through some sort of tunnel. I felt the air turn to ice and close in around us. The wolf clawed at the back of my shoulders. I pushed off and the two of us tumbled through the painfully bright shaft for several seconds. I was spinning through the air, with a giant wolf snarling and growling just a few feet below me.

It was simple luck that ended this particular threat. The portal opened up over a stone floor on the other side. I heard the wolf snarl again and then there was a sort of wet thump followed by a cracking sound. I flew out of the chute a moment later and landed on the wolf's neck. All two hundred and seventy pounds of my bulk crashed down on the giant animal. There was another crunch, this time the wolf's vertebrae snapping in its neck, and then everything was quiet. I shook my head and glanced around.

I was in what I could only imagine was some sort of temple. Stone floor, large altar in the middle, stone pillars holding up the roof. It certainly looked like some sort of archaic temple. I wasn't sure what to do. I slowly stood up and rubbed my arms. I was still left cold and a little stiff from the strange portal.

That was when I heard the scream.

I turned and leapt through the portal.

I may not have started fights growing up, and I might have run from more than a few, but there was always one exception. If someone else was being picked on and hopelessly outmatched, then I would jump in. Even if it was to save the man that had once left me and my mother at the side of a road.

I aimed my feet and legs so that I could, hopefully, hit the ground running once I reached the alley. The coldness was growing more frigid, and the space in the chute was closing even faster than it had the first time I went through. Fortunately, I managed to squeeze out just before the portal clapped shut behind me. Other than hair standing on end from the static electricity, I was unruffled physically. I charged toward the man, who was now holding my father by the hair and pointing one of his swords at his chest.

"I don't know where it is, I swear!" my father said.

The man in the mask plunged the sword deep into my father's chest. He then pulled the blade back out and lopped off my father's head before his corpse had even started to fall.

I don't know why I felt the primal rage inside that I did. It boiled up and propelled my legs even faster. The man in the mask turned and regarded me. He *laughed* at me. Then he raised his sword and took three steps toward me.

At that moment, a lesson came back to me. I once had a sensei who thought it would be fun to make me dodge sword strikes in class. It led to quite a few welts the first few times, but I learned quickly. At the time, I thought the lessons ridiculous, but at this particular moment, I was hoping my muscles would remember how to do those same tricks one more time just as easily as my legs had remembered my football coach's teachings.

The masked man stepped in and sliced down. I turned sideways, allowing the blade to sail harmlessly in front of me, and then I spun around so as to use my momentum. The attacker dodged away, and I tackled nothing but empty air. I grunted as I hit the ground, and instinctively rolled quickly away. The sword came down and threw out orange sparks as it struck the asphalt. The man growled and ran after me.

This was the part that I remembered the most from my lesson. My only task was to continue rolling on the ground as the sword kept chopping down. Once on the left, then twice on the right. I rolled out of the way easily for a man of my size.

The masked man then shifted his grip and was about to come in with a sweeping chop that would go sideways rather than straight down. This was decision time. In training, I had been taught that this was the correct time to get back onto your feet if downed in a sword fight. The first option was to somersault backward and hope that the attacker didn't anticipate your move and adjust accordingly.

The second was even riskier.

I went for option two.

I kicked my legs forward, simultaneously performing a sit-up. My right leg was aimed at the man's groin, while my left was just for propulsion. I connected with my attacker and he stumbled backwards. His attack was interrupted, and the swinging sweep of his sword never reached me. Better than that, I had just managed to grab the handle of his spare sword. As the attacker stumbled backward, I had pulled the blade out with ease.

I quickly jumped to my feet and held the blade out.

The upside was I had a weapon, but the downside was we were far from evenly matched. My sword training had pretty much ended at this point. In training, my sensei had always bowed with a smile on his face once I had taken his spare rattan sword, but I had a feeling this fight was only just beginning.

The masked man swished his sword from side to side. Lightning streaked across the blade.

On the inside I was freaking out. I just saw *lightning* shooting around on his sword like something out of a fantasy novel. On the outside, I tried my best to ignore the display and scowl menacingly. It must not have worked, for the masked man came charging in. He swung and I moved to parry. Our swords connected and a terrible crack of thunder echoed through the alley. The man spun around, changing directions. I blocked that strike as well, but had failed to see the masked man's foot sailing for my stomach.

The kick tossed me up into the air and against the building on the other side of the alley as easily as if I had been a sack of straw. Whoever this man was, he was strong.

He came at me again, but I managed to get my weapon into position to block that strike as well. Without even thinking about it, I launched a left fist and pummeled the man in the stomach. His body bent a little, but nothing like when he had kicked me. The sword came in again, I raised mine up and had to use two hands to block it this time. Even still, his blade cut into my left shoulder. The blade burned my skin and streaks of lightning fired off around the swords. My eyes then landed on the corpse of my father. I suppose stopping to think while in the middle of a fight is not the smartest thing to do, but that is probably what saved my life. In my mind's eye I saw myself lying where my father was. I saw *my* head a few yards away, grotesquely connected to the rest of the body by a line of dark, crimson dots of blood stretching across the dark pavement. I then thought of my wife and son seeing that kind of image.

In that moment a rush of adrenaline surged through my body like never before. I kicked again, this time pushing the masked man back several feet. I rose up quickly, angling the sword up and out. The man charged in and I put my feet to the wall behind me and pushed off. His sword went over my backside so quickly that I felt the wind behind it on my back. My sword, however, plunged deeply into the man's lower abdomen.

He howled in pain and we both crumpled to the ground. I let go of my weapon and climbed up his body until I grabbed hold of his sword arm. He was strong, but I had never met anyone with arms stronger than mine. Before he could angle for another strike, I pressed his wrist to the ground with my left hand and then I began wailing on the side of his head with my right. After two punches I heard a *crunch!* The sound raised my spirits, so I kept slamming my fist down. The man tried to fight back with his free hand, so I hit the sword handle sticking out from his gut with my leg. The man roared out in pain.

I was winning. Whoever this psycho was, I had killed his wolf and now I was about to beat him too!

It only took an instant, but at that moment my mind replayed that thought in my head. I had just *killed* something, and I was happy about *killing* something else. Except, this wasn't a thing. The masked man was a person. I was happy about killing a man. The terrified realization only lasted for a half of a second. I was back in fighting mode right after that, but a lot can happen in half a second. The next thing I knew there was a flash of light and searing pain ripped through my chest. My heart beat maybe forty times in the space of a mere couple of seconds and my body was flying toward that building again, only this time I hardly noticed the slamming against the bricks because of how terrible the lightning was.

I looked down and realized that the man had fired lightning with his hand. His freaking hand! It was like some sort of Star Wars movie. A giant wolf man and some sword wielding jack-tard who was now shooting me with lightning!

My mind slipped. Maybe I had eaten bad food at the restaurant. Or, maybe my plane had crashed and I was in a coma, dreaming some terrible nightmare based upon all those monster books I read during breaks at work.

The lightning stopped and I slid to the ground.

Neither one of us moved.

In the distance I heard a familiar sound. Sirens. Help was coming. Unfortunately, it wasn't coming fast enough. My estranged father was dead in an alley, and I was not far off from that same fate. A part of me cursed myself for not listening to my grandfather. He had always said that a gun was like toilet paper. Carrying an extra roll around and not needing it is no big deal. However, not carrying it and suddenly getting the runs can leave you in an awful mess real quick.

He was right. Right now I was elbows deep in "mess" and I had no clear way out. I could barely move my fingers and toes. The masked man, however, was turning over and starting to press up to all fours. It was impossible. The son of a gun had a sword sticking straight through him, but he was still moving. He stood and staggered forward two steps. He was still holding his other sword in his right hand. He turned and raised the sword.

I still couldn't move. My jaw went up and down, but I couldn't even scream for help.

Where were all the crazy Texans with guns when you needed them? Walker Texas Ranger would be a welcome sight right about now.

The man took a step toward me and I knew what was coming. I was about to die, killed by something out of a B-movie, or a Power Rangers show with really good costumes. Then the mask fell from the man's face. The eyes were almond shaped, slanted horizontally. The skin had some sort of strange pattern on it, almost like the rough lines a crocodile has along its skin. The man smiled to reveal short, but very sharp teeth.

Something about realizing that my enemy was not human put the strength back into my muscles. I pushed up, using the wall for support as the monster staggered toward me. He came in with a forward thrust, but he was much slower now, and easy to dodge. I slipped left and then snatched out and yanked the handle sticking out of his abdomen straight up with my left hand while my right seized his sword arm once more. The creature hissed at me, so I answered by head-butting the ugly little prick. His nose was flattened and began oozing blood a few seconds later.

The sirens were growing ever closer now. I just had to hang on for a few more seconds.

So long as I wasn't hallucinating, I'd be famous. I'd be a hero!

The creature spat in my face. The liquid hit the skin just between my eyebrows and started to burn. I recoiled, but still tried to hold the creature fast. It easily yanked its sword arm free, so I ripped my sword out of it and prepared to fight. Instead, the creature turned and leapt for its portal. The hole in space closed and I was left alone with a sword in my hand and my dead father's corpse behind me.

I had barely managed to wipe away the acidic spit when a flood of lights hit me from both sides of the alley.

"Drop the sword!"

"Drop the weapon!"

"Down on your knees you son of a—"

All of the commands came at once. I couldn't clearly hear any of them. The next few moments are still a blur. All I really remember clearly is the sensation of three small pinches in my back, followed by something hot and stabbing. According to the papers, I had been hit by six tasers at once, but I only felt three, I think. I guess I should count myself lucky that they hadn't used their lethal sidearms.

Everything that followed can best be described as hell. Hours in interrogation. Threats of the chair or firing squad. I knew no one would believe my story of aliens, or monsters, or whatever the heck they were. So I told them we were jumped by a guy with swords. I said that I had managed to get one of the swords and fight off the attacker, but that he got away. It was mostly accurate. I just left out the parts that would ensure a quick trip to a padded cell and very tight jackets.

In the end, it was the sword and the strange wounds on my back that had the jury convinced I was innocent. My sword had blood on it, but it didn't match my father's nor my own. Not to mention the claw marks in my back couldn't have been made by an old man in his early seventies.

Still, somehow an acquittal didn't seem like nearly the right compensation for what I had been through. Not to mention, I wasn't entirely sure that I *wasn't* crazy. Terrible Tuesday had wrecked my life, and now I was sitting on a park bench near a jail house and trying to figure out how to pick up the pieces.

CHAPTER 2

Later that night, I decided to head to a motel for a bit of sleep rather than take a late night bus back to Utah. Frankly, I wasn't sure I wanted to go back to Utah anyway. I was no longer married, and what with being in jail during the divorce proceedings, there had never been hope for custody of my son in any part. At the moment I wasn't even allowed visitation rights. I may have been acquitted, but that didn't mean I was innocent in the people's court.

I tried to go as easy as possible on that thousand dollars Susan left me on my credit card. I bought some cereal and milk, a set of four Styrofoam bowls, and some plastic spoons. I got a rather judgmental look from the cashier, a hipster by the looks of it, who was wearing an old "Save the Rainforest" shirt that he probably bought back in the 90's.

"You could use a cloth bag, y'know," the bearded cashier said from behind his thick rimmed spectacles. I looked him up and down, snickered at his bright yellow jeans, and just shook my head. I wanted to say something, but since I had literally just gotten out of jail a few hours earlier, it was probably best not to be caught on camera harassing a wimpy little cashier who had to use both hands, and arched his back, to lift the jug of milk.

I carried my dinner of champions to the nearest no-name motel. The letters N and C were out on the neon sign, so instead of displaying "Vacancy," it simply read "Vacay." I laughed to myself as I rang the bell situated outside the iron bar-infused window and waited for the manager. I had to imagine they got quite a few people coming out of the jail, either that, or the same interior designer had set up both this manager's booth and the one at the jail where I had collected my personal effects.

A short, fat man came waddling around the corner. He reached up and wiped a thick forearm over the sweat on his forehead.

"How many nights?"

"Just one, I think."

The fat man nodded and wiped his forehead again. Oddly enough, it needed it. Don't get me wrong, it's hot in Texas, and the AC was not working in the office, but even with that this poor man was huffing and puffing just from walking to the counter. He stopped typing on his computer just long enough to turn on a black metal fan clipped to the front of the counter and aimed it up at himself.

"How many people?" he asked.

"Just me."

The fat man looked up and eyed me with a suspicious glare. "Don't let me catch you with anyone else in your room, y'hear? If I see one hooker in there, I swear I'll beat your backside with a switch like my grandad used to do."

Somehow, I doubted the man could even walk to the room, let alone have enough power to pose any real harm, but I kept my mouth shut. It wasn't polite to judge, and he was only trying to look out for his wallet.

"Just me, I promise," I said as I pulled out my credit card and slid it into the metal pass-tray that dipped into the counter below the window.

"Need yer ID too," the manager said as he kept typing on his computer.

Reluctantly, I pulled out my driver's license. I had hoped the motel was run down enough that I wouldn't need to show my identity. I was not sure how I would react if the manager recognized my name. I passed the license under the window, this time catching my knuckles on the window itself. There wasn't a lot of space in the pass-tray.

I caught a lucky break. The manager didn't recognize me. He just click-clacked away on the keyboard and then ran the credit card through his ancient card reader that may have been white at some point in history, but certainly not in the last decade. I frowned as the man swiped the card through seven times. He was cursing at the reader, and I was praying it wasn't taking the payment every single time he moved his hand. Finally, he passed everything back to me, along with a key attached to a plastic plaque that had most of the number rubbed off.

"Room three," the manager said. Then he cursed the heat and walked away. If I wanted a receipt, it was too late now. The light in the room beyond the doorway flicked off and I heard stomping, heavy footsteps ascending a set of stairs somewhere in the back.

"Here's hoping I'm not paying Ritz rates," I muttered to myself as I took the key and my card and license. I walked out from the office, passing under one of those annoying bells that rings when the door hits it. Room three. Well, three was my favorite number, and it was a Friday after all, so perhaps things would go smoothly for a night.

Boy, was I wrong.

I took a shower in what can be described as interestingly brown water that came out a smidge warmer than room temperature. I chose to believe that the brown tinge was rust from old pipes. After the brief shower, I toweled off with something that felt more like eighty-grit sandpaper than cotton and moved to the AC unit. I turned the dial and cranked that puppy all the way up. It made a bubbling sound and then sputtered out decently cool air. The only problem was I couldn't feel the air if I was standing more than eight inches away.

Well, at least I didn't have to listen to Slim brag about the things he had gotten away with. Part of me had wondered several times if I could wear a wire and cut my processing short by trading dirt on Slim. Contrary to popular culture, I had no problem snitching on a druggie, especially one that dealt to kids. Unfortunately, that opportunity never presented itself. Let's just say that Slim had a couple tin stars on his side at the county jail house as well. Not all of them of course, but it was enough of a deterrent to keep my mouth shut. Besides, I'm not sure they would have given me a favorable deal anyhow. I wasn't exactly an honored guest, what with being accused of hacking my old man down with a sword in an alleyway and all. Texans are big on family. Blood is thicker than water down there. Suspected patricide had actually put me lower down the list than Slim when it came to how valuable a person's life was inside the jail.

But, that was all behind me now. I jumped onto the bed. It creaked and groaned. Not sure what I was hoping for, but a plush deluxe mattress this was not. I tried to lay down and get comfortable, but my cell bed had more firmness to it than this thing, and, believe it or not, the mattress in my cell smelled better than this one too.

I got up and put my pants on, tossed my towel onto the bathroom floor. No need to clean up after myself in this place. I poured a bowl of cereal and flipped through the channels. The TV was so old I actually had to turn a dial to choose between one of the twelve channels. Aside from an old local news station, everything else was just static. Shoot, even the jail didn't use analog TVs anymore. A part of me thought about asking for my cell back for one more night, not the serious part of me, mind you, but the thought did cross my mind.

I made do with the granular picture of some suited up weather man standing in front of his little weather board and pointing at images I assumed were little yellow suns. It was hard to tell with the picture quality, but he was talking about lows in the 80's for the next day and no chance of precipitation. As it switched from weather to local high school sports, I was nearly half-way done with my cereal.

That was when my door opened.

Two men walked in and smiled. One was wearing slim jeans and a pair of stiff, tan cowboy boots. The other was wearing carpenter jeans and a checkered button-up shirt.

I jumped up from the bed and glanced at the door. I was certain I had locked it before taking a shower. "This room is occupied," I said, hoping that maybe the manager had overbooked the room.

"Joshua Mills?" one of them asked.

The man with the button-up shirt pulled a glock from his back pocket and started screwing a silencer into the barrel.

"Whoa, what is this?"

"Calm down, we're from the government, and we're here to help," the man in slim jeans said.

Really, he was going with that *line?*

"We aren't here to hurt you."

"Fooled me," I said as I looked to the pistol.

"Here, let me show you my badge." The man in slim jeans pulled out a black wallet and opened up to show a shiny badge with the number four emblazoned on it and an ID card below in a separate section of the wallet.

"I haven't done anything," I said, still not entirely sure they were real agents.

The guy with the gun gently closed and locked the door behind him. He then moved to lean against the wall, pointing his gun down and resting his left hand over his right wrist as if this was nothing more than a casual conversation.

"If you're feds, shouldn't you be wearing suits?" I asked as I took a step back.

"Suits in a place like this would draw attention," the man in slim jeans said. "Now, jeans and a pair of cowboy boots are about as Texan as a man can get."

"Except you don't have an accent," I noted.

"Pitch it," the man with the gun said.

"Pitch what?" I asked, glancing to the gun and making sure he wasn't preparing to shoot me. I had had guns pulled on me before, but never by someone pretending to be a law enforcement officer.

"We know what really happened in that alley," the man in slim jeans said.

"I didn't kill my father," I said quickly.

The man smiled and shook his head. "No, you didn't. I know that, and so does Briggs here."

"Don't give him my name," Briggs said. "It makes it more personal."

The other man shrugged. "I'm Jones. Special Agent Jones from Section Four."

This was either some deranged idiot's idea of a fun time, or I was about to get merced by these two clowns. I kept running through the past eight months, trying to think of any inmate that I might have offended badly enough to warrant this. I couldn't come up with anyone.

"You know, you were at the best steak house in Dallas, fine eating."

"What does this have to do with anything?" I said.

"Cameras, my friend, cameras. Don't you think it odd that a fine restaurant wouldn't have any cameras pointed in the alleyway?"

"The DA said the cameras went out due to a power surge right after we entered the alley. They were there, they just hadn't been working."

"On the contrary," Jones said as he pulled out his phone. He typed a few keys and then turned the screen to face me. There, in jerky black and white, I saw me and my father enter the alley. I had seen this part before. I had tried to use it to show that I was unarmed going into the alley. The tape was going to die in 3…2…1…

But it didn't. There was a bright flare, followed a moment later by another. My mouth dropped open and my cereal fell to the floor. On this man's phone was the proof that I hadn't killed my father. It showed the wolf creature, and then it showed me tackling it and then disappearing. It then showed me remerging just before the masked man killed my father. I then tangled with the masked man.

"I think he gets the point," Briggs said.

"Quite right," Jones replied as he turned the screen off.

"You knew?" I was both relieved and infuriated at the same time. "How could you let me rot in there and go through all of that?!" I started toward Jones, but Briggs whipped his pistol up and aimed it at me faster than I could blink.

"Careful, boy, I wouldn't mind making a mess of your brains," Briggs said. From his cold tone and the wicked sneer on his face, I knew he wasn't bluffing.

"The simple answer is this, we had to know what kind of person you were. We wanted to see if you would talk about the real experience or not."

"Okay," I said, realizing that they must be feds if they had the footage and had managed to erase it from existence elsewhere. "Why?"

"Well, Section Four is a very secret organization. In the plainest terms, we don't exist. The FBI doesn't know about us, the CIA wishes they were us. We deal with incidents like the one you encountered in the alley."

"We clean up the messes left behind too," Briggs said, still pointing his pistol at my face.

I didn't like him.

"Had you tried to tell the authorities, we would have worked within the system to have you transferred to Rusk State Hospital; they handle the criminally insane. Then, we would have had this very same meeting with you, except we'd be dressed in lab coats and you'd be strapped to a table and hooked up to a few powerful electrical devices," Jones said.

"So the gun is like the table and the straps then?" I asked.

"Except I get more fun this way," Briggs put in.

Jones nodded. "I am rather impressed that you *didn't* tell the authorities about the encounter. It shows discretion, and it shows that you can still think while under pressure. Not to mention the fact that you survived the encounter in the first place; that is usually enough to warrant an interview."

"Interview? You make it sound like a job offer," I said sarcastically.

"It is," Jones said flatly. He smiled briefly and then motioned toward the bed. "Have a seat."

"I'd rather stand," I said. They had the gun, but it didn't mean I had to be totally compliant.

"He said sit," Briggs said with a twitch of his gun toward the bed.

"It's fine, Briggs," Jones said. He then folded his arms and looked me dead in the eye. "Listen, we're here to offer you a spot with Section Four. Normally we hire through other channels, but when we get ahold of footage that shows the tenacity you displayed, we tend to make exceptions."

"And so you barge in on me with weapons drawn and want me to believe we're gonna be friends?" I asked. "Seems far-fetched, and mind you I lived through the events on that tape, so I think I know what a ridiculous story looks like."

"Briggs, put the piece away," Jones said.

Briggs frowned and was slow to comply, but he did put the weapon into the back of his waist band, though I noticed he didn't bother to remove the silencer.

"I get it, believe me, I do. I actually joined Section Four under similar circumstances. A portal opened up and one of those wolf creatures came through and attacked my boss. Killed him in the blink of an eye. I lived thanks to my .44." Jones smiled. "It was not easy trying to come up with a story that explained the bullet holes in the wall and my boss' body on the ground. I went to jail too. Section Four showed up the day after my release and offered me the same thing I am offering you. It's a good gig, great benefits, good pay, and you get to play with some amazing toys. Best of all, we investigate and mitigate the kinds of incidents that upended your life."

"So, what? If I say yes, is there some kind of training involved?"

Jones nodded. "We have a facility where we train new hires. Those who pass become agents, those who fail the training become administrative staff. It's a win-win either way."

"And if I say no, do you pull out a little pen and flash away my memory?"

"We aren't the men in black," Briggs said dryly.

"No, that's the downside," Jones said with a nod. "Memory wipes are horribly expensive. Besides that, they are never absolute. There's always the chance of the subject regaining their lost memories, and I'm sure you understand why we can't have people running around talking about monsters and Section Four and all of that."

"So what then, I sign a document of some kind and swear myself to secrecy?" I asked.

Jones shook his head. "In the rare case that a civilian survives an encounter similar to yours and wants to keep to themselves, that usually works. However, yours is a ...*special* case. You see, the individual hunting you is part of a larger group that we are working against. It seems they have taken a special interest in you, and your father. Frankly, to explain it all now would be giving you access to information that is classified at such a level that the president doesn't have routine access to it, so you'll forgive me if I say you just have to trust me on this. To put it in terms that you can understand, the encounter you had is likely the first of many. They want you dead. So, either you work with us and we see if we can put the puzzle pieces together and stop them, or, we kill you to avoid future incidents like Dallas where more lives are lost in the cross-fire.

"I'm sorry, what was that?" I asked.

Jones sighed. "If you say no, then Briggs will kill you. I'm not going to sugar-coat it. We'll make it look like a suicide, or some sort of armed robbery gone wrong, but you'll be just as dead either way. Believe me, that isn't the option I want you to take."

"You'd shoot me right here, in a motel room?"

"Rather naïve question," Briggs said as he reached for his pistol.

"Don't say no," Jones said. "Come with us. Try it out, you'll like it. What else have you got to live for anyway? Your wife left you, you'll never see your kid again. This could be your fresh start."

He wasn't wrong. The idea of having a job offer was certainly more tempting than discovering whether I would hear the pistol report before the bullet struck my brain. Still, none of it sat well with me. The idea that someday I could be Briggs or Jones, barging in on some poor guy in a motel who barely had escaped a death penalty for a murder he had tried to stop, was not something that I could swallow. On top of that, the way he tried to use my family as leverage sickened me.

"You'll have to shoot me then," I said. The words flew out of my mouth before I fully realized what I was saying. I had always been like that. Once I was sure I was on the right side of an argument, it had never mattered to me if I lost, so long as I stood up for what I believed in. Right now, I was very much against the manipulation and abuse of power these two had already displayed and admitted to.

"Would it help if we discussed the pay?" Jones asked. "I do have some power to get you a slightly higher starting salary, seeing as how you already killed a—"

"No," I said sternly. "All I want is to pick up what's left and forget any of this ever happened."

"You can't forget this," Jones said. "It doesn't work like that! These are the things of nightmares. These are the beings that we base our horror movies and camp fire tales on. They have been around as long as we have, and they are not going anywhere anytime soon unless we make them leave."

"They tried to kill me, you are threatening to finish what they started. I don't see much difference," I said.

Briggs smiled and cracked his neck. "Can I do it yet?" he asked.

"No!" Jones yelled. He put a frustrated hand to his head. "Come on, Mr. Mills, think this through. We are the good guys here. We fight the monsters and keep people safe. You can join our team. What's not to like about that?"

"Can you promise I won't be pointing a gun at an innocent man five or ten years from now, just like Briggs?"

Jones glanced to Briggs and then back to me. "Sometimes a bit of coercion is necessary. I get that you're upset, but if you like, you can volunteer for an admin position. You wouldn't even carry a gun doing that line of work, but you'd still be helping Section Four with its mission."

"And I would be supporting other thugs like Briggs," I argued.

"All right, I'm doing it now."

"Briggs, I said no!" Jones yelled.

Fists pounded on the wall from the next room over.

"Shut up in there!" someone called out.

"Briggs," Jones said in a calm, yet deadly voice. "We've already woken the neighbors, let's just simmer a bit."

Briggs shrugged. "I could do them too," he said casually. Just like with the threat against me, I could tell he meant it. The man had no soul.

"I said no." I folded my arms for emphasis. Certainly I was anything but intimidating to either agent, standing there shirtless with a spilled bowl of cereal at my feet in a rat-dump motel room.

The door opened again and someone came in with a very exuberant, "Why helloooo Briggs and Jones!"

Briggs pulled the pistol up, and Jones reached to his waistband as he turned around. As I got a better view, I could see that Jones was holding a snub-nose .38. My grandfather had one of those.

"What do you want, Hank? This is official business," Jones growled.

Hank? As in the man with the bent business card? I craned around to see and sure enough, it was the same man. He smiled and winked as he waved at me. He kicked the door wide open and then stuck his foot there to keep it open. Briggs stepped closer to the wall and Jones put his .38 back in his pancake holster.

"I came to say hello to my new friend here, and make sure you weren't going to cause him any trouble."

"Are you with them?" I asked.

Hank shook his head. Jones tried to close the door, but Hank leaned on it and winked at Jones. "Door stays open, Jones, and I have three cameras pointed at you right now."

"One maybe," Briggs said. "We can take care of one camera."

"Three," Hank said with a cocky nod. "One through the door, another through the small window in the back there."

I glanced over my shoulder and saw the long, sixties style narrow window that ran horizontally along the back wall of the room.

"And the third?" Jones asked.

"A thermal camera scanning the whole room, and it has a reeeeaaaally sweet microphone on it too. Did you know, that we can pick up voices simply by pointing a laser at a window? Amazing how technology has changed, right boys?"

Briggs cursed and unscrewed the silencer.

I was confused terribly, but at least the silencer was being put away. That was certainly a step in the right direction.

"What do you want Hank?" Jones asked.

"Well, he turned you down, as any man or woman of upright character would, and I just thought, rather than waste a man's life, you could let me see if he wants to work with us."

"Bloody Guardians," Jones said with a shake of his head. He turned back to me. "You sure you won't come with us?"

I answered him with a silent glare.

Jones threw his hands up. "Hank, you know I'll catch hell for this."

"And *you* know that I saved your life back in '96, '99, and '05."

"Cocky little –" Briggs started, but was cut off by Hank.

"Saved *your* tail in '07, Briggs. Twice." Hank smiled and folded his arms. "And let's not forget how much dirt we have on Section Four," he whispered with his hands to his mouth, making a show of being quiet.

Suddenly, I found myself liking Hank a lot.

"You'll wipe his memory if he refuses?" Jones asked.

"Only tonight's memories," Hank said. "Anything more than that would be unnecessary and intrusive. Can't have him not knowing what happened at all."

"You'd be responsible for him then," Jones said. "You would have to ensure that any future assaults were dealt with discreetly, and without collateral damage. If you fail, we'd have to finish the job."

"Yes yes, big scary agents with guns, I know the drill. Now, if you don't mind I would like to speak with Mr. Mills alone. I think he has finished with you."

"Keep your mouth shut," Briggs said as he glowered at me. I wasn't sure if he was more upset about the possibility of me talking about the "incident" or the lost opportunity to shoot me. If I had to guess, I would say it was number two.

Jones shook his head and waited until Briggs left the room. Then he leaned toward Hank. "You can't keep playing the 'I saved your life card' forever, Hank. One day your favors will run out."

Hank nodded. "Exactly how many favors is your life worth? I want to make sure I keep a solid tally," he said with a twinkle in his eye.

Jones took in a deep, loud breath, and then left the room.

Hank looked to me and then pointed at the door. "Mind if I come in and close this?"

"I imagine you just saved my life, so you can do what you like," I said with a wave of my hand.

"Imagine?" Hank echoed as he closed the door and locked it. "You didn't imagine it, I *did* save your life, and I arrived not a second too soon I might add."

I nodded. "So, you can wipe memories too huh? What part of the government are you from?"

Hank shook his head. "Not government at all," Hank said. "Closest I get to that is if we have to rescue their sorry cans when something goes really sour. They have toys and a lot of man power, but we have brains, and better people."

"But you can wipe memories?"

"Only if needed, and even then I try and just take the most recent twenty-four hours, just enough to erase any memory of me, or of Section Four. It protects us, and you. After that I can try to have you put into our protection program, and guard against future attacks like the one in Dallas. However, I am hoping you won't turn me down like you did them."

"So this is the part where you tell me you pay better?" I scoffed.

Hank shook his head. "We pay a marginal stipend, but it's just enough to get you fancy mac-n-cheese instead of ramen noodles."

I frowned. "So, no toys, no stacks of cash?"

"Some toys, and a bit of cash, but not much more than thirty K a year. We do provide housing though, so that helps."

"Well, I am in between houses at the moment," I said. At least my sense of humor wasn't entirely destroyed. "Those two said something about a vendetta or something like that. They said the lizard man, or others like him, would continue to hunt me. Do you know why?"

Hank nodded. "I have an associate who can give you quite a bit of information to shed light on that topic. We'll do our best to answer any questions you have."

"It would be nice to have some answers," I admitted. "I tried to do some research from the library back in county, but other than a few twisted memoirs about big foot, I didn't find much."

Hank smiled and stifled a laugh. "I can promise you two things," Hank said. "First, we never threaten people to join us, and so you will never need to be in that position."

I perked up at this. I wondered just how long he had been listening. "And second?"

Hank smiled and wrinkled his nose a bit, then he looked me straight in the face and without blinking said, "We fight to help those who cannot fight for themselves. We don't do it for glory, 'cause we can't talk about it. We don't do it for the money, 'cause there ain't much. We do it for those who would fall victim to the others. We fight for them, and help them stay blissfully unaware so that the nightmares only affect their dreams. In the simplest terms, we try to rescue people. That's it. We are the Guardians."

Not the best pitch I had ever heard, but it rang true, if a bit over-rehearsed. "What about people like me? Do you recruit all of the survivors of attacks?"

Hank shook his head. "First of all, if a gateway is opened, there are usually no survivors. Second, we try to get to the gate before it opens. We clear the innocents out of the area and then stop the intruders from coming into our world." He reached up and stroked his cheek. "In your case, we hadn't seen that portal opening until it was too late. We didn't have enough time to get to you. I'm sorry about your dad, and for the past eight months. If I could have stopped any of that from happening, I would have."

I nodded, thinking on his words for a moment. I was still confused about everything, but at least Hank seemed sincere. I just had one more question. "What do you do with survivors who turn you down?"

"Most of the time we wipe their most recent day, like I said."

"But Briggs and Jones said memories can come back, aren't you afraid of exposure?"

"There was once a time when we didn't have to skulk about," Hank said. "Personally, I don't care so much about secrecy. If I had my way, the whole world would know the truth, but there are other complications that make that a less than ideal option for now. In any case, we try to work with the survivors as best we can. A couple of times we did wipe a few months of memories, but that was because the survivor asked for it. The trauma they had been through was more than they wanted to deal with. We then relocated them and set them up as best we could to keep Section Four off their backs."

"So you look out for the little guy, even if they don't want to join up with you?"

Hank nodded. "It may sound idealistic, or cliché even, but that's what the Guardians are. We protect people. Don't get me wrong, we don't hold little tea parties or diplomatic galas with those who try to open gateways into our world. We are as rough and dirty as circumstances dictate, but we're not thugs like Briggs and Jones."

"All right," I said. "Just let me get my shirt."

CHAPTER 3

Hank put me on a plane bound for Sea-Tac airport. I hadn't ever been out that way before. All I knew about the Emerald City was that it rained a lot. As I expected, it was raining when I left the plane. I went out to the baggage claim area and pushed through the crowd as politely as I could. I was more than anxious to get out of the airport though, and I had pretty much sworn off planes for life.

If you think TSA is bad normally, try going through airport security after barely beating a murder charge. I was screened twice, and I don't mean the polite pat down they give to the "random" grumpy people. I was special, so I got to go and visit the special screening room. VIPs only. Apparently it took six TSA agents to do the job too. The plane wasn't much better. I was seated next to the window on a smaller plane, which meant the wall of the cabin curved in sharper than it does on larger planes. Wide shoulders are a blessing when lifting and doing hard work, but they are a curse in confined quarters. The seat itself wasn't much better. I have twenty-nine inch thighs, and they aren't the jiggly, squishy kind of large legs, so trying to fit between the narrow armrests that were so wisely fitted with divider walls was fairly painful.

To top things off, the air marshal introduced himself to me and then took the seat right next to mine. Needless to say, he took the armrest right away. I suppose he was testing my sharing skills. I would have put on headphones, but I didn't own any now. I didn't even have a cell phone. In-flight entertainment? Sure, but the headphones weren't coming around before take-off. I sighed and tried to lean my head against the cabin wall and close my eyes. Before I could get too comfortable, the air marshal leaned over and whispered into my ear. Apparently he felt the need to tell me that there were three marines on the flight returning home from a training exercise. He had already spoken to them about me, and they promised to be ready if I proved any trouble.

As I said, an acquittal doesn't mean jack in the people's court.

I couldn't help but sigh in relief as I walked out to the pick up area and beyond the last row of TSA agents and cops. I needed space to breathe. Hank was there as he promised, leaning up against a green sedan, arms folded and a big smile on his face.

"Welcome to Washington," Hank said.

I nodded and got into the car. "Thanks for the ride," I said as Hank jumped in and buckled up.

"Well, normally we make the trainees walk to HQ, but it can be a bit tricky to find."

HQ – it sounded like some sort of giant concrete bunker hidden deep in the woods or something. Hank drove and turned up the radio. I was surprised to learn that he was a devout ABBA fan. Let me tell you, you have never lived until you've hear Hank sing Dancing Queen. I had to look out the window to keep from laughing, yet even I have to admit it was just the thing I needed to lift my spirits after that flight.

We drove for about two hours south. We stopped for a late lunch at a two-story KFC where the top floor was where most people preferred to eat as it overlooked the southern end of Puget Sound. So, after eight months in county jail for allegedly cutting off my deadbeat father's head, I was eating fried chicken and mashed potatoes from a box while watching seals play in the water down below in a rainstorm. Definitely not where I thought I would be when the interviewer at my old job asked me where I saw myself in five years. You know the saying, life is what happens while you are making other plans.

We ate quickly, and I turned to leave, but Hank reached out and grabbed my wrist before I could remove the tray from the table.

"You aren't timed for meals anymore, son," he said.

I don't like being called "son." Never have. Still, I could swallow my pride a bit for someone like Hank, so I just nodded and tried to sit down. Within seconds I was tapping my thumb on the table faster than The Offspring's drummer.

"Try to relax," Hank said. "Look at the water, how it moves in and out. Watch the seals."

I was trying to relax, but it wasn't easy.

"Are you nervous about what's coming?" Hank asked.

"A little," I said. Frankly I wasn't sure I had actually wrapped my head around it entirely. I still wasn't completely sure I wasn't losing my mind. It's hard to explain, but when the whole world says you are guilty, and probes you and interrogates you for hours, then days, then months, you start to break down. You start to wonder if they're right. Hell, there was a part of me that thought perhaps I had made up the creatures in the portal to shield myself from the truth that I had in fact murdered my own father. I could push the thoughts away mostly, but they were always there, nagging at the back of my mind and eating away at who I knew myself to be. Seeds of doubt had been planted, and just like dandelions in a large lawn, the doubts were hard to kill, no matter how many times you tried to pull them out by the roots.

"You'll be all right, in time," Hank said as he leaned back and pulled a toothpick out of his wallet. He had chosen corn on the cob for one of his sides, so it took him a while to work at the little bits of yellow stuck in his teeth. When he finished, he chewed on the piece of wood and watched the seals play. We didn't speak. We just stared out the window. It was probably only two minutes, but it felt like I was there for hours. It wasn't long before I *had* to get up and take care of my tray.

Hank didn't try to stop me this time, he just smiled and led the way back to the car. We drove down I-5 for a little while longer and then took exit 104 to get onto Highway 101 heading north. As we rounded the curve and crossed over a large body of water, Hank pointed over his left shoulder.

"Remind me to take you over to Tumwater Falls next spring. Beautiful cherry trees there in the spring time. Decent restaurant too. I used to take an old girlfriend there sometimes. It's a fun place."

I tried to look to where he was pointing, but I couldn't see anything over the divider and several lanes of I-5. What I did see though, was trees. As we went north, the highway was lined with trees. Thick, tall pine trees covered the ground everywhere. It was far greener than anything I had ever seen in Utah. Utah has its own natural beauty, don't get me wrong. Zions Park, Arches Monument, the Wasatch Front, they're all nice, but this blew me away. Anything that didn't have a building, road, or parking lot was covered in trees and big ferns. It was a stark contrast to the Seattle metro area.

"Sometimes I take the ferry across, but I thought driving might help you reset a bit better. Besides, I wasn't sure if you get sea-sick or not," Hank said. "Some people are real sensitive to that kind of thing. You ever get motion sickness or seasick?"

I shrugged. I had never been on a boat before, so I had no idea.

"Well, we'll find out soon enough I suppose. We have our own chopper, and even a plane, of sorts."

I looked at him with wide eyes. I had kind of expected them to have a helicopter I guess, just judging from the way he talked about the Guardians, but it was the words "of sorts" when he mentioned the plane that got my attention. Were we talking a prop plane with wings duct taped on?

A part of me wondered if maybe I should have gone with Section Four and their big toys. Maybe then I could have flown in some UFO-based jet they designed in Area 51 or something.

Hank winked at me and then cranked up the volume and began singing Fernando at the top of his lungs, complete with hand gestures as if performing in front of a stage audience. I shook my head and resigned myself to watching the trees fly by on the side of the road. Another thing I noticed about this area, cops. A lot of them. I think I counted seven state patrol cars from Sea-Tac to Olympia, and another four on Highway 101. Most of them were marked cars, but not all of them. I saw bright red dodge chargers fitted with tinted windows and lights in the grille. I saw a pair of blue Ford Expeditions, both hilariously parked at a donut shop off of I-5. I drooled with envy when I saw a gray Mustang GT with baby blue racing stripes. I wasn't sure how that officer had scored a car like that, but he must have done something very, very right. I was about to ask Hank what it was all about, but as we drove further up 101, I saw a sign for the State Patrol Academy. It all made sense then.

We passed through a couple of smaller towns, or perhaps they were simply houses set back from the highway, I wasn't sure. There weren't any signs. We turned off and pulled into a town called Shelton. It didn't look like much. Mostly commercial and industrial space. Wood mills, fisheries, that sort of thing. Hank said most people lived outside of the town itself.

"The town's bigger than it looks. The high school is listed as a 3A for sports. The football team can get a bit rowdy. They once threw a log off an overpass onto a rival team's bus."

I looked at him incredulously.

"One hell of a powerlifting team though. They take state more often than not."

I thought back to my high school football team. Our coaches made us dress up in suits for game days, and the craziest trouble we ever got into was towel-snapping each other in the locker room. Our coaches would have killed us if we had thrown pebbles at a bus, let alone a frickin log.

Before I had finished my thought, we had passed through the town and were driving out to the north. We drove along the coastline of Oakland Bay, which was fed by Hammersley Inlet and still a part of the Puget Sound. I watched as people stabbed the thick mud during the low tide.

"Clamming," Hank shouted over the chorus of Take a Chance on Me. "If they're lucky, they'll find a gooeyduck."

"A what?"

"Well, it's spelled GEO-duck, but we pronounce it goo-ey-duck. It's the largest burrowing clam in the world. Right here." Hank pointed out the window for emphasis. "Good eatin' to be sure."

"How big?" I asked, mostly out of the hope that conversation would force Hank to turn down Abba.

"Biggest one I found was seven pounds, that's just under the record. Most are one to three pounds though."

Whoa! That is a big clam!

"Anyway, we're getting close."

Close must have been a relative term. We drove another twenty minutes or so before peeling off toward the west. We drove down a paved road that eventually turned into a single lane gravel road before coming to a stop at a small cemetery deep in the woods. Hank flicked the ignition off and yanked the keys out as he undid his belt and swiveled out of his seat.

I followed him and looked around. Most of the gravestones were old, faded and worn by time. Some of them had lichen and moss growing on them. The graves themselves were indiscriminate. There were no mounds of earth or borders to mark the actual area where the coffin was buried. Grass had grown up to overtake the grounds, with ferns and ivy invading from the north.

A large angel statue stood in the center of the cemetery. Her wings were folded in and her arms were outstretched. I noticed right away that her right hand had broken off. As I looked closer, I realized she was missing her nose as well. I know it wasn't real, but for the life of me an old Dr. Who episode came back to me and I started to wonder if Weeping Angels were real. The very idea sent goosebumps down my forearms, and I found myself involuntarily staring at the statue, trying not to blink.

"Over here," Hank said, ripping me away from my childish fear. The man was walking toward a large tree. I know what you're thinking. Most trees are large in the lush forests, especially out so close to Olympic National Forest, and you'd be correct, but this one was different. You know those photos of massive redwoods that had tunnels cut through them to let cars pass? This one was *that* kind of large, except it was an oak tree. Its bark was gray with white splotches. Its branches stretched out, thick and strong, and its leaves grew bright and green. Hank moved to the tree and knocked on it.

Curious to see what was going on, I walked up to him. "So, is this like a secret tree or something? Is there a machine in the bottom that will suck fifty years of my life away?"

"Cute," Hank said. The tree then opened up and Hank walked down a set of stairs.

My eyes shot wide and I stood there, staring at the open staircase and wondering how badly I had just insulted Hank. It took me a few moments, but I recomposed myself and walked in. I went down a few steps and then the tree closed behind me.

"Come on down," Hank shouted from below. "I have some people I want you to meet."

My heart jumped in my chest and suddenly I felt a bit nervous. The reality of what was happening was too hard to suppress any longer. I was in a magic tree, somewhere in the Olympic Peninsula, going into an underground lair beneath an abandoned cemetery.

What had I gotten myself into?

"Come on, Mills, time's wastin' and we have other things to do."

I moved my feet. My shoes, a nice pair of sneakers that Hank had bought me just before my flight so I would have something other than the flimsy slippers I wore at the county jail, made soft echoing sounds as I stepped on each metal stair. I followed the spiral down until it opened up into a castle-like chamber. The walls were made of stone. Lights dangled from the low ceiling, but the bulbs weren't the new daylight kind, they were the old, yellow light bulbs that gave the room a more gritty feel to it, like a nineteenth century mining shaft.

Hank was standing at the head of a rectangular table made of wood. How they had gotten the thing down the stairs was beyond me, but he motioned for me to sit in a chair at his left. I complied and sat quietly. I didn't see any others present with us. I looked around the room again, and this time caught just a glimpse of a pair of swords hanging on a far wall with a shield covering them.

I sat there, nervously bouncing the heel of my foot on the floor. After another minute or two, a door opened somewhere in the back of the chamber, around a wall of stone. I couldn't see them yet, but I could hear them chattering away. Hank gestured for me to stand up, so I did. I crossed my hands in front of myself and tried to put on a friendly face.

The group came around the corner and walked toward the table where Hank and I waited. As I looked at them, each and every one of them eyed me as well, as if second-guessing Hank's decision to bring me in.

"This is Dan Schmidt," Hank said, indicating a tall man with light red hair. He looked to be in his late forties. He was wearing a polo shirt that fit snugly around his chest and shoulders, but was very loose at the waist.

"Good to meet you," Dan said as he offered his hand across the table. I reached out and shook it. The man had the grip of a bear! Not wanting to show any weakness, I smiled and tried to strengthen my grip against his.

"Dan is former HRT with the FBI," Hank said. "He knows his stuff. He's been called all over the world to handle problems."

Dan smiled and sat down.

Hank then pointed to a short man that was maybe five foot five if he really stretched his back straight. "This is Robert Williams, our tech guru. You can call him Mack, though, as that's what he goes by."

"What's up?" Robert said with a nod as he moved to sit next to Dan. "You're a Mormon right?" he asked while obnoxiously chewing on a wad of gum.

I nodded.

"Well, I'm an atheist, so don't even think about trying to preach around here, or I'll have to beat you down with logic and scientific reasoning. Got it?"

"Crap, Mack, the only one ever bringing up religion is you," Dan said with a shake of his head.

"It's all right," I said with a laugh. "I hadn't thought of this as a place to proselytize." Mack gave a curt nod, as if he had won some sort of epic battle. So, just for fun I poked him a bit. "Though, honestly, doesn't science and logic point to a higher power than our own?"

Mack threw his hands up. "You see, I told you. Mormons never shut up about this." Mack shook his head and pointed at me. "Listen, I have heard all about intelligent design, but you aren't going to change my mind. Not one bit."

I shrugged. "I just find it funny that I am sitting in an underground chamber with a magic tree for a front door, and that you all hunt monsters from other worlds, and you are unable to admit that somewhere out there, there might be a higher power. You're a tech guy right? So with all the advances of science on our own planet, isn't it possible that somewhere, in the vast and unending universe, another civilization figured out how to unlock immortality? If they did that, then conceivably they could have plenty of time to unlock mysteries of physics that we can't even approach at this point. Would not such a civilization be considered gods to people like us?"

Mack frowned. He looked at me and then smiled. "Well, that is a new angle I haven't heard before." He glanced to Hank. "Let's just move on with the introductions."

"Well I'll be a monkey's uncle, I have never heard Mack shut down before," Dan said as he put the back of his hand to Mack's forehead. "You feeling okay buddy?"

"Stop," Mack said.

"You ever watch the movie Independence Day?" Hank asked me.

"Sure, who hasn't?" I said with a nod.

"Remember how Goldblum's character stopped the mother ship with an old mac laptop?"

I nodded.

Hank thumbed at Mack. "He could do it with two paper clips and a rotary phone. Also, he wouldn't ever admit it, but he's a good operator as well. Used to run all the missions with us in the field."

"Yeah, and then I took a horn to the chest," Mack said as he rubbed the right side of his chest. "Lung never fully healed after that. So, now I sit back with the computers and fun toys while you guys do all the hard work."

Hank then pointed to a tall black man with a shaved head. "That's Marcus Brown. He used to be an army ranger. He's been places most people couldn't point to on a map. More than that, he's one of the best field medics I have ever seen. He can cut down the enemy as well as anyone else I know, but if you're bleeding out,

Marcus is the only man you want to call on for help." Hank pointed to Mack. "You ever hear of someone else living through being stabbed in the lung in battle?"

I shook my head. I was sure there were such stories, but I wasn't about to break Hank's momentum.

"Well, let's just say that Marcus not only saved Mack's life, he did it while fighting off three harbinger wolves."

"What's that?" I asked.

"It's that big wolf-man creature you pushed back into the portal in Dallas," Dan said quickly.

"Three of them?" I asked.

"Well, I had already killed their master," Mack put in. "So I did all the hard work."

Marcus offered a half smile and sat down next to Mack. "You keep telling yourself that, brother. Maybe I won't be there the next time you get gored by a Borelian."

"A what?" I asked.

"We'll get to that later," Hank said. "For now, just focus on remembering the names of the people here.

A tall, very fit man came around Marcus and sat down at the end of the table opposite Hank. He had thick, black hair and bright blue eyes, but unlike the others he did not smile or even nod toward me. He just stared.

"I don't like you," he said flatly.

You ever have one of those instant repulsions to someone for no apparent reason whatsoever? In that moment, I sure did. "The feeling's mutual," I said before I even knew the words were forming in my mouth.

"Shut your hole, Flint," Hank said. Hank then turned to me. "Mr. Mills, this is Flint. Don't let him get to you. He tells all the new people that he doesn't like them. Uses it to size them up by their response."

I stared at Flint until he looked away and gestured for Hank to continue.

"Flint was also an army ranger, for a while," Hank said. "He completed six years with the army and then joined up with a merc group. You ever hear of Blackwater?"

I nodded. I had seen the name in the news a few times since the war in Iraq started.

"It was a group like that, but a bit more secretive," Hank said.

"He's a bit rough around the edges, but you ever get into a place where you're holed up against insurmountable odds, Flint is the one you want to come in after you."

Hank then looked around the room. "Where's Amber?"

"She's out on a bounty with the three vikings today," Dan said.

The three Vikings? With a group as rough as this one, how does someone earn *that* kind of title?

Hank sighed. "Amber is our resident sniper. No formal training, as such. However, her father spent thirty years as a marine forward recon sniper. He trained her up from the age of three."

"Katya is going over the file one more time," Dan put in quickly.

Hank nodded. "Katya, you ready yet?"

"Da!" a thick, sultry voice called out from the back room. A slender woman with black hair and a very fit, curvy figure came into the room with a small manila folder in one hand. I noticed she had a pistol strapped on the right side of her waist in a tactical holster that had a durable cordura strap around her leg for extra stability. I wasn't much of a gun guru, so I couldn't tell what it was she carried, but it looked bigger than the glock Briggs had pointed at my face.

"Katya is former FSB," Hank said.

"That's Russian intelligence," Dan clarified for me. "Think KGB, but with better tech."

I nodded.

"I don't play those games anymore," Katya said in her thick accent as she whacked Dan playfully on the top of the head.

"I'd know if you tried," Dan said.

Katya winked at him and then handed the file to Hank. "No you wouldn't. We Russians only get caught if we want to. How long did it take you to uncover the Great Seal Bug given to your ambassador in Moscow?"

"Seven years," Dan muttered.

"All right, get a room you two lovebirds," Hank said as he opened the file. "Now, on to business. Mr. Mills, think of this as a kind of placement interview, if you will. You have already been assigned instructors, but the people around this table, including myself, will be responsible for deciding which team you join upon completing your training."

"Fifty says he washes out in three weeks or less," Flint said as he leaned forward and put his head down on his hand as if extremely bored by being in the room.

"I'll take that bet," said Dan. "I saw the video. This guy has fight in him."

"You saw the video?" I asked. "But how did you get it? I thought Section Four had the only copy?"

"Bah, Section Four, smexion four," Mack said. "If I explained how I took it, you wouldn't understand, but it's enough to know that I did."

"You hacked into their systems?" I asked.

"Hacked is such a dirty word," Mack protested. "It sounds like I am just creating cheat mods on a video game or something. I prefer the term—"

"Nobody cares, Mack," Flint said.

Mack huffed and folded his arms.

"All right, back to the issue at hand," Hank said as he held up the folder.

Katya walked around Hank and moved to sit next to me. She smiled when I glanced to her. I smiled back, and then promptly turned back to see what Hank had in his hands.

"Here we go," Hank announced as he opened the folder. "Born in '84. Lived in Phoenix until he was four years old. Parents divorced during his early childhood. Moved thirty-eight times before his seventeenth birthday. Finally settled down long enough at that point to finish the last bit of his junior year, and actually all of his senior year at the same high school."

I straightened in my chair. The file was about me.

"Suspended thirteen times for fighting, but never expelled because all of the fights were self-defense, save for one."

"He lost that one," Katya interjected.

The others chuckled and I just put on a smile. I hadn't *lost* that fight. I just realized after the first punch that I was picking on someone who didn't deserve it. I *let* him win. I had gone through a lot of teasing after that, but it had been better than living with the guilt of pounding some poor twerp's face out of peer pressure. Besides, as Hank already noted, I moved around a lot anyway. I was outta that place only a few weeks later.

"Continuing on," Hank said as he cleared his throat and lifted the file to the light. "One fight was actually with a computer science teacher in the seventh grade." A few of the guys laughed at that too.

"Last recorded fight in the file was your sophomore year at a new school."

Yeah. I remembered that one well.

"Says on your second day at Allbright Academy, you took it upon yourself to stop a group of kids, all of whom were part of the local gang, the Lucky Sevens with extensive rap sheets, from picking on another student."

"It was more than that," I said quickly.

Hank nodded. "Yes, the file mentions that you claimed the students were trying to pull a young lady into a restroom with them." Hank tilted his head and looked back at the file. "Out of eight young men ranging from fourteen to nineteen in age, three of them were unconscious, two had broken arms and noses, one had a switchblade stabbed into his backside, one was vomiting blood, and the last one was barely coherent, but missing several teeth."

"Holy –" Mack started, but was cut short as Hank continued.

"Also found at the scene were two additional knives, a semi-automatic .22, and drug paraphernalia."

"That record is supposed to be sealed," I said. "The police said they wouldn't reveal my involvement to anyone."

"Yes, it says that too," Hank stated. "Apparently six of the eight you pummeled were under investigation for an unsolved murder at the time."

"Pay up," Mack told Marcus.

"Gentlemen?" Hank said.

I looked over and saw Marcus shake his head. "You don't know you're right," he said.

"Yeah I do. You heard *that* and you still think Hank got him here with the 'come see the world and explore the universe speech?'" Mack shook his head and looked to me. "Hank suckered you in with the whole, 'come and help us protect the little guys' line, didn't he?"

I looked to Hank.

"You can settle this later." His tone had shifted noticeably. Mack and Marcus straightened up and fell silent.

"Now, also says Mills played football. Started out as wide receiver, had a 4.6 forty—"

"I still run that in 4.4," Flint said.

"Nobody cares," Mack said sourly. Dan and Katya laughed. Marcus smiled and patted Flint on the shoulder. "I care about ya, Flint,

I care." Flint shook Marcus' hand off of him and grunted.

"Broke his hand in freshman year, then was team captain the last three years of high school after gaining forty pounds and switching to defensive end. Placed third in state powerlifting meet senior year. Also ejected from wrestling for body-slamming his opponent."

"What, like the wrestling on TV kind of body slam?" Mack asked.

I nodded. "He tried to grab and squeeze something he shouldn't have, so I picked him up over my head and then slammed him down. He deserved it."

Mack whistled.

"Apparently that move was quite a popular one," Hank continued. "Mr. Mills worked in security after the age of eighteen. He caught someone trying to steal auto parts from the service shop and chased the man down. The thief pulled out a socket wrench and Mills did the same body slam, only this time the opponent suffered a fractured neck afterward."

"Play stupid games, win stupid prizes," Dan said.

Hank nodded. "He also served on the local search and rescue unit, and helped to find a young six year old girl that had gotten lost in the woods. Served a mission for the LDS church in Russia, where the fights continued."

"I'm sorry, but where are you getting all of this?" I cut in. "Most of that stuff I don't talk about. Some of it was sealed, and the stuff in Russia... nobody knows about that except the other missionary who was with me at the time. I mean, I reported it to the mission president, but that's it."

Hank smiled and pointed to Mack.

"Anything the government has, I can get a copy," he said. "Sealed records, expunged records, classified records, it doesn't matter. I can dig up all sorts of bones."

"Well, that's enough to make a guy turn into a conspiracy theorist," I said with a shake of my head.

"I'll cut this short," Hank said as he set the file down. "Four fights during your mission. One started by a group of skinheads who tried to mug you. Your companion at the time had a sprained ankle, so your choice was to run or fight. You fought. Second fight was a pair of drunks you saw slapping a homeless lady on the street. After knocking them out, you escorted the woman to a shelter of sorts. Third fight was a mafia enforcer."

"Really?" I blurted out before I thought about it.

Hank nodded.

"I thought he was just trying to scare us," I said under my breath, now realizing how badly that particular event might have gone.

"The enforcer pulled a knife on Mills, Mills broke his arm, twisted it, and then took the knife. He then broke the man's jaw with a knockout punch."

Mack whistled again. "I don't think that's what the bible means when it says turn the other cheek," he said with a wink.

"Fourth fight was on public transport. Three drunks tried to attack a marshrootka driver."

"A what?" Marcus asked.

"It's like a bus, but it's a large van that you can get on or off anywhere along a specified route," Katya explained.

"Anyway, Mills threw two of the drunks out of the sliding door while it was moving when the driver shouted for help. The third nearly pushed Mills out, but Mills was able to get back in and subdue the final assailant."

"Why did they attack the driver?" Marcus asked.

I shrugged. "They were fine for the first ten minutes, then they just went off."

"Crazy Russians," Dan said as he looked at Katya. The woman just made a kissy face back at him.

"Mills married two years after he returned from his mission. Went to join the Air Force, got into ROTC, and then quit after the first year. Tried to get into the Marines as a fighter pilot, but then decided not to sign the papers when he was offered a slot at OCS.

"See," Flint said. "I guarantee he'll be gone in three weeks. He's a quitter."

Hank smiled and shrugged. "His latest fight was with a bull. He was passing by a farm in rural Utah and saw a bull break free from its pen. It then charged and attacked a woman. Mills stopped his car, jumped the fence, and fought the bull with his bare hands until the woman escaped."

"Why not just ram it with your car?" Dan asked.

"Ditch was too deep," I replied. "My car would've gotten stuck." I then turned to Hank. "You're missing one," I said quickly. "I tried to join the army before my mission."

Hank nodded. "I left it out on purpose. I was going to bring it up last, for Flint's benefit." Hank looked directly at Flint and then said, "Mr. Mills was offered a training slot at the Defense Language Institute in Monterey California. More than that, he had a hefty sign on bonus and his pick of several choice bases."

"But he didn't sign because he can't commit," Flint said. "Isn't that right?"

I had no idea what was up this guy's backside, but I had a big part of me wondering if now might be a good time to forget about my rule of not starting fights. Trying to keep my cool, I just shook my head. "I didn't follow through because the recruiter had promised me a waiver that guaranteed I would be allowed to go on my mission for my church. When the day came to sign all the papers, he told me he didn't have that one. He tried to get me to sign the papers without it, so I walked out. I can commit, I just have to believe in the cause."

"Fine, still doesn't explain the Air Force or Marines," Flint said.

"After getting into the ROTC program, I discovered that a pilot slot wasn't guaranteed in the Air Force. Worse than that, the competitions weren't entirely skill based. There was a lot of politics involved, and some luck. So I left the program after hearing that Marines offered a guaranteed aviation contract. Better, their system was skills based. If I passed the tests and did better than others, I could choose my aircraft."

"So why'd you bail then?" Flint pressed.

"I was married by then," I said. An aviation contract with the Marines was guaranteed to send me away from home for eight to twelve months at a stretch even if I wasn't called to the front lines. Then, I'd get a couple months home and then go back out again. My wife and I were pregnant, and I didn't want to leave my family behind. So again, it was for a bigger commitment."

"Fat lot of good that did you," Flint said. "If you're so upstanding, then why'd your wife dump your sorry can?"

That took the wind out of me. I knew everyone could see the pain stamped across my face, but there wasn't anything I could do about it. It was a lot like getting sucker-punched from the side.

"That's enough," Hank shouted. "That's below the belt, even for you, Flint."

There was a tangible silence, and then Hank took a seat. "We have four teams waiting for a replacement. Mills, do you have any preference between San Antonio, Miami, London, or Budapest?"

I looked up. "I thought I was going to stay here," I replied.

Hank shook his head. "I run the team here, and it's already full. There are four positions open, and I have three other noobs that have joined us in the last couple of weeks. The four of you will fill our current vacancies."

"Assuming Mills doesn't wuss out," Flint muttered under his breath.

I thought about Susan and my son. The likelihood of seeing them again was very, very small, so it didn't really matter where I went. "I'll go wherever," I said.

"Russian won't be useful in Budapest," Dan said. "Maybe we could make a lateral transfer and move someone off of the team in Moscow, send them to Budapest, and then have Mills go to Moscow."

Hank shook his head. "Budapest is the central and eastern European hub for us. Putting him in Budapest would allow him to use his language in some of the former soviet bloc countries."

Dan nodded.

The group openly debated the assignment process for several more minutes. I was happy to stay out of the discussion though. I had just met these people, yet all of them had my entire life summed up onto a single sheet of paper sitting on the table. It was more than a little surreal. I didn't bother paying attention as they settled in on a place to send me.

It was just as well, looking back on it now, because I was never actually going to make it to any of the teams they had listed.

CHAPTER 4

I spent the night in a room that reminded me a lot of my old jail cell, except there wasn't a window. I slept on a stiff cot and was woken up at an inhumanely early hour the next morning.

"Wake up, sleepy head," Katya cooed in her sultry voice. "Come on. You have lessons now."

"Lessons?" I asked as I rolled lazily off of the cot. I struggled to put my clothes on in the dark, and then followed her back through the room with the long table to a large metal door. She punched a series of numbers into a lock and then the sound of hissing gasses and scraping metal vibrated through the door just a moment before it opened. Inside was a small room with a projector and three desks. I sat at the desk on the far left.

Katya closed the door behind us and the locks reengaged.

"Today, I will tell you about those creatures you saw in the alley," she said as she pulled a remote off of a pedestal at the back of the classroom. The whirring sound of the fans inside the projector filled the room and was followed by a bright light on the wall in front of me.

"You already know the harbinger wolf."

As she spoke, an image of a wolf-man similar to the one I had fought popped up on the screen. He was hideous. Massive claws and fangs. Sitting there in that seat, I had to wonder if I had actually tangled with one of those, because my feet were already itching to run away just from the image.

"They are very fast. Usually, they are used as scouts, or forerunners. That's why we call them harbinger wolves," Katya explained. "The only way to kill it is to stab it through the heart, or take its head."

I turned and looked at her. "The one I fought died after hitting its head on the stone, and then I broke its neck."

Katya shook her head. "No, that just takes him out of the fight for a bit until he can regenerate. They have amazing healing abilities."

"So, like a werewolf then?" I asked.

Katya nodded. "A werewolf is a lower level creature. Harbinger wolves can create lycanthropes by turning a human. However, a werewolf, for all of its power, can never open a gate like a harbinger wolf can."

"So if that portal hadn't closed, it would have come after me?" I said. I had hardly heard anything else she had said as I was too lost in my own realization of how close to death I had come that night in Dallas.

"The portal closed because the harbinger wolf had gone back through. Had he not been unconscious, he would have reopened the passage with a mere thought and come through for you."

"Pleasant thought," I said.

"I should warn you, harbinger wolves don't forget a scent. The likelihood that it will come for you at some point is pretty high."

"Wait? It's going to hunt me down?"

Katya nodded. "Probably. So, I would suggest you do well in training. Moving on." She clicked a button and a new picture popped up. I saw something that looked like a demon. It had the right kind of horns on its head, the thick, meaty body, with fangs and wings to boot. The bottom half had a thin covering of fur, and looked like it came from a bull.

"Minotaur," I guessed.

"Similar," Katya said. "Minotaurs are the foot soldiers, and they look nearly the same, except the faces are still bull-like, rather than human. This is a greater demon known as a borelian."

Dang. Something like that is what had gored Mack. No wonder his lung hadn't healed. The beast was at least four hundred pounds. It was incredible anyone could survive that kind of blow at all.

"They can control portals. If you thought the harbinger wolf was bad, the borelian makes that look like a slightly misbehaved puppy in comparison."

"How do you kill it?" I asked.

Katya smiled approvingly. "I like you, straight to the point. You kill it by putting a fifty cal through its skull and into its brain. You can try to sever the head, but unless you have a tractor mounted tree saw, you are not going to cut through its bones. Other option is to hit the heart, but this is another difference between a minotaur and a borelian. A minotaur can be shot through the heart as easily as a moose, elephant, or other large animal, which isn't to say that it's easy, but that it is possible. The borelian has a thick layer of bone around its heart, like a second skull. Best option is to have a pair of snipers. One goes for the brain, the other for the heart. If I am the one shooting the heart, I prefer the OSV-96."

"What's that?" I asked. I knew a little about guns, but not a lot, and I had never even heard of that kind.

"It's Russian weapon. Very powerful, like the Browning fifty caliber BMG, but instead of a twelve point seven by ninety-nine millimeter cartridge, the OSV fires a twelve point seven by one oh eight. It will knock a borelian down at one thousand meters. The others have successfully used a Barret M-98, but sometimes even that doesn't get through the heart bone."

I nodded. I had never fired one, but I had a vague conception of what a fifty caliber rifle looked like. It was not something I would want to be on the receiving end of.

"In addition to minotaurs, the borelian can use satyrs and centaurs as foot soldiers as well. Unlike the other creatures on this list, the borelian is native to this planet. At one point, it was nearly hunted to extinction, until it joined up with other dark forces and escaped."

"How many are left now?" I asked.

Katya shrugged. "Too many. The three Vikings will have a more precise count, they are the ones who keep those kinds of records."

She clicked the remote again and I saw a tall, gaunt man with wild hair and long fangs. He had been photographed mid-flight, jumping off of a tipping van and toward the cameraman.

"This is a vampire. Dangerous creature with a love of violence and a hatred for humanity. The bystander who took this photo was ripped in half only a second after taking this picture. The van being tipped in the photo is a Section Four vehicle. Unlike harbinger wolves, vampires are not afraid of direct confrontation with the larger agencies. They'll cling to the shadows as their first choice, but if you back one into a corner, they'll be sure to take out as many as they can before they finally die."

She clicked the remote again.

The humanoid in this picture gave me chills. He had a long, thick green tail, and a face much like the reptilian face I had seen on the masked assailant. He had two swords as well. He wore a fitted robe of blue silk. In front of him was a man. Behind him was a tall, open portal like the one I had seen in the alley. Through the portal I could see many dozens of the same reptile-men waiting on the other side.

"This is a Drakkul, a fierce and deadly opponent. However, unlike vampires and borelians, they are not without honor."

"What honor could a creature like that have?" I asked with a shake of my head. "I watched one slice the head off of an old man who was on his knees begging for mercy."

"There are bad apples in every basket," Katya said flatly. "Usually the drakkul do not fight with unarmed opponents, thinking it dishonorable."

"They made an exception in Dallas," I said.

Katya nodded. "Perhaps there was a reason. Could be that he perceived your father as a thief or some other kind of threat, an enemy without honor."

Thief? How could my father, a drunken con-man for all intents and purposes, ever steal something from a race that lived on another planet? Sure, he had told me about taking *something*, but I just assumed he stole some sort of plans to a proprietary engine. Aliens and monsters had never crossed my mind. As I sat here listening to Katya, however, it did start to make sense. It was almost funny actually. My mother had always said that his schemes would eventually get him into too much trouble with the wrong kind of people.

Katya continued. "Either way, it is not entirely unheard of for rogue drakkul to go off on their own. If he were banished from his tribe, or forced to flee, then he would have been very desperate. You are fortunate to have survived the encounter. Drakkul are excellent swordsmen, and they do not yield. Normally, when a raiding party of drakkul comes to this planet, they open a gate and challenge the guardian."

"Didn't Hank call our entire group guardians?" I asked.

"Yes, but there is one senior guardian who is responsible for the gate. The group exists to act as a buffer, and fight off the creatures that sneak into our world, but the senior guardian is a sort of champion for our world. He or she fights one on one against enemies who initiate an open claim on our world. If our champion wins, then they leave for a period of time. If we lose, then their invading force has earned the right to assault our home."

"Who makes these rules?"

"The Ancient Ones," Katya said. "There is a race of being out there that has always been fighting for control of our universe. Some faiths refer to them as angels and demons, but they are essentially the same thing, just some fight for what we would call good, and the others fight for evil, or darkness."

"So angels and demons set down rules that govern duels fought whenever someone opens a portal to our world?" I asked.

"Not just our world, but any world," Katya corrected. "It is a vast universe out there. Most believe that the dangerous aliens will come on large spaceships, but those are cockroaches, nothing more. The dangerous ones use an ancient power to teleport directly into the world they wish to conquer. They are the ones who can topple empires with only a handful of soldiers. The other ones we see in the movies, that come in massive spaceships and invade our skies with fighter spacecraft, they are nothing. They're more like fleas jumping from planet to planet, and are easily defended against."

"Defended against?" I pressed.

"Come, you didn't think the international space station was really orbiting the earth in some sort of peace-keeping initiative did you?" She smiled coyly and sat in the desk next to mine. "It is there to warn us of extraterrestrial threats, and to eliminate them. There is also a base on the dark side of the moon, lovingly nicknamed Fort Floyd, for obvious reasons."

I smirked. "And all of the countries of the world just sing koombiah and get along with massive weapons overhead?"

Katya shook her head. "You have heard of mutually assured destruction, yes?"

I nodded. "The theory that one nuke fired will set off a chain reaction wherein all nuclear powers will launch nukes and everybody dies."

"The weapons up there," she said as she pointed upward, "would burn our atmosphere in seconds. No government will call it down on an earthly enemy, as everyone would die. Humans, plants, animals, everything."

"What if a crazy guy gets his hands on it?"

"Let's hope that doesn't happen," Katya said with a wink. "Besides, there are safety measures. Keys, codes, all of that. Only the permanent U.N. Security Council states know of the weapons, and it would take their vote to fire it. Unanimous decision. No exceptions."

"You know a lot about that," I said.

"Don't tell anyone else, or I will slit your throat like a goat and hang you up to make blood pudding," she said. I couldn't tell if she was joking, so I nodded. "Now, there is something else you should know about the portals. When they open…"

WEEEEEEE-OOOOOOO, WEEEEEEE-OOOOOO!

I covered my ears as a siren blasted through the room. A blue light flashed, stabbing my eyes painfully.

"Come," Katya said as she yanked me up by the arm.

I had to run to keep pace with her as she dashed through a series of halls. I wasn't sure whether the alarm signaled a true emergency or some sort of training lesson. She stopped in a side chamber and disappeared for a moment, only to return three seconds later with several weapons. I realized that this wasn't a drill when she offered me a glock. I took the handgun and looked at her as she adjusted the tactical strap on an AK-47 so that the weapon sat evenly over her back. She tucked what looked like a futuristic Uzi into a holster on her left hip and held a strange, long barreled rifle in her left hand. When I looked I saw that the stock was folded up. The thing looked like it would be well over three feet long when unfolded. I wanted to know what it was, but she motioned for me to follow and didn't bother explaining.

We ran up a set of stairs I hadn't seen before and out through a steel door that was several inches thick and took a hefty tug to pull open.

There, in the cemetery, was another portal. My heart caught in my throat. It was widening slowly, with blue and silver lightning crackling and popping as bolts shot across the black void. Had Katya not turned back and grabbed my arm again, I would have stood there staring like an idiot for a long time before realizing that she was moving us to a grassy knoll near the back of the cemetery.

She dropped into a squat and unfolded the rifle. She clicked a few things into place and then loaded massive bullets into a large magazine. She then stuffed the magazine up into the bottom of the rifle and yanked the bolt back.

"Take this," Katya said as she handed me something that looked like a scope.

"What do I do?" I asked.

"Put your gun away, it's only if they get close to us. You are the spotter. Keep your eyes on the target."

I didn't bother asking which target. At that moment, a large drakkul stepped through. Two swords hung from belts tied around his red robes. This one wore a mask like the first one I had seen, but did not have a tail like the one in the picture.

"Where is the guardian of this world?" the drakkul asked in raspy, but otherwise perfect English.

"Here, you stinking goat-sucker," someone yelled back.

I put the monocular up to my right eye. There was a thin layer of fog rolling above the grass and snaking between the headstones where the drakkul stood. Beyond that, I saw a group walking toward the portal. Flint, Hank, and Dan were there, armed to the teeth. Flint was holding an M4, while Dan had a Bushmaster ACR held at the low ready. Hank, on the other hand, had some sort of lever-action rifle I couldn't identify.

"The guardian is coming, he asks that you wait a moment," Hank said.

"I don't like waiting," the drakkul said.

Hank worked the lever on his rifle and smiled confidently. "I'm sure a minute or two won't be worth the hassle of breaking the Shadow Concordance."

"What's the Shadow Concordance?" I whispered.

"Shut up," Katya hissed. "Keep eyes on the drakkul. If any other forms step through the portal, you tell me and I will shoot them."

Feeling like an idiot, I closed my mouth and concentrated on the portal. After two minutes, three other men joined Hank and the others. I hadn't seen them before. They had weapons as well, but nothing modern.

It was like something straight out of the Viking era. Three men, all about the same height, broad shouldered and heavily armed, approached the portal. One of them led the three. In his left hand he held a massive, round shield with a studded buckler in the middle. In his right hand he wielded a large axe. As he walked I caught glimpses of a gladius hanging at his side. Over his right shoulder I saw the narrow tips of two javelins, while a thick and sturdy spear poked out over his left shoulder. He wore chainmail under several thick furs. The two marching in lockstep behind him were equally as menacing. One had leather armor augmented with the kind of metal plates one would expect to find on a roman soldier. He had a large sword and shield, with several knives along his belt. The third wore thick hides, with iron plates attached by sturdy chains that rattled as he walked. Instead of a shield, he carried only a massive, two-handed axe in his hands.

The three walked up to the drakkul and regarded him silently for a moment.

"I am the gatekeeper," the man in the front said. "I am Rolf, son of Einar, the last of the great chiefs of the north." He motioned toward the others. "These are my cousins, Arne and Bjorn. They have fought at my side in every battle, and we stand in command of this world."

In command of this world? Strange concept of global rule if they were hiding out underground like the rest of us.

"I am Hek'tar Bar'Sule," the drakkul said with a slight nod of his head. "I have come to collect on a bounty. Your world is harboring a criminal, and I have come for recompense."

"Our world has many criminals," Rolf said stoically. "Of whom do you speak?"

"A man," Hek'tar said. "A man who murdered my brother."

Rolf shook his head. "We control the portals," he said. "No human from this planet has gone to yours, so unless your brother was trespassing on our world, we have nothing further to discuss."

Hek'tar roared and his hand went down to his sword, but stopped short of pulling it. "You would dishonor me by hiding the criminal!"

"So be dishonored," Rolf said. "Your brother dishonored himself by coming here without invitation or permission." Rolf set his large shield down and let it lean against his left hip. He then held out his hand. The large man with the massive axe dug under his armor and pulled a piece of paper. Rolf flipped it open. "There was an incident involving a drakkul in a city known to us as Dallas. Is this the drakkul you speak of?"

"Yes!" Hek'tar spat.

My heart skipped a beat. The drakkul was here for me. I had been the one to kill his brother.

"Easy, Mills," Katya whispered to me. "Try not to think about Dallas."

How could I not? This drakkul was the other's brother. He came here asking for me, and now a trio of strange men who looked like they should be battling it out at some sort of ren-fair were all that stood between me and another encounter. Sweat formed on my brow.

I saw the image of the drakkul I had stabbed. I felt the pain of the lightning on my skin once again. My hand trembled and the monocular shook too much for me to watch. I pulled it down and tried to take a steadying breath.

"There! Him! I demand his blood!"

"Mills, I told you not to think about it!" Katya said as she sat up. "Now they know where you are."

I felt my stomach churn as the drakkul pointed right at me. "How?"

"They can sense memories," Katya said. "Go on, we have already lost the element of surprise."

"Go?" I asked.

"Come HERE HUMAN!" Hek'tar shouted.

Rolf pointed his sword at Hek'tar. A dozen drakkul hissed from the other side of the portal.

"Your brother trespassed on our world," Rolf said. "If you want to take this human, you will have to fight me for the right to take him."

"Go on," Katya said. "You'll only make it worse by hiding here."

Bjorn, who appeared ever more massive the closer he got, began walking toward me and waving for me to meet him. I slowly got up to my feet and walked toward him. Were they going to send me off to die? I did have the glock with me. Perhaps I could just run for it and shoot any drakkul who came after me? I wasn't sure what to do. I couldn't say why, but my feet numbly continued forward. Bjorn patted me on the shoulder, which felt more like a bear with a steel paw slapping me downward than anything a comrade might do. Then he gently pushed me forward.

"This human murdered my brother!" Hek'tar accused.

"Your brother attacked and murdered an unarmed man," Rolf said flatly. "This man acted in defense. The criminal here is your brother."

I glanced to Hank. His normally confident smile was gone, replaced by a worried frown.

That was not a good sign.

"How do you answer?" Rolf asked me.

I stared back at the large man and arched a brow. How was I supposed to answer? I looked to the drakkul warrior. His features were not human, but the narrowed glare and the curled lips were more than enough to display the creature's hate.

"Your brother murdered my father. He came with one of those harbinger wolves, and they attacked us. We didn't have any weapons."

"Liar!" Hek'tar shouted. "My brother would not attack unprovoked. You had weapons! How else could you murder my brother?"

I wasn't sure if it was the fact that the threat was now in my face, or perhaps the false accusation that I was a liar that set me off, but my fear was suddenly replaced by hot anger. "I don't lie," I snarled. "Your brother attacked two innocent people, and I killed him with his own sword after he attacked us!"

Hek'tar stepped forward as if to strike, but Rolf's sword stopped the large drakkul. "I have seen proof," Rolf said. "This man speaks the truth."

"Indeed?" Hek'tar said. "Then what of the engine his partner stole?"

My self-righteous anger faded as I recalled the words my father had said. He had mentioned something about stealing an engine, and then when the portal opened, he hadn't acted surprised by the portal itself, but fearful about the fact he had been found. Even in death, the lousy deadbeat was only good for getting me into trouble. "I didn't have any part of that," I said.

"Ah! You admit that you knew!" Hek'tar said.

"Is this true?" Rolf asked as he turned to me.

My heart started to beat faster and harder than any other time in my life. "No, I mean, yes, but not the way he says. I didn't know about it until right before they came into the alley. My dad mentioned something about one of his previous jobs, and that he had taken something, but that's it. Then, the portals opened and the giant wolf and lizard-man came through."

"You are the thief's child?" Hek'tar growled.

"No, well, yes, but he hasn't been my father for a long time. My mom raised me."

"Mills, shut up," Hank called out from the back. I glanced over and saw that Hank and the others had shouldered their rifles. Rolf put a hand on my chest and pushed me back. Bjorn stepped in front of me and made a point of stamping his axe in the ground.

"He didn't know," Rolf said.

"But he is the child," Hek'tar said. "The sins of the father pass to

53

the sons. I will take him, or you will give me the engine. Those are the only two solutions to our problem."

"Do you have it?" Rolf asked.

"Have it?" I shook my head. "I don't even know what it is. Not really. I swear. I haven't been in contact with my dad for years. I had no part in this."

"No matter!" Hek'tar shouted. "He is guilty by blood!"

The dozen drakkul behind him shouted and raised swords.

"According to our laws, he is innocent," Rolf said firmly. He bent down and picked up his shield. "If you wish to contest this, then there is only one way."

"Foolish human," Hek'tar said as he backed away and slowly drew his sword. "I come from a long line of conquerors. I have destroyed three worlds myself. Their gatekeepers begged for mercy. I feasted myself on their screams. I will enjoy spilling your blood upon the ground, and then I will devour your body and consume your strength."

Rolf laughed and motioned for us to get back. "You may have conquered worlds, but you have never faced a chieftain of the north before. I shall send you to Hell, and you shall be thrust down into the darkness forever."

"This duel is in agreement with the Shadow Concordance," Arne said. "None shall interfere until it is finished. You all know the rules. Break them, and we shall destroy you."

A second drakkul came to the edge of the portal and drew his sword. "We agree," he said. "No one shall break the rules. For honor. For Glory!"

The others behind him took up the chant. "For honor, for glory!"

Rolf jerked his head to the side and I heard several popping noises. Then he shrugged and rolled his shoulders. "I'll make this fair," he said as he kicked his large shield away. "Here I am, Hek'tar. Come and get me."

Bjorn pulled me back just as a translucent shell of energy fell on the area in front of the portal.

Hek'tar advanced without any hesitation. The lizard thrusted his sword with one hand and blasted a bolt of lightning out from his other. Rolf somersaulted to the left, allowing the lightning to slam into the translucent shell. The electricity crackled and sparked across the barrier as wisps of smoke rose upward. Rolf lunged in and the two clashed swords. The sound was distorted through the barrier, seeming almost like a bad 80's electronica drum. I watched as the two danced back and forth. Their swords flashed and darted in and out, but neither scored a hit on the other.

"He plays with him," Bjorn said. "Wants to make a point for the others."

I looked at the large man silently. Bjorn was smiling, obviously not nearly as afraid as I was of the whole situation. I glanced across to Arne and saw a similar, contented expression. I soon learned why.

Rolf let out a mighty cry. I swear he called out to Thor. *Man, he really takes this Viking thing seriously.* He charged in and lashed out with his axe. The heavy weapon knocked Hek'tar's sword down toward the ground. Rolf then leapt over the weapon and drove his knee into the lizard-man's nose. The drakkul's head snapped back and blood shot out to splatter against the barrier just in front of me.

Bjorn and Arne raised their weapons and hooted like a couple of hockey fans.

Hek'tar stumbled back and drew his other sword, but Rolf had other plans. He threw his axe, forcing the drakkul to duck, and then he launched a javelin before the creature knew what was coming.

Screams and angry hisses came out from the portal as their champion was struck through the left shoulder. The narrow point exploded out through the back, easily tearing through Hek'tar's scales and muscle. Hek'tar let out a cry and used both hands to send lightning toward Rolf. The large man turned and ran up the barrier, executing the most graceful backflip I had ever seen anyone do, and then he whirled around and threw his second javelin. This one went through Hek'tar's right shoulder. The creature fell to his knees and could no longer keep his arms up.

Rolf drew his spear and stamped the butt on the ground.

Bjorn and Arne were chanting in unison, "Rolf, Rolf, Rolf!"

Rolf walked slowly toward the drakkul. He lowered the spear just inches away from the creature's face. Through the barrier, I could see Rolf's mouth moving, but I couldn't hear the words he spoke. Hek'tar then glanced in my direction. He flicked a forked tongue out and then sneered at me. I got the impression that even now, with javelins sticking out of his body like some sort of scaled pin-cushion, he was threatening me. Hek'tar then looked up to Rolf and spoke, but again the barrier prevented me from hearing the words.

The spear plunged in. The front of Hek'tar's robes pressed in, and then tore loose as the spear drove through the drakkul's body and exploded out the back with a small spray of blood. Then, in a move so fast I barely knew what was happening, Rolf unsheathed his gladius and took Hek'tar's head.

A column of green and red light poured upward from the neck hole and collided with the magical shell around them. The light washed over the surface and then the shell melted away. Rolf sheathed his gladius and then picked up the head in both hands and showed it to the drakkul on the other side of the portal. They all hissed and shouted at him.

"I have won. This portal will now be shut. You are not to come back again for seven weeks!" Rolf bellowed.

"Seven weeks?" I repeated softly.

Bjorn nodded. "Seven sets of seven days. It is the prescribed period of time after a challenger has been defeated."

A bolt of silver lightning shot out from the portal and struck Hek'tar's lifeless head, melting the flesh away in a sick, Indiana Jones kind of way. Then, the portal closed and the light was gone.

Bjorn and Arne moved to the headless corpse and knelt beside it.

"Honorable foe," Arne said softly.

"Return to the hall of your fathers. You fought bravely," Bjorn added. The two removed the javelins from the corpse and cleaned up the weapons in the area. Then they picked up the body and carried it away.

Rolf approached me with the severed head. I couldn't help but stare at the empty eye sockets.

"I need to know about this engine," Rolf said.

I shrugged. "Honestly, I don't know," I replied. "I told you everything I know." I pointed to Hank. "You saw the tape right? That's it, that's all I know about any of this."

"Rolf, if I may," Hank said as he stepped forward.

Rolf held up a hand and shook his head. That was all it took to shut Hank up. I was confused. Hank didn't seem the type to ruffle easily, but when he saw Rolf's signal, he didn't just stop talking, he *bowed* his head. What was I getting myself into now?

"You're coming with me," Rolf said. "The king will know what to do."

Great. As if these three Viking wannabes wasn't enough, now I had to go and meet "the king."

"He's a friend," Hank put in.

Rolf didn't listen. He just wrapped his fingers around my arm so tight it was like a mechanical vice. He dragged me along without hardly any effort on his part.

"I got ten bucks that says newbie doesn't live through the meeting," Flint said.

I heard Dan curse under his breath.

CHAPTER 5

I was taken back down through the main meeting room in the underground bunker, and toward the back where a secret door opened with a wave of Rolf's hand. A cool breeze rushed out to meet us as the stone slid to the side and opened into a hallway lit with torches that burned blue. We hurried through the hallway and to a large door of bronze. On the face of the door was a carved image of a large portal. In front of the portal was a single man holding a sword drawn and out to the side. Something that looked like either fire or lightning was rising from his free hand.

Could Rolf summon lightning like the drakkul? I wondered.

A voice came from the door. "The darkness comes," it said.

"But I am the light, and I will pierce its heart," Rolf replied.

The door swung open.

We passed through and into a large chamber. How any of this was kept hidden from the world was beyond me. The forests of this area were thick, but surely someone must have noticed the strange trees with doors and the random cars parked in the cemetery by now. More than that, how could anyone have excavated this massive underground compound without Section Four shutting them down?

Rolf led me through the large chamber and then into a side passageway that curved and wound through the earth. The walls of stone turned to clay as we descended down a spiraling staircase. It seemed we went down for three or four stories before the stairs opened out into another hallway. We walked for twenty yards and came to a three-way fork. The door on the left was blue. The one in the middle was gold. The door on the right was red. In front of each door was a box of black stone set upon a pedestal of gold. Rolf moved toward the red door and placed his hand atop the box.

I watched as a yellow light grew from within the stone and enveloped his hand. It was like some kind of biometric scanner, but it didn't use any technology that I recognized. The light faded and the red door opened. We walked inside and I was directed to a wooden chair. There were five other chairs in the room, four more along my side of a half-moon shaped table, and one large, high-backed chair on the opposite side. I expected Rolf to take that one, as it was obviously meant for whoever was in charge, but he didn't. He sat next to me.

A door at the back of the room opened and two women entered. They were gorgeous. Brilliantly bright blonde hair, sharp facial features, and tight, athletic builds. Their clothes were equally magnificent. Robes of green silk with gold and silver designs woven into the trim around the cuffs and hem lines. They only came in a few feet, and then moved to take positions on either side of the doorway.

Rolf stood up.

I did likewise.

A tall man entered. His eyebrows were thick and dark. His face was stern, with angular features like the women, but a much wider jaw and nearly square chin. He looked at me with eyes that appeared to be purple. He wore a silver robe with red trim that matched the women's in design. A long, slightly curved scimitar hung from his left hip. My eyes locked onto the blade as he moved toward the high-backed chair. As a boy, I had collected swords of all kinds. I had claymores, katanas, longswords, you name it, but I had never seen one like this. The scabbard was leather, not the cheap kind that only maintains its lacquer for a year or two before cracking, but expensive, supple leather. The hand guard was made of steel, and had a leaf-and-vine design carved into it. The handle itself appeared to be a mix of wood and ivory. I had this intense longing to see what the blade itself looked like, but I didn't dare do something so bold as ask to see it.

Whoever this man was, if Rolf was showing deference, then I would keep my mouth shut until spoken to.

"Be seated," the man said with a wave of his hand.

Rolf and I sat.

The man moved into the high backed chair and looked at me for a moment. Then he turned to Rolf. Neither of them spoke. They just stared at each other. I shifted in my seat and glanced to the two women at the back of the room. They were watching me carefully. I put on a smile and offered them a nod. They didn't respond at all.

My stomach was growing into a knotted mess as I sat quietly, waiting for whatever this silent period was to be over. Then, after a few minutes, the man reached up and pulled his hair back. It had been too long to see before, but now that the hair was moved I could see tall, pointed ears.

"My name is Indyrith, I am the Oracle of the Gates."

I nodded. I heard the words, and had I not been stuck staring at the man's ears, I might have responded. I had read many fantasy novels as a kid. Indyrith was the spitting image of every wise elf I had ever read about. The long hair, the sharp features. The graceful walk. The pointed ears and the vibrantly colored eyes. It was as if I had stepped out of reality completely now. Rolf had to nudge me to break my fixation.

"I am Joshua Mills," I said, rubbing my ribs a bit.

"It is my understanding that the drakkul believe you have stolen something of theirs."

"No, I didn't take anything," I said. Why was nobody understanding this?

Indyrith waved a hand. "The drakkul have laws that allow the direct descendants of criminals to be punished in the event that the criminal has either died, escaped, or is otherwise beyond their grasp."

"But they killed him," I replied. "He already paid for his crime, if he actually stole something from them."

Indyrith shook his head. "I'm afraid that is not how the drakkul see it. They will continue to maintain that they have a right to claim recompense until they are satisfied. The more valuable the object stolen, or the greater the crime committed, the more the drakkul will demand as fair repayment. In most cases, blood is considered fair payment for theft, murder, and other acts that dishonor the victim." Indyrith laced his fingers together on the table and leaned forward a bit. "I have seen them carry on feuds for generations, both in their worlds, and in ours. To put it into terms that are readily understandable, you are familiar with the fact that there are groups of people who seek reparation from the U.S. government for the slavery of African Americans, yes?"

I nodded.

"If this situation was the same, but drakkul people had been enslaved, they would be demanding the deaths of each and every direct descendant of every slave owner not only now, but for another three hundred years, or until their descendants were destroyed."

My eyes shot open wide. Suddenly the couple of complaints I had heard from my crazy uncle about affirmative action seemed pathetically paltry by comparison.

"I don't even know what was stolen," I said.

Indyrith nodded. "Yes, I have the details that Rolf gave me." He reached across the table and held out his hands for me. "Come, give me your hands. I will search your memories. If we can find any clues that will help us, then I can maybe present a solution to the drakkul."

"But, I thought Rolf won the fight. Doesn't that mean they can't come back?"

Rolf shook his head. "Seven weeks. That's all the longer a portal closure is good for. In seven weeks, they can return with another champion."

"Yet, I fear they will not wait," Indyrith said. "The first drakkul came covertly to find your father. Whatever he stole is of such vital importance that some drakkul individuals are willing to risk their own honor and deceitfully gain entry into our world. If we do not stop them, it will open the way for further attacks. If other races see that we are unable to protect ourselves, they may also try to take advantage of the situation."

I reached my hands across the table. I wasn't sure what to expect, but I didn't see the harm in allowing Indyrith to look into my thoughts. "I don't think you'll find anything new," I said.

Indyrith smiled. "We shall see."

The instant my hands touched his, there was a power that seized my wrists and held them fast. My vision went dark. A rush of wind whirled about me in the blackness, and then there was a flash of silver light, followed by a second, and then a third flash. It was like a lightning storm off in the distance, breaking into a moonless night, except I knew it wasn't nighttime. I could no longer feel my chair, or the floor beneath my feet. There was only the rush of air, and a stirring in the dark that I could not see.

"Calm your mind. Try to relax. The longer you fight it, the harder it will be for me to find what I need," a voice said in the darkness. It took me a moment to realize that it was Indyrith speaking. "Focus on your breathing. Take a deep breath in, hold it, and then slowly let it out."

I tried, but it was like taking a breath while sticking your head out the window of a car moving at high speeds on the freeway. The air assaulted my face, and my body was resisting against it.

"Calm," Indyrith said again.

I tried to open my mouth to speak, but it was filled with a gust of air that blew out my cheeks and made my lips flap about. Forget the car metaphor. This was like that Chevy Chase movie with the g-force machine. My hair was whipping back behind me. I squinted my eyes shut. My stomach flipped and I felt as though I would retch last week's breakfast.

"Clear your mind," Indyrith said.

Clear it? How does one clear their mind after seeing the things I had seen in the last couple of days? A secret government organization that wanted to kill me if I refused to work for them, a random team of super soldiers that fight the monsters that keep children awake at night, lizard-men that visit our planet through massive portals, and elves. Let's not forget there was an elf holding my hands at this very moment. Being raised Mormon, I had never taken drugs, but I was starting to wonder if someone had slipped me something back in jail. Maybe I was still there. Or, maybe I really was in the mental hospital. That would explain a lot of this.

"You must clear your thoughts!" Indyrith shouted. The voice echoed in the darkness. I tried to focus on my breathing, but it was still coming in short gasps. I couldn't simply think of nothing. It was impossible. There was far too much going on. Still, I wanted to work with Indyrith as best I could. If he could devise a way to appease the drakkul, then I had to try.

I thought of Susan. Our wedding day. It had been the best day of my life. The ceremony had been wonderful, with friends and family gathered into the temple in American Fork, Utah. The reception had been held at an outdoor park. It had made for wonderful pictures, but I could still remember how hot it had been wearing a tux outside during the last weekend of June. In my mind's eye, I saw Susan's face. She was smiling, brushing a stray bit of hair from her face as we went to cut the cake. We didn't shove the pieces into each other's faces like some do. After the reception someone had told us that not doing so was a sign of good luck, that we would be strong as a couple. I guess there was no omen to warn us about me being charged with murder.

Soon the line between memory and reality faded. I wasn't just seeing the past. I was *reliving* it. I held her close for our first dance. She laughed as we focused only on ourselves. She was radiant in her gown. It was like dancing with a star. She laid her head on my shoulder and we finished out the song before giving each other a kiss.

I fast forwarded to the day Tommy was born. It was a cool day in late September. Susan went through thirty-six hours of labor while I sat there holding her hand and wishing I could have taken the pain for her. I could still feel the overwhelming sense of joy, pride, and love that filled the room when little Tommy finally emerged. He wasn't overly large, but he was the most beautiful thing I had ever seen. The nurses cleaned him up and performed their measurements and tests. Everything had worked out better than I had ever anticipated.

Next I saw his second birthday. We had stuffed dragon's hanging from the ceiling. At the time, Tommy was so into the movie How to Train Your Dragon, that he hardly talked of anything else *but* dragons. We were happy. Life had been perfect.

"Good, now let me direct you," a voice said.

I turned around and saw Indyrith standing in the living room of the small apartment we had been living in during the time of Tommy's second birthday.

"How did you get here?" I asked. I had almost forgotten that I was inside a memory.

Indyrith smiled. "Come with me."

The tall elf led me to the front door. I looked back into the apartment. Susan and Tommy were playing, and then I saw myself, as if watching a family movie. The past version of me filled the void in the memory as I left it behind.

"Come," Indyrith said. "We cannot stay long, or you will get lost in your own mind." I nodded, but there was a part of me that thought it might not be so bad. If I could relive those early years again, before the alley in Dallas, before the...

I shook my head. No. I had a job to do now. The real Tommy and Susan were still out there, and they were going to need me if this drakkul feud was going to involve *all* of my father's direct descendants.

I stepped out the open door, but instead of reaching the apartment balcony, I found that we were in the alleyway in Dallas. I saw the old me and my father come around the corner. I stayed quiet as Indyrith walked around them, listening intently to their words.

The portals opened. The fight ensued. I had been able to detach myself somewhat from the videotaped version of the past, but seeing the memory played out around me was entirely different. While the old me ran for the harbinger wolf, I sprinted toward the drakkul warrior. I lunged for him from behind, and then sailed through his body as if I were nothing more than a ghost. I hit the ground and rolled to a stop. I jumped up and made to attack again, but Indyrith suddenly was at my side and held me still.

"There is nothing you can do," he said.

"I have to try."

Indyrith held tight.

We were both pulled through the portal along with the old me. I guess since my mind didn't see what happened in the alley until I returned, we weren't able to stay where we were and help. I watched as I struggled with the harbinger wolf. I felt the same rage as I watched it tear into my back. Then, in the blink of an eye we landed on the other side of the portal. The harbinger wolf went down first and then I crashed onto it and finished the fight, or at least I thought I had. In that moment I remembered Katya's warning that the creature would heal from the injuries I inflicted on it.

We rushed back through the portal once more.

"I don't know where it is, I swear!" my father said. I already knew how this was going to play out.

The masked drakkul plunged the sword deep into my father's chest. He then pulled the blade back out and cut off my father's head.

I saw my old self charge the drakkul. The drakkul turned, laughed at my old self, and then raised his sword and took three steps toward the old me.

I watched helplessly as the old me engaged the drakkul. The only saving grace was I knew how this was going to play out. I would win and survive, and the drakkul would get stabbed through the gut. It would be a slow death for him, and an agonizing murder charge that would change my life.

"Study everything," Indyrith said as he motioned for me to walk with him to survey the battle up close. "The human mind picks up on things that you cannot always recall clearly. That is why I prefer to walk among memories myself, rather than discuss important questions."

"And I thought it was 'cause you didn't trust me," I said sarcastically.

Indyrith nodded. "It is harder to lie in such situations, yes. That is part of it. I trust that you would tell me what you could, but I am looking for something you can't tell me. A lie of omission because your subconscious recorded a detail you can't remember. I trust you,

Joshua Mills; it is the failings of the human mind in general that I distrust."

I shrugged and watched as the masked drakkul stepped in and sliced down. The past me turned sideways, allowing the blade to sail harmlessly in front of me, and then I spun around so as to use my momentum. The attacker dodged away, and I tackled nothing. The old me grunted as I hit the ground, and rolled away. The sword came down and threw out orange sparks as it struck the asphalt. The drakkul growled and ran after me.

"You aren't going to win, snake-face," I said as I grinned. I would never call myself a fighter, but watching the moves I executed in the alley, I had to admit that I was doing a fine job of it, especially considering the circumstances.

The old me kept rolling out of the way as the drakkul continued his assault. After a few more near misses, the old me kicked my legs forward. My right leg connected with the drakkul's groin. The drakkul stumbled backwards. The old me masterfully pulled the spare blade and jumped up.

The masked drakkul swished his sword from side to side. Lightning streaked across the blade. Then, he charged in. The drakkul swung and the old me moved to parry. The swords connected and that terrible thunderous sound rocked the alleyway again. The drakkul spun around, changing directions. The old me blocked that strike as well, and then the drakkul kicked the old me in the stomach.

"You were doing well," Indyrith commented as I watched my old self fly into the building and slide down the wall.

"Until this point," I replied.

The drakkul charged, but the old me blocked that strike as well. As I watched the old me punch the drakkul, I mimed a savage left as if fighting again. It was hard not to get into the action, despite having already sailed through the memory-produced image of the drakkul once.

The drakkul came down with a hard chop that despite the block, cut down into old me's shoulder. Streaks of lightning fired off around the swords. Then, I noticed that the old me drifted his gaze to my father's corpse.

I stepped forward. "No, don't lose your focus. Get back in the fight. Think of Susan and Tommy, fight for them! Don't let them find you here in an alley like some gutter-rat! Get up!" I shouted at my old self.

Old me set his jaw and kicked again, this time pushing the drakkul back several feet. Old me shot upward, angling the sword up and out. The masked drakkul charged in. Old me leaned forward and prepared to launch off the wall with the sword, but I could no longer contain myself. Indyrith had already told me there was nothing I could do but watch, and I had already discovered that myself when I tried to tackle the drakkul, but something urged my feet forward.

The angle of the drakkul's sword was not where it should have been. In the alleyway, the sword had flashed over my back horizontally, but now the memory-produced version was angling for a diagonal chop. There was no way the old me was going to avoid being hit.

I rushed forward with speed like I had never had before. The drakkul was fast, but with all of my rage focused on him I swung at the back of his head. My fist *connected* with his skull. He stumbled forward and in an attempt to correct himself, he shifted the angle of the sword.

The old me stabbed the drakkul through the chest, and the drakkul swished his sword through the air, just missing old me by a hair.

The drakkul howled in pain and crumpled to the ground with old me. Old me let go of the sword and climbed up the drakkul's body and seized the creature's sword arm. Old me pressed his wrist to the ground with his left hand and then began wailing on the side of the drakkul's head with the right.

As for me, I was too caught up in the moment to realize I *shouldn't* have been able to strike a memory. I rushed in just after the second downward punch by old me and kicked the drakkul in the head. I heard a sickening *crunch!*

Old me kept raining down knuckle-bombs while the drakkul tried to fight back with his free hand.

"Go for the sword handle!" I shouted.

Old me shifted his leg and hit the sword sticking out of the drakkul's abdomen. The lizard-man roared out in pain.

Old me sat up sat up just a bit and smiled. Then the smile faded. The moment was only a fraction of a second, but I remembered what was coming.

"Stay in the fight!" I screamed at old me. "Don't let up now!"

Too late.

The drakkul aimed his hand and fired a blast of lightning into old me. Old me went flying through the air once more. There was a *thump* as old me collided with the wall once more. The lightning intensified and old me was losing consciousness fast.

I hesitated for only a second before I realized that the lightning was not stopping. The drakkul was advancing and maintaining his power over old me.

I rushed in again and pummeled the drakkul in the side of the head. His skull snapped to his left shoulder. I then kicked him in the stomach. He roared out and doubled over. The lightning stopped.

Old me slid to the ground.

Neither old me nor the drakkul moved.

I could hear the sirens coming now and knew the fight was almost over.

"Get up!" I shouted at old me.

Old me just stared at the drakkul.

The drakkul was now straightening himself, breathing heavily and flexing his fingers.

"Get up!" I shouted again.

Old me mouthed something inaudible.

The drakkul took a step toward old me and I knew what had to be done. I swung again, but this time my hand sailed through the drakkul's image harmlessly.

NO! I had to finish this. I couldn't lose my focus now! I tried to concentrate and swing again. Again nothing happened. I cried out for Indyrith to help, but the elf didn't move. The drakkul was going to kill old me, and whatever had allowed me to hit him before was now gone.

Old me looked up at the mask.

The mask! It had fallen before.

Instead of punching at the figure, I moved around the drakkul and snatched at the mask. I failed to grab it, but I did manage to knock it loose. The mask fell, and old me now realized what he was fighting.

The drakkul smiled, but this time I realized he hadn't ever smiled at old me. He was smiling at *me*. He was looking me in the eyes! In the heat of battle, I must not have noticed that detail, but it was clear now. The drakkul had seen me, reaching back in time somehow.

Katya's words about the drakkul seeing memories came back into my mind.

Old me pushed up, using the wall for support as the drakkul

staggered forward. The drakkul thrusted forward. In my memory, I thought the stab had been slower and indirect. Only now did I realize the truth of it. The blade had appeared slow to old me because the drakkul wasn't aiming for old me. The blade slid through me as I looked down in horror. I had just been stabbed by my own memory. I cried out in pain.

Old me dodged and then then snatched out and yanked the handle sticking out of the drakkul's abdomen straight up. The drakkul hissed again. I flinched as old me lunged forward and head-butted the creature in the face.

The sirens were growing ever closer now. I just had to hang on for a few more seconds.

The drakkul spat at old me. Old me recoiled, and ripped the sword out of the drakkul's abdomen at the same moment the drakkul pulled his other sword out of me.

I sank to my knees while the drakkul turned and leapt for its portal. The hole in space closed. My vision started to go dark. Even as the headlights and sirens poured into the alley, I slumped to the side, clutching at my stomach.

The first time I had been in this alley, I had ended up going to jail, but now, I was about to die. My body felt cold and I shivered. My muscles cramped and burned all through my body.

I barely noticed the hand slip under my head and lift me up.

"Come, Joshua Mills, it is not your time yet," Indyrith whispered into my ear.

CHAPTER 6

I don't know how I got into my bed. I assume Indyrith carried me, or perhaps Rolf. All I knew is I woke up in my bed, covered in thick sweat that slimed the sheets and slicked my hair to my scalp. I looked down at my stomach. There was no visible wound, but I could still feel the blade coursing through me. I tried to sit up, but only managed to move an inch or so before screaming in pain and flopping back down.

The door opened and Katya came in. gun in one hand and a book in the other. "You alone?" she asked.

I nodded. "Yeah. What are you, my bodyguard?" I asked. I almost laughed, but that sent burning pains shooting through my abdomen as well.

Katya arched a brow and shook her head. "I am guarding the people out here. If you get attacked in your dreams, it will be too late for you."

I looked at her with wide eyes.

"Just kidding," she added, a wicked sneer curling the corners of her mouth upward.

"Not funny," I replied.

"Well, I was half joking. I will try to save you too, but I am here to keep intruders out. You have been marked."

"Marked?" I said as I reached down and gently placed a finger over the spot where the sword had entered my body. "I was stabbed."

"Not really," Katya said. "I've been stabbed. You were just…*dream stabbed*…"

"Tell that to my stomach. Feels like a piece of rebar is running through me."

"Is he awake?" a voice called from behind the door.

Katya nodded. "He's awake."

"Bout time," Hank said as he moved in around her. "It's been three days."

"Three days?" I blinked and looked back at my stomach.

"Aw, sit up, it's all in your head." Hank reached down and pulled me up.

Trying to sit up by myself was an eight out of ten on the pain scale, and I don't complain easily. I once had a broken finger and the doctor had to x-ray it to make sure it was broken because I was playing with the detached portion of the bone. I could feel it move, but it wasn't painful. But, if trying to sit up by myself had been an eight out of ten, Hank yanking me up was an eleven. I squealed and screeched. I couldn't breathe. My vision began tunneling and I think I might have tried to punch Hank in the stomach. I'm still a bit hazy on that part. All I know for sure is Hank called me a few choice words, and then I passed out again.

The next time I awoke, I was not in a bed. I was on a table in a room I had not been in before. It was cold, and my shirt was off. I had to blink the darkness out of my eyes a few times before I could look around. I was on a medical examination table. No IVs, no wires, and thankfully no bloody rags or organs hanging out. I took in a deep breath, slowly at first, allowing the air to expand my diaphragm, figuring that would be the least impactful test of how my stomach was feeling.

No pain.

I moved my arms, then my legs. Finally, feeling brave enough to try once more, I moved to sit up. This time there was only minimal pain. A sharp stab right next to my navel, but nothing I couldn't push through. That was followed by a dull ache that radiated through my entire torso. Fun times.

The door opened after a minute or so and Hank entered the room. He didn't mention anything about the last time he had tried to get me up. He just smiled and held up a steaming cup.

"I have some soup. You should try to eat."

"Sorry… 'bout before, I mean," I said.

Hank shrugged. "Don't trip on that. Here, drink your soup. You'll need your strength."

"How long was I out this time?" I asked. "Another three days?"

Hank shook his head. "No, it's been seven."

I stared at him incredulously. "A week?"

Hank nodded. He pressed the soup into my right hand. "Drink the soup."

"How am I still alive?" I looked around again, sure I had missed an IV somewhere, or a feeding tube perhaps.

"Indyrith saw to that," Hank said. "He and his daughters have been tending to you each day."

I lifted the cup and sniffed it. Sometimes, there is nothing better than a cheap, hot cup of chicken soup. I scarfed it down without coming up for air, and then I set the cup down.

"Thanks," I said.

Hank smiled. "He has some questions," he said. "Says you might be a dream walker, or something like that."

"A dream walker?" I asked.

Hank shrugged. "It isn't my place to talk for Indyrith. Once you feel up to it, let's go and talk to him together."

I pushed forward and slid off the table, landing solidly on my feet. "I'm good now," I said.

Hank's smile widened. "All right then, let's go."

We walked through a series of corridors while Hank quietly whistled the melody from Dancing Queen. Man, this guy *really* liked Abba. We went into the main hall where I first met the others and sat at the table. A minute or so later, a door opened and a big, hairy thing came out from the back. I started to panic, as it looked like some sort of bad wookie costume, but Hank was quick to steady me.

"He's a friendly," Hank said.

I studied the creature. His hair was thick and long, covering every inch of him from head to toe, even his face. He walked slightly leaning forward, but I wasn't sure if that was how he walked all the time, or if it was to keep his head from smacking the doorways and ceiling. His visage was unmistakable, though I could hardly believe my eyes. "Bigfoot?" I asked.

The large, hairy creature grunted and came toward the table.

"He prefers Nick," Hank said.

"Nick?"

Hank nodded. "What, you think all squatches run around calling themselves Bigfoot? That'd be like all humans running around calling themselves Human."

"But, his name is Nick?"

"Not what you expected?"

Nick draped a white towel over his left arm and approached the table. "Drinks?" he asked in a very low voice.

"I'll take a whiskey on the rocks," Hank said. He then pointed at me with his left thumb while making a circular motion next to his head with his right index finger. "He doesn't drink, he's a Mormon."

Nick made a sound that seemed a mix of laughter and growling. "Milk," Nick said with a nod.

"And a shirt," Hank added.

"I'm being waited on by Bigfoot," I said with a shake of my head. Elves can read minds, and Bigfoot is going to fetch me a milk."

"You forgot the Vikings," Hank said.

"Yeah, the ren-fair guys are a bit over the top, but I'm sure not going to tell them that."

Hank burst into laughter. "Ren-faire?" he echoed with a shake of his head. "No, son, you got it all wrong. Those are three *actual* Vikings."

"No," I said. "Impossible."

"With all you have seen and you are hung up on *that* as being impossible?" Hank whistled through his teeth.

"They'd be hundreds of years old," I said.

"Yep," Hank replied.

"But…" I shook my head and decided to let it go. Hank was right. Why get hung up on *that*? "So they're like some kind of Highlander kind of Vikings then?" I asked. "Or are they more like Wolverine?"

"Bit of both, I suppose," Hank said. "A bit meaner, perhaps."

Nick returned with a shirt draped over the white towel on his arm and a tray with two drinks balanced on his other hand. "Drinks," he said.

Hank and I thanked him. I slipped the shirt on, wincing as a sudden jolt ripped through my body where the sword had stabbed me.

"It'll wear off," Hank promised.

"So you've been wounded in memories too?"

Hank shook his head. "Nope. I've only ever gone into my memories a few times. Never been able to interact with them though."

I was about to ask another question, but as Nick moved his giant bulk out of the way, I saw Indyrith. I moved to stand as Rolf and I had done before, but the tall elf held out a hand and shook his head.

"Remain seated, please," he said.

I nodded.

"How are you feeling?"

"Hungry," Hank said with a smirk.

Indyrith smiled slightly. "That is good. There has been no sign of fever or infection. You should be completely healed within another day or two."

"Infection? How can I get an infection from a memory?" I asked.

Indyrith nodded once and his smile faded. "I had thought this gift lost. I have searched many times for one such as yourself. Unfortunately, the minds of men are not as open as they once were, even among the reservations."

"The reservations?" I glanced to Hank. The man picked up his whiskey and took a small sip after swirling the amber liquid around the giant cube of ice in the cup.

"A dream walker is most commonly found among the Native Americans."

"Well, obviously there is an exception to that rule too," Hank said as he set the glass down. "This guy is as white as they come. Look at him, I bet if he went outside without his shirt, he'd reflect sunlight better than a mirror."

Indyrith tolerated the joke with a nod, but barely offered any hint of a smile. He turned back to me. "But you have Native American heritage, do you not?"

I nodded. "Cherokee," I said.

"Bah, everyone has Cherokee blood," Hank dismissed with a wave.

"Tell me your line," Indyrith said.

"How's he supposed to do that?" Hank asked.

I smiled. I guess he didn't know how much genealogy Mormons did. "I am the direct descendant of a long line of chiefs," I said. My sixth-great-grandfather fought with Andrew Jackson in the Creek and Indian Wars. After Jackson became president, that same ancestor went to Washington D.C. to try and stop the trail of tears. When Andrew Jackson refused to listen, my sixth-great-grandfather led one of the detachments across the Trail of Tears. In addition to being a chief, he was also one of the Cherokee judges. They had a very well organized system of laws, complete with courts."

"How far back does your line go?" Indyrith pressed.

I shrugged. "The records I found stop with a Chief Onai in the sixteen hundreds. The trail goes a bit cold after that."

Indyrith nodded. He held out his right hand. A moment later, one of the blonde elves from before entered the room, carrying a large, green leather book. She set it in his hand and then bowed her head as she backed away. "This is a record of the dream walkers who have joined our ranks over the years," Indyrith said. "I also have a Chief Onai listed in my records. He had a daughter, her name was A Li Onai. She was a formidable dream walker."

I nodded. "I have her in my family tree," I said.

Indyrith placed the book on the table. "I am not the best teacher. Traditionally, a dream walker should be taught by another, but as I have said, those I have tried to work with in recent decades have not proven successful. Their minds are too rigid, formed by the world as they understand it now. Even the purest traditionalists have trouble believing in what you would term the supernatural." Indyrith smiled and traced a finger over the symbol of a tree on the front of the book. "Perhaps you have not been chosen by accident."

"We know that already," Hank said. "His father stole something."

"Your father, did he come from the Cherokee lineage?" Indyrith asked.

I shook my head. "No, the Cherokee are on my mother's side."

Indyrith nodded. "I think we have been looking at this the wrong way," he told Hank. "I suspect the harbinger wolf came independently of the drakkul when they attacked in Dallas."

"Why would they do that?" Hank asked.

Indyrith pointed to me. "Dream walkers have many things in common. Among the most prevalent are dreams of a wolf."

I sat back in my chair. "A large wolf?" I asked.

Indyrith nodded. "One that would start at a young age, and continue to torment the dream walker during the nights."

"I first saw one when I was four," I said.

"Oh please, you don't remember things from when you were four," Hank said as he finished his whiskey.

"Knowing all that *you* do, and you're hung up on *that*, Hank?" I asked.

Indyrith held up a hand to keep Hank silent. "Please, tell me what you saw."

I nodded. "I was asleep in my bed. My room was at the end of a hall, with a big window that went from the floor all the way up to the ceiling. I can still see the wolf. His face took up the entire window. His big, yellow eyes stared at me from the other side of the glass. I couldn't move. I was stuck in my bed, as if something was holding me in place. The wolf turned and then growled. He opened his mouth and glass shattered inward like an explosion. I screamed, and then I woke up. My parents ran into my room like any child's parents would."

"But that was not the last time you had the dream?" Indyrith asked.

I shook my head. "I had the same dream several more times. We moved around a lot, living in different houses while I was growing up, but the dream was always the same. I was back in that room. The wolf came and roared, and then the window would explode inward."

"Always the same?" Hank asked.

I nodded. "Except once, when I was fourteen."

Indyrith cocked his head to the side. "Tell me about that one."

"I woke up, or, at least it felt like I was awake. I'm sure it was just a dream like the others. This time, the wolf was large, but not as large as the other dreams. It stood with its hind feet on the floor, and its front paws on my bed, on my legs, actually. It leaned forward in the moonlight. It was a massive, muscular gray wolf. It bared its fangs and slowly came toward me. I knew it was going to bite me. Its teeth were long and sharp, and it was staring at me with hungry eyes. Like in the other dreams, I couldn't move."

Indyrith nodded. "And then the wolf bit you, and you screamed in pain until the dream subsided," he concluded for me. "It is the same with each dream walker I worked with in the last two hundred years. Always the same dream up until the age of fourteen, and then they are finally killed by the wolf." He opened the book and started to turn it around for me. "Here, read these accounts and see for yourself."

"But I didn't die," I said emphatically.

Indyrith stopped and stared at me. "What did you say?"

"I said, I didn't die."

Indyrith stopped turning the book and sat back in his chair. "What happened then?"

"Somehow, I knew the wolf was coming for me, so I banished all of my fear, and I sat up and took a swing at it."

"You tried to punch it?" Indyrith asked.

"I did," I said. "I almost connected, but then it disappeared and I was just sitting upright in my bed. Shook me to my core though. Even as a proud teenager I had to go to my mom that night. I explained the whole thing to her."

"After two hundred years, finally there is a dream walker strong enough to defeat a harbinger wolf while in the world of dreams."

"What do you mean?" Hank asked. "Harbinger wolves don't attack people in their dreams."

Indyrith nodded. "They attack *some* people in their dreams. You see, the harbinger wolves fear the dream walkers. That's why they attack while the dream walker is young and undeveloped. There are many accounts of dream walkers being attacked in the same way. Not just for the last two hundred years I have recorded here, but for centuries before that as well. The oldest tribes have legends of such events. Some of them now confuse the event with the choosing of a spirit animal, but that is not what it is."

"What does it mean then?" I asked.

"It means that you have the potential to become a very powerful dream walker. Powerful enough that the harbinger wolves have been watching you. You moved around a lot as a child, tell me why."

"I dunno," I said flatly. "At first it was because my dad moved us around. After that, it was to keep us safe from him. He wasn't a good man. Threatened us with a lot of bad things, tried to follow us."

"I suspect there is more to it than that," Indyrith said. "Did your mother ever have dreams of you dying while still a child?"

I shook my head. "No, that's…" I stopped mid-sentence as I recalled three such events that I had long forgotten about. "Yes, a couple times."

Indyrith nodded. "Your ancestors knew the danger you were in. Your mother moving you away from your father helped throw off the harbinger wolves as well. But, if ever the wolves came close to finding you, then your mother would be given a dream to let her know you were in danger."

"What? But why? What is so great about a dream walker?"

Indyrith smiled. "You already know the answer to that," he said. "A dream walker, if properly trained, has the power to fight enemies through many planes and dimensions. You experienced that when you fought the drakkul in your memories."

I nodded. "So, if I hadn't hit the lizard-man,"

"Drakkul," Hank corrected.

"Whatever," I replied impatiently. "If I hadn't hit him while inside my memories, I would have died in Dallas?"

Indyrith nodded.

"But how is that possible?" I asked. "Isn't that a paradox or something? How can a future me save an old me?"

"Time is not as linear as men believe," Indyrith said. "It appears so, and it acts that way, but there is more to it than a simple line of progression. Even I do not know all of time's mysteries, but I can tell you that if you had not found your inner power, you would have died in Dallas. Furthermore, I am now certain that the harbinger wolf came separate from the drakkul. The drakkul came for your father, the harbinger wolf came for you."

"And now both of them are pissed off at you, greeeat," Hank said. "I'm gonna need another drink."

"What do I do now?" I asked.

"I will help you along as best I can, but then you will have to hone your powers on your own. I have some records, but without a dream walker to teach you the path, I am not sure how far you can develop."

"Then why worry about it at all?" Hank cut in. "I mean, we have been doing just fine with the three Vikings and our team. We keep the baddies out, or put down the ones that sneak in. Why all the fuss about a dream walker? I haven't even heard you talk about one before."

Hank seemed a bit jealous with that last bit.

Indyrith nodded. "Those questions are more complicated than they appear," the elf said. "I have not spoken of it before, because I was not sure I would ever find one again. The last candidate failed to even exist within the dream world for more than a few minutes at a time before losing his focus. We never even progressed to the first test, which is to draw water from a stream in the dream world." Indyrith turned and gestured to me with his hand. "Joshua Mills, on the other hand, was able to call upon his power to change time itself, and defeat a drakkul that otherwise would have killed him in the flesh. I have not seen this level of raw power since I first met A Li Onai."

"Wait, you knew her?" I asked.

"She was a powerful warrior, and a great healer." Indyrith sighed and closed the large book. "Dream walkers were first and foremost healers. They could use the energy of the dream world to heal physical, emotional, and mental wounds. However, as the harbinger wolves closed in on them and began attacking, the dream walkers were forced to become warriors themselves. They eventually became the best fighters this world has ever known."

"Except for Rolf, you mean," Hank said. "After all, Rolf not only fought monsters with his cousins, but they killed an entire tribe of ice giants, and were granted a boon by Thor, himself. They even killed Ogedei Khan, and then thwarted all of the other Mongol princes until the Mongol Empire fell. That's to say nothing of the other monsters they have fought."

Indyrith smiled. "And yet, if Joshua Mills can reach his full potential, he could slip into Ogedei's dreams and kill him from there, as well as all of his followers. More than that, he could travel to other worlds without ever needing the portals that the drakkul and other master races employ. They would never see him coming, and he would be like a cloud of death, killing them while they slept."

"So, he'd basically be like Freddy Krueger?" Hank asked.

Indyrith looked puzzled. "I am not aware of a dream walker by that name."

"Forget it," Hank said. "Not important." He turned and examined me. "You're here to fight for the right reasons, yeah?"

I nodded. "Protect the little guys, like you said."

Hank rubbed his chin and then folded his arms. He turned back to the tall elf. "So, if we help Mills reach his potential, then we can stop the invasions forever?"

Indyrith nodded. "I believe so. There is nothing by the way of prophecy, but there are several oracles before me who have proposed such a solution. That is why I have devoted much of my efforts to finding a dream walker."

"I still don't get it, why not tell us?" Hank asked. "I could have helped."

Indyrith shook his head. "It had to be kept secret. Even now, we can only discuss it with those in this circle who need to know. You may tell Flint," Indyrith told Hank. "I will tell Rolf, and my daughters as well but no one else can know of this yet."

"Why the hell not?" Hank asked.

"Think of it this way. Imagine that you are a general of a large army, and you hear that your enemy is developing a weapon of terrible power, one that could destroy your entire army, and against which there is no defense. What would you do?"

"Well, I would take every soldier I had and attack first," Hank said.

Indyrith nodded. "If the others discover Joshua Mills' power, and his potential, then they will do the same. Many will come to the portal, and Rolf will do his best to keep them out, but the line will grow so long that he will not have the time to rest. Eventually he will lose."

"And that's assuming that other enemies don't come in the same way the two in Dallas did," Hank said.

Indyrith nodded. "Like a wounded and cornered tiger, they will fight with every method at their disposal."

"Armageddon," Hank said. "We'll be swamped by millions of invaders, and they will all have the same goal."

"To kill me," I said with a nod. Suddenly I was feeling very unwell.

CHAPTER 7

The following day I was taken out to a large shooting range. Berms had been put into place, piled high on the sides and much higher in the back. There were seven shooting stalls, but only one of them was occupied. Flint was busy placing weapons onto a table off to the side. Loaded magazines sat next to each rifle or pistol he had with him. He saw me coming and smiled.

"Well, if it isn't the puny human who gets hurt in dreams," he said as he racked a glock 9mm. "Come on, let's see if you have any skills we can actually use."

I was going to say something about asking whether he had ever had an entire sword pass through his gut, but I thought better of it. We were supposed to be on the same side. Sinking down to play his games wasn't going to help that along at all.

Besides, I had served as a Mormon missionary in Russia. Russians have swear words that will make your blood curdle, and they aren't half as restrained in using them as Americans are. Flint wasn't going to toss anything my way I couldn't just let roll off my back.

I walked up to the stall and kept behind the red line drawn at the back end of the stall.

"You ever been taught how to shoot?" Flint asked.

"Nope," I lied. The truth was my grandfather had taught me as a kid, but that was a long time ago, and I didn't want to say I had been taught only to realize that I had then forgotten. Besides, most of these weapons were things my grandfather never showed me. Black powder? Sure. Old school lever action and bolt-action rifles that were made pre 1970? All day long. Semiautomatic handgun? No chance. My grandfather didn't even own one. But then again, I bet I could throw a tomahawk better than Flint. Grandpa had plenty of tomahawks.

"Well, this is about as basic as it gets," Flint said as he set the 9mm on the table. This is a glock eighteen. It has a four point-four-nine inch barrel. That's nearly half an inch longer than the nineteen, so hopefully it will help you hit something. Normal trigger pull is five and a half pounds, but I have reworked mine so it's a full six pounds. Don't want you shooting yourself in the foot by accident when you get excited. Holds fifteen rounds in the magazine. I loaded ten just to see how you shoot. When you're ready, pick it up and aim at the target."

I looked out and saw a paper silhouette mounted against a thick rubber backing. I moved forward and then picked up the weapon. "Where's the safety?" I asked.

"It's on the trigger," Flint said. "Originally it was planned to have no external safety. When he was forced to make one, Gaston Glock figured that a smart warrior would know that the only real safety for a weapon is the man or woman handling it. Keep your finger out of the trigger guard until you're ready to shoot, then fire when ready."

Made sense. I had once heard that you didn't have any business carrying a firearm until you knew it as well as you knew a roll of toilet paper. The man who had said that explained that you could be drunk and upside-down in a swimming pool, but you would still know how to use toilet paper. I guess he was hoping to get the same point across as Gaston Glock. The only safety on a weapon that matters, is the training the operator has employed to develop his skills.

I aimed at the head and fired the first shot.

Flint laughed. "High and left," he said.

Funny, the round had hit the head, so I would have counted it for a beginner.

I took more careful aim at the white oval where the eyes would be and fired again. The bullet tore into the left side of the oval, but not centered in the white.

"Still high and left," Flint said impatiently. "Listen, build your castle with your sights, and then squeeze the trigger. Don't yank it. Don't jerk it. Just softly squeeze it back to you. Don't try to anticipate the shot."

I aligned the sights carefully and then tried to slowly squeeze the trigger. It didn't matter. My muscles in my arms tensed just before the shot and pulled the whole weapon down. The round hit the white space to the left of the neck on the target.

"And you're dead," Flint said. "Too bad, so sad. Thanks for stopping by."

I set the weapon down and folded my arms. "You have any additional tips?" I asked.

Flint smiled and stuck a toothpick between his teeth. "Sure, go back home and leave the fighting to the grown-ups."

I nodded. I had never been a great focused shooter. I could never quiet my brain enough to simply be in the moment with a pistol. However, there had been one method I used with my grandfather that had worked. Of course, I had been using a .44 magnum at the time and it was a very different animal from the glock sitting in front of me, but still. I had to see if it would work.

"Don't overthink it," my grandfather had said. "See the target, raise the weapon, and shoot the target. Put your eyes on the target and fire as soon as your weapon is aligned. Simple as that. Don't hold it and wait. Don't try to put everything through the same hole. Just go for a grouping that fits within a quarter. Try to touch three bullet holes together. Do that, and you'll be fine."

It was almost as if he was standing with me now, telling me to ignore the arrogant prick to my left who was snickering and asking if I wanted to pack up and call it a day.

"Three shots," I said aloud, more in response to my grandfather's memory than anything else.

"Yep," Flint said. "You fired three shots and they all sucked. One of them missed, the other two wouldn't take down a borelian. You'd be dead three times over."

I ignored him. I concentrated on the red plus sign in the middle of the oval on the target. I stretched out my hand and picked the glock up. I held it at the low ready and took a breath. I looked at my target, and then I pulled the weapon up fast and steady. *Pop pop pop!*

I lowered the weapon.

"How in the…" Flint muttered.

I smiled. Three holes on the plus sign, each of them touching and forming a kind of shamrock design.

"That has to be a fluke," Flint said. "Do it again."

I took in a breath, enjoying the smell of gunpowder. It had been far too long since I had smelled that beautiful aroma. As I took it in, it brought with it a flood of memories, and suddenly I was having the time of my life. I brought the weapon up again and fired three quick shots. Another shamrock blasted into the first, obscuring the design, but no less compact in the grouping.

"Beginner's luck," Flint said.

"This one's for you, Flint," I said as I pulled the weapon up one more time and fired the last round.

"Now that's just cruel," Flint replied when he saw the bullet hole in the silhouette's crotch. He took the empty pistol from me and then turned to grab a light tan colored rifle. "Let's move to the next stall on our left and see what you do with the scar." We shifted to the adjacent stall and he pointed out a target set half way down the range. "That's fifty yards. Think you can hit it?"

I shrugged and held my hands out for the weapon. Flint popped the magazine into place and then racked a round into the chamber.

I took the rifle in hand and held it up the way I would if I were shooting with my grandfather. The holographic sight was amazingly easy to get used to. I fired the first round to get a feel for it, and heard Flint swear under his breath. I pulled my trigger finger out and to the side as I lowered the weapon and tried to see precisely where my shout had gone. Flint put the binoculars up in front of me. The bullet had torn through the plus sign in the white oval.

"You sure you never fired one of these before?" Flint asked.

I shook my head. "Last rifle I fired was a thirty-aught six my grandpa had, but that was back in high school."

"Put three shots in center mass," Flint said.

I nodded and raised the rifle after he pulled the binoculars away. I put three into center mass. The holes didn't touch, but they were still grouped roughly close enough to fit inside a fifty cent piece.

"Not bad, Mills," Flint said. "Perhaps we can use you after all."

We spent the rest of the day blasting paper targets with various kinds of weapons. I was like a kid in a candy store. It felt like I had spent hours playing. He introduced several different rifles and handguns to me that I had never fired. The only one I didn't like was the Taurus 9mm. The magazine release button was put in a strange location that didn't fit my hand quite right, so I would fire it only to have the recoil send the button into my thumb and release the magazine in the middle of the action, thus causing a malfunction nearly every time I used it.

"Don't worry about it," Flint said. "You can stick with the glock if you need too. However, I wanted to see how you do with this." Flint reached to a holster on his left side and pulled up what I recognized to be a model 1911. "This is a Springfield 1911 .45 ACP," Flint said proudly. "This beauty has been with me in every battle. When I first found out about the things that go bump in the night, I was deep in the bad parts of Afghanistan."

"Are there good parts?" I asked with a scoff.

Flint nodded. "There's good parts everywhere. Afghanistan is a wonderful place, as long as you make it past the camel spiders and the jihadis trying to kill you. There is beauty there."

The way he said it sounded like my third grade teacher scolding me. I nodded and ceded the point. I hadn't been trying to offend, but I hadn't met anyone who had enjoyed their time in Afghanistan, and I had spoken with several friends after their deployments.

"Anyway, if it wasn't for this," Flint said as he held up the 1911. "A harbinger wolf would have ripped my throat out."

"You met a harbinger wolf in Afghanistan?" I asked.

Flint nodded. "Evil piece of scum-sucking filth too. We had heard reports of insurgents killing local people who sympathized with us. I was sent to investigate and report back if I found evidence. Thing is, it wasn't no dang jihadi. The harbinger wolf had killed an entire family of thirteen. Shredded them apart and ate bits of them. Killed their goats too. Came after me and broke my rifle in two." Flint reached up and pulled the collar of his green t-shirt down to reveal a long set of jagged scars on his chest. "Sliced me up a bit, and that was through my body armor. Knocked me to the floor and I only barely managed to pull this up. I put it to the harbinger wolf's chest as it lunged to finish me off. I pumped everything I had into it."

Flint went quiet for a bit. "I made it out, carrying the monster's head with me as proof. I had thought I was going to get a prize or something, but instead I was rewarded with solitary confinement. My CO called in Section Four. Apparently Afghanistan was crawling with activity at the time, so there were standing orders to call the feds in for cases like that."

"They tried to recruit you?" I pressed.

"They did," Flint said.

"So how did you end up here with Hank and the others?" I asked.

Flint took a breath and shook his head. "Long story, and one I don't like to tell."

"Sorry," I said.

"Move to the first stall. Let's see if you can keep up with something." We moved and he set up a clean target fifteen feet out. "This time, I want you to run a drill I make up," Flint said. "I'll call out five shots, and then you do them as quick as you can." Flint stood off to my side and then pointed at the target. "Your targets are left shoulder, then right shoulder, abdomen, head, and then two in center mass. Remember, do it quick."

I looked at the target. I hadn't done anything like this before, but it sounded pretty fun. The 1911 felt good in my hands. Not just good, but almost as if my hands had been made to hold it. It was a perfect fit.

"Go!" Flint shouted.

The pistol came up. I fired and moved smoothly through the designated targets. It was *a lot* of fun. After the last shot I set the pistol down and looked at my work. Each shot was placed right where it was supposed to be. Both shoulders had holes in the center. The abdomen had a new belly button. The head had been hit dead center in the forehead area, and the two in center mass were touching each other and sitting just to the left of dead center.

"Well then," Flint said as he put a stopwatch in front of me. "You're good, but I can beat you by about a quarter of a second."

I read the numbers. One point eight seconds. I had no idea if that was good or bad, but I would like to think that it would have made my grandfather proud to see I had not forgotten how to shoot, even if I wasn't perfect. Either way the day was spent and my initial training session was over.

CHAPTER 8

You would think that with all the things that had happened in my life, I would have been racked with nightmares or strange dreams at night, but I wasn't. I found it hard to fall asleep, as I would overthink and analyze everything, but once I finally was able to sleep, it was restful and deep. I spent three weeks training. Breakfast was at five a.m. After breakfast there were briefing classes. Most of the materials that predated 1960 were supplied by the three Vikings. They had information dating back to their time. They had hunted monsters and blocked invasions on every continent, if I was to believe their records. They fought ice giants in Norway. They fought werewolves in France and Germany. They fought wild yetis in the Himalayas. And that was only scratching the surface. I learned of something called the Rift Wars, a terrible event where seven portals opened simultaneously in Antarctica in the late fifteen hundreds.

Katya had told me that the Rift Wars had been devastating for the elves, with only a small fraction of them surviving. In the end, a total of three thousand invaders had been slain, but a few larger ones had escaped. The three Vikings spent the next hundred and fifty years tracking down each of the invading demons before they were finally able to put an end to the last creature that had come through.

"I didn't even know we had ships capable of sailing down there at that time," I said as I shook my head.

Katya smiled and winked. "We didn't," she said. "The elves did. However, after the initial battle was won, most of the elves sailed off to the Taiga Forest in Russia. They vowed not to get involved anymore."

"But Indyrith is here," I said.

Katya nodded. "A small group of elves remained faithful to their covenants to protect our world."

"Our world?" I asked. Something about the way she said those words made it seem as if the elves were not a part of Earth.

"They are native to our world, but they have always been reclusive. The Rift Wars was the final straw for many of them. You see, they have terribly long lives, just as you would expect from fantasy fiction, and without war, they could live very happily. The Rift Wars are aptly named not only because of the massive inpouring of invaders, but also because it created a schism within the elves. Most believed that humans had advanced enough to protect themselves. More than that, the elves demanded that humans start to work for their own protection rather than waste the precious blood of elves. So, they sailed away en masse. No one has ever found their home in the Taiga Forest."

"Well, it is the largest forest on Earth," I said. "Not to mention hard to reach."

Katya nodded. "Indyrith and his order have been the loyal ones. They remained engaged, even when all of their kind rebelled against them and shunned them."

"Shunned them?"

"We call Indyrith the king because by birth he is the rightful king of the elves. However, after the Rift War, the elves forced him to abdicate his throne. Indyrith was young then, only fifty years old at the time. Rather than allow his people to engage in a civil war, he agreed to let them choose a new ruler. Indyrith was allowed to leave, but warned never to try and follow them. A couple dozen faithful elves went with him, and now they live here. They help us and teach us, but their numbers dwindle as the years drone on."

"I suppose the other elves were right," I said. "I mean, with groups like Section Four, the elves didn't need to sacrifice themselves."

"Section Four!" Katya scoffed. "They are imbeciles. Incompetent, arrogant…" she broke into Russian and used words that were anything but nice. Something more was there than a simple rivalry of ideologies, but based on her current reaction just to mentioning Section Four, I was not about to press the issue. I let her finish vomiting out a long string of curse words that would have made a trucker blush, and waited for her to recompose herself.

The door opened.

Hank was holding an old Winchester lever action rifle and looking as serious he had when the gate had opened in the cemetery. "You are being called up," Hank told me.

"Called up to where?" I asked.

"He isn't ready," Katya said. "He is, how you say, green."

"Flint says he can shoot, and we already know he can fight. Either way it isn't my call. It's Rolf's."

I hesitated for a second. There was something about the hardness in Rolf that still unnerved me even during the times I could get the image of the fight with the drakkul out of my mind.

"Good luck," Katya said in Russian.

I nodded and moved to follow Hank.

"Has another portal opened?" I asked.

Hank shook his head. "Nope."

I waited for a moment. It wasn't like Hank to give short answers. At least, not unless he was busy whistling some Abba tune. "Did I do something wrong?" I asked, unsure what else could be going on.

"You're going hunting," Hank said. "Listen," he began as he stopped and put a hand on my shoulder. "You haven't finished your training yet, so I wouldn't put you in this position, but Rolf has located something bad, and he seems to think that you can help him kill it."

"What is it?"

Hank reached up and scratched his head. "All right, I guess since you are about to go into battle, you should know the full truth of it. You know all those posters for missing children and such?"

"Sure," I said with a nod. The local Walmart was plastered with nearly twenty of the things.

"People are bad, really bad sometimes. We can be downright evil to each other on a level that makes the orneriest animal look like a saint by comparison, but not every missing child is the work of some kidnapper or serial killer. Some are taken by other things."

"Like harbinger wolves?" I asked.

Hank shook his head. "No, those kind of monsters have an origin, and a place. As contemptible as they are, they have a kind of order, and a set of laws that governs them. Sure, once in a while we might see a rogue harbinger wolf like the one who came for you in Dallas, but there are other things that exist in this world that are much darker by nature. They exist only to create misery and pain for the living. Some of them come from other worlds, but most of them have always existed on our world, born in the shadows and thriving upon our agony."

A chill ran down my spine. I'm nearly three hundred pounds of good muscle, and I don't scare at bedtime stories, but the way Hank spoke seemed to bring with it an air of pure evil. As if simply talking about these other things was enough to call their attention to us.

"Most of them are physical, but not all," Hank said.

"What do you mean, like ghosts?" I asked.

Hank shrugged. "I suppose you might think of it that way. That isn't exactly correct, but that's as good an understanding as one can be expected to have until they encounter one."

"A ghost took a child, and now Rolf wants to hunt it with me?" I asked. I had seen a lot in the last few days, but this was a bit much for me to believe.

"Rolf isn't going to fight it with you," Hank said with a shake of his head. "You are going to fight it alone."

"What?"

A door opened down the hallway and Rolf stepped out and pointed at me. "You, come. We have work to do."

"You're up, dream walker," Hank said with a shove on my back.

I walked toward Rolf as the large Viking turned and disappeared into the side room. When I followed after him, I saw Indyrith sitting near a large stone table. Arne and Bjorn were in the room as well, sitting in the far corner and apparently praying in some language I didn't understand.

"My cousins and I will pray that Thor will grant you strength," Rolf said as he motioned toward the stone table.

"Thor?" I said softly without really thinking about it.

"You have your god, and we have ours," Rolf said with a bit more patience than I would have expected. "Go to the table and lie down."

I looked to Indyrith for clarification.

The elf gestured to the table. "I had hoped to have more time with you, but there is a matter that requires your help."

"Now we'll see if you are a true warrior, or if you turn tail and run," Flint said as he slipped in behind me and closed the door.

"What do I need to do?" I asked. I went to the table and got into position. I had expected the stone to be cold, but it was warm instead. It vibrated and hummed against my body.

"There is not much time to explain," Indyrith said. "A mile to the west, a pair of teenagers are camping. They have been attacked by an alp, a kind of creature that is somewhat like mixing an incubus and vampire together."

"Then why not charge out and help?" I asked. "Why are we *here* in this room?"

"An alp attacks people in their sleep," Indyrith said. "We could go out and slay it, but in so doing we would kill his victims. We are hoping that you can go into the nightmare he has spun for them, and fight the demon on his own terms."

"How do I kill it?" I asked.

"No, don't try to kill it. It will be more powerful than you," Indyrith said. "Instead, try to steal its hat. The tarnkappe is its source of power. Take that, and the alp will no longer have a hold over the two teenagers."

"Hank and Dan have already gone out to flank the demon," Flint said. "If you fail, they'll kill it quick."

"This one is strong," Rolf said. "He will not fail. Thor will guide him."

I looked to the elf and nodded. "I'm ready to try, but I don't know how to start."

Indyrith placed a hand on either side of my head. "This is going to hurt a bit."

That was an understatement. I once had a large wart frozen off of my finger with liquid nitrogen. The sucker was big and stubborn, so it required three separate trips to the doctor. If you could somehow combine the experiences all together and focus the intense, stabbing cold of that process, it would come close to describing the initial two seconds after Indyrith put his hands near me.

The cold shot through my temples, and ripped into my head. I found it hard to breath, despite the fact that my mouth opened and I gasped for air. Rolf held me down with his massive hands. He shouted something about courage in the face of battle, and then I blacked out.

My consciousness was no longer inside my body, but that didn't stop the pain. I was falling through darkness, and plunging through such bitter cold that every joint locked up. I pulled myself into the fetal position and focused solely on trying to breathe as I fell through nothingness.

"Relax," Indyrith's voice called out around me. I looked around, but there was no light to see with.

I continued to fall. There was nothing to slow me, and the cold was seeping into my body to such a degree that the burning and aching was starting to pass and I was losing interest in staying focused.

That's when I heard the drums. They were distant at first, then they grew closer. A single man sang in the darkness in some language that I had never heard before, and yet it seemed familiar. The drums woke my heart and the singing put strength into my body again. As I concentrated on that melody, I was able to stretch out. I stood up and suddenly found that I was not falling anymore.

"This way, boy," a voice said in the darkness. It wasn't Indyrith, but rather it sounded like the man that had been singing. I still could not see, but he kept calling me to him as I walked. I followed his voice for a few seconds and then there was a hand on my shoulder. "I will open the way, the elf is not as good at this as I am. I will watch over you."

I could feel a sense of strength and warmth coming from the man. "Who are you?" I asked.

"Not important. You are here to save the two boys, yes?"

I nodded in the darkness. "I am."

"Then take the creature's hat. Try to sneak up on him from behind. Take it, and then they will be free."

A point of light opened in front of me. A tanned, wrinkled hand pulled the curtain of blackness away and the hand on my shoulder gently pushed me through. I turned back around to look at my helper, but the rift was gone and I saw only a snow-filled forest of pine trees. All around me was a blizzard. The snow was so thick that it blew in through the trees and obscured my vision. This kind of snow wasn't likely for this area of the Olympic national forest. It was nearly up to my knees and there was no sign of letting up. I rubbed my shoulders and then thought better of it. I was inside a dream. Perhaps I had powers like Neo did in the Matrix. I could run faster, turn bullets away, and just maybe clear the snow. I tried to think of how I would even perform such an experiment, but nothing I thought of worked. I did try to jump up into the air, thinking that maybe I could at least fly, but nothing happened.

A snarl came from my left and I turned to see a strange pair of glowing eyes staring at me from the darkness under a snow-laden bough. I looked down and realized I was without weapons. I bent down for a stick just as a large lynx leapt out toward me. With every bit of strength I had, I clocked that animal in the face as if I was going for a home-run record. The stick shattered across the lynx's face and the animal fell to the ground.

It then shook its head and turned to stalk around my left.

I needed something, anything!

There was no time to look for another weapon. The lynx charged in. I cocked one leg back and waited for the right moment before putting everything I had into a massive kick. I caught the animal in the throat and it flipped backward to flop into the snow. It yowled and then faded away to be reabsorbed by the nightmare.

I heard a scream in the distance.

I ran toward it through the snow and the trees.

There was a large bonfire that rose twenty feet high in the air. A pair of young boys were tied to pillars near the fire. Their shirts had been torn free and they were being whipped by a haggard, two-legged beast that had a long, spined tail and wild fur covering its body. Was this the alp? I crouched low just to make sure I wouldn't be seen while I studied the scene before me. The creature whipped one of the boys and he cried out in pain as the whip tore through his flesh and caused blood to spill out over his left shoulder blade.

I couldn't just sit and watch. I had to act, but I didn't see a hat on the creature's head. The monster did a little dance as it squawked and chirped loudly. It whipped the other boy and then danced again. It spun around and howled at the night, revealing to me a long snout and not two, but six orange eyes as bright as the fire behind them all.

Then another creature came into the light from the trees on the left. Two curled and twisted horns extended out from its head. It walked upon two legs like a man. Its arms were lean and muscular. Its face though, was hideous. Two black eyes reflected the fire-light and sat on either side of a wide, flat nose with flared nostrils. The creature smiled wickedly, revealing a mess of teeth that would easily tear into anything. Atop its head, sitting between the two horns, was a small green cap.

I could only guess that this was the alp that Indyrith had spoken of. It went to the first young teenager and licked at the blood running along his upper back. The alp clicked and groaned with satisfaction. It took every ounce of focus I had to keep from turning and running away. There was something about this creature that felt like pure evil, even more so than the harbinger wolf that I had fought.

The other creature bowed to the alp and took several steps back.

The alp licked at the blood again and the young man screamed in pain. "Let me go!"

I couldn't watch any longer. I had to act. The problem was that there was no way of getting to the hat without one or both of the monsters seeing me. So I devised a different plan. I ran for the bowing servant. It was still holding the whip as it knelt down in the snow and worshipped its master.

I'm a big man, but I'm also fast. I crossed the distance in two seconds and somehow managed to lunge in and wrap the whip around the monster's neck. I pulled back with my upper body while pressing down into the creature's spine with my legs. The whip bit into my fingers the way a small cord does when you pull it against something thick and sturdy, but I didn't dare let go.

The monster tried to fight back, but to my happy surprise I discovered that it was very weak. I heard a crisp *snap!* The monster's head lolled off to the right and the body went limp. I slid the whip out from under the lifeless body and turned to see the alp already watching me. It stretched a clawed hand toward me and muttered something that I didn't understand. It sounded more like angry snarls and clicks than any language I had heard.

"Help us, please!" one of the boys shouted.

I gave a practice swing of the whip. It let out a satisfactory pop. The alp snarled at me as a long cane appeared in its left hand. I had never used a whip before, but I had seen Indiana Jones. I got the general idea. I cracked the whip at the alp, but the creature only laughed as the strike fell horribly short. The alp then lunged through forty feet of air faster than I could prepare for another strike. The cane came down and struck me in the chest. The world spun around me several times, and then I found myself lying face down in the deep snow. A massive weight fell on my back. Claws dug into my skin and I cried out. My mind was a flurry of thoughts. The snow was too close to my face, I couldn't breathe. The weight on my back pinned me down. Any moment now, the alp was going to club me like a baby seal and that would be the end of my pathetic rescue attempt.

A pain jabbed into my spine. The creature atop me snarled and pressed down harder. All I could do was eat away the snow around my face to try and make room enough to breath without sucking frozen ice crystals down my throat.

The alp grew heavier and heavier. It was like being stuck under a tractor. I knew this because I had once been caught under a tractor that had tipped. It had taken me several minutes to worm my way out of that one. My current predicament was worse.

I tried to flick the whip at my attacker, but it was useless. There was no way for me to get a proper angle. Suddenly the whip was ripped from my hands and the alp started to coil the cord around my neck. The monster was laughing now, enjoying himself fully while I frantically thought of how to escape. I tried to twist and slither out from under him, but the weight continued to grow until I could only manage wheezing breaths.

In the distance, I heard the drums once more.

Hurry! I thought.

Boy, why did you attack? I told you to sneak up on the creature and take his hat. The man's voice was in my head now.

The pressure grew and my vertebrae began to pop and crack. Sharp pain shot through my ribs as they bent unnaturally under the pressure.

Help! I cried out with my thoughts.

You must help yourself, I am only a guide.

Oh, well that's a steaming pile of crap! I thought angrily. *Give me a sword or something!* My mind recalled a beautiful sword I had seen in a shop once. It was fashioned in the style of a katana blade. Long and nimble with a black, lacquered sheath. The actual blade itself had an eastern dragon carved into it, swirling in and out of the clouds. The hand guard was a coiled dragon, and the pommel was the face of a demon. If ever there was a sword fit for slaying a nightmare monster, that would be it.

Something hard appeared in my right hand. I couldn't see it through the snow, but I knew by its feel exactly what it was. Somehow, I was more like Neo than I thought. I was now armed with a sword. I couldn't swing it, but I had enough room to angle my wrist back and try to poke the alp. I moved as quickly as I could and stabbed at the creature.

"GEEEARRGH!" the alp shrieked. It leapt off of me and suddenly I could breathe again. I stood up, chest burning and ribs aching. I tried to push the pain out of my mind. It was just a dream, after all. My real body was fine. I just had to persevere through the dream, and everything would be fine.

The alp was bleeding from his right arm. The scarlet liquid coursed through his white fur, matting it and giving it a slick appearance. The monster raised his arm to his mouth and licked at the wound. The blood hissed and sizzled, and then the wound closed itself. The beast came at me fast, swinging the cane like a club. I blocked with my sword and then spun around to chop at the alp's side. The thing was unearthly fast. I didn't even see the legs move, but somehow it was now standing four feet beyond the reach of my sword.

The drums became louder in my head, and I heard the man singing once again.

I took confidence from the song and let out a war cry as I charged in. The alp dodged left as I swung my sword. He countered with a massive chop to my left shoulder. I felt the bone pop out of its socket, but I don't think it broke. I launched a fast snap kick that caught the alp in its furry stomach. It doubled over, granting me a shot at its face. I kicked it in the teeth and also came in with a one-handed chop of my sword. I sliced through the fleshy chest and the alp staggered backward in pain.

The drums were pounding all around me now. The alp's face twisted in confusion and then fear as it looked around for the source of the drums. It narrowed its black eyes on me and pointed a shaky finger at my face.

"Dream walker?" it said.

I nodded. "That's right sucker. I'm a dream walker."

The alp turned over and tried to scurry away. It may not have been the most honorable thing to do, but I knew to take a good shot when presented with one. I jumped forward and brought the tip of my sword down hard into the creature's back. It howled in pain as I pinned it to the snowy ground. I left my sword quivering in the monster's back and took the small hat from the alp's head.

The creature howled horribly and then melted away as a burst of golden fire consumed his body. I jumped back, pulling my sword with me, but found that the flames had not spontaneously exploded out around the alp. They were attached to me. They swirled around me in dazzling purple, gold, and white streaks. Then, after the alp was devoured by the flame, the fire died out and the blizzard stopped.

The drums stopped.

The boys, help the boys. The stranger's voice said inside my head.

I turned and ran to them.

"Don't kill us," One of them said.

I shook my head. "No, it's all right now. The monsters are dead." I cut the first down and he collapsed on the ground.

"Where are we?" he asked.

"Don't worry about that now," I replied as I moved to the second one. How was I supposed to explain that he was stuck in a nightmare that had the power to actually kill him?

The second teenager was only barely conscious when I cut him down. He crumpled to the snowy ground and groaned. I turned him over and was relieved to see that he was still breathing. I had had CPR training a long time ago, but I doubt I remembered everything I would need to in order to bring him back had he not been breathing. Besides, could someone be revived in a dream?

A flash of white light cut through the air a few feet away and I stood at the ready, sword in hand and hoping it wasn't another portal ripping open. Indyrith stepped through along with his two daughters. They ignored me entirely and went straight to the young boys. They whispered and waved their hands over them. The wounds in their backs closed and the boys disappeared.

"They are taking them into other dreams," Indyrith said. "They will be sore when they wake in the morning, but they will think they just slept on rocks. The human mind is fairly easy to give suggestions to," he said with a nod.

"So they won't remember any of this?" I asked.

Indyrith shook his head. "It is our way, protecting the innocent from the darkness. We not only stop the monsters physically, but we erase the memory of the pain they inflict."

"But, if everyone knew, then we could all band together," I suggested.

Indyrith shook his head. "No. Think of it this way. There are slightly more than seven billion humans on the world today. Do you know how many ants there are?"

I shrugged. "A lot."

"Over ten trillion," Indyrith said. "That is one thousand three hundred and eighty-eight ants for each human on this world. Now, instead of insects, imagine there were that many creatures hiding in the shadows. How would you fight such a host?"

I stopped and stared at him. "How many are there?" I asked, wanting a more precise number so I knew exactly what we were up against.

"For each human, there are somewhere between ten and one hundred creatures seeking to bring them down. Some of them are not strong enough, for even an unaware human still has some power to resist the darkness, but there are many who are far more capable than this alp you faced off against." Indyrith smiled and folded his arms into the sleeves of his robes. "How many dreams do you think you could fight in at one time? How many beds can you look under? Even with Hank and the others, and all of Section Four, how long do you really think the world would survive if it came to total war?"

"So then what, are they just letting us live?" I asked.

Indyrith nodded. "To a certain extent, yes. It is more complicated than that, but there is a degree of safety that is preserved by ensuring the population at large does not know the danger in which they are constantly found. It helps us avoid unnecessary attention. The more powerful demons and monsters have specific regions of power that they maintain with almost absolute control." Indyrith pointed to the slain alp. "As for good news, I did not expect you to be powerful enough to slay the alp. Where did you get your sword?"

I looked down and saw the sword. I looked at it for the first time since somehow summoning it. It was the exact same as the one I had thought of, carvings and all. "I am not sure," I said honestly. "It just came to me."

"Interesting," Indyrith said. "Normally a dream walker conjures the weapon of his ancestors. I would have expected to see something used by the Cherokee side of your lineage."

"Did the other dream walkers summon bows or things like that?" I asked.

Indyrith shook his head. "None of the others whom I taught were able to conjure anything. You are the first to forge a weapon in the world of dreams. I believe the balance of power is tipping in our favor, Joshua Mills. There may be more to your destiny than even I had suspected."

"What do you mean?" I asked.

Indyrith held up his hand. "Come, our time grows short. We must go."

I started to walk, but as soon as my left shoulder moved it reminded me how badly it was hurt. "Can you fix my wounds?" I asked. "You know, like your daughters did with the teenagers?"

Indyrith shook his head. "Unfortunately, a dream walker is

different. Our magic can heal those who are injured in nightmares, but only those who are in a normal sleep state. As you are awake inside the dream world, and fully aware of everything around you, your injuries are beyond our ability to heal."

"So every battle I go through, I will have to recuperate on the other side?" I asked.

"Until you learn to heal yourself," Indyrith clarified. "You are the only one who can heal your wounds from the dream world. I can help ease your pain once you wake, but it is your mind that will decide how injured you truly are."

"Great," I said. "So, save the world, but don't tell anyone, and get hurt in dreams that would normally just scare others, but are going to leave me with some serious pain. How much am I getting paid again?"

CHAPTER 9

I awoke with a terrible pain in my shoulder. I rolled off the table and struggled to stand up.

"What happened to you?" Flint asked.

"He slew an alp in melee combat," Indyrith said. "He needs rest."

I expected another flip comment out of the ex-special forces operator, but instead he whistled through his teeth and moved toward me, holding out a hand. "Well, that's one way to cut your teeth I suppose," Flint said as he helped me stand straight. "To your room?"

I nodded. As I moved around the table I saw the three Vikings stand and each give a solemn nod. It seemed that I had earned a lot of respect that day. Flint helped me into my room and then shut off the light and closed the door. I had no trouble falling asleep. My body was tired, and racked with pain. More than that, my mind was tired. I could barely think straight at all. With the darkness of the room, sleep overtook me within seconds, something that had only happened maybe twice in my life up to that point.

I slept peacefully at first. No dreams at all. Then, I relived a dream I had had when I was a child. I saw the harbinger wolf come to my childhood window. He was as big and nasty as I could remember. Thick black fur. Mean, yellow eyes. Teeth that seemed to grow as the beast snarled at me. The window exploded into the room and the wolf roared as if it were a mighty lion.

I tried to sit up, but I was paralyzed.

The wolf stood on its hind legs and stepped through the shattered glass. From its belt it drew a long, red-bladed sword. It pointed the tip at me and growled ferociously. "You must never enter the dream world again," it snarled.

Finally, I broke the spell and sat up. "You know I won't stop," I said with a swell of courage that helped me ignore the pain in my shoulder. "I will never stop."

"Then your son will die," the harbinger wolf said. "I will slay and eat your child, and I will consume his mother also." My heart flitted with fear and my stomach churned into a thick, sour knot. Three additional harbinger wolves came into the room through the broken window. Each of them had their eyes fixed on me. "We are not as strong as you are yet, but we will be when we enter your world again. We will be able to fight you in your world, and in the dream world. But, even if you defeat us, we will kill your son."

"I will drink his blood," another said.

"And I shall subdue your wife before I rip out her heart," said a third.

The fear left my heart, replaced by anger. I jumped up and ran toward them, shouting and fists ready for a fight. The ground stretched out before me. No matter how fast I ran, I could not reach the harbinger wolves. They were forever out of my reach.

"Go to the elf, wipe your memories of this, and we will spare your child," the first harbinger wolf said. "Do this now, or we will destroy everything you hold dear in this world!"

Lightning streaked in through the window and blasted me in the chest. I flew backward several hundred yards, for I had sprinted a long way in the dream world trying to reach them, and crashed into the wall above my bed. I slid down slowly and slumped onto the mattress. I looked down, heaving and gasping for air. I could see that the quilt on my bed was the same yellow quilt with circus animals in trains that I had had as a small child. Whoever these harbinger wolves were, they had picked the earliest location of my encounters with nightmares to try and scare me.

I tried to struggle to my feet. I slid off the bed and stood up. I was not about to let them go without a fight. The ground shrank back to its normal size. The wolves were only ten feet away now. From around their hulking bodies, I noticed something new. It was another alp. Unlike the one I had just slain, this one had brown fur and three horns.

It pointed at me and clicked in its guttural language. "You murdered my mate," it hissed. "Go to the elf, or I will destroy your blood. You have one hour from now to comply, or we will kill them all." It stamped its feet and a great earthquake shook the room. I fell to the ground as the house crumbled around me.

I woke just before a massive slab fell onto my dream self. I was panting and sweating. The red numbers on the clock on the far side of the room red six o'clock on the button. I swung my feet over the edge of the bed and went to the door. My left shoulder was still sore, but I shook it off. I had much more to worry about now. I threw my door open and went down the hallway and to the main chamber.

I saw Nick sitting on the table playing with a collection of rocks.

"What are you doing?" I asked.

The furry creature looked up and smiled and snorted. "I paint rocks like me," he said as he held one up. "I then put in forest for professor to find."

"Professor who?" I asked.

"He's toying with a lecturer at one of the local colleges," Mack said from the far side of the room.

"Where's Indyrith?" I asked. "I need to see him."

Mack shrugged. "I dunno. Only Rolf or Hank can summon the elf."

"Then where's Hank?" I asked.

Mack set down his laptop and rubbed his face. Then he stood up and motioned for me to follow him. We wandered down a long corridor and into a library. Hank was sitting at a table with a pile of books on his right and an open book in front of him.

"Dang it, Mack, I thought I said I didn't want to be disturbed," Hank said as he set down his reading glasses.

"Newbie is looking for you," Mack said. "Seemed important."

I walked past Mack and pulled up a chair before Hank could mouth his protest. "I had a dream, and I need to speak with Indyrith. Now."

Hank dismissed Mack with a wave and then got up and closed the door to the library. "Given the special circumstances, I will let this one slide, but if you ever speak to me like that in front of my men again, I'll pull your tongue out with a pair of pliers and use it as chum the next time I go fishing, you understand?"

I ignored the threat. "Four harbinger wolves and an alp came to me in my dream and said they would attack and kill my wife and son unless I wipe my memory and stay out of the dream world."

"Ex-wife," Hank corrected.

"Bite me, Hank," I spat.

Hank bristled and then nodded his head. "All right, I can see this has you shaken up. I can call Indyrith if you like, but wiping your memory isn't the right thing to do."

"Tommy isn't even old enough to go to school yet," I said hotly. "If the choice is between fighting to save the world and saving my son, then the whole world can burn for all I care."

"You don't know what you're saying," Hank said as he patted the air.

"Call Indyrith!" I shouted.

Hank took in a breath and then turned on his heels and left the room. The slamming door echoed several times in the library. I turned and looked at the books Hank was reading. Each of them were old books on legends and scary stories. Two of the books focused on Native American legends, while most of the others centered on German lore. I looked at the page Hank was reading. I was slightly impressed to see that the passage was actually written in German. I knew a few languages, but German was not one of them. I closed the book and shoved it aside so I could set my elbows on the table and rest my head in my hands.

It was a long time before Indyrith and his daughters came into the library.

"Joshua Mills, we must discuss this," Indyrith said.

"Just answer one question," I said quickly as I stood up to show the elf respect as he entered. "If I refuse to do as they say, will they kill my son?"

Indyrith nodded. "I will never lie to you, my friend. If you defy them, they will hunt your son and your ex-wife as they said."

"Then I have no choice. They will get to them faster than I can. There is only one way to protect them."

"Just hold on a moment," Hank said as he closed the door again. "Don't you realize how special you are? A dream walker is what we need to close the rifts. A dream walker can end the invasions forever. That's why they're after you. They want to scare you away. That means you have real power!"

"It worked," I said quickly. "They have my attention."

Hank began to speak, but Indyrith put a hand out in front of the man. The tall elf then stepped closer to me and placed a hand on each shoulder. "This choice is one that only you can make," Indyrith said. "However, you should know that if you do as they have demanded, they will still come after you. You will be defenseless. They will kill you."

"And they'll still go after your family, you dense little —"

"That's enough," Indyrith said with surprising force. "This choice belongs to Joshua Mills."

"Will they leave my family alone if I do what they ask?" I implored.

Indyrith shrugged. "Tell me of the dream, leave no detail out."

I recited everything I could remember. Unlike most dreams that vanish once you wake, each and every detail was still fresh and clear in my mind. I told the elf everything.

"The sword was red, you're sure?" Indyrith asked.

I nodded.

Indyrith took in a deep breath and then turned to the others. "Hank, I need to be alone with Joshua now."

"Nope, I'm staying. I want to know what this little twerp stepped in and how bad the stench is going to dirty the rest of us."

Indyrith shook his head and motioned to his daughters. "I need to be alone with Mr. Mills."

The two daughters turned around and escorted Hank out of the library. He resisted at first, but once they touched his hands, he cooperated and seemed to forget where he was.

"You wiped his memory, didn't you?" I asked.

"Only for the last two hours," Indyrith said. "My daughters will give him the memory of falling asleep in the library while conducting research. He will then believe that he went back to his room to lie down. No harm done."

"Have you erased my mind before?" I asked.

"No."

"But if you didn't tell me, I wouldn't know the difference would I?" I pressed. "You just walk around putting spells on people as easily as the MIB use their little flashy-stick things."

"I am not aware of the MIB," Indyrith said.

I rubbed my forehead and groaned. "Never mind. Just, tell me, will the harbinger wolves leave my family alone if I do what they want?"

Indyrith nodded. "Under normal circumstances, I would say no. They can be treacherous, as any race can. However, with the presence of a red sword in the dream, I am confident that they will not attack them."

"What's special about the red sword?" I asked.

"It is made with the blood of a harbinger patriarch. It is not used often in battle, except when a harbinger wolf wishes to call upon its ancestral line for additional strength. However, it is used as a powerful symbol in oath making. Should the harbinger wolves that made the oath seek to attack your son and ex-wife after you do as they have demanded, then the sword would require their deaths. Their dishonor would be cleansed from their world, and they would be no more, as if they had never been born. More than that, it will extend to their descendants. It is, as you would say, a cleansing of the blood."

"So they can't lie?" I asked, not quite grasping the concept Indyrith was trying to get across.

"No, it isn't that. It is that the blood sword requires promises to be fulfilled. Usually they are used to broker peace between rival clans. It is a safety feature. The fact that they used it with you, means that they expect you to have already understood its meaning."

"Why would they assume that?"

"Because your powers in the dream world are beyond anything they have seen for centuries. They fear you. You are the last of a powerful warrior type that has the power to destroy them. For example, it took four of them working together with an alp to find you in your sleep and come to you. Even then, they dared not attack you while in the dream world. Instead, they made a bargain. They will let your family live, if you stop fighting."

"You make it sound as though I am some sort of cosmic assassin," I said with a scoff. "I'm just me. I sell memberships for a local gym, or, at least I did, before Dallas."

Indyrith nodded. "It isn't about what you see yourself as. This is about the threat they see in you."

"But you're sure that if I do as they say, my family will be safe?"

Indyrith nodded. "They will come for you, and so will the drakkul, but your family will be safe."

"The drakkul," I said softly. "I forgot about them. They want my blood for killing the other one." I tossed my head back toward the ceiling. "They won't honor the harbinger promise will they?"

Indyrith shook his head. "If they feel your family is guilty as you are, then they will come for them, but they are more honorable than the harbinger wolves. The drakkul will usually come through the portals first. Rolf will not let them get to you or your family."

"But the one in Dallas didn't come through Rolf," I interjected. "He tracked us down and came for us."

"He was after your father," Indyrith said. "If you knew what it was your father stole, then perhaps we could help come to an arrangement with the drakkul."

"I don't know what it was," I said. "Just some engine thing. That's all he said before the portals opened." I sighed. "What if we wipe my memory, and then send me through a portal to the drakkul? Then, they can kill me and be satisfied, and the harbinger wolves will be happy that I forgot."

Indyrith shook his head. "If you were to see a portal again, it would likely bring your memories back. The mind, even a human one, can be quite resilient. If your memories returned, then the harbinger wolves would be free of their oath. They would come for your family."

"So we wipe my memory and then hope that I die before I see a portal again, is that it?"

"Or, perhaps you can hide long enough to create a new life," Indyrith said. "I could erase years of your life. I could go back four or five years. If I did that, and Hank took you somewhere far away, then it could work."

"No," I said. "Take away my memories of this place, and the thing that happened in Dallas, but don't take away the memory of my family. I can't live without that."

"If I did as you ask, then you would not remember that you are divorced. You would go looking for them again. I have to send you farther back in time. Or, you can choose to stay and fight."

I thought for a moment. "If I stay and fight, will I be able to reach my family in time to save them?"

Indyrith shook his head.

"What about Section Four?" I asked.

Again, the elf shook his head. "The harbinger wolves will strike soon. They will beat us unless you do as they say. My guess is that they already have assassins in place, and that is why they gave you the time limit of one hour."

"So I have to forget all about them in order to save them, and even then I will likely be hunted down and killed by the harbinger wolf that has haunted me since I was a child?"

Indyrith nodded. "Also, I will need to know when you met your ex-wife. I will have to go far enough back to ensure you don't remember anything about her."

I nodded sullenly. What choice did I have? "The harbinger

wolves gave me an hour, can I have a phone?"

Indyrith smiled. "You won't remember saying good-bye," he said.

"I can't do it without at least trying," I replied.

Indyrith left the room and came back with Hank's cell phone.

I picked it up and dialed my wife's number. Ex-wife, that is, but even now it was hard to get used to the new title. I felt the same sort of jittery butterflies in my stomach as I had the first time I had called this number to ask her out to dinner. Now I was dialing to say good-bye forever to her, and to my little boy. What would he think of me? What would she think?

One ring.

I thought of Tommy's birth and the first few months we had him in our little apartment. Watching him learn to crawl. Looking back on it now, I should have changed more diapers. I should have read more bedtime stories.

Two rings.

My mind went back to a few days after the wedding. We had been so happy. Two young adults out to conquer the world together. Our whole lives had been ahead of us. Even going out into the town we hardly noticed anyone else even existed those first few months. It was all about having fun and enjoying being around each other. We liked to say that our honeymoon phase never ended. It just changed to include another person once Tommy was born.

Three rings.

Maybe she wasn't there. What if she was in the shower, or asleep? It was still early morning in Utah. This might be the only chance I had to speak with them again, and she might not even have her phone turned on.

Four rings.

Someone picked up.

"Hello?" a woman said on the other end. It was Jill, Susan's older sister. I had never gotten along with Jill even in the best of times. It had only gotten worse after Dallas.

"Hi Jill, listen, I need to speak with Susan," I said in as polite a tone as I could muster. I even tried smiling on my end. I had heard during my job training for selling gym memberships that customers could hear a difference if you smiled on the phone. I hoped the fake cheese I put on for Jill would work.

"You have some brass ones calling here," Jill said.

My smile faded. "Jill, please, it's important."

"Yeah, well, right now she's asleep, and you don't need to be calling around here anymore."

"No, Jill, please. I need to speak with her, just for a minute. I promise, I'll be quick."

"Don't care," Jill replied. "I knew you were no good the moment I met you. You have hurt her enough. You can just go to—"

A young voice called out in the background and I ignored Jill for a moment to focus in on it. "Is that Tommy?" I asked. "Put him on, please."

"You can't talk to him," Jill said flatly.

"Phone!" Tommy's little voice shouted. I could picture him reaching for the cell phone as he always used to do whenever Susan or I were on the phone around him.

"Jill, listen," I began.

"No, you listen," Jill said. "According to the court, you can't even see Tommy, so why would I give him the phone. Go take a long walk off a short pier somewhere. Don't bother calling again."

She hung up.

I hit redial, but all I got was a busy signal. She had shut off the phone.

"Time is short," Indyrith said.

I nodded. At least I had gotten to hear Tommy one more time. He would never know that I had tried to reach out one last time, heck, I wouldn't even remember, but at least I knew it for now. I looked to Indyrith and slid Hank's phone across the table. "Can you watch over them?" I asked. "Just in case?"

Indyrith nodded. "We have several weeks yet before the drakkul are allowed to return. We will do what we can to protect your family in the meantime. I'm sure Hank will be eager to search for the engine your father stole as well." he said.

"Maybe Mack could dig it up," I offered. "I mean, you all know about my entire life, so why not dig up my father's skeletons?"

Indyrith offered a soft smile. "We have been investigating your father. We have not turned up any useful evidence as of yet. Come on, we only have a few minutes left to give the harbinger wolves what they wanted."

Flashes of memories with my family flooded my mind. It felt as though I was betraying them somehow. That, even in saving them, I was failing them.

"Close your eyes," Indyrith said.

I complied as the memories kept rushing through my mind's eye.

"Clear your thoughts as best you can," Indyrith said.

Fat chance of that.

"I will enter your mind and see how far back we need to go," the elf said.

The door opened and closed. I opened my eyes for a second to see his daughters. They locked the door and came to stand on either side of me. They placed their hands on the top of my head. I could feel a warm power pouring into me.

"It will start soon," Indyrith said.

That was when I heard the drums again. They started as a faint beating in the back of my mind. They grew louder and louder. The stranger from before was singing again. Suddenly I found myself inside my mind. It was like being in the dream world, but instead of dreams I saw memories floating around me. I peered through them to see a tall, muscular man sprinting toward me as the drums grew louder and louder.

"Wait, boy, you must wait!" he shouted. "There is another way!"

I stepped toward him, fascinated by the clothing he wore of animal skins and beads. Who was he?

"Wait!" he shouted again.

I could hardly hear him over the drums.

"All right, Joshua," Indyrith said in a voice that sounded like thunder around me. I looked up, as if expecting to see a giant elf head inside my mind, but nothing was there except for a bright light. The feeling of vibrating warmth permeated the whole of my being. "I know where to begin now," Indyrith said. "This time, it will not hurt. Allow yourself to relax, and all will be well."

"No boy!" the sprinting stranger said. "Wait for ME!"

A flash of white light ripped through my mind, and everything was gone.

CHAPTER 10

I woke in a park. Newspaper covered my lower legs. A dog was curled up beneath the bench I was on. I pushed up and rubbed the lines out of my cheek that had been pressed into my skin from the metal on the bench and yawned. I put my feet on the ground and felt the cool dirt on my toes.

That's right. I slept here last night.

I looked around and saw a mostly empty park. There was one lady jogging by. She was nice looking, fit and kind of cute. She made sure to stay as far away on the other side of the walkway from me as possible when she jogged by. I looked down at myself and agreed with the woman. I looked a little worse for wear. My clothes were torn in several places.

I stretched my arms and recoiled sharply as pain shot through my left shoulder.

Must have slept on it wrong. I thought.

I got up and the dog obediently went with me as I walked in the opposite direction from the jogging woman. Heaven knows how badly I would have scared her if I walked the same direction. I went to a nearby garbage can and robotically bent down to pull a piece of cardboard out from underneath. I unfolded it. It was a good sign. I always hid it under the garbage so none of the others would take it from me. I walked out of the park and onto the nearest street corner. I sat at the light and held out my sign.

It was rush hour, so if today was a good day, I could pull in maybe one or two hundred dollars. I decided that if I did, I was going to sleep in a motel for once. I was getting tired of the park bench.

A black beamer pulled up to the light. Tinted windows, chrome rims, classical music wafting out the slightly cracked driver's side window. I walked past that one without even another thought when the light turned red. Drivers in beamers never helped out. However, when I saw the ford escort pull up with a slightly dented door and paint missing from the bumper, I made sure to make eye contact.

She gave me a twenty.

Boom! There's food for today and tomorrow. Things were looking up.

I spent three hours waiting for red lights and then walking alongside the cars that stopped. Then my shift was over. Two other panhandlers came to the corner. I never did catch their names, but I remembered the beating they had given the other guy who used to be allowed to walk the street in the morning before them when he ran over his allowed shift. I was a big guy. Too big for most people to realize that I really was homeless and needed the money, but not big enough to take these two clowns. Rumor was they carried heat. Either way, I thought little of them. Fighting over turf to panhandle was a low thing to do. More than that, the two panhandlers working the light now were better off than I was. One of them even drove a BMW. Like I said, BMW drivers never help out. They all think the world owes them.

I made my way down the street toward the nearest McDonalds. The morning manager never seemed to mind about me not having shoes so long as I made my order to go. I ordered a sausage mcmuffin with cheese. I split it with my dog, Dozer. Then we walked down to a shoe store and I found myself a pair of cheap Chuck Taylor knock offs. They weren't perfect, but they were a whole world better than walking along the side of a busy road barefoot.

Me and Dozer finished off the day by visiting the local train yard. I found a caboose that was empty and unlocked. I went inside and took a nap on the bed there. Then, we made our way out to the pier and spent the rest of the day on the beach.

I watched families come and play in the water, young couples cuddle and kiss in the waves, and the occasional fortune hunter with his metal detector as the day passed me by.

It wasn't much, and for the life of me I couldn't remember all the decisions I must have made that led me to this point, but it wasn't terrible either. I followed that routine for about two weeks before something started nagging at me.

It started as a throbbing headache. The back of my head would pound and pulse for a minute or two, and then go away. I assumed I needed more fluids. Southern California can be hot in the summer time. So, I made sure to buy extra water each day with the money I got from folks nice enough to offer me some help. Each day the headaches would get worse, lasting longer and pounding harder. Once I even lost part of my vision. That was probably the scariest thing I had ever experienced. I had reached down to pet Dozer's head and then realized that I couldn't see his face. It was just a blur of nothingness. I put my hand in front of my face, but could only see my wrist and the tips of my fingers.

I didn't dare go panhandling that day. Instead, I went to the beach and stripped down to my boxers. I went into the waves and tried to relax. It must have worked, because my sight was back by the time I emerged from the water. Dozer and I fell asleep under the pier that day. I woke up to him barking on the beach and staring out at the water.

"Dozer! Knock it off!" I called out. Sleeping overnight wasn't allowed on the beach. If he got us caught, it would mean jail for me and the pound for him.

Jail.

That sounded familiar. Had I been in jail before?

I stopped and looked down at the fingerless gloves on my hands. *That's right. I had been arrested for vagrancy before. I had been caught sleeping on a parked bus one time.* That had not gone over well. K-9 units are wound fairly tight. I still had claw marks on my back from the stupid dog that had been unleashed.

"Dozer," I called out again. "Shut it!"

A pair of headlights sparked to life, illuminating Dozer and the area around him. I froze. The red and blue lights came next. The vehicle started forward.

"Dozer! Come on!" I said as I clapped my leg with my hand.

The foolish dog wouldn't turn away from the water.

I ran for it. I was not about to go back into jail. Dozer would survive a night in the pound. I could bail him out in the morning, but I had to get away from there.

I stumbled in the sand. It wasn't easy running on the beach. The engine roared louder and the lights grew brighter. I knew they would catch me unless I was extremely lucky. I said a quick prayer for help.

Does god help homeless beggars who break minor laws?

Then I heard a yelp.

I turned around to see Dozer roll through the sand. He tried to get back up, but only flailed his head and tail.

"No!" I shouted. I turned back and ran toward him. He was the only friend I had in all the world. How could they have been so careless? He wouldn't ever hurt anyone. "You sons of—"

The spotlight turned on me and blinded me. The engine roared and the vehicle shot forward, spraying sand everywhere.

"Stay there!" a voice called out over the PA system.

I stood with my hands up over my eyes. The truck was coming straight for me. At the last minute, I dodged to the side as the truck sped over the spot where I had just been standing. I heard the wheels lock up and the tires tore into the sand as the truck skidded to a halt.

They had tried to hit me too!

The passenger side door opened and someone jumped out.

"I wasn't doing anything wrong!" I shouted as I ran for the pier.

Dozer was still whimpering helplessly on the beach, but I couldn't get to him. One cop was chasing me on foot while the other worked the truck and turned it around.

"Don't move!" the cop shouted.

Not likely! They had just tried to run me over. I was going to get out any way I could.

"Stop or I'll shoot!" I heard the cop shout.

I dodged around a pillar to break line of sight and tried to catch my breath.

The cop came running up and I did the only thing my adrenaline-filled body could think to do. I jumped out and sucker-punched the prick right in the nose.

His head snapped back and he groaned as he hit the ground.

The truck was roaring toward me, but I knew I could get behind a pillar or two and try to hide.

I looked up and saw something flash out of the window. A blue streak shot out and slammed into my left side. I dropped to the ground, falling behind the pillar. Electricity coursed through my body as I convulsed.

Taser?

The truck got closer. I could hear the tires ripping up the sand and then there was a massive *slam!* The pillar broke out and nearly collapsed. Smoke and steam hissed around the pillar, dancing in the light from the sirens and headlights. I looked up and saw the front end of the truck wrapped around the pillar.

"Should have bought American," I said as I pushed myself up to my feet. I walked to the side of the Toyota and saw the driver slumped over the wheel. Blood was pouring out from a gash in the cop's forehead. I couldn't understand it. What were these two thinking? They ran over my dog, and then tried to kill me. I wasn't hurting anyone.

I checked the cop's pulse and then tried to reach in for the radio. I was a fighter, but I wasn't heartless. I tried to call in. I pressed buttons and turned the dial until I got someone on the radio.

"Officers need assistance," I said.

"Who is this?" a surly voice grunted on the other end.

"Officers got into a wreck down under pier seven. They look hurt. Hurry!"

"Who is this? Identify yourself!" the voice shouted.

Not a chance! I had called in for help. That was all the more involved I was going to be. I ran over to Dozer. He was barely breathing. Panting in short, frantic breaths, each one ending in a whimper. There was nothing I could do for him, but I wasn't about to leave him behind. I scooped the old lab into my arms and picked him up. I then sprinted away from the scene as fast as my cheap knock-off shoes would carry me.

It was morning by the time I stopped running. Big guys were never meant to run any distance longer than from a couch to the kitchen. My knees hurt, my shins hurt, my lungs were on fire, and my arms were all but dead from carrying Dozer. He had long since given up his last breath, but I didn't have the heart to dump him anywhere. He deserved a proper burial. On the south side of town, there was an old mine. I had been there before. I found an old abandoned shovel and began to dig in one of the shafts.

It took a long time, but I was able to dig far enough down that I was sure nothing would bother my friend. I climbed out of the hole and then went back to Dozer. I put my hand on his head and tried to think of something fitting to say.

"I'm not real good with words," I whispered to his lifeless body. "But, you were a good friend. Best a man could ask for." My eyes filled with tears as the sound of his yelp came back into my mind. "I don't know what those guys were thinking," I said. "There ain't much I can do about it now, but they got a little taste of what they deserved before we left. It isn't justice, but it will have to do."

I gently placed him down into the hole and then filled it with dirt.

I didn't leave a marker. I knew where he was. That was enough.

I exited the mine to find a tall man wearing a checkered shirt and faded blue jeans.

We both jumped a bit upon seeing each other. The man held his hands up and eyed my shovel.

"I don't have anything worth taking," the man said. "I own the mine and someone said they saw someone coming in. I thought it might be teenagers skipping school and getting drunk, so I came to check is all."

I set the shovel down. "Sorry, I didn't think anyone would mind if I was here," I said.

"You won't find anything in there," the man said. "The mine has been dry for decades. Ain't nothing valuable in there."

I smiled and nodded. Little did he know that there was something worth more than gold buried in the shaft now. "Sorry. Would it be all right if I left and you didn't tell anyone I was here?" I asked. "Been having a bit of a rough time lately."

The man nodded. "Yeah, I can see that for myself," he said. "Tell you what. I have twenty bucks back in my truck. Would that help you out?"

I shook my head. I still had twice that left over from the last time I panhandled. "No, thanks. I have enough for now."

"How bout a bus ticket, then?" the man said. "I have a colleague who might have work for you," he said. "It ain't easy work, but it pays well. Ever been to Dallas?"

I shook my head again. "No thanks," I said. "I best be on my way."

I started to leave, and the pounding came back into my head. This time, it sounded like drums.

CHAPTER 11

It was more than a week before I made my way back to my park bench. Worried that the cops might be able to identify me, I had tried to look for a new place, but to no avail. I couldn't find a corner worth working with my sign. Eventually my hunger forced me to go back. For the first week back at my spot I jumped every time I saw a cop car. After that, I was able to calm my nerves a bit. The employees were happy to see me again, asked about Dozer and gave me a full day of food for free when I explained he had been run over by a truck.

I took my hamburgers back to my park bench and ate while I watched joggers and moms with strollers pass by on the track. I didn't sleep well that night. Just kept staring up at the few stars I could see through the light pollution from the city and tried to fight the nagging feeling that there was something more I was supposed to be doing.

For the life of me I couldn't remember what that was.

When I finally did fall asleep, the sky was already brightening. I barely got any rest at all before the sun hit my face and the pounding of drums returned to my head. I got up, fighting the stiff aches that sleeping on park benches will give a person, and made my way out to the street. To my surprise, I saw a woman with a sign already working my spot. I shrugged it off and turned to go up the street. After all, I had had a full three meals the day before, so I could stand to miss a day if this lady needed some extra cash.

I hadn't gotten far when I heard shouting.

I turned to see a blue BMW stopped at the corner. The driver side door was open and a man was standing on the street berating the panhandler. When I looked closer, I realized it was one of the two men that scammed people for money at that spot.

I'm not sure what it was, but something inside said that the man's time was up. I was not going to walk away while someone was in trouble.

Cars passed the arguing couple as the light at the intersection turned green. Some people honked, others pretended not to notice, but nobody stopped to help the woman.

I sped up my pace and was only about fifteen feet away when the man slapped the woman and shoved her to the ground.

No. That isn't right.

I ran over and sucker-punched the man square in the nose before he had time to see me coming. His head jerked back and blood trickled down his face. He grunted and reached up to grab his nose, but I didn't let up. I came in with a hard left hook that blasted his jaw and dropped him to the ground. I then reached down to help the woman.

"It's all right, come with me," I said.

She took my hand and then let out a gasp as she looked back toward the car.

I looked up to see the passenger side was now open and a man was coming at us, baseball bat in hand. Fear rippled through my stomach. Cars passed us by. I was amazed that no one stopped. The man was shouting a string of curse words as fast as his breath would let him. With one hand I gently pushed the woman away from me, placing myself between her and the man with the bat.

"Go," I told her. "You need to go, now!"

The woman turned and ran, her sobs fading as she left.

The man with the bat came in hard and fast, swinging for my head. I ducked and stepped back out of the way, then, as the bat's momentum carried his arms up and to the side, I came in for the opening. Two quick shots to his exposed ribs. The man flinched, but answered my attack with a head-butt. I shook it off and managed to get my arm up just in time to stop the second swing of the bat. My forearm was going to be extremely sore, but at least my skull wasn't smashed in. I brought a knee up to the man's gut, but it had little effect. We pushed back and forth for a couple seconds, and then I managed to wrestle the bat free from the man. The man threw his hands up defensively and cowered away from me.

"Get outta here, and take this puke with you," I ordered as I pointed to the unconscious man that had assaulted the woman. The man nodded, so I turned and tossed the bat toward the park.

I was about to turn and offer one final parting shot at the thug, but something hot and heavy punched me in the gut. Blinding, searing pain ripped through my body and my legs went weak. I fell to my butt and looked up to see the man towering over me, gun in hand. I saw a bright flash and heard a loud, thunderous boom. I heard some frantic shouting, followed by screeching tires and a roaring engine. I dropped down to my side and tried to breathe. Something about the flash of the muzzle seemed familiar. The bright light opening up before my eyes. Had I seen something like that once before? Everything went black after that.

When my eyes opened next, there were bright lights above me. Dark greenish-blue figures were moving around me. I could hear voices, but didn't understand what they were saying. My lips were numb and my mouth wouldn't move when I tried to call out for help. A flash of pain made me squirm, and then something clamped down on my face and the darkness returned.

It was the beeping that woke me after that. It took a few minutes to cut through the drug induced haze and realize I was in a hospital. I was in a shared room. The other three men were either asleep or unconscious. I tried to reach for the remote on the side of my bed, but my stomach hurt too much to twist. I looked down and saw blood seeping through a thick layer of gauze. I tried twice more to grab the remote, and then I gave up and laid back, letting sleep take me.

The next thing I knew, I was in a house in the middle of a forest. I was in my room, filled with fantasy novels, an old super Nintendo, and a playstation. I heard someone scream. I walked out from my room and saw the house was empty, but the front door was open.

I walked outside. The sun was shining bright, but there were no birds singing in the trees around the house. There were no squirrels. Nothing. Not even a breeze. Everything was still. I exited the house and walked around to the back. My movements were slowed, as if stuck in some sort of unseen pool that held every motion back. Another scream filled the air, the panicked sound of a young woman terrified. Not just any young woman, but my baby sister. I had to find her. I stormed into the woods, doing my best to run, but held back by the heavy air around me. I wound my way through the trees. I saw a figure in black robes flash through the trees. He was terribly fast, and he was chasing my sister.

The only good news was that he hadn't seen me yet. I was slow, but I had the element of surprise.

I moved through the trees as quietly as I could. I rounded a grove of aspens and then a large pine tree. The figure nearly ran into me. His face was covered by a mask, a white one just like the one worn in the movie Scream. In his hand he held a long chef knife. He tilted his head to look at me, as if he hadn't expected to find me in the forest. Suddenly the realization came to me that I was also holding a chef knife. Knowing that he was hunting my sister, I plunged my knife into his chest. The blade ripped and tore through the flesh and sinew, slipping between the ribs and puncturing the tender organs deep within. The masked man let out a hiss, like air escaping a tire, and then collapsed to the ground.

I turned around triumphantly, calling out to my sister and telling her it was all right.

Then I remembered that I didn't have a sister. I had been an only child.

My face began to itch, so I reached up to scratch it and found something hard over my skin. I pulled at it, only to find that I had been wearing a mask identical to the one worn by the strange figure in black robes. I then felt a pain in my stomach and looked down.

A bloody chef knife was protruding from my stomach, just a few inches left of my navel.

I woke with a start as pain ripped through my abdomen.

"Easy now, we're just changing your bandages," a young nurse said as she pulled at the gauze on my bullet wound.

A male nurse moved in and forced me back down to the bed. "Try to relax buddy," he said.

I passed out again before they finished.

I woke once again sometime after the sun had gone down. A tray of food sat at the side of my bed, only everything had been eaten, except for the salad.

I scanned the room and found a man sitting in a chair next to my bed, drinking chocolate milk from a container that was surely supposed to have been on my tray.

"I hope you don't mind," the man said. "I figured you weren't hungry anyway, on account of you snoring like a lumberjack and all."

I squinted at him, and then recognized him. He was the man from the mine. He had been wearing different clothes then, but it was the same man. I was sure of it. I was about to say something about my food, but then a thought occurred to me, had he found Dozer? Had he changed his mind about pressing charges for trespassing?

"Do you remember me?" he asked.

I nodded. "You own the mine," I said soberly.

The man nodded. "And…?"

I frowned. *And what?*

"You don't know me from anywhere else?"

I shook my head. "Should I?"

The man tapped the bottom of the milk container and then tossed the empty carton into the trash. He stood up and pulled a pair of photographs out of his suit pocket. "What about these two?"

I looked and saw the images of the men I had fought with on the corner of the street. A rash of worries flooded my mind. Were they related? Did those men work for him or know him somehow? I looked up at his blue eyes, but I didn't say anything or move a muscle.

"Relax, I'm not a cop," he said. "Think of me more as a guardian angel."

A guardian? That word seemed to stand out to me for some reason. "I'm all right," I said.

"Sure, you've been shot twice in the stomach, why wouldn't you be all right?"

The door to the room opened and closed. A man came in wearing a long white coat. "How is he doing?" the man said in a grim tone.

For some reason, I had an instant, deep dislike for the man. He looked at me and offered a smile, but I felt no sincerity behind the gesture.

"Doesn't remember a thing," the man in the suit said.

"Well, this is your lawyer, and I am your doctor," the man in the lab coat said.

"Lawyer?" I asked. "He owns a mine outside of town," I put in.

"Yeah, well, news of your condition spread fast," the man in the suit said. "I do own the mine, but I am a lawyer by profession. I happen to know the DA quite well actually, and I came to support you after I saw you on the news."

"We put out a bulletin asking for anyone with information about your identity to come forward," the doctor explained. "Your lawyer has been kind enough to take care of your bills as well."

I nodded and said, "Thank you, but you didn't have to do that."

"Actually I did," the lawyer said. "You see, I wanted to see how much you remembered."

"About the fight?" I asked.

119

"Cut the horse-crap Mills," the doctor said harshly. "Enough with the theatrics. Just let me do it my way this time." The doctor reached into his coat and pulled out a gun with a silencer.

I tried to scream, but the lawyer was on me faster than I could even blink. One hand covered my mouth, and his other put pressure on my bullet wound. Pain ripped through me so intensely that I nearly passed out. Only problem was, the "doctor" ran smelling salts under my nose to keep me conscious.

"No shots until I have what I need," the lawyer told the doctor. He then turned to me. "What kind of game are you playing at?" the lawyer asked.

My eyes shot around the room, hoping that any of the other patients in the room would wake up. None of them did.

The doctor moved in toward my ear. "If you think I won't shoot in here…" He put the gun next to my waist and fired three rounds into the bed. "You're dead wrong!" The doctor then put the hot barrel against my knee for emphasis.

"That's enough, Briggs, now back off!" the lawyer shouted.

Briggs, I had heard that name before, but I couldn't remember where from.

The lawyer leaned on me, pressing harder into my wound. "You may be out of the group, but if that's the case, then why are your friends chasing down leads about your father?" the lawyer asked. "What are they looking for? What does it do? Is it a weapon?"

My mind was racing. I had no idea what this man was talking about. I kept hoping this was some terrible reaction to the pain meds I had been given, but this was all too real.

"What are they looking for?" the lawyer growled.

The PA system in the hospital came on. At first it was just static, as if someone were tuning the radio on an old car. Then, of all things, ABBA came blaring to life. The entire hospital erupted in full volume as Waterloo came on.

"Check the hallway, now!" the lawyer shouted. He eased the pressure on my wound enough so I could finally take a breath without the urge to scream into his hand, which was still placed firmly over my mouth. The man with the gun ran toward the door.

The lights went out, but ABBA continued to play on the PA.

"It's them!" the gunman said.

I noticed a red dot appear on the back of the lawyer's arm. There was a strange sound, like someone hitting a pane of glass with an icepick, and then a fuzzy, red-feathered dart appeared in the back of the lawyer's arm. He slumped over, his head slamming onto my wound. There was an explosion of light, sound, and smoke, then the door blew off its hinges and the gunman was thrown to the floor.

"You son of a—"

Two masked men stormed in and stomped the gunman in the face while a third disarmed him before he could even finish his sentence.

"Got him," one of the masked men said as he reached up toward his ear with his left hand.

The next thing I know, I was being wheeled out through the pitch-black halls by the masked men. The taller one was racing through the corridors like there was no tomorrow while I held on for dear life. The third masked man in the back was whistling along to ABBA.

I kept my mouth shut as I rode in the back of a van. I had no idea who these people were, but the way they handled the two back at the hospital told me everything I needed to know. They kept their masks on and made a quick getaway from the city. Within ten minutes, we were on a freeway and headed north. A woman's voice called out from the driver's seat.

"How is the noob?"

"The quitter is fine," one of the masked men said.

Quitter? Noob?

The third masked man reached over to the radio and started playing ABBA again. Seriously, not my idea of raiding music, but I was not about to tell them to turn it off.

"You doing all right brother?" one of them asked me.

I nodded and found the courage to speak. "Who are you guys?"

The masked man puffed air through his teeth and elbowed the one that had called me a quitter. "That elf did a number on this one, huh?"

"Shut up back there," the man in the front said. Everyone quieted down. Which unfortunately meant that the masked man in the front was now free to sing at the top of his lungs. I was starting to wonder if there was a spare tranquilizer dart to put me out of my misery.

No such luck. We drove for at least seven hours, and then pulled off the freeway. I saw a couple signs, but couldn't see what they said.

At last, we reached a place called Fort Ord. To say I was confused was a gross understatement. I had just been rescued from two goons in a hospital by a real life A-Team and now was headed into the residential area of a military base. I kept waiting for Mr. T to rip his mask off and kiss his gold chains.

We pulled into the driveway of a long, rectangular house at the end of a cul-de-sac. The masked men ushered me inside under the cover of night. We had only been inside maybe ten minutes when another vehicle pulled into the drive. A few moments after that, the door opened and a group of large men came in, carrying the two goons from the hospital.

"Man, we are gonna catch hell for this," someone said.

"Couldn't leave him to the likes of Briggs and Jones," said the ABBA lover. "Besides, we need him."

"Section Four is gonna be up our –"

I tuned them out and watched as the two goons were stuffed into a closet. It was only then that I realized that the goons were bound with zip ties and gags. I was not. The only thing holding me in the chair I had been given was my own bewilderment. I moved to stand and then realized that there was something else that would make an escape impossible. A stabbing pain ripped through my stomach. I wasn't going anywhere.

The female driver minced over to me and knelt in front of me. "Don't tell me you forgot me? Krasavits."

Russian. She spoke Russian. I spoke Russian as well, but I was fairly certain I didn't know this woman. The Russians I met all lived *in* Russia. Not to mention the fact that I didn't normally hang out with paramilitary folk.

One of the masked men returned from stuffing the goons in the closet and struck a match to light a cigarette. The flare of the flame grabbed my attention. My eyes saw the orange and red burst, but my mind saw something else. A white explosion in an alleyway. I winced away as the pounding headache returned.

"He doesn't remember anything," the tall masked man said. "He can't help us now."

The ABBA fan walked toward me and removed his mask. His face was familiar, but I couldn't quite place it. "Your name is Joshua Mills," he stated dryly.

"I know my name," I replied. "But who are you?"

"Your father, he stole an engine from a company in California, a place called Twin Turbo, do you know anything about that?"

This was about my father? Good grief that man had a knack for getting into trouble. "I don't know what you're talking about."

"Show him the film," the man said. "Come on, Mack, reboot this newbie so we can move forward."

A shorter man, maybe only five and a half feet tall, came over with an iPad in his hands. "Here, let's see if this will jog your memory."

I watched the screen, and as I saw myself and my father enter an alley, everything came flooding back to me. The drums in my head sounded louder and louder, and my heart filled with dread as I realized what was happening.

"NO!" I shouted as I stood up and knocked the iPad away from Mack. "Hank! You can't do this to me! My family will be in danger!"

Hank held up his hands and patted the air. "Whoa, hold on, Mills, you don't think I'd risk that do you?" One by one the masks all came off. Marcus, Dan, Flint, and Katya were all there, along with several people I didn't know.

"What exactly do you think we've been doing the last several weeks while you've been vacationing in So-Cal, Newbie?" Flint asked.

"Some vacation," I said as the pain in my stomach pulled me back down to my seat.

Hank happily slapped my back. "The point is, we found it. We know what your father stole, and we know where it is. We have a plan that will get the drakkul off your back."

"And the harbinger wolves?" I asked. "What about Susan and Tommy?"

"We have a plan for that too," Hank said with a smile. "Everything is in place. I have a team protecting Susan and Tommy."

"More than that, they are in a pretty safe place," Mack cut in. "I might have messed with the Mexican Star Cruise tickets give-away this year."

"You put my wife on a cruise?" I asked, bewildered.

"A ship is a pretty safe place," Hank explained. Physically they are unreachable by the normal portals that harbinger wolves use."

"But the dream world?" I pressed.

Hank shook his head. "Even the dream world is connected to where your physical body is. With them always changing places, it will be nearly impossible to get a lock on them."

"But there is a chance," I said.

"Indyrith and his daughters are aboard the cruise liner, along with three teams. They're safe," Hank promised. "Now, we have to get our tasks done before they make landfall in two weeks when they will be more vulnerable."

"Assuming we have two weeks to begin with," Dan jumped in. "Or do I need to remind you that we not only assaulted Briggs and Jones, but we kidnapped them?"

"So, all we need to do is get the engine for the drakkul, and then hunt down the harbinger wolf that hates me before Section Four finds and massacres us all, is that it?" I asked.

Hank beamed from ear to ear. "That's it."

CHAPTER 12

The morning came fast. The smell of instant coffee filled the three bedroom house along with bacon and eggs. Everyone gathered in the back bedroom around a table with a paper plate full of food and a mug full of piping hot coffee. As a Mormon, I never drank coffee, but even if I hadn't been Mormon, I doubt I would have taken up the habit. Could never stand the smell. So, I made do with a cup of tap water.

"After Indyrith filled me in on what had happened with you, Mills, I selected the spot for you to hide out based upon proximity to where you used to live as a child. It gave us an easy way to keep tabs on you while we looked into your father's past."

"Indyrith told me to dig into his employers and find what I could," Mack said. "There were only two that could have anything to do with engines, and Twin Turbo was the best fit."

"Once we found what we were looking for, we came to get you."

"If you were keeping an eye on me, then where were you when those cops tried to kill me?"

"Those weren't cops," Dan put in. "They were werewolves, sent by the harbinger wolf that wants you dead."

"Okay, but, where were you?" I pressed.

Hank frowned. "We were there," he said flatly. "We were fighting a second group of werewolves that were led by a harbinger wolf. They had opened a portal two miles north of your position. I guess they thought they could divert us with the larger force and send others after you."

"So it was luck then?" I asked.

Hank shook his head. "Amber was watching you. She was able to hit the driver of the truck, that's why he recklessly slammed into the pillar under the pier. She also shot the other one that you punched in the face."

"Sorry to deflate your sails," Flint cut in. "But if Amber hadn't

125

been there, your punch wouldn't have done jack-crap to that werewolf. Even in human form they are strong as hell."

I looked around. I had heard of Amber at my first introductory meeting, but I had not yet met her. "Where is she?" I asked. "I would like to thank her."

"She is a bit tied up at the moment," Hank said. "Anyhow, let's move on. So, we have located the engine your father stole. The problem is, he sold it to a rival company who has been trying to implement it into their rocket designs."

"Rockets?" I asked.

Hank nodded. "Your father thought it was a rocket engine that would allow for multiple takeoffs and re-entry. He sold it to a billionaire by the name of Brent Rathison."

"The guy who has the commercials saying they want to take people to Mars?" I asked.

"That's the one," Mack said. "Problem is, they don't know what they really have. It is an engine, but it was never designed to be put onto a rocket. It's a trans-dimensional unification engine."

Everyone looked at me as if I was supposed to know what that meant. I just shook my head and waved my hand over the top. "Yeah, that one sailed right over me," I said. "I have no idea what that means."

Katya stepped to the table and set her plate and coffee mug down. "You remember when I told you about aliens and Fort Floyd?" she asked in her thick accent.

I nodded.

"Well, there is more. Truth is, there are many worlds out there to be conquered, but we aren't just fighting to protect our world. The Earth exists in seven parallel dimensions. Each one is stacked atop the other, like a transparent overlay for projectors they used to use in schools. We live in the fourth dimension, right in the middle. The dimensions below us are increasingly evil and dark. The fifth dimension is home to the drakkul, the sixth is the plane of harbinger wolves, and the seventh is the home of terrible monsters. It is also where the borelians fled to when the humans chased them out of this world."

Hank sighed and set his empty mug down with a *clank*. "You see, when the world was formed, Michael, the Arch Angel, fought against the Dragon, as it says in the bible, but, what it doesn't say is that he was not alone. Yes there were angels, but the dragon had his demons. As they fought over control of the Earth, the world shattered into several dimensions. Michael and his angels reside upon the highest dimension. The second dimension is home to what the three Vikings call Asgard. Thor, and warriors like him, do in fact reside there and from time to time do visit and help our world. The third dimension is that of the elves."

"Wait, I thought you said the elves were native to this world?" I cut in.

Katya nodded. "It was easier to explain it that way. But the truth is that the elves were the first race to master the portals. They came and dwelled here from the earliest of times. They aided the humans in fighting the borelians and expelling the beasts. As this dimension is in the middle of the light and dark planes, it has always been the front lines of the battle for control of all the dimensions. In fact, the battle in Antarctica was fought against a more primitive trans-dimensional unification engine. The seven portals that were opened were each calling the champions of the seven dimensions. The great war fought there was one of unparalleled loss. Other than Indyrith and his followers, the other elves that were trapped in this dimension fled to the Taiga."

"Why don't the angels come down and wipe out the bad guys then?" I asked, trying to wrap my head around everything.

"All Indyrith could tell us was that the angels are so powerful, that their weapons would be extremely harmful to us. If someone were to succeed in unifying the dimensions, the battle between angels and demons would rage again, but no matter which side won, ultimately it would mean the destruction of all races in the middle."

"So why are we giving the engine back to the drakkul? And how did Twin Turbo get their hands on it in the first place?"

Flint finished his eggs and set his paper plate down on the table before washing down the last bite with his coffee. "That's where you come in, Dream walker."

"Me?" I said. "What am I supposed to do?"

"Indyrith could explain it better than I, but essentially, the reason dream walkers are feared is because they are the only beings who can master the dream world to such a degree that you can flow between the dimensions unseen. Harbinger wolves can sometimes use the dream world, but not to the same degree a dream walker can. They can only inflict psychological harm on most beings in their dreams, and sometimes more physical harm, but a dream walker can slip in and out and kill enemies without detection."

"The drakkul and other master races that dominate each dimension mainly rely on portals," Flint said. "They are like the amphibious assault teams. Everyone can see them coming, or at least it's easier to see them coming. The harbinger wolves are like paratroopers in the dream world. Sometimes they can use it to their advantage, but they have to use smaller strikes. But you, you are like a stealth tactical nuke. No one can see you coming, and no one knows about your arrival until after the flash."

I shook my head and waved my hand. "But, I'm not ready," I said. "I... I've only had a couple of fights in the dream world, and I nearly died both times. I need training, I..." The drums sounded in the back of my head. A voice whispered something to me in a language I didn't know, and I swear it felt as though a hand squeezed my shoulder.

"We're out of time, Mills," Hank said, pulling me back to the conversation. "The plan is simple. We steal the engine, take it through the portal to the drakkul, but Mack here is going to rig it to malfunction when they try to use it. Your job is going to be keeping the drakkul off our trail, and using the dream world to eliminate key targets. Then, once the engine is out of commission, we will launch an assault on the sixth dimension. Rolf and his brothers will fight for the right to challenge those hunting your family, but you will simultaneously use the dream world to make sure they don't escape."

"So, we're back to using me as a cosmic assassin?" I asked.

Hank shrugged. "We have bullets and blades here, but none of us can even come close to doing what you did to that alp. I won't lie, it might be impossible, but if we fail, it will mean that someone is going to use that engine to link all of our dimensions. It won't just be your family, or even our world at stake. It will be seven parallel dimensions, and everything on them."

"The collision alone could create a cosmic event that would be second only to the big bang," Mack put in.

I shook my head. "And here I thought Mack didn't believe in anything bigger or greater than himself."

"I still don't," Mack said. "If there is a god, then he shouldn't have let the world break apart in the first place."

"Or maybe that was the point all along," I replied without thinking. "To see how hard we would fight to reach the light." There was a moment of silence, and for the briefest of seconds I thought that perhaps I had stunned them all with something clever. Flint put that notion to rest by hiking his leg and letting out a rank, juicy fart.

"Yeah, well, all I see are targets and objectives. Let's just stick with that instead of debating philosophy," Flint announced. "We need to move. Section Four is likely going to be on our doorstep any minute."

Hank nodded. "Mills, there is more I need to tell you. The rest of you, you know your assignments. Gear up in the next room, and get to work."

The room cleared out fast. The door closed, leaving me alone with Hank. The man smiled sheepishly and glanced at the closed door before letting out a huge sigh. "Indyrith filled me in on everything, including the fact that he wiped my memory after I had a bit of a meltdown. I wanted to apologize for that. I understand the love for your family is a powerful force."

Wow. I mean, I knew Hank was more human than Briggs just from the night he saved me at the hotel, but this was way beyond anything I expected, even from Hank. "It's all right. On the other side, I can see that what I was doing would seem selfish to anyone else."

Hank nodded and slapped the table. "The trouble is, now when you go to sleep at night, you are going to be hunted. The harbinger wolves will need to find you physically to inflict real harm. They know they are no match for you in the dream world, but there are other things out there. We are about to go into the muddy waters, and we're wading in fully aware that there are crocs and snakes waiting for us. This isn't going to be easy, but you have our full support."

I nodded. "I'll do what I can, but..." I pointed down to my side. "I still have a hole from that scuffle on the street."

Hank sucked his teeth and glanced down at my torso. "Yeah, someone ought to tell you that you don't bring fists to a gun fight."

I smirked. "Will I feel this in my dreams?" I knew that wounds received in the dream world left me sore and hurting in the physical world. If that worked both ways, then it was going to make things a lot more difficult.

"I honestly have no idea. Indyrith never let me in on his little secret about dream walkers. We've always dealt with the monsters in the real world with bullets and knives. All I know is, we're in for a helluva fight. Brent Rathison isn't just a billionaire. He is the son of a powerful vampire family. His wealth is dirty, and he has more powers than his silk shirts might make you think."

"So, my father sold an engine to the son of a vampire?" I smiled and nodded my head. "He never was very lucky with his schemes."

"What we haven't figured out is how the drakkul consider it theirs. From everything we discovered, it appears as though Twin Turbo invented the designs. There is nothing inherently alien in its mechanics. Furthermore, Brent Rathison has had it in his possession since the day your father sold it to him well over two decades ago, and only in the last couple of months have they come close to a working prototype."

"How would they know of the other dimensions?" I asked.

"Vampires are crafty devils," Hank replied. "They know far too much about everything. They have their fingers in just about any pie worth having, and they control most of the world banks."

"Sounds like a conspiracy my uncle would believe," I commented wryly.

"This one's true. They're hard to hunt. They have learned to live in the shadows and remain hidden. They let their human offspring be their faces when they have something they really want to accomplish, though. Brent Rathison attends charities, galas, you name it. He has many allies. If we go after him, it won't just be vampires chasing us, it will be all of his political allies, and his reach is far and wide."

"Why not team up with Section Four then?" I asked. "I mean, surely they don't want the engine to make the dimensions collide do they?"

"Indyrith tried," Hank said flatly. "I called in a favor with Jones. Jones arranged for his boss to meet with me and Indyrith. Problem is, the meeting was a failure. Jones' boss was hit before he reached us. Some creature we never heard of ripped into his convoy and killed thirty-two men. Since then, Section Four has clammed up tight. They put eyes on you and then you know the rest. Doesn't help that the two men you trounced were actually Section Four agents."

"Wait, the beggars beating people up were from Section Four?"

"They wanted to get close to you, thought you were scheming something. We told them you were out of the group; that your memory had been wiped clean going back several years, but they didn't trust that, not after what happened with that convoy."

"They don't think you had anything to do with it, do they?"

Hank shrugged. "Oh they probably think we did something stupid to piss some demon off somewhere. I doubt they think we helped ambush the convoy, but I think they blame us all the same." Hank ran a hand through his hair and took in a deep breath. "The thing I really need to tell you is—"

The door flew open and Marcus stormed in, cell phone to his ear. "Hank, Houston just got hit!"

Hank spun around. "What?!"

Marcus held the phone out on speaker. Gunshots and curses came through the speakers.

"Tell Hank to activate Alamo! I repeat, activate Alamo!" someone shouted on the other end. A loud snarl smothered the shouting as the rapid gunfire continued to *pop pop pop!* There were explosions, and then the line went dead.

"That was the safe house," Marcus said soberly. "They're all gone."

Hank snatched the phone from Marcus and frantically worked the buttons. When the phone failed to ring, Hank swore at it and turned it off. "Go, activate Alamo now!" Marcus nodded and rushed out the door. Hank turned to me. "Mills, you better come with me right now!"

A shadow flew across the window to my left. I looked just in time to see a four-legged beast with dark purple skin crash through the glass. I turned the table up and over to use as a barricade. Hank pulled a .357 magnum from his hip and fired six shots into the creature's face. Blood and bits of flesh splattered out around the room, but the thing kept coming. It slammed into the table and threw me against the wall. The stitches in my side ripped open and along with the blinding pain I could feel the rush of fresh blood pouring out.

Hank shouted at the creature and went for a bowie knife. I struggled to get to my feet and help, but the muscles in my core wouldn't work. I was wracked with spasms that rendered me useless in the fight. The door flew open again and Dan was there with a massive weapon that looked like a shotgun but had a drum magazine attached to the bottom.

Sparks and flames exploded from the barrel as a deafening thunder echoed off the walls. Goo and blood painted the room as Dan unleashed everything he could with his automatic weapon. The creature, what was left of it after the gun stopped roaring, flopped to the floor in a torn heap. Hank was on his back, leaning against the other wall with a mess of blood matting his shirt to his chest.

I could hear gunshots coming from other areas in the house as well. People shouted orders as guns popped off and creatures snarled and roared, but for the moment my eyes locked with Hank's. All the chaos out there seemed miles away as the man who had rescued me twice slumped lower to the floor. Only as he fell to his side did I see that his right arm had been ripped away at the shoulder, along with much of the flesh on his upper chest and back. His face was white as a sheet, except for the spots of purple blood that had gotten on him from the creature.

Dan was working to stop the bleeding, but ultimately there was nothing he could do.

I watched, helplessly clutching what now seemed a miniscule hole in my stomach, as Hank died in front of me. His once vibrant eyes turned to a dull shine. He was gone.

Dan jumped up, rage conjuring swear words that would have made Katya blink, as he left Hank's broken body. He barely stopped long enough to toss me a pistol before running down the hall and joining in the fight. I held the weapon, a glock 23, and stared at Hank's body. I kept wishing he would get up. I had seen people die before, but they had been old and in hospitals. This was the first time I had seen this side of death. It filled me with both regret, and fear, but I wasn't left alone to those feelings for long.

A slender shape stepped through the hole where the window had once been. It was a woman, or female at least, for I could see the shapely curves, but there was little about her that looked human in a normal sense. Her skin was pale gray, her hair long and dark, but covering much of her neck and face as well as her head. As she stepped into the room, I realized that she was not clothed, but instead covered by a thick coat of dark fur. Long, sharp claws protruded out from the ends of her massive fingers. I wasn't sure whether it was a harbinger wolf or a werewolf, but I didn't care. My stomach wouldn't allow me to run, but my arms were ready and willing to do their jobs.

I snapped the gun up and peppered the wolf creature with three shots to the face. She fell backward and tumbled out the open window. Her body fell out of view. I grunted, struggling to push myself up to a better position. I had to be ready if she came back inside. I used the corner for support, leaning my left shoulder into it and breathing heavily as blood continued to trickle out from the wound in my stomach.

A mess of dark fur launched up and into the window so quickly I barely had time to react. I fired seven more times, and then the slide cocked back, indicating the magazine was spent. A moment later, the wolf crashed into me. Her arms reached around me, but the claws did not dig in. Her head slammed into my chest, but she did not bite me. Not wanting to wait and see if she would regenerate, and pushed her away and forced myself to stand. I made for the door quick as I could, but a hand wrapped around my ankle and dropped me to the floor. I hit hard, but quickly turned over to try and kick at her with my free leg. I hit her three times in the top of the head. I'm a strong guy, but my kicks did little more than slow her down.

She started to come more fully to her senses. Her grasp on my ankle tightened until it felt as though the pressure had cut through my skin and was now crushing my bones directly. She turned her ugly face toward me and sneered, blood seeping out from the several bullet holes I had given her. My ankle popped, and then a burning pain washed over me as I felt the bones succumb to her grip. She started to advance, slowly at first, still dazed from the shots, but she was gaining strength with every passing second. I looked around for something, anything to use as a weapon. I saw Hank's knife, still clutched in his left hand. I wrenched it free just as the wolf lunged for my throat. I plunged the knife up under her jaw and deeply into her neck. She yelped and then tried to push my hands away.

I drove it in with everything I had. She raised a hand as if to claw down at my face and neck, but at that moment I heard the loudest, deepest *boom!* A spray of blood and tissue plastered the wall. All that was left of the wolf's head was her lower jaw. Everything above that had been obliterated by the obscenely long rifle in Katya's hands. The wolf's arms and legs twitched and convulsed, but the danger had passed. I turned over and dumped the body on the ground with great effort, heaving and gasping for breath.

Katya set the large rifle down and came in with a machete to finish severing the neck, kicking the lower jaw and bit of neck away from the rest of the corpse as she cursed it in her native tongue.

"Still alive?" she asked me.

I nodded and reached up for her hand. She pulled me up and then helped me through the hallway. I could see Marcus patching up a wound on Flint's arm. Dan had the back of his shirt ripped off and there were gashes over his shoulder blade, but he didn't seem to mind them. Mack was holding a wad of gauze to his head, and I could see a bit of blood oozing downward over his left eye.

Three of the other men whom I had not met prior to my rescue from the hospital were dead. Briggs was standing over Jones' headless body, staring at it silently. He had a shotgun in his left hand, and a very bloody knife in his right. A creature that looked like the purple monster that had killed Hank was dead at Briggs' feet. There were two more werewolves in the house as well. The southern wall of the house was missing, blown off by explosions and gunfire. In the lawn in front of the house were several mangled creatures.

Flint walked away from Marcus and out to the yard where one of the purple monsters was trying to crawl away. He pulled his 1911 and poured everything into the monster's head. Flint then returned to the house. "Briggs, you can call it in, but you're coming with us."

Briggs dropped the shotgun, sheathed his knife, and walked toward Flint. For a moment, I thought they were about to fight, but Briggs walked past Flint and out into the yard.

"Briggs, stop or I'll shoot!" Flint shouted. Flint reloaded his 1911 and aimed it at Briggs. Briggs held his arms out and kept walking away. "Dang it Briggs, you can't make it on your own!" Flint yelled as he lowered his weapon.

One of the other operators ran into the house and motioned for everyone to follow him. "I got one of the armored vans to turn over. Come on, we have to go."

"Briggs!" Flint called out.

"Let's go," Katya said to me as she turned to aim me for the hole that had previously been the door to the driveway. Within two minutes, we were all in the van, except for Briggs, and speeding out of there. I had a million questions about how an incident like this was going to be kept a secret, but no one was in the mood to answer questions.

We drove northward without stopping until we could hit I-80 heading east into Nevada.

Exhausted from the day's ordeal, and drowsy from the pain meds Marcus gave me to calm my broken ankle and ruptured sutures, I fell asleep.

CHAPTER 13

I could tell I was dreaming. It was the kind of scenery that seemed to melt with every movement, moving fluidly in response to my actions. I was in a desert somewhere. I didn't recognize the area. It was nothing like Utah. The dirt was red and orange, with massive, gray rocks dotting the ground. Large cacti rose up with great spines and simple, bright yellow flowers. A pair of birds tweeted and chirped at each other as one hovered just in front of a hole in one large cactus and the other sat inside. The sun sat high in the sky, but it wasn't as hot as the setting would have suggested in real life. A mirage rose up to my right. I stopped and watch the wavy illusions for a moment, watching them start to take form and approach.

The creature wasn't overly tall, but the three horns and brown fur put a rock in my stomach that threatened to pull me down into the desert floor. The alp that had threatened my family was here.

On my left, behind me, and off to the north, three flashes of light ripped through my dreamscape. Before the harbinger wolves stepped through their portals, I knew what they wanted.

I took in a deep breath, trying to focus my mind and take control of my dream. I was relieved to find that my broken ankle and other injuries did not transfer over into the dream world. My sword materialized in my right hand and I watched and waited as the monsters approached.

"You broke your word?" the alp hissed as it stopped some twenty yards in front of me. The harbinger wolves snarled and paced back and forth as they locked their eyes on me and licked their lips. "What have you done with your family?"

I was more than a little comforted to find out that Hank's plan to keep Susan and Tommy safe was working. Too bad the same couldn't be said for Hank, but there was no time for sadness now. I was about to face off with four creatures who knew the dream world far better than I did. Frankly, the scene reminded me of the showdown in The

Good, The Bad, and The Ugly. I was starting to think that I should have wished for a gun.

The alp clicked and held out its hands. "First you, and then your family." The creature's nails grew longer and then a layer of purple and gray smoke covered the desert floor. The sand dropped out from beneath me, and I found myself falling downward as the alp laughed and the harbinger wolves lunged toward me.

I twisted in the air and slashed through the fleshy shoulder of the closest harbinger wolf. The beast snarled and recoiled as the clouds enveloped us and we crashed downward into a new scene. My body broke through an old barn roof. I landed hard on the aged wooden planks of the upper floor where bales of stale hay were kept. Out the corner of my eye, I saw the wounded harbinger wolf burst through the upper floor and crash down to the dirt below. He howled in pain, and then I heard the claws ripping at the ground and pounding the stairs as he made his way back to me.

Jumping up to my feet, I took stock of where I was. I knew this place. I had lived here as a boy. This barn was situated deep in the northwestern corner of Montana, smack in the middle of twenty of the most fertile acres on God's green earth. I smiled. The alp was manipulating the dream, but he had miscalculated. This barn had been my fortress as a boy. I had won many imaginary battles within its walls, and I knew all the secret places to hide, and to escape. I raced over two bales of hay and came down with the point of my blade. I hadn't needed to look before I struck, I knew that this would put me right over the top of the stairs. The beast unwittingly raced toward his own doom. As I came down, my bodyweight easily sank my sword into the harbinger wolf's spine. The monster yipped and fell limp. I wrenched the sword free and then came down with a heavy chop to sever the harbinger wolf's head. For good measure, I kicked the head down the stairs.

A second wolf was climbing the walls outside the barn, headed for a large gap where age and weather had torn away a section of the upper wall. He charged in as I gave him a wink. I raced up the last couple stairs and slid my sword back into its sheath upon my back. I clambered over a short stack of hay bales and leapt outward. I had done this many times as a boy, much to my mother's chagrin. If only she had known that this exact move would save my life one day, perhaps she wouldn't have scolded me for it. My hands found the familiar, strong rope hanging from the top of the barn. In years past, it had been used as part of a pulley to hoist up the hay bales, but I used it the way Robin Hood might have used a similar device to swing from tree to tree, only I was making a wide arc. At the apex, I kicked my legs back toward the barn to pick up momentum. The harbinger wolf had leapt out after me, but he had not known about the rope. The heel of my boot connected with the harbinger wolf's lower jaw and snapped the creature's head back as my momentum drove me through the beast. The large monster grunted and flipped over backward, landing hard upon the ground below. No sooner had my feet touched the edge of the barn than I jumped down, pulling my blade and aiming it for my next target. My feet drove into the harbinger wolf and kept it pinned as I pierced its chest with my sword.

I grinned victoriously. This was going much better than I had thought.

The next thing I know there was an explosion of gray wood from behind me. Splinters teeth and claws shot out at me back as the third harbinger wolf flew at me. I managed to duck and roll to the side just in time to avoid the beast's menacing fangs, though the claws did tear a gash in my right shoulder, causing an immense, hot pain to shoot along my arm. I hit the ground hard and watched in horror as the harbinger wolf I had just stabbed through the heart slowly rose to its feet and shook off the debris. It turned and sneered.

"You heal faster in the dream world..." I huffed. "Fantastic." I jumped to my feet in time to raise the sword as the wounded wolf lunged for me. His right arm was a blur of gray and brown as the claws came sailing at my face. I pulled back and managed to hit the arm with my sword, but I had made a mistake. I had lost sight of the harbinger wolf that had broken through the wall.

The creature seemed to come out of nowhere, as if the grass in the dream had grown longer just to hide his movements. He jumped up at my side, his gaping maw filled with yellowed fangs dripping with spittle. I felt the hot breath on my face as the monstrosity came within striking distance, but instead of finishing me, a flash of green zipped in, followed by a crackle of lightning. The harbinger wolf's head stopped in midair and then fell to the ground, mouth still open wide.

"Don't stare, fight!" a stern voice shouted.

A large foot slammed into my abdomen, claws ripping at the front of my shirt as the force of the blow threw me back through the opening in the barn wall. The wolf howled and turned to fight the newcomer. After I bounced across the dirt floor of the barn and came to a stop, I looked up, expecting to see Flint, or Indyrith, but the man I saw fighting in my stead was neither human, nor elf.

A drakkul was standing toe-to-toe, working his blades as quickly as the wolf could strike with its massive claws. I could hardly believe my eyes, but growing up a bit on the poorer end of things, I knew better than to reject such a generous gift. I jumped up and rushed in. With the two of us together, the final harbinger wolf didn't stand a chance. My sword lopped off the wolf's right hand just below the elbow, which then created an opening for the drakkul. The lizard-man thrusted one sword through the wolf's heart, and planted his second up higher in the creature's left shoulder.

"I have him pinned, take the head!" the drakkul shouted.

I was already in motion by the time the lizard had spoken. My sword whistled through the air and then took the harbinger wolf's head with one *thwack!* A spray of blood hit the ground, and then the monster went limp, easily sliding backward off of the drakkul's swords.

A thousand thoughts ran through my mind. Was the drakkul here to kill me himself? Was he related to the others who had died already? Or was he simply here to make sure I didn't die before he could retrieve the precious engine of theirs?

I opened my mouth to speak, but the world melted away again. Instead of the ground falling out, as it had in the desert, the horizons seemed to liquefy and flow downward, mixing together as if made of nothing more than wax that had been put into a furnace.

A great rumbling shook the ground and I fell to my knees. When it stopped, I was in a barren, brown valley filled with rocks and tall, black trees.

"The alp is taking us to my homeland," the drakkul said. "He will try to use my memories to disorient you."

"Why are you helping me?" I asked.

The large drakkul turned and offered a toothy grin that revealed his many sharp fangs as he swished his tail back and forth. "Focus on the alp, if we survive, I will tell you."

If we survive? We had already killed the harbinger wolves. I had killed an alp already by myself. The rest of this fight was going to be easy.

The knocking sound of falling rocks rose up from the mountains behind me. I turned and saw several large boulders tumbling downward.

"Get down!" the drakkul hissed. The creature then flattened himself to the earth. I almost did likewise, but my doubts got the better of me. Why was this drakkul helping me? Or, was it even a drakkul at all? Alps were able to manipulate dreams. What if this was some sort of trap?

I clutched my sword and scanned the area, keeping a wary eye on the drakkul who was still motioning for me to lie flat on the ground.

A great screech rent the air. A massive, four-winged creature exploded out from the mountainside and dove toward my position. The largest bird I had seen in real life was a California Condor. It was massive, with a nine foot wingspan. The thing soaring my way now could easily make a snack of a condor with one bite of its giant, pterodactyl-like beak.

I ran and dove behind a large boulder. A wave of air kicked up dust and small bits of sand and gravel as the winged terror sailed just a foot or two over the boulder. Because of its size, the thing couldn't turn around in a tight corner. It had to sail off toward the other side of the valley and then careen around in a wide arc as it prepared for the next dive.

"Come on!" the drakkul hissed.

This time I didn't question my unlikely partner. We ran. The drakkul led me to a pile of rocks and pointed to a space between them. I scrambled down inside and peeked around to see what the drakkul was doing. The green-skinned creature sheathed his second sword and held up his left hand. A mass of swirling, crackling lightning bolts gathered in his hand. He waited as the winged monster came closer, and then fired his spell a second before diving down into the space between the rocks with me.

I heard an agonized squawk, and then there was a great crash as the massive thing scraped and scratched across the surface, dragging rocks and dirt with it until its momentum was broken.

"Come, we must kill it now!" the drakkul said as he clambered out from the rocks.

I wormed my way up to the surface and rushed after him. This being his native environment, the drakkul was much more adept than I at climbing out of the small space. He was already atop the great beast's back and stabbing at the creature's spine by the time I had climbed out and made it to my feet. I ran into the fray, seeing that the winged beast was thrashing about and trying to shake off the spell it had been hit with. Its long neck craned around, bringing the deadly beak directly toward me. Out of reflex rather than experience, I dropped to slide on my knees and bent low to the ground as I thrusted my sword up into the soft spot just at the back of the beak. My blade easily tore into the creature. Before I could pull my weapon out and prepare for another strike, the creature made a hissing sound and flipped its head back the other way, flinging me and my sword several yards away. I tumbled across the hard dirt and slammed into one of those tall, black trees. Stars went around my head as if I was in an old Looney Tunes show, followed by a terrible ringing in my ears that made me clench my eyes shut until it passed.

Stabbing pain ripped through my left shoulder and something picked me up as easily as if I were a doll. I opened my eyes to see the alp, but it was not the small creature I had seen before. It was twenty feet tall, and easily heavier than several bull elephants. He laughed at me and then threw me to the ground. His claws pulled at my flesh as they were rent from my body, and then there was a terrible *crack!* I bounced once on the dirt, and then came to a twisted stop. I tried to force myself to remember that this was just a dream, but the wounds were too real. I could barely breathe. My left arm was dead and useless. I was only vaguely aware that my sword was no longer with me.

Blackness was closing around my vision as the blood poured from my shoulder.

"I'm not through with you yet," the alp said.

A great, pink tongue stretched out and licked at my shoulder, bringing with it a pain that could only be described as fire. The heat rolled into me like a ball, and then expanded through my body in waves. I cried out in agony, and then I nearly lost consciousness. Somehow, the alp was keeping me awake, reveling in my pain. It seized me by my left ankle, twisting the joint as it brought me up into the air. I heard the bones crack, but the pain was nothing compared to the burning in my shoulder.

"A dream walker," the alp hissed. "I had forgotten how good the blood of a dream walker tastes."

A flash of green ran at the alp from below. I tried to warn the drakkul off, but it was too late. The alp swatted the drakkul away with his free hand, sending my ally flying through the air and away from the battle. The beast then brought me closer to his large, brown eye. I dangled helplessly, racked with pain and void of the will to live or even move. There was nothing I could do. The plate-sized pupil dilated and then narrowed as I came within a few feet of the great eye.

"I will not eat you quickly," the alp promised. "Your body will die in only a few hours, but in the dream world it shall feel as years to you. I will relish in this kill."

I'm not sure what it was. Fatigue, the brink of consciousness I was at, I can't say, but for whatever reason, I started laughing. The alp shook my limp body, but still I laughed.

"What is wrong with you!" the alp shouted so loudly that rocks tumbled from the nearby mountainsides.

I shook my head and despite the pain, answered the creature. "My name is Joshua Mills. I am nobody. I sell memberships at a local gym, and here I am fighting monsters and waging war against creatures that create nightmares. It's ridiculous. No one would ever believe me."

The alp dropped me and then stabbed a single claw through my right leg. The wound went down into my bone and caused my back to arch with the most intense, massive spasm I could imagine. A moment later the creature pulled me back up to its eyes and licked the blood flowing from the new wound. A fire started in my leg, just as it had when the alp licked my shoulder.

"There, was that enough to help you believe your eyes?" the alp hissed.

I clenched my jaw against the pain and focused my eyes on the great orb in front of me. My strength was draining faster than I had ever experienced before in my life, but the anger and indignation rising within my soul gave me a bit of strength. I wasn't going to win the fight, but I was not about to go down easily either.

"Go to hell," I whispered. I jabbed the great eye with my index and middle finger on my right hand, pushing into the soft, wet surface as much as I could before curling my fingers and raking my nails across the orb.

"GARGH!" the alp shouted as it flung me to the side. I hit the ground and skidded to a halt just before slamming into a large rock. I smiled. That had felt good. I struggled to crane my neck around and watch as the alp was holding its eye and thrashing about angrily.

"What's the matter, something in your eye you big oaf!" I shouted.

Drums sounded in the valley.

I looked around, expecting to see the drakkul, but he was nowhere to be seen. The drums grew louder.

"Get up boy," a man said. "Get up and fight."

I laughed the notion off at first, but then a great swell of energy filled my lungs.

"GET UP!" the man shouted. In that moment, I forgot about the pain in my body. I pushed up to my feet as the drums grew louder and louder. "This is your dream," the voice said. "Bend it to *your* will."

I looked around, but saw no one except the alp, who was still holding his eye and gnashing his teeth. That was when I realized that there was a tall, brown hat on the ground near me. In all of the alp's thrashing and jumping around, he had lost his tarnkappe. I bent down and took the hat, remembering that Indyrith had said the hat was the source of the alp's power. No sooner had I taken it, than a cool breeze wrapped around my body. All of my wounds healed. More than that, I could feel my muscles grow thicker and stronger. My head cleared, and my sword appeared back in my hand. I tucked the hat into the back of my pants and whistled at the alp.

"Hey there One-Eye-McFatty, I'm not through with you yet!" I shouted.

The alp turned then and wailed at me, raising its claws angrily and preparing to strike, but when it saw me standing, it stopped and stood still.

"No, this cannot be!" the alp hissed. It clicked and glanced nervously to the side, and then it tried to run away.

"No," I said calmly.

The alp smacked into an invisible wall.

"Let me out!" the alp shouted. The creature turned to run another way, but again slammed into an invisible wall. It then wheeled around on me, its one eye bloodshot and red. "I will not let you do this!"

The ground fell away once more and a cloud of smoke surrounded the alp.

"No!" I shouted.

The ground returned.

The smoke hiding the large alp disappeared. Then the creature shrank back to its original size.

"NO!" the alp hissed. "How are you doing this?!"

I reached back with my left hand and pulled out the tarnkappe. The alp's eyes went wide and the creature shook with fear.

"No, no, give it back! Give it back!" It charged toward me, but knowing that I had the power over this nightmare, I had a bit of fun of my own. As the alp dashed in, I imagined a column of rock rising up in front of it. In answer to my imagination, a column sprang up and the alp ran headlong into the stone, knocking itself back onto its rump and nearly losing consciousness.

I tucked the hat back into my waistband and advanced on the dazed creature, sword at the ready.

"No!" the drakkul shouted as he came around a group of black trees, limping badly and holding his left arm close to his side. "Keep the hat and the beast will be your slave."

I shook my head and walked up to the wide-eyed, three-horned alp. Its lower jaw quivered as it stared at my blade. "I have no need for slaves," I said decisively. I brought my sword down and took the alp's head in one fell swoop. As the alp's head rolled across the ground, I turned back to the drakkul. "The first time I saw one of you, it ruined my life."

The drakkul nodded. "I know of Hek'tar Bar'Sule, but I am not one of his kin. I am Drendarin, First Talon of the House of Grena." The lizard-man puffed out his chest and stood straight. It was obvious that in his home such a title would carry great meaning. In the middle of a nightmare that had almost killed me, I couldn't care less.

"Get to the point," I said impatiently. "Why did you show up and help?" I threw up a finger and pointed at the creature. "*And*, while you're at it, go ahead and tell me just how you got into my dream in the first place."

Drendarin nodded and his proud shoulders fell. "The house that hunts you is a mighty clan. They have always been quick to fight, but slow to listen to reason. They seek what your father stole from them, but they ignore the consequences of reclaiming such a device."

I knew he was talking about the trans-dimensional unification engine, but I wasn't going to feed him any information by filling in holes. He was going to have to explain everything to me. "What do you want?" I asked bluntly.

"The machine belongs not only to the Bar'Sule clan, but to mine as well," Drendarin stated. "My father's father worked with Hek'tar Bar'Sule's grandfather on the invention. It took many years, and much sacrifice to create it. They knew it would be a challenging endeavor, but neither of the original inventors guessed that it would lead to a war between our clans. When it was near completion, my grandfather realized that using the machine would not simply unify the seven worlds into one, but that it would destroy nearly every living thing in all seven dimensions. Seeing that he could not complete his work, he spoke with Hek'tar Bar'Sule's grandfather, a great and marvelous scientist known as Taragoth the Quick. Taragoth agreed with my grandfather, but Taragoth's son would not see reason. In a fit of rage, Taragoth was slain by his own son during an argument about the fate of the machine. It was then that my grandfather knew he had to dispose of the machine."

Drendarin swished his tail behind himself nervously. "My grandfather arranged to deposit the machine in this dimension."

"Why in the bloody hell would he do that?" I shouted. "Hey, I just invented a giant doomsday machine, oh, I have an idea, let's give it to the humans!" I went on in my best evil scientist impression, rubbing my hands together and everything.

"You misunderstand!" Drendarin said with a snort. "He never thought that anyone in this dimension would be able to actually complete his work. He destroyed all of the notes and diagrams, and only deposited the machine itself in this dimension."

"So, let me get this straight, your grandfather thought humans were too dumb to figure it out?"

Drendarin nodded and flicked his forked tongue. "In his defense, we did invent the wheel some ten thousand years before humans. Technically, you never actually invented it. The elves gave it to…"

"I really don't care," I snapped. "So, you are telling me that my family is innocent, that *I* am not the son of a thief?"

"Well… no," Drendarin said with a shrug. "My grandfather placed the machine within an organization that would have used its parts to fuel some sort of crude engine. Your father did, in fact, steal the machine from them."

I shook my head and waved it all off. "Still, I'm blaming you that I am right here, right now." A swell of anger boiled up inside my chest. Drendarin was still speaking, but I was no longer listening. I sheathed my sword, walked up to the six-foot-tall lizard-man, and belted him straight in the face with all the power my three hundred pound body could. Drendarin hit the dirt, hard. He hissed in a predictably snakelike fashion, but he didn't draw his weapons or move to fight back.

"You are like Hek'tar Bar'Sule and his clan, slow to reason," Drendarin hissed.

"And you are an idiot," I shot back. Not my most creative insult, but I can't always come up with the right thing to say when I'm flustered. "If not for you and your stupid grandpa, I could be home with my wife and son. I would never have gone to jail. Everything would be perfect!"

Drendarin held a clawed hand out to me and sighed. "If my grandfather had not hidden the machine when he did, the others would have already used it. Your world would not exist, nor would your family. At least you have had some piece of happiness, even if you lost it in the end. What is it you humans say? It is better to have loved and lost, than to have not loved at all?"

Great, I'm stuck in a dream with a giant lizard-philosopher. I grunted and reached down for his hand. Drendarin nodded his appreciation and then looked to the horizon.

"This is what my world looks like in the barren parts," he said. "Come, I will show you more." There was a flash of light as Drendarin played with a ring on his left index finger. Suddenly I was in a city of sorts. I stood upon a gray street. Houses lined the sides and drakkul were out in the sunlight. To my right, four children kicked a ball in the street. To my left, a pair of adult drakkul were discussing the sale of a rather large animal with six legs and two heads.

"We are not so different, you and I," Drendarin said. "We each have families. We both have communities. Look there," he said as he pointed to a conical building with windows of green and blue glass. "That is our primary school where our younglings attend until their tenth summer. When I was young, I attended there. My mother taught in that school until she died of old age."

Drendarin played with his ring again and we were whisked up into a high mountain overlooking a coastal city with towering buildings and sprawling streets separated by rectangular green spaces.

"Even our larger cities are similar," Drendarin noted. "Down there you will find universities, churches, buildings of government, homes, and businesses of all kinds. We have vehicles that are like your automobiles, but ours run upon water, and do not pollute our skies, though, they are slower than your noisy contraptions."

"You seem to know a lot about my world," I said suspiciously.

"I am a student of science and history," Drendarin replied. "I study many subjects, but your home world is among my favorite topics, yes. Ever since the machine was placed in your home world, my family has endeavored to learn of your home, and its people."

"Why?"

Drendarin sighed and pointed down to the city emphatically. "Because, the more you understand your enemy, the easier it is to recognize that you should be friends. Ours is a society built upon honor. If my clan could take a more prominent role in governing our people, then the drakkul will learn that humans are not our enemies. They will see as I do, that we are more the same. Our bodies may look different, but we have the same desires and aspirations."

"Tell that to the drakkul who beheaded my father," I said.

Drendarin touched his ring and we were back in the barren valley where we had started. "Even if you cannot find mercy in your heart for my people, surely you must see the danger that the machine poses. If it is used to merge our worlds, none of us would survive. Imagine the chaos that would come to a barren place such as this when it merges with your home."

"I assume that would also come with those giant pterodactyl things?" I asked.

"And many more beasts the likes of which your world has never known," Drendarin answered.

I shook my head. "All right, so let's say I put aside my feelings for your grandpa and ask what your plan is, what would you say?"

Drendarin grinned, revealing his wickedly sharp fangs. "Find the machine, put it out of reach of the Bar'Sule clan, and then broker peace between your family and theirs."

"Oh, is that all?" I asked with a roll of my eyes.

"I have sacrificed much to stop the Bar'Sule clan from retrieving the machine. I must succeed where my grandfather failed. We must destroy it."

"If I destroy it, then the other drakkul will never stop coming after me and my family," I reminded him. "I'm not about to let them hunt my son."

Drendarin shook his head. "No, you help me get the machine back. I will report that you returned it, thus making amends for your father's sins. *I* will destroy it."

"And I am just supposed to trust you?" I scoffed. "Fat chance of

147

that."

"I saved your life," Drendarin put in. "The harbinger wolves had you cornered."

He was right of course, but that wasn't nearly enough to sway me into giving him the engine. "You may have saved my life," I said. "But, the machine of which you speak could destroy far more lives. The others I work with wouldn't allow it even if I did. They don't trust you. I assume you know of the three Viking guys right?"

Drendarin nodded and grinned slyly. "Yes, I have seen them in action. Also, Hank has told me a bit about them."

"Hank?" I spat out incredulously. "How do you know him?"

"I don't know him well," Drendarin said. "I only got into contact with him a week ago. We were working on a plan to find and take back the machine."

"Bull-crap," I said. "I think we're done here."

"Hank was planning on stealing the machine back from a man named Brent Rathison, was he not?" Drendarin pressed. "Exactly how did you think you were going to go up against the most powerful family of vampires without help?"

This was too much. Drendarin knew far more than he should. "You can read my mind can't you?" I accused. "In the dream you can get into my head. That's how you know this."

"No," Drendarin said with a shake of his head and impatient tail thump. "I am the first drakkul to walk in dreams. I used a modified version of one of my grandfather's inventions. We had made it as a way to guard against harbinger wolves, but I used it to find Hank. I watched the last several battles at the gates. I was there when you saw your first battle between Hek'tar Bar'Sule and one of your vikings. I saw something in Hank, an intelligence that wasn't as obvious with the others. I began working then on contacting him. He distrusted me at first as well, but eventually he came to see that I was right."

"You want me to believe that you and I are allies just because you can name Hank and some billionaire son of a vampire? You're going to have to do better than that."

"I cannot prove my words to you. Believe, or do not believe, the choice is yours. I will say that we need to help each other. If you assault Brent Rathison without my help, you will fail."

"And you have something that can give me the edge?" I asked. Drendarin nodded, keeping his gaze locked steady with mine. "If you know how to beat them, then why not do it yourself?"

"Simple," Drendarin said. "I am an honorable drakkul. I cannot sneak into your world in the physical sense. For me to do so would bring dishonor and shame upon my family. Additionally, thanks to the recent defeat at the hands of your viking guardian, I cannot open the gate from our world to yours and challenge your gatekeeper for several more months. So, as you can plainly see, I need your help."

"So we're supposed to become friends then?"

"A friendship between two people can grow into peace between two nations," Drendarin said as he stretched out his hand.

CHAPTER 14

I woke with a sudden start, coughing and gasping for air while my eyes filled with tears. There was a terrible, acrid odor assaulting my nose and burning my lungs. I looked down and saw a bottle of Nose Tork. Reflexively I slapped at it, but Marcus moved the bottle out of the way before I could hit it.

"Sorry brother, just looked like you were having a bad dream so we thought we'd get you out of it," Marcus said.

"You could have just used smelling salts," I said. "The little ones aren't as bad as the crap you put under my nose." I coughed again and wiped away the water building up in my eyes.

"Didn't have anything weaker on hand," Marcus said with a shrug.

"Just be happy we made it out alive," Katya said. "We got word that our Moscow team was hit same time we were. No one lived."

"Who attacked the Moscow team?" I asked.

No one answered.

The vehicle stopped moving and doors popped open on all sides as people jumped out. I moved to follow, but a sharp pain in my ankle reminded me that I was not in perfect shape. Marcus helped me limp my way out. Now that I was essentially living two lives, one in the real world and one in dreams, it was difficult to keep up with all of the injuries I had and remember which ones applied in which life.

"It'll take some time to heal," Marcus said as he motioned to my ankle. "I stitched up the puncture wounds, but the bones are broken."

I looked down and saw a mass of purple skin bulging out through the gauze that had been wrapped around my limb. "Thanks for patching me up," I said.

Marcus nodded and continued helping me until we passed through a steel door that was several inches thick and into a small room. Katya flicked on the light and a warm, faint yellow bulb began humming as it hung from the ceiling, doing its best to light up the racks of weapons on the walls to either side.

"Where are we?" I asked.

"Safe house in Nevada," Katya replied. "Come on, get the dream walker into the sleeping quarters."

Marcus pulled me toward another metal door on the opposite side of the room as a pair of men pulled the thick steel door closed and sealed the safe house off from the outside world. Katya turned to Mack and asked him for a full report.

Mack was holding an ice pack to his head, and still had some dried blood matting his left eyebrow down. "Moscow was hit by a pair of drakkul leading a horde of beasts," he said. "From what I could see it was similar to the ambush we got, except a lot bigger."

Katya swore in Russian and put two fingers to her mouth as she spat. She opened her mouth to say something, but I cut in first.

"Are you sure there were drakkul?" I asked Mack.

The short man nodded. "Positive."

"I need to tell you all something," I said.

"It can wait," Katya said dismissively.

"No, it can't," I argued. "While I slept on the way over here, I had a battle in the dream world."

Katya eyed me carefully and then finally nodded. "Go on," she said.

I relayed to them the entire dream, careful to go into as much detail as I could. When I finished, Katya spat again.

"You should have killed that egg-sucking lizard!" Dan said as he pulled his ripped shirt off over his head and went to a metal chest near the back wall to retrieve a new, forest-green shirt.

I nodded in agreement.

"So, you two shook hands and became best buds while Moscow was getting their cans kicked, is that it?" Flint asked angrily.

"No, I didn't shake hands with him. He offered me his hand, but I ended the dream there. I didn't trust him. And, now that I hear about Moscow, I think that was the right decision. I think he was only there to try and pump me for information about the engine."

Katya nodded. "Sounds accurate enough, but how did they get to Moscow without our team catching the illegal portal?"

Mack jumped in. "The portal opened in the Moscow safe house. Our team never stood a chance."

"In the safe house?" Flint spat. "How in the he—"

"Can they get to us here?" Dan asked, cutting Flint off.

Mack shrugged. "I don't know," he said. "I only know that Moscow was hit because I was trying to contact them just before we all got hit. I was going to set up a coordination meeting to follow up on Hank's plans. When no one answered, I was able to get into the security camera footage. That's what I was going to explain before Mills interrupted. I saw the bodies in the live feed, and then we got hit before I could say another word. After we escaped in the van, I accessed the camera footage and rewound it. The attack was quick and brutal. They knew exactly where to go."

"The safe house in Moscow is four hundred feet below ground," Katya said. "I helped arrange for the purchase of the facility from an old... acquaintance."

"You mean your FSB connections," Dan quipped.

"Don't be jealous," Katya replied coyly.

"All right, then we supply ourselves and move on," Flint said.

"Who put you in charge?" Dan asked.

"It doesn't matter where we go," I cut in. "The drakkul know our plans. They know we are going after Brent Rathison, they will do whatever they can to get there before us unless we act quickly."

"So what are you suggesting?" Flint asked. "Shall we storm the billionaire's mansion with a handful of operatives and some dream walker who can't even walk without help in the real world? Oh, and did I mention there is a family of ancient vampires guarding both Brent and the engine?"

"We could call Section Four," Mack said in a voice that was almost too quiet. Everyone turned and stared at the bloodied hacker.

"Briggs will have us all flayed alive," Flint said. "Jones was..." Flint's words caught in his throat. As I watched the towering soldier, I could see tears welling in his eyes. He turned and walked out through the back door and disappeared down a dark hallway.

Dan sighed and shook his head. "We've lost some good men today," he said. "Perhaps it's best if we all catch some sleep and then decide what to do after we have regrouped a bit."

Easy for him to say. He didn't have to spend his sleep time fighting demons from other worlds.

"Katya, see if you can contact the other teams and warn them. Mack, try and find Indyrith. We could use his help." The former FBI operative then looked at me with stern eyes and a sour expression on his face. "You come with me," he said. "Let's see if we can't do something about these dreams you are having."

Marcus helped me limp after Dan as the large man walked through the corridors as easily as if the safe house had been his childhood home. I took in the rusted hinges on the doors, the lightbulbs hanging by their cords and sloppily stapled to the ceilings, and felt more than a little apprehensive as I watched the shadows around us. Toward the end of a particularly long hallway, Dan opened a green door that screeched in protest as he pulled on it.

For a moment, I wondered if he had something like Professor X's Cerebro… but I was soon disappointed to discover that it was a simple conference room. It was like something out of the Cold War era. A single table sat in the middle of the room. Some old contraption that appeared to be a recording device was sitting atop the table. Marcus helped me to a chair and then left the room, closing and locking the door from the outside.

"What's going on?" I asked as Dan crossed his arms and began pacing on the other side of the table.

The large man shook his head. "Interrogation rooms help me think," he replied. "I'll ask questions, and you answer them."

"That sounds like an actual interrogation," I said.

Dan nodded and shrugged. "Your father stole the engine from Twin Turbo, right?"

I nodded. "That's what they say," I replied.

"And the drakkul, what was his name again?"

"Drendarin," I said.

"Right," Dan said. "Drendarin said that it was *his* grandfather who created the engine."

"With the help of Taragoth the Quick," I supplied.

"And once they discovered the engine was too powerful, they wanted to destroy it, but Taragoth's family started fighting for it, killing Taragoth." Dan tapped his forehead. "What year did your father steal the engine?"

I shrugged. "I don't know. I was in kindergarten maybe so…"

"That's right, I remember your file now. So about twenty, maybe thirty-two years ago."

I sat back in the chair and folded my arms. This seemed to be going nowhere to me, and I was finding it more than a little bothersome to be sitting in some mock interrogation while my ankle was throbbing and aching. "I thought you said you were going to help with my dreams?" I asked.

Dan held up a finger and kept staring at the floor while he paced back and forth. "Drendarin came to you while the others went to Moscow. He wasn't just pumping you for information, he was trying to buy them time. But why? What were they after?"

"After?" I echoed.

Dan nodded. "They attacked one of our best teams," Dan replied. "As far as I know, there isn't anything over there that would be of…" Dan broke off and snapped his fingers. He turned suddenly and slapped his palms on the table. "Of course! Twenty-one years ago! I should have seen it! I have to talk with Katya."

"Want to clue me in?"

Dan smiled. "Remember who provided the safe house in Moscow? We have only been using it for the last five or six years. Before that, it was a base for Russian Intelligence. The Russians are excellent at spy craft. Corporate espionage is one of their strong suits. Think about it- a massive engine that promises sustained speeds the likes of which no one has ever attempted before? Of course they would have sought the plans. I bet the Russians knew where to find the engine. The drakkul went to Moscow to look for the files!" Dan moved for the door and motioned for me to follow.

"And my dreams?" I asked. The door squealed as its old hinges were pried open and Dan left the room, practically running down the corridor. It took me several minutes to catch him, what with my ankle crippling me and all. By the time I reached Dan, he was in the middle of a conversation with Katya and the two were absolutely ecstatic.

"Then that would mean the files were there all along!" Dan said happily.

"Mack, run a search on the third subfloor of the safe house," Katya instructed. "Focus on the western hallways."

Mack sighed and cracked his knuckles before plunging into his keyboard and clicking out a series of commands. In less than three minutes, he turned his laptop around and set it on the table. Katya smiled coyly and Dan clapped his hands together. I walked around to see the static image of a camera showing a hole blown into a wall. Beyond the blast site was an archive of sorts. Tall, green metal safes and file cabinets were pried and cut open. Papers were strewn about the floor as well.

"They were after the engine's location," Dan said.

Flint spoke up then. "But any intel they had on it would be out of date by now. Surely the vampires have it in a secure location that not even the Russians could get to."

Katya shook her head. "Russia is known for many things, but ask any soldier who has fought against Russia and they will all tell you the same things. Moscow winters are darker and colder than any place on earth, and vodka is the only thing that staves off the cold."

"Meaning?" Flint pressed impatiently.

"Meaning the long and dark winters create a wonderland for vampires," Katya said.

"Not to mention the plentiful feeding options," Dan said.

Katya nodded. "In winter, drunk men can be seen walking the streets, or passed out on dark roads. Sometimes you will see others kick them to wake them up enough so they don't freeze, but a vampire could easily take them in."

"Scratch Moscow off my bucket list," Flint said decisively.

"I thought Brent Rathison was in California?" I said. "Aren't we going to hit his mansion there?"

Katya shook her head. "By nationality, he is British."

"He summers in St. Petersburg," Dan said. "He has a stretch of five hundred acres along the seashore just thirty miles to the west of the city. He collects big statues there. You know, old fifty-foot tall Lenins and massive granite structures that symbolize the worker's party."

"The perfect place to move a large engine to, and hide it," Flint said. "But we have to be sure that's where the engine is before we go off gallivanting to Russia. They may give us a bit of discretion given what we do, but they still aren't the greatest hosts to foreign paramilitary operators."

"I thought you only fought in the Middle East," Mack said.

Flint shrugged and let the thread die unanswered.

Dan turned to Katya. "Do you have any friends who could look into it before we go in? Flint's right, we have to be sure the engine is there before we move. It could just as easily be in Rathison's Argentinian ranch for all we know."

"Hank was pretty sure it was here on U.S. soil," Mack said. "I have the schematics for a large structure that could be used to house the engine."

155

Katya waved her hand and everyone fell silent. "It would be smart to have a lab here. Rathison has access to money and equipment that are second to none, but to launch the rocket, he will need a host country that is... how you say, lax in their administration of space and air laws."

"So, with NASA defunded, and the strict FAA rules here, that leaves Russia as the best launching position," Flint guessed.

"Or one of the 'stans," Dan cut in. "Russia might be a great staging spot for assembling materials and conducting additional pre-launch research, but Kazakhstan or Uzbekistan might be better for a rogue rocket launch. It puts them farther out of reach of various organizations that might be opposed to it. Plus, it makes for good publicity for the Rathison brand."

"So, I thought Hank was going to have us storm the mansion in California," I said, trying to wrap my head around what seemed like a pretty sudden shift away from Hank's plans.

Dan shook his head. "Hank wanted you to infiltrate Rathison himself, while we staked out the mansion," he explained. "He wanted you to use your dream walking magic to get into the billionaire's head and dig for more information. The reason he was intent on the mansion was because there is a gala there next week. Rathison is throwing a final pre-launch party before announcing the details of his operation."

"I heard it's ten thousand per plate," Flint said.

"Naw, it's twenty," Mack corrected. "Ten thousand is just for entrance to the after party."

"Dang, I couldn't even throw a proper birthday party as a teenager, let alone get people to pay *me* to come to my house." Everyone turned and looked at me as if expecting more of an explanation for my comment. I shrugged and offered a sheepish smile. "As a Mormon, I couldn't offer alcohol, so my parties were pretty lame. Just music, video games, and maybe a pizza or two."

Mack started snickering and the others turned back to the image on the laptop.

"Katya, can you call this in?"

Katya nodded. "Give me twenty minutes. I know a guy who... owes me a favor." She patted Dan on the back and then walked out of the room as she pulled an old flip phone from a hidden pocket in her waistband.

"Heaven help any man that owes *her* a favor," Dan muttered.

Flint and Mack shared a look, and then did their best to hide their smirks. I understood immediately that I was missing some great inside joke. The pain in my leg became unbearable, so I hobbled to sit down on a large crate and lean back against the wall. I rubbed my lower thigh and a bit down below my knee, but I didn't dare get closer than that to the bulging mass throbbing beneath the bloodied gauze.

"Hank would have been proud of how you fought," Flint said to me as he approached. "Going hand to hand against a werewolf is a bit on the insane side of things, but it's impressive nonetheless."

"Well, you know, I figured I already crossed swords with a drakkul and tackled a harbinger wolf so…" I offered a cock-sure smile that Flint wasn't buying. The hardened man pulled out his 1911 and turned it over in his hands. Seeing the weapon made me think of how Flint had pointed it at Briggs just the day before.

"What do you think Briggs will do?" I asked quietly as Dan and Mack carried on trying to analyze the secret room that had been hidden in the Moscow safe house.

"He'll survive," Flint said coldly. "Look, if you're trying to have a bonding moment by digging into my personal life, you can forget it." Flint holstered the weapon and then stomped out of the room, slamming the door on his way out.

"Did you try to preach to him?" Mack called out over his shoulder. Dan sniggered at the joke but kept pointing at something on the screen.

"No, I just asked him about Briggs, that's all," I replied.

Mack and Dan turned on me. Dan whistled through his teeth and slapped Mack on the back. "You can handle this alone yeah?"

Mack nodded.

"I'll go after Flint," Dan said.

Mack came and sat next to me, but kept quiet until Dan had left and closed the door once more. "Probably would have been better if you *had* tried to convert Flint to Mormonism," Mack started.

"Why?"

"Flint didn't come directly to us after his… incident. He went to Section Four first." Mack rubbed the bruise that was forming on his forehead and sighed. "I don't like spreading gossip or talking about others behind their backs, but let's just say that Briggs is a sensitive subject with Flint. You can talk about the man insofar as he is a

Section Four agent and we might bump into him, but try to dig up their past dealings with each other, and you may as well go digging for honey badgers with your bare hands. The honey badger will leave more of you behind after he has finished than Flint will if you push too hard."

I could tell Mack was serious, but, unlike Mack, I was always up for digging in the dirt. Besides, if I was supposed to trust Flint with my life, then I wanted to know who the man really was. "So you tell me then," I probed.

"No."

"I see, so you can dig up my file, read my life story as if it's some comic book, but I am not allowed to ask any questions about any of you?"

"There isn't much to tell..." Mack started.

"Sure, nothing to tell about a midget hacker, a bunch of ex-special forces guys, a former Russian spy that even Dan, our resident FBI guy doesn't trust, and a frickin sasquatch that fetches me milk when I ask for it. Let's not even mention the elf king and his daughters."

"Actually, I can tell you something about Indyrith's daughters," Mack said. I stopped in my rant and looked to the short man. He smiled at me mischievously. "They're smokin' hot!" His smile widened and I couldn't help myself. My resolve was busted and I broke out laughing.

"Yeah, I guess that's true," I said.

"But it would be good to have Nick out here. I could go for a beer right about now. I doubt there's anything here except stale M.R.E.s and a bunch of canned water that tastes a bit more metallic than it should."

"Yeah, I could use a good drink too," I said.

"Let me guess, you need something hard, like a *chocolate* milk right?" Mack quipped.

"Bite me," I said through a chuckle. "But seriously, Mack. I have done everything you guys have asked. I even had my memory wiped and lived as a freakin bum on the street. I didn't ask for any of this."

"Ah, that may be true, but I bet there is a part of you that loves the adventure of it all. Think about it, cosmic monsters that come to earth and the only people in their way are a bunch of rag-tag has-beens. There is no cooler job out there."

"Yeah, I guess it'd be hard to sell gym memberships now," I said. Even with my swollen leg and mashed up ankle I had to admit he was right. I missed my wife and son to death, but other than that, there was nothing I missed from my former life. In fact, this was the first time I could recall when I truly felt like I belonged. "So, you aren't gonna tell me about Flint and Briggs?"

"Not a word," Mack replied. "The envelope isn't just sealed on that file, it's on fire. So just let it go."

"Can you at least point me to a bed?" I asked. I was tired.

Mack shrugged. "I think Dan had someone working on a room for you."

The two of us pushed up to our feet and Mack opened the door for me. We turned down a side passage and walked to a small room that had a single cot. You know the kind. Bare steel frame and a thick bit of fabric the color of old, faded fatigues stretched in the middle. A white blanket was folded at one end, with a small travel pillow set atop.

"What's the desk for?" I asked, pointing to a table and chair set next to the bed. It wasn't so much the table that was weird, but rather what was on it. There was some sort of contraption with knobs and wires spewing out from it and dangling all over the table.

"It's a dream regulator," Mack said proudly.

I looked under the table and saw an old car battery hooked up to a pair of thick cords. "You sure it isn't a torture device?" I asked.

Mack shrugged. "Don't worry. Katya and Dan won't be running the machine while you sleep. I will. But, yes it is designed to give you a bit of a shock if needed."

"Electric shock therapy went out of style a few decades ago," I said sarcastically as I limped my way to the cot.

"No, the machine will monitor your sleep cycle. I won't bore you with the details but—"

"Oh, no, if you are going to hook something up to me that is going to shock the hell out of me, I think you can 'bore' me with the details." I smiled. "Or you can tell me about Briggs."

"Let it go, Mills," Mack said. "So, the machine will monitor your brain activity during sleep. I'll be able to tell once you hit your R.E.M. cycles. If it looks like you are having an intense nightmare, I'll wake you up. I'll try shaking you first, followed by that Nose Tork crap that Marcus used earlier. If those don't work, then I'll administer a shock that will hopefully disrupt your brain activity enough to pull you out of the dream."

"Sounds pleasant," I said.

"Things are heating up pretty quickly," Mack said. "If it were me, I'd rather have a safety net like this so I didn't die in my dreams."

"Sure, sure, much better to die in the real world by werewolves than in a nightmare," I quipped.

"Sarcasm doesn't win many friends," Mack pointed out as he took his seat at the table.

"You're going to stay awake all night?" I asked as I slowly let myself down onto the cot.

"I am a master of my craft," Mack said. "Part of that art is staying awake to dial into things when others are asleep and less able to defend themselves."

"Great, while you're at it, can you conjure me up a nice dream, you know, like from the Matrix? Shoot, I'll just settle for a nice boring dream in a steak restaurant somewhere."

"Right, so you can tell Agent Smith where to find us? I don't think so, Cypher."

"No, just, I'd rather have a good last meal, that's all," I said.

"Just relax. Get some rest."

Sure. Get some rest. Nothing about dream walking was restful. At this point, the title was more a curse than a blessing. I had no way of knowing how to initiate my own assaults on others. I was helplessly at the mercy of those creatures that lived in the shadows and lurked in the dark corners of our minds. I was in my early thirties, and I was starting to intimately fear the dark.

CHAPTER 15

Drums sounded in the darkness. I turned to look for them, but the fog of the dream world was thick, almost too dense to penetrate. The rhythm was both familiar and foreign. It sounded like the same kind of drums that had played in my mind before, but they were playing something new. *Thump-ta-thump, thump-ta-thump-ta-thump.* It played over and over, growing louder as an orange glow appeared in the distance. I walked toward the light, crossing miles in a matter of seconds. An old man with long, gray hair sat on the other side of the fire. His shoulders were wrapped in a hide of some sort with colored drawings of men with spears riding horses. In his left hand he held a large spear that had a bit of fur wrapped around the shaft just under the spear-head. Attached to that was a long leather cord from which a pair of feathers waved lazily in the shifting air. In front of him was a strange leather shield that had a drawing of a buffalo with a crescent moon above it on one side, and was painted black on the other side.

The old man looked at me and waved for me to join him at the fire.

I moved in closer, and was going to sit at the man's side to speak with him, but another man appeared from the darkness, standing in my way. This man was dressed similarly, with a hide draped over his left shoulder. His neck and the visible parts of his chest were tattooed with various designs, and his face was painted red from the eyes up. A single black feather was tied into his hair, which was fashioned into a Mohawk. Instead of a spear, this warrior held an old muzzle-loaded rifle. He pointed in the dirt a few feet away and grunted something that I didn't understand. I assumed he was telling me where to sit, so I shifted to the side and sat down. The whole time I moved the second man stared at me. Twice, he spoke to the first man while watching me. I had no way of knowing what he was saying, but it didn't seem to be approving.

Two more men came from the darkness to sit near the fire. One was dressed in a white tunic of sorts with blue beads woven into it. A leather pouch hung from his shoulder, and he held a strange, mace-like object with a single spike protruding out from the front. The other was dressed similarly, except the only color on his otherwise brown attire was a necklace of silver dangling over his chest and red beads woven into his hair.

The four of them looked at me expectantly for a while. I smiled, but none of them returned the gesture. Instead, the warrior with the rifle gestured with his hand at me and spoke with the others. The two that had come last nodded and seemed to agree with whatever the warrior said. The old man sat quietly for a long while. At last a fifth man joined us at the fire. He was dressed similarly to the others, but I easily recognized him when he spoke.

"Hello boy," he said in that familiar tone.

"You were the one who helped me," I said.

He nodded. "You are hard to reach, slow of hearing," he said. He reached down and pulled a large stick from the fire. "Come with us." The others rose up and walked a few yards in front of him. As I walked along with him, the drums stopped, replaced by a soft, but energetic, flute.

"Where is the music coming from?" I asked.

"Where else does music come from, but from the heart?" the old man said.

"From my heart?" I asked.

He shook his head. "The music is part of you, but it comes from us, passed to you as a gift. Come, we must walk into the forest."

I surveyed the darkness as the glowing fire atop the branch pierced through it to reveal the edge of a dense forest thick with trees and bushes. A warm wind blew around us as we entered the woods. A pair of elk stood grazing not too far off, but as I watched them, a pack of wolves took them down. I jumped, and felt my hand reach for my sword.

The old man turned around with a stern look on his face. "Tonight, you may not use your weapon."

"But why not?" I asked.

"Because, you have taken the power of the dream walker. It has not been given to you yet."

"What?" I asked. "But you helped me before, why would you stop me now?"

He put a large, strong hand on my shoulder and smiled with his great, brown eyes boring into my own. "Before, I could not assemble the council. Now, we are all here. We are not come to stop you, but to test you, and give you a gift after you have proven your worth."

"What kind of test?"

"Do you know how a Cherokee becomes a man?" he asked.

I shook my head.

"Follow me, boy, and you will learn."

We walked through the forest, crossing streams and winding around large hillocks until we came to a dark and desolate mountain. It alone in the midst of the green woods stood black and scarred, as if a fire had ravaged everything upon it. We climbed the mountain until we came to a large stump, and then we stopped.

The warrior with the rifle pointed off to the distance and said something in his language that I couldn't understand, but I looked where he pointed and saw another pack of wolves, this time led by what appeared to be a werewolf. They were watching us.

One of the other younger warriors pointed off in another direction. I looked over there and caught only a glimpse of something that appeared to have wings, but walked upon the ground and was much taller than the werewolf.

"Boy, here you will learn what it is to be a dream walker," the old man said.

"What do I do?" I asked, thinking I was meant to fight the creatures hiding in the shadows while the other warriors judged my skill.

"You are to sit upon the stump." The old man pointed to the stump and smiled.

I didn't know what to think or do. "But why?" was all I could think to say.

The warrior with the rifle began to shout and stamp the butt of his rifle on the ground.

The old man patiently held up his free hand to quiet the others. "To be given the full power of a dream walker, you must pass this test. That should be answer enough. Sit upon the stump."

I moved to the stump and sat down.

"Face the north," the old man said, pointing in the direction I should face. I adjusted myself on the stump and rested my hands on my knees.

163

"And now what should I do?" I asked.

"In life, a Cherokee boy must do this same test. It shows that he has the courage to become a man, and the wisdom to join in his world, to become a part of it. For those who walk in dreams, the challenge is different. A dream walker must sit upon the stump, but the forest is one of nightmares." The old man pulled a long, black cloth from a leather pouch and held it out to me. "You must tie this around your eyes."

"A blindfold?"

The old man nodded. "To show that you have true courage, you must show the enemy that you have no fear." I took the cloth, but I felt more than a little scared as I brought it up to my face. "After you have tied the blindfold and each of us inspects it, we will leave you until the sun rises."

I looked at him incredulously. "What if the wolves attack?" I asked.

"You must sit upon the stump, and show them that you have no fear. If you try to run, they will catch you. If you try to fight them, they will defeat you. You must sit still and courageous in the face of evil. Do not remove your blindfold, or you will lose your eyes. Sit and remain still until the sun warms your face and you hear the call of the birds in the forest below the mountain."

I looked down at the black cloth and shook my head. This was madness. I had already seen the wolves take down a pair of elk. That was to say nothing of the werewolf or the winged thing lurking nearby. I already knew enough about the dream world to know that I could very easily die here and never live through the night.

"Tell me, why should I risk this?" I asked.

The warrior with the rifle fired a shot into the air and shouted angrily, but the old man pulled a hatchet from the air and held it out. He didn't say anything. He just pointed the hatchet at the other warrior. The others all bowed their heads. The old man then turned to me. As he did so, I could see strange writing along the edge of the hatchet that glowed in blue.

"I cannot say what it is," he told me. "I can only say that it will be worth it."

"Will it help me protect my family?" I asked.

"And so much more," he said with a nod.

I looked back to the blindfold and took in a deep breath. "Well

164

then, let's see what the night brings." I raised it up and tied it tightly around my eyes. The old man stepped close, his feet crunching in the burned twigs and branches littered around the stump. He tested the blindfold in a couple places.

"Good. Now, don't untie it until the morning."

I nodded.

I heard footsteps approach and then there were hands around my head and eyes checking the blindfold for weak spots. I assumed that I passed their inspections because after that I heard their footsteps grow distant.

"Boy," the old man called out. "If you survive, we will welcome you into our midst as not only a man, but a dream walker."

I nodded and sat still as I was told. Silence filled my ears. I wondered how close the wolves would come to me in the night, but tried to shake the thought from my mind almost as soon as it had come. The warm breeze turned decidedly cold, prickling my skin with goosebumps. It was startling how vivid the dream world could be in terms of senses.

A twig snapped from somewhere behind me, startling me and sending a shiver up my spine. My adrenaline surged and my heart beat faster and harder. I strained my ears, barely catching the soft pads of something stepping along the burned ground a few yards behind me. It circled up around to the right, and then seemed to walk away, with the quiet footsteps growing more distant.

Show no fear. I kept reminding myself over and over that the old man had said I would live through the night so long as I showed no fear. *Don't run, and don't call for help. Just sit still.*

Something large flapped through the air above me. At first, my fear was that the winged monster was coming to snatch me from above, but the rational side of me reasoned that the wings were far too small to be whatever creature I had caught a glimpse of in the forest. *An owl. It must be an owl.*

As the night wore on, my mind began losing its grip on logic. Every small crack became the harbinger of a werewolf running toward me. Every flap of the breeze or rustle of the leaves made my brain envision the winged beast attacking from behind. Several times, my feet almost shot out without my permission. My very core was nearly yelling at me to rip the blindfold off and run down the mountain. My right hand was aching for my sword. Would it really disqualify me to summon my sword so long as I remained upon the stump?

A loud thump hit the ground.

Something growled nearby.

My breath caught in my throat. This was insane. After all that I had been through so far, I was going to sit here like an idiot and let something kill me without a fight? Ridiculous. My hand left my knee and went up a few inches, on a path to take my blindfold from my eyes, but I stopped as an image of Tommy came into my mind. My son was sitting upon a white sand beach building a sand castle with Susan. In that moment, the old man's words came back to me. If I passed the test, I would be better able to protect my family.

Something brushed against the hairs of my right arm.

I concentrated on Tommy and Susan. I had to pass this test, for them.

Something snarled in front of me. I could feel its hot, putrid breath on my face. My adrenaline surged again, and my muscles begged to be let loose on whatever beast was taunting me, but this was not a battle of strength. It was a test of will.

I focused on the image of my son playing on the beach and imagined myself walking up to them and playing in the sand as if nothing had ever split us apart. My beating heart slowed and my muscles relaxed. The snarling monster walked around to my back and sniffed me. I worried for a moment that perhaps pretending not to be afraid wouldn't be enough. If a dog could smell fear, then what could a werewolf smell?

My worries proved unfounded when the thing stomped away, snarling and hissing as it moved.

I sighed with relief, but my rest was short lived, for not more than a minute later I heard great wings beating the air above my head. The air itself slapped down atop me, and then the creature landed with a mighty crash just a few feet away. Dust and dirt was flung into my face. I flinched and shook my head, but I stayed on my stump. I tried to call up an image of Tommy and Susan again, but this time I couldn't concentrate.

Something sharp set upon my left forearm. It poked into my flesh, pressing it inward but stopping just short of piercing my skin. I froze, holding as still as I could while under such a threat. A strange sound, like a wet noodle slapping the wall, assaulted my left ear. I heard the noise twice more, and then the sharp thing on my arm dragged downward. It was a feeling like a cat scratch, roughly pulling at the top layer of skin and tearing my arm just a bit.

"I will tear your world apart," a rough voice hissed. "I will feast upon your loved ones."

The voice was something I didn't recognize, and the breath was most foul, like raw sewage and halitosis had gotten together and created some sort of unholy offspring that could be used in chemical warfare. My stomach twisted into a knot and I nearly gagged as the beast came closer and exhaled. "Don't you know who I am?" the voice asked. "I am death, here to take the flesh from your bones and the light from your eyes. You cannot escape me, not in the dream world, and not in the mortal realm either. I shall always find you. No matter what you do, I shall win, and you will fail."

In that moment, a quote that had made its way around an email chain a few years prior came to mind. Essentially, the quote said that if you have a negative thought about yourself, tell it to go back to hell where it came from. I'm pretty sure that the quote proved to be one of those made up things attributed to someone who was never actually recorded as saying it, but nevertheless it helped me as the thing in front of me kept laughing at me with its horrid breath.

I steeled my mind and sat up straight, convincing myself that not only was I going to live through the nightmare, but I was going to end this threat from the bunch of bloodthirsty drakkul hunting me down. No one was going to lay a finger upon my family, and I certainly wasn't about to let some billionaire son-of-a-vampire launch a world-ending rocket into space. I was going to win.

Without warning, the thing in front of me roared mightily, spittle flinging onto my face and hot breath washing over my front. Then, when I didn't react, it ranted upon the ground and screamed angrily before flapping its great wings and leaving me in peace.

After that, I could still hear things moving in the distance. Sometimes they came within a few yards, but nothing dared come as close to me as the winged creature had. I sat upon the stump and waited until I felt the golden, warm rays of sun on my face. I almost took the blindfold off right away, but thought I should probably wait until some light illuminated the areas around the edge of my blindfold, just to be sure it wasn't something else breathing on me.

After I heard the first birds start to sing and my eyes at last discerned that there was, in fact, sunlight, I reached up and smoothly pulled the blindfold down. To my amazement, what had been a barren, burnt hillside, was now sprouting with small flowers and seedlings. I reached down and took a small blue bell and picked it. Never before had a flower seemed so bright to me as this one did after the long night on the stump. I stood up from my spot and stretched my back. Then I surveyed the slope leading back down into the forest. I realized that the entire mountain was now starting to bloom and blossom with life. I turned around and saw a single, green shoot sprouting up from the center of the stump and marveled as it grew and unfurled right there before my eyes. It grew four feet tall and then thickened out into a tree. Branches shot out to the sides as I stepped back to give it room.

Within a few more moments it began bursting with lush green leaves and brilliant, white flowers.

"A dogwood," the old man said as he came from a few yards away.

"Where did you come from?" I asked.

"I never left," he said with a hearty smile. The old man pointed to a few spots around the mountain and in each spot I saw one of the other four warriors. They each smiled and nodded to me as I spotted them. Even the warrior with the rifle seemed happy to see me.

"I thought I was alone," I said.

"In the real world, a young boy's father remains with him in the forest through the night, watching over him. It serves as a reminder that none of us are truly alone, even when we feel most vulnerable."

"So you all watched over me, all night?"

The old man nodded. "In the dream world, each member of the council of dream walkers remains throughout the test. It serves much the same function, in reminding you that you are never alone. Now, you shall be able to call upon our strength, and we shall come to aid you, when we can."

"So the prize is a team of dream walkers then?"

The old man shook his head. "No. What you have gained now is the permission to be a dream walker. Pull your sword." I summoned my fancy katana from the air and held it out to the old man when he reached for it. He pulled the blade from the black sheath and smiled. "You are an interesting man," he said.

Man. He called me a man, not boy.

"A dogwood is an interesting tree for a dream walker to conjure.

I suspect it is because you are a blend of Cherokee and Irish ancestry, and therefore the tree that grows upon your mountain is a symbol that can flourish in both lands."

"My mountain?" I asked.

The old man nodded. "This mountain has lain barren for some time now, but as you have passed the test, it is now yours. The council of dream walkers is now complete. Six are required for the council to be at its full strength. Though we have passed on from the mortal world, we each were the dream walkers of our times. You are the dream walker for yours."

He looked down at the blade again and held his right hand over the metal. Above the engraving of the dragon that was on the lower half of the blade, a series of letters burned into the steel, glowing a bright blue. "Now, you are one of us. You are entrusted with the strength of our people to fight the shadows. Long may you live, and righteously may you judge." He held the sword out for me and I took it, staring at the letters. Many of them were similar to the inscriptions on the old man's hatchet that I had seen the night before.

"What do they mean?"

"They are emblems of your spirit and power. You will have to discover their meaning for yourself."

I nodded and gave a light swing of the sword. It felt different, stronger somehow. "How do I call upon you and the others if I need to?"

"We cannot always come to your aid, but we will be there when we can. Our council works on both sides of life and death. Those of us who serve after mortality strive to pass our experience and our foresight onto those who yet live."

Another question came to my mind then, one that I figured only he could answer. "How do I initiate a dream? I mean, if there is someone I need to find or fight, how do I make that happen?"

The old man smiled. "You must find the place between sleeping and waking. Focus on that, and you will get it in time."

I nodded and was about to ask for a demonstration, but then the old man's smile disappeared.

The warrior with the rifle came running up the mountainside and he anxiously told the old man something while pointing and gesturing at me.

The old man nodded and turned to me. "All right, brother, it is time for you to go back. The harbinger wolves have found your family."

"Susan and Tommy?" I asked. "But, Hank said they were safe, and Indyrith is with them."

"The elf is wise, but he is not a dream walker. The ship upon which they sail has been stalled. Go, you must go to them."

"Do the wolves come in the dream world?" I asked. "Can't you send me there right now?"

"No," the old man said. "They found them using the dream world, but they are going to them in the real world. Go, now, you don't have much time."

"How am I supposed to help them with a broken ankle?" I shouted. "I can't even walk."

CHAPTER 16

I woke from my dream and pushed up in my bed.

"Bad dream?" Mack asked. "I didn't notice anything on the machine."

"Your machine sucks," I hissed angrily as I forced myself to stand on my feet. Pain ripped up through my leg, but adrenaline pushed me through it. "Do we have a helicopter or something?"

"Helicopter?" Mack asked.

"Go get Dan, the cruise ship is about to be attacked."

"No, that's not possible, we have teams there."

"We had a team in Moscow too," I said.

Mack's expression changed and he turned to run out of the room.

I had made it half way to the main exit when Dan came running up from behind with Flint close behind.

"Hold up, Mills, what's going on?" Dan shouted.

"The cruise ship is stalled and about to be attacked. We have to get there."

"We're in Nevada, and they're in the Mexican seas," Flint put in.

"Yes, I understand, but I was told specifically that we need to get to them," I said. "Either come with me or stay out of my way."

"I just checked," Mack shouted as he caught up, laptop in hand. "The ship is running fine. It hasn't stopped. Currently about one hundred miles south, southwest of Tijuana."

"There, see, maybe your dream magic is off," Dan said.

I turned and looked at them. "I met other dream walkers in my sleep," I said. "They taught me how to project my dreams and target specific people and locations, but I'm not doing any of that until we go to the cruise ship, and I mean right now!" I wasn't one to stretch the truth, in fact it had been pretty hard-wired into my system to always tell the truth, but this was one time I was willing to let all the rules hang until I made sure my family was safe. "Now, do we have a chopper or Quinjet, or something super cool or do I call Section Four and see what Briggs can scrounge up for me?"

Dan and Mack blanched and looked at Flint.

Flint pulled his 1911. For a second I thought he was going to blast me then and there, but much to my relief he checked the magazine and then holstered it. "You don't want to count on Briggs at a time like this. I can take you."

"Well son-of-a-" Dan shook his head and didn't bother finishing his sentence. "I'll get my rifle."

"Mack, better suit up," Flint said.

"I'll get Marcus too," Dan said.

The four of them were in the van and ready to go in less than three minutes, almost faster than I could hobble to the vehicle with my broken ankle. Flint drove us away from the safe house and out toward a small airstrip in the middle of the desert. Flint turned off the lights before we reached the outer fence and parked the van just a few feet from a big sign that read "No Trespassing, Violators WILL BE SHOT."

Marcus pulled a pair of wire cutters out of a green duffle bag and the group moved toward the fence.

"Mack, could you cover their eyes?" Dan asked as he nodded with his head toward a security camera.

"You kidding?" Mack said as he flipped open his laptop. "Everyone loves having Wireless security cameras, but no one loves them more than me. So easy to hack and disrupt!" He clacked on his keyboard for a few seconds and then he smiled and flipped the lid down. "They're blind."

Dan nodded to Marcus. The large field medic snipped a hole in the chain link big enough for all of us to make it through, though I needed a bit of help to make it, as crouching put more pressure on my leg than I could fight through. We made our way to the nearest hangar and Dan had the lock undone in under sixty seconds.

"We gotta be quick," Flint said. "Cameras or no, the owner will hear the engine."

We slipped into the doorway and made our way through an office and into the area where the planes were kept. My jaw dropped open when I saw what was sitting there. Right in the middle of the Nevada desert, just fifteen minutes away from our safe house, was a massive helicopter. I wasn't nearly as fanatic as some history buffs, but I knew aircraft.

"That's a chinook!" I said excitedly.

"Yeah, it's been decommissioned and retired to a peaceful life of firefighting, but if we hurry and get it going before the owner catches us, we can use it to reach your family," Flint said.

"But don't they have a commercial version for fighting fires?" I asked. "Boeing makes a Vertol Model 234 for that I think."

"Yeah well, this one used to be the real deal. Which means it's faster," Flint explained.

"You better be right about the danger," Dan warned me.

We scrambled into the aircraft and Flint hopped into the pilot seat, with Marcus quickly sitting next to him. They began flipping switches and checking gauges as Dan ran out and pushed the heavy hangar doors open.

"I've always wanted to steal a helicopter," Mack said as he rubbed his hands together. "Ever since that one Grand Theft Auto game where you could steal the tank!" He started laughing as he strapped into a seat. "I love this!" He looked over to me and pointed at me. "See, no better job in the world!"

Within a few minutes we were out on the runway and the blades were spinning above us. Mack was laughing like a giddy schoolboy, but I was busy watching the lights turn on in a house in the distance.

"Mack, did you already cut the phones?" Dan yelled.

Mack was still laughing and stomping his legs as he stared out the window.

Dan reached back and smacked Mack in the shoulder. "Hey! Grow up!"

"What?!" Mack shouted.

"Did you cut the phone lines?" Dan pointed out the left side of the helicopter. Mack saw the lights and nodded. "Yeah, man, I cut all communications in and out of here while we were driving up."

"Incoming!" Flint yelled.

I looked out the window and saw the outline of a pot-bellied man in boxers bringing a rifle up to his shoulder. I never heard the report, but I saw the muzzle flash. A bunch of sparks shot out near the front, but Flint and Marcus were already down on the deck, reaching up with just their arms to control the aircraft. Another flash was followed by more sparks on the side of the chinook.

"Dan! Where you at?" Flint shouted.

Dan threw open the door and dropped to a knee. He brought a

rifle up to his shoulder and a pit grew in my stomach.

"You're gonna shoot him?!" I tried to rush Dan, but my ankle stopped me after my first step and I fell to the deck.

Dan pulled the trigger. Less than a second later, the man in the doorway staggered backward. I saw the muzzle flash fire toward the roof of the house as he toppled over. Flint and Marcus jumped back into their chairs and Dan closed the door.

"What the hell!" I shouted.

Dan turned and winked as he threw something to me. I caught a strange dart and stared at it. "Tranquilizer," Dan explained. "I knew Jeremy might give us some trouble, so I thought it best to bring these along."

"Tranquilizer..." I continued staring at the dart and then tossed it to the ground. "Wait, you know the guy's name?"

Dan set the rifle down and nodded. "Jeremy used to be one of us. That's how we knew where the Chinook was in the first place. He spent three years with us, and then asked to be retired."

"So we're stealing a helicopter from a former team mate?" I looked to Mack who was back to laughing and stomping his feet as the helicopter left the ground.

"WOO!" Mack shouted.

"Nah, we're just borrowing it. We have permission," Dan said.

"Permission? Then why'd he shoot at us?"

Dan shrugged. "When Jeremy retired he said we could use his helicopter any time we needed, but the problem is he wanted his memory wiped so he wouldn't remember the monsters we fought with."

"So he can't remember that he gave you permission? So you are stealing," I shouted.

"Depends on how you look at it I guess," Dan said. "Either way, it's the best we have access to without going back up to Washington."

Flint called out from the front and Dan moved up closer to hear him. Then he came back to me and Mack and knelt by us. "We should reach the ship in about four hours. We'll have to stop to refuel once, but I have a contact in Mexico that should be willing to do it for us. Just hang tight."

The helicopter tilted and spun around and then we tore off through the night. In all of my haste, I hadn't thought about how we were going to get across the border. Heck, I hadn't even thought of

U.S. airspace. I was about to ask Mack about it, but I caught a glimpse of his laptop and noticed what looked like a map of flight patterns. I figured the less I knew about the specifics of this particular trip, the better.

I spent the flight with a basket of snakes squirming inside my stomach. Would we reach them in time? Were we going to get shot down if Mack made a mistake with his computer? After we made it to the ship, then what? How was I going to warn Susan? I couldn't even walk.

The only thread of hope I had to hang on to was the fact that the old man had warned me in my dream, so that had to mean we would get there in time. Every few minutes Dan would ask for a status report on the cruise ship. Mack would check in and assure everyone that the ship was still sailing normally. Dan shot me the evil eye a few times, but about an hour into the trip he pulled out a satellite phone and got in touch with the team on the ship. He had them set up a defensive posture and prepare for an assault. Problem was, when they asked for more details, he couldn't give them any.

"New guy says there will be an attack," Dan shouted into the phone while holding a hand to his other ear. "Yeah, he learned about it in a dream." Dan looked up at me. "I'm not sure. Frankly I'm doubtful, but if he's right..." Dan was quiet for a minute. "Listen, after what happened in Moscow and to us in California, how about we play it safe and you just hop to? Got it?" Dan nodded then and hung up. He came over to me and reported on the conversation. "They've set up their equipment. If anything opens a gate, they'll detect it. They're ready. Your wife and kid will be fine."

I nodded, but I couldn't shake the worry that was settling deep in my bowels and making me nauseous. "Can we go any faster?" I asked.

Dan shook his head. "Maybe if we had a plane, but I can't shoot from a plane. I need a helicopter to cover from above." He patted me on the shoulder and went back to his seat.

I looked down at my watch. In the rush I hadn't even bothered to see what time it was. I was more than a little surprised when I saw it was only a minute after three in the morning. My dream had been an entire night long, and yet only a couple hours had passed in the real world. At least the darkness would help hide the behemoth we were flying through the sky.

Dan strapped into his seat and leaned back to try and catch some sleep. I watched him for a few moments and then turned to look out the window. I kept checking my watching and wishing that the Chinook would somehow grow jet engines. By the time five o'clock rolled around, I was sitting with my arms folded over my chest and tapping my outside thumb against my inside arm. Flint called out to Mack and Mack flipped open his laptop to check on the cruise ship.

I turned to watch, just as I had the last hundred times he had given a status report. Only, this time Mack's giddy smile faded from his face. His fingers worked the keyboard quickly and then he turned to me.

"The ship is stopped." Mack jumped up and ran toward Dan. "Dan, wake up, the ship is stopped!"

Dan snorted awake and rubbed his eyes. "Are we there?"

"The ship is stopped," Mack said once more.

Dan's eyes snapped open and he got onto the satellite phone. "Give me a report, why are the engines stopped?" he shouted over the deafening whir of the blades above us. The veteran FBI operator nodded and then hung up. "They say the engine has stalled. No paranormal activity though. Just a malfunction."

"You saying it's a coincidence?" Mack asked.

The pit in my stomach grew to the size of a large, spiky jackfruit and threatened to make me hurl, but my anger rose up to subdue my nerves. "It's no coincidence. This is what he told me would happen. We have to hurry!"

"She's going as fast as she can," Dan shouted. He undid his seatbelt and stood up to go speak with Flint. When he came back, he had the most serious look on his face that I had ever seen. There was no playful smile, no twinkle in his eyes. He was down to business. He set aside his tranquilizer rifle and pulled up a rifle that I didn't recognize. It didn't look half as big as Katya's rifle that had blown the head off of a werewolf, but Dan treated it like it was made of gold. He strapped himself to a hook in the ceiling and then threw the door open.

"What are you doing?" I asked.

"Setting up for over watch," Dan replied evenly. "What exactly did you think I did with HRT?" Within a few moments he was braced against the side of the open doorway and sighting in his scope.

Mack came to squat next to me and tried to pull my attention away from Dan with his laptop. "Look here, you can see the ship sent out a distress call. They aren't taking on water or anything, but their generators have died. They're on backup power only."

"What is he going to do with that?" I asked. "Doesn't he need something bigger?"

Mack smirked. "That is a GA Precision HRT rifle. It's built to custom specs to match HRT operator needs. It may not look as impressive as some of Katya's toys, but it will get the job done. Besides, when you're shooting from a helicopter, you don't want to be swinging something massively heavy."

That made sense to me if you were fighting humans, but werewolves and drakkul were another matter. I shook my head and grunted. "I wish I could get to them from the dream world," I said.

"Dan will take care of anything he sees," Mack assured me. "Our teams on the ship will keep your family safe. Don't worry."

"Target, six o'clock!" Dan shouted.

Already?

I tried to jump up, but Mack put a hand on my bad ankle and squeezed. I cried out in pain, but just then the chinook pitched and banked hard to the side.

BOOM! BOOM! BOOM! Dan worked the bolt action rifle so quickly it sounded like a semi-automatic.

"Three tangos down," Dan shouted into his mouthpiece.

"Sorry 'bout the leg, just didn't want you to fall out the door," Mack said as the Chinook leveled out. He scampered over to his seat and kept working the keyboard on his laptop. "Ship doesn't report anything unusual," Mack said into his mouthpiece.

BOOM! BOOM!...BOOM!

"That looks like everyone, confirm," Dan said.

I heard Flint loud and clear in my headphones. "Nice shootin' Dan, looks like you got 'em all. I'll circle once to make sure."

Marcus left his seat and slowly made his way to the open door with his green duffle bug.

"It's just a little F470," Flint called out. "Don't waste more than you have to."

Marcus said, "Understood," and then pulled something out of the bag and dropped it out the door. The chinook then banked the other way and we started getting back on course. Even with the deafening rotors I could hear the explosion down below.

"What's an F470?" I called out to Mack.

177

"You know those rubber inflatable motor boats the Navy Seals use?" Mack asked.

"So who was on this one?" I pressed.

"Six drakkul," Dan answered as he changed the magazine. "Looks like you were right. No portal, no warning, but they're headed for the ship."

The final hour of travel time was horrible. I was helpless. A prisoner of distance that separated me from the ones I loved while they were in great danger. Mack had hoped that I would feel better with the drakkul dead, but instead it only made me feel worse. The angst and anxiety grew to the boiling point, and then I retched onto the deck until I got the dry heaves.

"Marcus, Mills needs a shot," Dan called out.

I barely heard the words as my stomach convulsed and twisted my body down toward the deck once more and I made a grotesque gargling sound.

"Holy sh-" Flint started. "Someone pull his mouthpiece off so I don't have to hear it, bloody hell!"

Someone, probably Mack, pulled my headset off and then a moment later I felt a prick in my shoulder. Just like that, I was out. Lights were gone and I felt numb and cold. When I came to, Marcus had that blasted bottle of Nose Tork under my face again and Dan was leaning out the side of the chinook working his rifle as if unused bullets would blow up our aircraft.

"He's up," Marcus called out. The large black man then went to the door on the right side of the helicopter and strapped in just before throwing the portal open.

"What's going on?" I asked.

Mack was at my side, satellite phone in hand. "Here, the man on the other end is Alexi, he's one of ours. We've got multiple boats inbound."

"Like the one we saw before?" I asked.

Mack nodded. "Alexi will call in where they need us, then you shout it out to Flint so he can maneuver the Chinook, got it?"

I nodded. "What about you?"

Mack didn't answer. He just jumped back to his seat and frantically worked the keyboard on his laptop while simultaneously speaking into some other communication device. I realized then that my own headset was in my lap, so I grabbed it and put it on. To my dismay, the mouthpiece was covered in wet, cold vomit, but there was no time to clean it off.

"Hello?! We need support starboard aft, deck three. They're climbing up the side of the ship!"

I shouted the directions into my dirty mouthpiece. Dan and Marcus braced themselves as Flint took the helicopter into a sharp turn.

Ga-BOOM-ga-BOOM-ga-BOOM!

I looked up to see Marcus firing an M60 from his shoulder.

We were right in the thick of it.

Screaming could be heard on the other end of the phone. It wasn't Alexi, but someone nearby. My thoughts were flooded with Susan and Tommy, but I realized that asking about them would only interrupt the rescue operation. I had to trust my team.

BOOM! BOOM!

Dan's rifle tore into the waning night. As the helicopter pitched to the side I was able to catch a glimpse of the fighting through the window to my left. Werewolves were climbing the side of the ship. Security personnel were standing their ground, blasting the monsters as best they could. I watched helplessly as one werewolf vaulted over the side of a lower deck's railing and tore into the guard with his claws and teeth. The man's chest was ripped open and then his body fell to the deck.

"Reload!" Dan shouted into the headset.

The helicopter leveled out once again for a moment before turning to put the right side toward the ship. Marcus went to work with his heavy gun. The belt fed machine ate up the bullets quickly, spitting out the empty shells like discarded bones at an all you can eat BBQ rib shack.

"They're coming in through the windows!" Alexi shouted. "We need more support! There's too many of them!"

"What side?" I shouted. "Tell me where to put the helicopter!" I ordered.

KABOOM! CLICK-KA-CLICK... KABOOM!

Alexi's weapon barked so loudly that it blocked out our communication. I kept shouting at him, but he didn't respond. Then, there was a terrible scream and Alexi's gun went silent. Something picked up the phone, breathing heavily through its mouth.

"I told you," a deep, throaty voice said through the satellite phone. "I warned you," the voice said. "I will subdue your wife before I tear out her throat."

"No, you're dead!" I shouted. "You died in the fight with the other harbinger wolves and the alp!"

Laughing came from the other end. "You killed only the alp. You slew illusions that only looked like us. They were his creations. My brothers and I remain, and we will make good on our oath." A loud crunching sound was followed immediately by static.

"NO!" I shouted.

"What is it?" Dan asked as he looked to me. "Which way do we go?"

"Down!" I shouted. "We have to get Susan and Tommy."

"I can't set her down," Flint called out. "The heli pad is only meant for life flights. It can't handle this chopper."

"Then get me a rope!" I shouted.

"Mills, your ankle is busted up, we have to stay up here," Marcus yelled.

"Blue team is gone," Mack shouted. "I'm only getting three life signs from Red Team."

"What about Indyrith?" Flint shouted.

"Can't find him or his daughters," Mack replied.

The rage rose up inside me. I threw my headset off and unhitched my seatbelt.

"Mills, we're fifty meters above the ship," Mack shouted. "What are you doing?"

Drums pounded in my head. The throbbing in my ankle disappeared. The swelling went down to normal and the gauze fell off my leg.

"Take your sword," a voice called out to me. The roaring rotor overhead made it hard to recognize, but when the voice spoke again, I realized it was the same old man that had helped me before.

"This isn't a dream," I said.

"A dream walker can walk in both worlds," the old man said. "Come, brother, your family needs you now."

I held my hand out. A flash of blue light erupted in the helicopter and my sword appeared in my hand.

"Holy freakin sh—" Mack started as I pulled the blade free of its sheath. I smiled, knowing exactly what I needed to do. I strapped the sheath across my back by sliding my arm through the loop and then turned to Mack. "What cabin is my family in?"

"Uh… 402…" Mack said. "Why?"

"Where is that?"

Mack punched in a few keys and his screen displayed a cross-section of the ship.

"Flint, move this baby to the rear of the ship, close to deck four as you can," I said.

"Mills, what are you doing?" Dan called out. He then turned to see me standing on a healed leg and his mouth fell open. "Flint, do what he says," Dan said.

"Hang on to yer butts," Flint said. The chinook looped around once more and came in lower. "I can't get closer than that," Flint shouted. "If you have to go down, get a rope, we're still a good seventy feet up."

I shook my head as the drums pounded louder. These were war drums, and I was the dream walker. I didn't need a rope. I ran to the cockpit and reached down to Flint's hip. "I'll bring it back!" I shouted.

"Hey, you little—"

I'm sure Flint had a few choice words for me when I stole his 1911, but I shook off my headset and was racing out the open door before he could finish the sentence. Dan started to reach out to stop me, but with the door being so wide, I easily sidestepped his sweeping hand and leapt out into the night air.

The air enveloped me and tore at my face and clothes as I shouted on the way down. I landed on deck four and rolled to a stop near a bewildered werewolf that had just leapt over the railing himself. I stood on my feet and winked at the beast.

"That's right, I'm the dream walker," I said. Its stupid expression was still on its face when I lopped its head off with my glowing sword. The body hit the deck and then I turned and jumped in through a hole in the glass of the cabin next to me. I was met with a ghastly scene, an elderly couple had been slain in their beds and their door had been ripped open from the inside. The number on the door was hanging by a single nail.

434.

Susan and Tommy wouldn't be far from here.

I rushed out through the open door and found another werewolf on my left, tearing at a door, trying to get into a different cabin. Part of the door had been ripped away, but I could see a coffee table through the hole propped up to barricade the opening. I lifted the 1911 with my left hand and fired twice. Two shots to the head put the beast down. I ran to it and hacked at the neck with the sword for good measure.

Then I heard a scream that nearly stopped my heart. It was Susan.

I turned and raced down the corridor. The inner cabins were odd numbers, the outer cabins, those with windows facing the sea, were on my right. 428…426…424… I was running as quickly as I could, and then a door in front of me exploded as a security officer flew out and slammed into the opposite side of the hallway. He reached for a sidearm with a shaky hand, but a werewolf was already emerging from the cabin. It snarled and glowered hungrily at the man, licking its bloody lips.

I fired twice more with the 1911. The werewolf's head snapped back, giving the security guard just enough time to pull his sidearm.

"Thanks mate," the man offered as he unloaded four shots into the beast. "Give 'em hell. Is Dan still on over watch?"

He wasn't security. He was one of us. Our teams had infiltrated the ship and were posing as ship's security! I nodded and told him Dan had the skies covered as I ran past.

"NOOOO!" Susan shrieked.

I heard a terribly loud growl that shook me to my core as I ran toward my ex-wife's cabin.

418…416…414…

"Get away!" Susan shouted.

"Pretty thing!"

My feet moved faster than I had ever run before. Her cabin door was open, but I refused to let my mind believe that anything had happened yet. I had to reach her in time. That was the only way I could see it. I turned and sprinted in. My heart leapt to my throat at first glance. The room was in shambles. Claw marks marred the walls, furniture was torn to shreds. A large werewolf stood angrily ripping at the bathroom door.

Tommy was crying inside as Susan shouted at the monster trying to get in.

I took courage at hearing his crying, for that meant he was still alive. I made it, and nothing was going to reach them now.

"Get away from my family!" I shouted.

The werewolf turned and snarled at me. I fired three rounds into the monster's face and then the slide clicked open. The magazine was spent. The werewolf staggered backward, howling in rage and pain, but I didn't stop. I threw the 1911 at it and then charge in with my sword. It slashed up with its left paw, but I cut off the creature's arm and then came down and stabbed into the monster's chest. The werewolf tensed and yipped, and then went still. I ripped the blade free and then took the werewolf's head.

I then looked up as lightning flashed outside. I saw a massive head outside the cabin window. Great white teeth shining in the brief light as a snarl curled into a sly, evil grin. The harbinger wolf growled and the window shattered inward, just as it had when I was a child watching the scene unfold in my nightmares. Bits of glass cut my face and arms, but otherwise I was unharmed. The harbinger wolf was much larger than the other werewolves I had slain. He leapt through the window with the grace of an acrobat, but when he stood up fully erect his ears scraped the cabin ceiling.

The harbinger wolf snarled and I found myself frozen with fear, just as I had many times in my childhood nightmares.

"Now I will make you pay for your crimes," the harbinger wolf said. He pulled a glowing, red sword from the air. Lightning and smoke popped and hissed around the blade as it materialized in the cabin. "I made a blood oath, and now I am here to collect on it."

I stumbled back two steps and thumped into the bathroom door. Susan gasped and Tommy started crying louder inside. Their fear shook me from my own, granting me courage and strength to move once more.

"No," I said. "Your oath dies here, now, with you, you ganky scum-licking mutt."

"If that is your attempt to scare me, you have failed," the wolf snarled in its throaty voice.

I smirked and shook my head. "That was an insult, one my mother told me to hurl at you in my nightmares when you scared me as a child. It's funny because it means you are a crippled mutt that eats only putrid muck."

The harbinger wolf roared and advanced, but his spell of terror was completely dissolved now. I countered his sword with my own. Sparks showered the cabin as our blades connected. The wolf roared and I shouted back at it just before snapping up with a quick kick to its groin. The harbinger wolf recoiled and jumped back, doubling over just slightly.

I advanced on it slowly, not wanting to underestimate it. I made a feint to the right and the wolf answered by dropping down on all fours and swiping out at me with its free paw while raising the sword up to block with the other. I managed to step just out of reach, but then the wolf jumped up and lunged toward me. I blocked one, two, then three swipes of the sword, and then the wolf snapped out with its gaping maw. I barely managed to duck out of range, but the bottom of the wolf's snout struck my shoulder and knocked me back into the wall. Time seemed to slow and the drums in my head pounded louder and louder. The wolf roared and then came forward again. I was in no position to block effectively, as I was still leaning back against the wall and would not be able to regain my balance before it reached me. It seemed as though I was doomed to watch my death unfurl painfully slowly. For an instant, I wondered if this was when normal people would see their lives flash before their eyes, but then I remembered an activity I had gone to at church once as a teenager. A fencing bout came into my mind and I knew what I had to do.

I let my feet slide out from under me and fell to my rear on the floor while thrusting up and out with my sword. The harbinger wolf, unable to stop mid-lunge, skewered himself on my blade. Lightning struck my blade from all around the room as the tip exploded out the back of the beast. Its head crashed into the bathroom door and busted a chunk of it open, much to Susan's terror. She cried out in horror and Tommy began wailing. I looked up, about to assure her that the beast was dead, but then I saw a steak knife held in her hand come out and stab the beast in the side of the head.

I smiled proudly and nodded. *That's my girl!* I pushed the monster away and then pulled my sword free. I could hear Susan climbing into the bath tub to put distance between them and the monster, so I didn't worry about the knife coming out of the hole as I pushed up to my feet.

"It's all right," I called out. "I'm here. I got it!"

"Is it dead?" Susan cried.

"Yep," I said. Remembering what Katya told me about harbinger wolves and their ability to regenerate, I raised my sword and brought it down hard on the neck. Unlike the werewolves, this took three full chops before the sword finally cut through the bone. The head lolled to the side and teetered back and forth for a moment. "It's dead. You guys okay?"

"We're all right. Can you check on my boyfriend?"

My throat went dry and a mix of sadness and anger mixed in my chest so that my voice came out as little more than a mousy squeak. "Boyfriend?"

"Yeah, he's in room 311," Susan said.

"Um… sure…"

Susan went back to shushing Tommy. I stepped away from the door and stared at it blankly. In the distance I could hear gunfire dying down. People were crying and wailing, but there weren't any more terrified screams. As I stood there, looking dumbly at the door that separated me from Susan and Tommy, Dan came into the cabin, armed with a Scar and followed closely by Marcus.

"You find them?" Dan asked.

I nodded.

"They okay?" Marcus asked.

I nodded again. "Yeah, but she wants us to check on her boyfriend in cabin 311," I said quietly.

Dan and Marcus shared a look and then Marcus moved in and bent down to look at my leg.

"I'm good," I said quickly as I pulled away." I sheathed my sword and the weapon vanished as easily as it had appeared.

"Mack said he located Indyrith, I'm gonna go check on him if you're good," Dan said.

I took in a breath and leaned back against the wall opposite the closed bathroom door.

Dan disappeared from the doorway.

Marcus stood up and looked at me, and then to the door. "I'll go to 311," he said. Marcus patted my shoulder and then turned and left me standing in the room. I stood there for a while, listening to Susan force herself to stop crying just enough so she could sing a lullaby to Tommy. A lullaby that the two of us had made up for our son not long after he was born. The words were a bit silly, and we had admittedly stolen the melody from another nursery rhyme, but it was still ours. Something we had created for a person that was part of us. The anger in my chest started to win out and I turned to grab the 1911 so I could just leave and return it to Flint as promised. I had to move the body of the first werewolf to recover it, but other than the streak of blood across the side the handgun was unharmed. I worked the slide back into place and was about to slip it into my waistband when I heard the lock on the bathroom door click open.

I turned just as Susan pulled the door open and peeked out. Her eyes stared at the headless monsters on the floor. She gasped, but forced herself to come out. She then looked up and caught sight of me, standing over one of the dead bodies and holding a pistol in my hand.

"Josh?" she breathed quietly. "What are… how did you…"

I slipped the pistol away and the rage left my chest, replaced by the impulse to rush in and hold my wife to comfort her. "I'm here," I said as I stepped toward her.

"No!" Susan snapped angrily as she stepped back into the bathroom and slammed the door. "No!"

"Suzie, it's me," I said.

"What are you doing here?"

"Please, can we talk?" I asked.

"Daddy!" a little voice called out. I heard the handle wiggle, as if a little hand was reaching up to grab it, but then the lock clicked into place.

"You can't be here!"

"Suzie, please, I need to tell you something," I pleaded. "Just, listen, okay, you don't have to say anything. Just let me explain what's going on."

"What's going on?! You were in jail for killing your father, and now there are monsters on a cruise ship and you're here!"

"I came to rescue you!" I said loudly. "The same thing happened in the alley in Dallas. I didn't kill my father. He was killed by a monster, like these. I couldn't tell you before, you wouldn't have ever believed me. But now, you can see that I'm not lying."

"I don't know what to think," she said. "How did you find us?"

"I have a team of people that I work with," I said. "We hunt monsters, and they have some guys who watch you to keep you safe."

"Keep us safe? You're having us watched?"

"Suzie, you're missing the point," I said.

"Go away!" she screamed. She started crying again, and so did Tommy.

"Please, let me see him," I asked. "Just, let me see Tommy and then I'll go if that's what you want."

"No!"

I fell against the outside of the door and slapped a palm to it. "Please, Suzie. Don't let it hang like this."

"I can't…" Susan said through her sobs. "I can't do this."

I sighed and turned just as Marcus came back into the doorway. "I found the boyfriend, he's all right," he said.

"Josh?!" a familiar voice said from the doorway.

Carter Rutherford. I should have known. Susan's mom had always been quick to voice her confusion as to why Susan had ever chosen me over him. Carter had grown up only a few blocks away from Susan, and like his father and grandfather before him, had become a highly successful lawyer. Big house, brand new BMW each year, the whole nine yards. I'm a bit fuzzy on the details, but rumor has it that he had tried to convince Susan to elope with him two days after I had proposed. Just another reasons I dislike beamer drivers.

"Hey Collin," I said with a fake smile. It wasn't a punch in the face, but calling Carter by the wrong name had always gotten to the egotistical prick's nerves.

"It's *Carter!*" he said.

"Right, well, so why didn't you come up here to help?" I asked.

"I found him barricaded in his cabin," Marcus supplied when Carter started fumbling for words.

On second thought, playing name games with Carter wasn't going to cut it this time. I walked up to him and put all of my weight into a straight punch to the jack-tard's nose. His head whipped back and he stumbled out into the hall and hit the wall on the other side.

"Hold up," Marcus said as he put a hand on my chest. I flicked Marcus' hand away like a fly and moved in to grab the sniveling snob by the front of his Ralph Lauren polo shirt and pulled him in close.

"The next time Susan's in danger, you had best get your sorry arse out and fight to find her, you understand me?"

"Uh-huh!" Carter said with a quick nod of his head. "I swear it."

I then yanked him around and forced him to look at the headless monsters in the room. "You see that?" I asked. "I killed them myself. That's what Susan deserves, someone who would jump into hell to save her, not some sniveling idiot who hides behind his Armani suits and fake friends." I shoved him into the room and he landed just short of the harbinger wolf's body. He shrieked and tried to get up, but slipped in the pool of blood that had accumulated around the body. Carter turned and gagged.

I stepped in and picked him back up. "You listen good," I whispered in his ear. "If you *ever* let them down, I will come for you, and I will find you, and there won't be enough money in the world to stop me from bringing hell to your door and ripping you apart. You understand?"

Carter nodded and then groaned and looked down. I followed his gaze and saw that he had wet himself. I released him, letting him fall back into the puddle of blood.

I left the cabin and walked into the hall just as Indyrith approached. The tall elf had blood streaking his clothes, and a scimitar hung loose at his hip.

"My apologies," Indyrith offered. "I was caught in an ambush."

I noticed the slice on his shoulder and nodded. "I understand," I said quickly. "What do we do now?" I asked. I had meant what we were going to do about keeping Susan and Tommy safe, but Indyrith must have been thinking about something else, because his answer caught me off guard.

"I will change their memories," he said. "There is nothing I can do for the loss of life, but I could make it so that the survivors believe that the ship hit something and began to take on water. It is still tragic, but the memory of a sinking ship is better than this." The tall elf made a gesture to the cabin.

"Wait, so Susan won't even remember that I was here, or what I did?" I asked.

Indyrith shook his head. "No. And would you want her to? Such memories would only haunt her for the rest of her life. They will give your son nightmares as well. Would you wish that upon them just so that you could take comfort knowing that they would remember your heroism?"

I sighed and shook my head. "No," I said quickly. "If you can take the pain away, then you should do that."

I then turned and looked at Carter, who was still shivering and staring at me. "Can you leave his memory intact?" I asked.

Indyrith arched a brow. "You would have this man tortured by nightmares?"

"I would have him remember my warning," I said coldly.

Indyrith shook his head. "Such wanton carelessness would only allow for him to break the spell I will use to help your wife and son."

"Not to mention call the attention of Section Four," Dan put in.

I groaned and kicked at the floor. "Fine," I said.

I walked back into the cabin and held a hand out for Carter. I put on a smile as best I could. The man looked to my hand, and then up to my eyes as if expecting me to hurt him again. When I stood still and held my hand out for him patiently, he finally took it. I pulled him up and smiled. "My whole world is in that room," I said as I thumbed to the bathroom where Susan was still crying. "You may forget what really happened here tonight, but you had better remember to treat them right, for as long as you live."

"I-I-I will," Carter stammered.

I nodded. "Good." Then, despite my knowing that I was crossing the line. I punched the worthless sack once more across the jaw, laying him out cold atop the harbinger wolf's body.

"Mills!" Dan shouted angrily.

"What?" I asked as I left the room. "It's not like he's going to remember anyway."

"I will work with the other team members to clean up the ship," Indyrith told Dan. The elf king then turned to me and said, "You need to work on your temper."

"Bite me, elf," is all I said as I pushed past and made my way back to where a rope ladder was hanging from the chinook.

CHAPTER 17

The flight back was uneventful, and quiet. Even Flint kept his mouth shut when I handed him back his 1911. The whirring rotors were the only sound as we crossed back over ocean and desert. The refueling stop was short, and we were back in the hangar by nine-thirty. Poor Jeremy was still lying unconscious in his own doorway.

Dan and Marcus saw to him, moving him to his bed and staging things a bit so that perhaps the man wouldn't call the cops when he finally woke. Apparently Jeremy had a drinking problem, so they poured a bit of whiskey on him, stuck a mostly empty bottle in his hands and tossed his rifle on the floor with a couple of extra, spent shells. It seemed a bit harsh to let the man think he had gone mad in a drunken stupor, but compared to the people who had lost their lives on the cruise ship, it was as merciful as it could be.

Marcus patched the fence where he had cut it and Mack went to work feeding the cameras with looped footage that would show none of our activities, while of course being edited just enough to show Jeremy ripping his door open and shooting out at the air field.

By the time we got back to the safe house, Katya had the news playing on the TV. Reports of an engine malfunction and a breach in the ship's hull were making the rounds on all the major networks. There were many fatalities, as well as several reported missing.

"Looks like Indyrith did a good job on clean up," Flint commented dryly. "I'm gonna catch some sleep."

Katya turned and looked at me for a moment. Whatever she was thinking, she kept her mouth silent. She went back to watching the reports. Dan moved to stand beside her.

"No mention of monsters at all?" he asked.

"Not yet. Of course, I'll have to check the National Enquirer for the next few weeks, but it looks like the event is clean." She turned back to me again and looked at my leg. "You're healed?"

I nodded. "Leg's good," I said flatly. I wasn't really in the mood for talking, so I walked back to my bed chamber and went straight to my cot. Mack followed me a few minutes later and started to grab the wires from the machine to hook them onto me, but I refused.

"It doesn't work anyway, just leave it off," I said.

"I can at least monitor your brain activity," Mack said. "I just thought..."

"Mack, I could use some alone time."

Mack nodded. "Yeah. I get it." He set the wires down and sighed. "I should have told you earlier, but I didn't want it to mess with your head."

I turned over and faced the far wall. I didn't want to hear anything more about Carter. I didn't want to know exactly how quickly after I had left he had finally wormed his way into Susan's life. I didn't want to know the details of their dates. Nothing. I just wanted to be left alone.

Mack exited the room and I raged internally about the injustice of it all. It had been less than a year since that dreadful day when I had left for Dallas. As far as I was concerned, the ink wasn't even dry on the divorce documents yet, and Susan was already happy to let Carter right in and take my place. I had been erased from her life. Tommy would likely forget me entirely in a couple more years as well. Carter, or some other prick just like him, would eventually replace me in Tommy's mind. Meanwhile, I was out fighting monsters to keep the world safe, and yet was known only for the alleged murder of my father.

I looked at my watch and laughed in disgust. It was ten-thirty on a sunny Tuesday morning.

Tuesdays suck.

*****

I spent the next several hours trying to quiet my mind enough to go back to sleep, but it didn't work. After the fortieth time of looking at my watch, I gave up and left the room. I found the others in a mess hall of sorts, ripping into M.R.E. packages and chewing on things that did not look like they were meant for human consumption. Marcus tossed me one. I caught it and looked down at the words stamped into the box. Supposedly, I had just been given spaghetti with meatballs.

"Water is in the crate over there," Marcus said as he pointed to a large wooden crate with the lid propped up beside it. The food looked like crap, so I went for the water. I popped open a can and guzzled it down. I grabbed a second and then went to sit with the others.

"You want the good news, or the bad news?" Dan asked as I tore into my package of "spaghetti."

"Hit me with both," I said. There wasn't much that seemed worse than discovering my family had already moved on without me. I knew logically it made sense. I tried to tell myself that the older Tommy got, the harder it would be for Susan to find someone new. I had lived through enough of that with my own mother. She'd date a guy for a couple weeks, and then they would meet me and suddenly they dropped off the face of the earth. Tommy was still in the cute toddler phase, and stood a better chance of cutting through a suitor's reluctance to taking on another man's child… but it would still be hard. Still, the idea that they had moved on so blindingly fast was incomprehensible. I found myself wondering whether the whole thing had been a sham. Maybe Carter had always been lurking around, poking and prodding to test whether he could horn his way in.

"You all right there?" Mack asked.

It was then that I realized I was still fumbling with the M.R.E. package. "Distracted," I said as I dropped the food. "Just thinking."

Mack nodded knowingly and pulled a knife from his pocket. "Here, I'll grab it, these can be a pain to open." He took the M.R.E. and began slicing it open for me while Dan continued.

"The good news is Katya got ahold of her contact and found out that the engine is still here in the states. Apparently, Rathison is planning to move it to Argentina. He's bought himself a veritable fortress down there and has been preparing it for some time now. The Argentine government is more than a little excited to host the launch, so they have rolled out the red carpet for him, figuring this event will put them in a better position on the world stage."

"The bad news?" I asked as I took the opened package from Mack and sniffed at the curiously orangey-red mush inside.

"Mix it with the water," Mack said. "And then just chew and swallow. Don't think about it too much."

Dan cleared his throat and Mack stopped talking. "The bad news is we have two days until Rathison moves the engine. Tomorrow he is loading it at the docks, and then he's off to Argentina. So, if we don't catch him now, then we'll have to mobilize our team in Brazil to try and intercept while it's still in international waters."

"But I thought Rathison was holding a gala next week?"

Dan nodded. "He is, but the engine will be gone by then," Dan clarified.

"So we're back to storming the mansion then?" I asked.

Dan nodded. "I know you have been through a lot, but can you clear your head enough to get to Rathison tonight?"

I knew what he meant. He was asking whether I could target Rathison through the dream world. The poor sod didn't know that I had been bluffing. The old man had told me it was possible, but he hadn't taught me *how* to initiate my dreams in a practical method. The best I could do was try. "I'll give it a shot," I said.

"Good. The three Vikings are on their way down to us now," Dan said. "They'll be here to make sure no drakkul sneak in through unauthorized portals."

I used the small fork provided to shovel some of the mush into my mouth after I mixed it with a bit of water. It tasted vaguely of meat mixed with tomato paste and noodles, but I wouldn't call it spaghetti. Still, my body was tired and hungry, so I managed to put the whole thing away in a couple of minutes and then washed it down with the rest of my water.

"So, um, how'd you fix your leg?" Mack asked when I finished.

I shrugged. "Honestly, no freaking clue," I answered. "I'm as new to the dream walking thing as you are. I don't know if I could do that again, or even if I am the one who did it."

"Meaning what, exactly?" Marcus cut in. "I'm the one who patched you up, so I know how extensive the damage was."

I shrugged again. "Meaning that there is a council of five other dream walkers that I met. They're the ones who warned me about the cruise ship. Anyway, they said that in times of great need, they would lend me their strength. Best I can figure is that one of them healed my leg."

"Five others?" Dan echoed. "Where are they? Can they help you with Rathison?"

"They're dead," I said bluntly. "They are dream walkers from the past. They said they form a council to help the living dream walker."

"And they healed your leg and then gave you super powers so you could leap out of the helicopter without splatting on the ship's deck like an egg, is that it?" Flint said.

I nodded. "Pretty much."

"So, do you still have your extra strength?" Dan asked.

I shook my head. "I don't think so. I think it was just temporary, while I needed it. I feel pretty normal now."

"Well, whatever the hell it was, I'm glad you had it," Dan said. "Indyrith said they were in a bad way, but you killed four werewolves and a harbinger wolf by yourself, which gave Marcus and I enough time to fast rope down and get into the mix as well."

"Where is he now?" I asked. "I was sure the news would have had a field day with an elf king and his two daughters."

"One daughter," Dan corrected. "Only one survived."

That took a bit of the wind out of my sails. I had been under the impression that all of them had survived. "I'm sorry, I didn't know."

Dan nodded soberly. "Let's just say that Indyrith can choose to whom he shows his true form. To everyone else out there, he has a kind of hypnosis, or illusion spell if you will, that tricks them into seeing just an average, every day human. He's in California now, waiting for the three Vikings."

"Too bad *they* don't have an illusion spell," Mack cut in. "Everywhere they go they look, act, and *smell* like Vikings. It gets tiring trying to convince people in diners and gas stations that they're performers in costume. You know most people just think we're all crazy."

"We are crazy," I said as I leaned back and folded my arms. "We're all certifiably crazy. Stealing helicopters from old friends, then letting them think they were on a bender and went over the edge, or hanging from said helicopter and sniping werewolves in little motor boats and charging in with swords. It's stupid. We don't even get paid well enough to make the skulking in the shadows worth it. I mean, what could you make as a security specialist, Dan? Or, Katya, what kind of money could you make with your background? Shoot, Mack could probably just create money by hacking into any bank he pleases, and Marcus should be a doctor somewhere. Instead, we're hunting monsters and then not even taking credit for it." I tapped my foot under the table and looked down at my now eaten M.R.E. and shook my head.

There was silence for several moments. Everyone just sat and chewed their food or looked at the table. It was Katya who broke the quiet first.

"I lost my sister, thirteen years ago," she said. "I was assigned to a special unit that investigated paranormal activity. I got too close once, and a harbinger wolf hunted down my sister in retaliation. I joined with the Guardians after that."

I looked at her and saw her wipe a single tear from her left eye.

Dan went next. "My wife left me just a few years into my job with the FBI. I guess I wasn't home enough for her. Our neighbor three doors down was," he said. "We had two kids. A boy and a girl. They have kids of their own now, and I'm not the one they invite to birthdays or parties. Anyway, a few years before retirement I became involved with a fellow agent. We talked about getting married after we retired and living in Panama or Belize. We were on a routine training op. The area was reported to be clear of all civilians. Well, I guess no one had told the resident group of vampires that we wanted to be alone, so they came out and hit us hard. I was on over watch, just like last night. I watched helplessly as every vampire I shot got right back up and kept coming at the assault team on the ground. I can still hear her, calling my name as they closed in on her."

"I pissed off the wrong hacker," Mack said. "I had been dueling with this punk kid for months. We were always trying to one up the other. Pushing boundaries or stealing jobs, that sort of thing. Anyway, you know how it is, people talk big when they hide behind a computer screen and keyboard. So, we got to trash talking one day and I guess I pushed him too hard. Turned out he wasn't some punk kid. He was a borelian. My whole house was leveled by a gang of minotaurs. And, being the stereotypical computer warrior, I was living in my parents' basement at the time. They didn't survive."

"I was married once too," Flint said.

Everyone turned and stared at the large man.

"Yes, special forces guys have wives too," Flint said defensively. "Anyway, I kept my mouth shut after my incident in the Middle East. Briggs was working with me and getting me into Section Four. What I didn't know, was that the monster I took down in the desert was the leader of a small pack. They're not just wolves, you know, they have brains, so they researched me. They found my wife and son. Briggs knew about it, but instead of getting my family into protection, he chose to use them as bait. I was entirely left in the dark about the danger to my family. The night that the monsters attacked, I was four hundred miles away, investigating a missing person's case that we suspected to be the work of a vampire. Briggs' strategy fell apart pretty quick when seven werewolves attacked my home, accompanied by three harbinger wolves." Flint picked at a spot on the table with his thumbnail and then reached into a small pouch and pulled out a single bullet. The casing had two hash marks drawn on it in red. "This bullet is for Briggs. One day, when the world no longer needs monsters like him to fight the monsters that prey upon the innocent, I'm going to give this to him, right in the back of his thick skull."

Flint fingered the bullet and then put it away once more. He looked at me and offered the faintest of smiles. "My point, Mills, is that all of us have lost family. Take a good look around the table. We may be crazy, we may be the most incompatible misfits you can think of, but we are the only family any of us have left. Each of us knows a portion of your pain. We share it, but we have a job to do, and we have to move through the pain."

I nodded. I understood now that I was indeed part of the circle. I was a Gatekeeper, just like the rest of them. "Well then, I had best get started on locating Rathison. I won't let any of you down."

We broke from the room. Mack followed me into my bedroom. I sat on the cot and Mack sat at the table. I reached out my hand and tried to conjure up my sword again. Nothing happened. Mack watched intently as I tried for several minutes. When nothing happened, I gave up on that and turned to Mack.

"Do you have a picture of the mansion or a map or something?" I asked. "This is the first time I have tried this, so anything you could give me would help."

Mack nodded and left the room. He came back a few minutes later with several print-outs and his laptop. I set the pictures on the cot in front of me and studied them. Meanwhile, he brought up a satellite image on his laptop and then spun it around for me.

"What else do you need?" he asked.

"Time, I guess," I replied. "I'll have to figure this out on my own."

Mack took the hint and left the room, stopping at the door only long enough to say that he would be waiting right outside in case I needed anything at all. I smiled. Mack was a lot kinder than what I had first judged him to be when I had met him. Sure, he was arrogant, but he had a good heart, and he wasn't nearly as off-putting as that first meeting would have suggested.

I sat on the cot and focused on the pictures and the map. I remembered the old man's counsel to find the place between sleeping and waking. I tried a modified meditation ritual and tried to lull my body into a more relaxed state. I was there until my feet were prickling from the lack of oxygen, but was met with no success. I stood and stomped out my feet to wake them up. After they felt normal again, I went back to the cot and started over. I was there for another hour before the door opened and in walked Indyrith.

The tall elf closed the door behind himself and came to sit at the table where Mack had been. He looked at me intently with his bright, violet eyes, but didn't speak. As he watched me, I felt a twinge of guilt squirm its way through my soul.

"I should not have spoken to you like that," I said with my eyes averted downward. "I was upset, but that was no excuse. If you have lost face in front of the others, I could make the apology a public one if—"

"No, Joshua Mills, that will not be necessary," Indyrith said. "I understand you are attempting to create your own portal into the dream world. I thought I might be able to help."

I wanted to extend my condolences for his daughter as well, but the words seemed to get caught between my brain and tongue, so instead, I nodded and accepted his offer. Like Flint said, we have all lost loved ones, but we had to persevere and finish the job.

"I can help you get into your trance, and even direct you to the mansion," Indyrith said. "But I will not go with you. I can dive into memories, but I cannot go into the actual dream world and actively use it. The best I can do is open the doorway for you."

"That will help a lot," I said. "I have been sitting here forever and I can't even find the door," I said.

Indyrith smiled. "Sometimes, we can try too hard, and thereby overlook the very thing we are searching to find." The elf reached out with his hands and placed them on either side of my head. A warmth flowed into my temples and then I felt a rush of air swirl around us. A fog rose up from the floor and we were swallowed in darkness. Then, there was a single point of light off in the distance. It grew larger and brighter as we sailed toward it. After a few moments, I realized it was a great, sprawling mansion.

The grounds were beyond enormous. There were gardens, pools, a river, a fairground, and several pavilions all along the land leading up to the massive, four-story building that was capped with a bright green and gold tile roof and set with turrets and towers. Great gargoyles clung to the white stone of the wall with one hand while reaching out toward the air with the other. Their snarling faces scanned the grounds, as if watching for intruders.

A blue fountain shot up into the air some thirty feet in front of the granite staircase leading up to the french doors of the mansion. Parked at the bottom of the stairs were three cars, a Rolls Royce Wraith, a Mcleran 570 GT, and a BMW i8. Even if I hadn't known that Brant Rathison was the son of a vampire family, the beamer would have made up my mind about him. As I dropped from the sky and set foot upon the driveway, I noticed that the license plate said "Vrum-Vrum."

Arrogant prick.

Indyrith's image waved to me and then faded away. "This is as far as I go," he said.

I watched him fade away and then looked around the grounds, wondering where I should go first to find the engine. Before going inside, I conjured up a nice, shiny key and made sure to redecorate the BMW. The dream world was turning out to be quite a bit of fun!

I floated up the steps and slipped through the doors as if I were a ghost. I nearly cried out as I found myself about to bump into some sort of servant carrying a tray of food, but just as with the door, the servant passed through without being disturbed. I looked down at the key still in my hand and marveled at the power I suddenly found at my disposal. I could interact with objects if I wished, but if not, then they would be entirely undisturbed by my presence. Wanting to test the limits just enough to know how careful I needed to be while in Rathison's mansion, I called out to the servant.

"Oi, fetch me a plate of olives gov'na!" Not my best line ever, but it served its purpose. The servant continued onward without even stopping to turn around. Next, I ran up in front of the servant once more and waved at him. This time, he did stop. The bald man turned and looked as if noticing something for the first time. I froze, hoping I hadn't made a terrible mistake.

"Just your imagination Stanley, as you were," the servant said to himself with a shake of his head. He then resumed walking toward a large door that was at least nine feet tall. He pulled the ring on the door and slid it open into a pocket in the wall.

Beyond the opening I could see Brant Rathison. He was standing in the room with another man, and they were eagerly looking down at something on a round table and laughing as they spoke.

"Ah! Stanley, good man!" Rathison said.

I crept up to the door and walked through it just as Stanley closed it once more.

"I took the liberty of making cucumber sandwiches and house lemonade, sir," Stanley said.

"That looks wonderful," Brant said. "Place them on the table there, will you? Thanks." Brant was not entirely what I expected. He had what could almost pass for a mullet, with his hair flowing down to his shoulders and a great goatee encircling his mouth. His eyes sparkled happily as he moved to grab two sandwiches and a drink. He turned to his guest and motioned toward the food. "You *must* try Stanley's lemonade. It's his own recipe. He won't tell me everything that's in it, but it does have a spritz of coconut rum, I can tell you that."

The guest turned around and nodded. "That sounds wonderful," he said with just the hint of an accent. "As I was saying, my government is prepared to offer you another seven hundred hectares, tax free, of course."

"Mateo, I have all the land I need, so while I thank you for the generous offer, I must decline. I need only the help with the launch, as previously discussed."

The man identified as Mateo sighed and held his hands out to the sides. "It is a pity to waste such a ripe opportunity, but, I understand you have your reasons. As for the help with the launch, everything is already in place. We have the personnel standing by as we speak. The facility preparations are ahead of schedule."

"So I will be able to launch three days after the gala?" Brant asked between bites of his sandwich.

"You can launch the day after, if you like, Señor Rathison."

"No, no, three days after will suffice."

Mateo took a drink of his lemonade. "This is most excellent," he said with a smack of his lips. "I shall have to ask for the full recipe."

"Alas," Brant began, "Stanley will not divulge the secret, not even to me. Now, back to the launch. Can you guarantee the fuel I have requested?"

"Yes, yes, everything is ready. You can rest easy, Señor Rathison.

My government is most anxious to make this leap with you. Sending men to Mars will dwarf even the moon landing. The whole world will see Argentina as a power player. Once we have established the colony there, you will continue to use the launch site as your only launch center for when the tourist flights begin, yes?"

"Of course, Mateo," Brant said. "Argentina will be known as the most important place for advancing space exploration the world has ever known."

"Pfft!" I scoffed. "You mean it will be known as the *last* launch center if you have your way."

"Can I see it?" Mateo asked.

"The rocket?" Brant asked. "My friend, you will see it soon enough, I promise."

"No, please, I want to see it. Come, just a peek. What can it hurt?"

"Mateo, please, I'd rather not."

"Come, after all my government is offering you, I think it's fair that I get to see the rocket. You owe me this," Mateo said, his tone becoming far less playful than before.

Brant popped the rest of his small sandwich into his mouth and promptly drank the rest of his lemonade. "Very well. If you insist."

"I insist, amigo."

Brant nodded. "Follow me." Brant pulled a smart phone out of his pocket and flicked through a couple screens. A few seconds later, classical music filled the home, piped in by speakers in each room and hallway. I followed the two of them through the grand entryway, and then down into an elevator that dropped several levels below ground. It opened into a dimly lit hallway. This part was unlike the rest of the house. Instead of polished marble and aged wood, the walls were bare concrete, with metal conduit running along the upper corners. Every ten yards there was a single bulb on the wall. Music played down here as well, but the speakers here were far more obvious, and looked to be part of a PA system rather than an expensive entertainment network.

"Amigo, you should not work in conditions like this," Mateo said. "It's too cold."

"The cold doesn't bother me," Brant replied calmly as he led Mateo down the long corridor to a single, red door. It opened before we reached it, and a pale skinned fellow came out from within. He wore a lab coat and held a clipboard in his hands.

"Ah, Bob, how are you doing today?" Brant asked.

"Fine," Bob replied with a nod of his head. "Just on my way to grab a bite to eat." The pale man looked at Mateo and offered a close-lipped smile.

"Señor, you should let your workers see the sun more often," Mateo said.

"Not to worry, amigo, they have grown accustomed to the darkness," Brant said.

Bob walked past them and then his lips opened as his soft smile turned into a wicked sneer. "Oh yes, the darkness suits me fine," he said with a laugh. I gasped when I saw the pointed fangs protruding from Bob's mouth. I suddenly realized that Mateo was walking into a great deal of danger.

They passed through the door and locked it. Feeling a sense of responsibility for Mateo, I rushed forward to warn him. Fully expecting to pass through this door as easily as all the others, I set into a full out sprint.

Thwack!

I bounced off the door and landed on my back, staring up at the ceiling and seeing through a pair of blurry, spinning eyes. *What the crap was that?* I sat up and tried again, but moved slower this time. My fingers stopped at the door. It was impermeable.

The speakers began playing Ave Maria loud enough to nearly deafen me. I glanced up to them, but then went back to the door. There was a small, round window through which I could see the other room. Brant and Mateo were talking as Brant pointed to a schematic hanging on a wall. Three more pale-faced "engineers" were in the room as well. Brant pointed off to a hallway to the right, and the engineers began to lead Mateo out of the room in front of me. Brant turned to the red door and walked a few paces toward it. Then he stopped, and looked directly at me and waved. He flashed his billion dollar smile and then said something to the others that I couldn't hear over the blaring music.

The engineers turned on Mateo in a fury of fangs and claws. The poor man never stood a chance.

Brant then smiled wider and offered me a casual middle finger before waving once more.

I turned away from the door and tried to float up. I knew I couldn't get through the door, but I had to get *out*. Somehow the man knew I was there. I had to warn the others that our attempt at covertly finding the engine had failed. I sailed upward and slammed into the ceiling as hard as I had the door.

What is going on?!

I turned and ran for the elevator, but that's when I saw them. A pair of gargoyles, statues no longer, were blocking the way and snarling at me.

The music paused and I heard the distinct sound of someone clearing his throat.

"Hello, intruder," Brant said. "I must commend you on your attempt to infiltrate my home. It was very brave, stupid, but brave. Now, as you can see, I have some urgent business to attend to, what with the Argentinian Ambassador now lying dead on my floor and a rocket to prepare. If you don't mind, I'll have you escorted out by my two friends there in the hall. Good day."

The speakers popped and then the music began playing once more.

It was the 'have a good day' part that pissed me off. It wasn't enough to trap someone, he had to rub it in my face. If I made it out of here, I was going to torch his frickin beamer, and then I was going to bring the three Vikings back to knock that smug smirk off his stupid face.

The gargoyle on the left stood up and roared. Great fangs dripped with spittle as I saw all the way down the beast's massive, black throat. I held my right hand out and called for my sword, but nothing happened. The gargoyles started laughing at me. The second one snapped its jaws together like some sort of monstrous Rottweiler. They began advancing slowly, prolonging the moments before the attack. I tried to summon my sword again, but still it wouldn't work. I didn't understand it. While it was true that I was walking through the real world, I was in the dream world, a world of spiritual essences that should allow me to do what I wanted. I glanced back to the door and had to wonder what kind of material it was made out of to prevent me from passing through it. Perhaps whatever it was also was in the walls of the tunnel.

The first gargoyle shook his body as he dropped to all fours and stalked along the corridor.

I looked up to the conduit running along the ceiling and an idea formed in my head. I launched up and ripped a section of it from the wall with superhuman strength. Sparks shot out as I pulled the cord from the last light in the hallway. The first gargoyle lunged toward me. I turned the metal piping around and held it like a spear. Tiny streaks of lightning shot out around the gargoyle's chest as the heavy body crashed into it. I could smell burning flesh as the electricity scorched and seared the gray skin. The beast hissed and fought to turn away from it, but I pushed forward, driving the conduit into its flesh until it burned through. It roared in anguish as lightning jumped between its fangs.

"How do you like that?!" I shouted as I drove my legs forward and pushed the behemoth back. The second gargoyle tried to squeeze past the first, but as its wing brushed against the first gargoyle's body, it received a jolt of electricity that knocked it into the wall. Its head hit the cement hard enough that the wall itself shattered to reveal a silvery layer of metal inside of it. The gargoyle hissed and walked backward.

"That's right, back, get back!" Brackets and bolts holding the conduit in place on the wall popped and shot out as I bent the long piping more with each step. I could hear the current humming and crackling as it searched out for targets, but with me being in the dream world, it didn't harm me. The gargoyles snarled and roared, even clawed out at me, but they couldn't get to me. When we finally reached the elevator shaft, I blew them a kiss and then bolted for the elevator. Having easily slipped through it on the way down, I knew that I could fly up.

I did my best Neo impression and shot upward through the shaft as quickly as I could imagine. I heard a crash below me and looked down to see the gargoyles ripping the elevator apart in order to access the shaft. I flew out and into the entryway.

Almost free!

I passed through the front door, smiling and almost laughing at my victory.

That was when I saw a massive, clawed hand sailing at my face. I turned to avoid it, but was caught in the left shoulder. Claws dug into my flesh, stopping my momentum as easily as one might snag a baseball from the air. A second later I was sailing backward, flung through the air by the gargoyle who had been lying in wait to catch me on the way out. I passed through the doors and watched as the portals shattered under the gargoyle's strike. Wood splintered out across the marble entryway as I slid backward.

I came to a stop in the middle of the room. The gargoyle from outside clawed his way into the house just as the two from below clambered out of the elevator shaft.

"I'd give anything to have Katya's big gun right about now," I said. My sword appeared in my right hand. "Not exactly a hand-cannon, but it'll have to do I guess." I jumped up and watched as the beasts closed in. Other than the smoldering hole in one of their chests, each of them were in far better shape than I was. Blood was running down my left arm and the puncture wounds burned terribly. I was starting to understand what Wolverine must have felt every time his claws came out.

The gargoyle with the hole in his chest leapt out at me, gliding the last several yards on its wings and screaming as it came in close for the attack. I brought my sword up and sliced at one of the wings as I spun out of the monster's path. The blade ate through the bone and tore the leathery wing apart as easily as stretched paper. The gargoyle crashed to the ground and winced away from me as its severed wing hit the ground and turned to stone.

The second monster took the opportunity to strike. I only narrowly avoided becoming its next meal by leaping behind a polished set of armor set on a pedestal near the wall. The armor crashed and clanged, echoing through the open room as the gargoyle smashed its head into the wall.

"You like hitting things with your head, don't you?" I teased.

The beast hissed and turned its blood-red eyes on me. It swiped out with a clawed hand and raked me across the chest. Fortunately, I was almost out of reach so the cuts were shallow, but they still stung as if someone had poured molten metal into my body. I had no chance to rest though. The gargoyle stalked toward me quickly, swiping and clawing at me as I backpedaled as quickly as I could.

The third gargoyle launched into the air and then angled down to dive at me. At the same time, the maimed gargoyle was circling around quickly on all fours. I didn't need a sword. I needed a frickin mini-gun, or maybe a howitzer! I leapt backward and closed my eyes, doing the only thing I could think of. Running away.

I flew through a far wall and then changed trajectory and headed up for the roof. I had to get out of the building. If I could do that, then I could outrun the gargoyles. I went up through rooms filled with artifacts and books, but I didn't look too closely. I could hear the monsters tearing at the walls and floors to follow me. I exploded from the roof like a missile headed for the clouds. Something was different though. The bright sunny day was now dark and filled with shadows. I looked around and saw a massive swarm of gargoyles circling the mansion.

There were scores of them.

My heart skipped a beat and my eyes shot wide as I saw several of them turn and dive toward me.

Instinct kicked in just a few seconds before it was too late and I dodged out of the way of the first two gargoyles. I then dropped down fifteen feet and let the next group of three crash into each other. Wood and tile exploded from below as the first three gargoyles shot upward. I couldn't see my way out of the mess, but I was never one to give up easily.

I shot out to the side and then dove down for the mansion once more. The swarm of gargoyles was hot on my heels. I passed through the roof, the next floor, and then the next, putting just a bit more distance between myself and the monsters with each passing floor or wall as they would have to spend the time and energy busting through the barriers. I dropped down into the first floor of the basement and then hooked outward. I couldn't escape them in the air, but if my theory about the dream world was correct, I wouldn't need the *air*. I passed through a couple of billiard halls and theaters stocked with full bars, and then I went right through the foundation and out into the ground itself.

It was dark, and nearly impossible for me to know where I was, but I didn't care. All that mattered was that the gargoyle would have to tunnel through the dirt to find me. I was at least eight feet down and shooting outward as fast as they could fly. With any luck, I'd be able to finally escape, which wasn't to say it wasn't unnerving to fly through the ground. I had to concentrate on keeping my focus to avoid slowing down and getting stuck. Any time I let my mind acknowledge the earthy, damp smell or the thickness of an underground root, the ground started to materialize enough to tug at my skin and clothing.

Being buried alive in a nightmare was not an ideal way to die, but risking that seemed smarter than facing a hundred raging gargoyles.

My unfettered escape was brought to a sudden halt when I exited the ground and found myself in the deep end of an outdoor pool. Ever since I had been a small boy, I had a fear of drowning. I had once jumped into a friend's pool not realizing what would happen if you jump in without taking the thick plastic covering off first. As I saw the water around me now, my fear disrupted my focus and a mouthful of water poured into my nose and lungs. My inertia was stopped and I slowly spun in the depths of the pool. The water burned my airways and stung my eyes. Pressure built in my lungs, trying to force the water back out while at the same time they yearned to suck in a breath.

I struggled to push off the bottom of the pool and claw my way to the surface. I gasped and choked, and then I fell below the surface once more. I frantically reached out for the edge of the pool, but it was several feet out of reach. It took me a while to remember that I needed to kick with my legs. I had never been a good swimmer. In fact, I had always compared myself to a rock when it came to swimming prowess. If you needed someone to float, or even just tread water, I was no good, but, if you wanted someone to dive in and sink to the bottom, I was your man.

Only when I heard the angry cries of the gargoyles did I remember that I wasn't in the real world. I willed myself to the edge, but still had to struggle to pull myself up and over the edge of the pool. I choked and then coughed up a few bouts of chlorinated water and then collapsed on the ground. My strength was entirely gone. Now all I had to do was figure out how to exit the dream. I closed my eyes and imagined myself sitting on the cot back at the safe house. I even tried clicking my heels. Nothing worked.

"Where's Mack's little electrocution machine when you need it?" I asked.

"Come, I will show you the way back, brother," a voice said.

I smiled and sat up, expecting to see the old man from my other dreams. Instead, I saw the warrior with the rifle. "Wait, you speak English?" I asked.

"Come, can't stay here. They're coming."

I looked over my shoulder and sure enough, about thirty gargoyles were sailing toward us at that moment. I had never gotten to my feet so fast in my life. I followed my fellow dream walker as he ran across the grounds and then jumped through a bright opening. There was no tunnel like with the harbinger wolf's portal in Dallas. Instead, we just jumped through like a doorway. We landed in the safe house, in my bedroom in fact. Indyrith was still sitting at the table, watching me carefully. I turned around to see the warrior close the portal with a wave of his hand. He then smiled to me and pointed to my body on the cot.

"Go, walk back to your body and sit into it. That will end the dream."

"Thank you," I said.

"There is much evil you have yet to face. Be strong, brother." With that, he disappeared.

I walked to my body, turned and sat into it like a chair. A warm feeling caressed me and then I opened my true eyes. My legs were stiff and my feet were well beyond the point of falling asleep. I groaned as I straightened out my knees and pushed up to my feet.

"You have returned," Indyrith said happily. "Did you find the engine?"

I held out my hand and gave him a wobbly gesture that meant "sort of" and then shook my head. "I found a tunnel leading to a room where Rathison said it would be, but I never saw the engine itself."

"Then why are you back?" Indyrith pressed. "You must try again, and find the engine."

"No, I really can't," I said emphatically. "We need to get the others. I have a *lot* to tell you guys."

CHAPTER 18

When I finished telling them everything that happened during my botched mission to find the engine, none of them were happy. Katya said a few choice Russian curses and then spat on the floor, and Mack just went off on a tirade.

"See, this is why religion is crap," Mack said to everyone. "Gargoyles are put on churches to ward off evil spirits, and guess what? They *are* the evil spirits! I mean come on, it's so obvious."

"That's enough, Mack," Dan said curtly.

Mack quieted down, but was still muttering under his breath for a few more seconds before he finally stopped.

"This is troubling, but there has to be a way around our problem," Indyrith said after a few moments.

"We attack from the front and kill everything inside," Rolf said eagerly. Arne and Bjorn quickly voiced their agreement.

"I think this calls for a more delicate approach," Indyrith said.

"Ah, hell, I don't see why," Flint cut in. "I'm with Rolf. We roll up on the mansion and burn the place down. In the past several weeks we have had more attacks than I have ever heard of. We have an engine capable of destroying the world, and the only thing standing between us and it are a bunch of stone gargoyles and a vampire clan. If we roll up, guns blazing, and take it out, then we're golden."

"Assaulting a fortress filled with vampires is no easy feat. Inside the confines of their own home, they do not have to hide from the light of the sun. They will be free to fight."

"What about the gargoyles?" Mack asked. "Do they fight in the real world too, or just in the dream world?"

Indyrith shrugged. "I have to admit that I am uncertain. What I can say, is sending Joshua Mills back through the dream world will not work. The metal you found in the lower level sounds as though it is a sheet of mithril."

"Mithril?" Mack asked. "As in, Frodo Baggins' shirt of mail kind of mithril?"

Indyrith nodded. "In addition to being exceptionally strong, it prevents the kind of travel that Joshua Mills uses while in the dream world. If the engine is still there, then it is hidden by that barrier. Furthermore, mithril prevents portals, so if they have a room encased in the material, neither the harbinger wolves nor the drakkul could get in without physically assaulting the mansion."

"Well, we'd stand a better chance in the real world than in the dream world, then," I said. "I mean, I'm good, but I can't fight off a swarm of gargoyles by myself."

"What about your council friends?" Dan asked. "Can they help you in the dream world?"

I sighed. "I'm not sure how it works yet, but it appears that they are fairly limited in the help they can offer. I don't think I can summon them to go in with me if that's what you're thinking. Even if I could, I'm not sure that would make much difference. Only one uses a rifle, and it's an old muzzle-loader."

"Well, either way, they know we're coming now," Flint said. "I still think it's better to hit them now, while they're still on our soil."

"We don't have enough evidence to go to Section Four for help, do we?"

"Why not?" I asked. "Just show him the footage from Moscow, tell him about the cruise ship, and then let them know that Rathison has the engine that the drakkul are looking for."

"Section Four will want to take the engine," Flint said sourly. "Briggs won't let something like that go without a fight. He might roll up with us with all sorts of firepower, but then he'll turn it on us as soon as we have the engine."

"You are forgetting something important," Indyrith said. All the others quieted down and waited for the elf king to speak. "Rathison comes from a family rich not only in wealth, but in power. They have purchased loyalty from many others to ensure their survival. I would not be surprised if Section Four had a few agents that would rather fight to keep the Rathison family safe. Their influence runs deep."

"I have a stupid idea," I said. "What if the drakkul I met wasn't lying? What if he was telling the truth about wanting to help us reach the engine? If he could help us get through the barrier, and assault the mansion, then we might be able to keep Briggs from getting his hands on the engine as well."

"Trust a drakkul?" Dan scoffed. "Have you lost your mind?"

"A drakkul is not without honor, that's what Katya told me," I replied. "What if he tells the truth?"

"I will not permit the drakkul to enter our world," Rolf said. "They shall find me waiting at any portal they open."

Indyrith held up a hand and silenced the others. "You met a drakkul who wished to ally himself with us?"

I nodded. "I told the others about it, but you were on the cruise ship."

Indyrith looked to his daughter and then gave a slight nod of his head. She stood up and moved to the door. "I wish to speak with Joshua Mills alone," Indyrith said. His daughter opened the door.

Rolf and the other Vikings were the first to obey. Their obedience to Indyrith was nearly absolute. Flint and Dan moved to follow, but not without a bit of grumbling. Katya and the others left after that. When everyone was gone, Indyrith's daughter stepped outside and closed the door.

"Tell me of this meeting you had with the drakkul," Indyrith said.

"I thought you would prefer to see it," I replied with a smile.

Indyrith tilted his head to the side. "For now, tell me. If I deem it necessary, then I will ask to look into your mind."

I relayed to him all that had happened in the nightmare with the alp. It took me a little while to recall all of the smaller details, but the elf king saw no need to peer into my memories after I had finished.

"The harbinger wolf on the ship had a red sword," Indyrith noted.

I nodded. "Yeah, he said the alp had only used illusions in the dream. He said he and his brothers were still ready to fulfill their oaths."

Indyrith frowned. "Then you must make a choice, Joshua Mills," he said. "There was only one harbinger wolf on the ship. All the others were werewolves. This would suggest that the other two will be ready to go after your family."

I slapped my forehead and spun around to kick the wall. *How could I have missed that?* Susan and Tommy were going to be easy pickings now that the cruise was over, and we weren't likely to get them onto another ship to try the same ploy to keep them from being found either. "Indyrith, I can't let that happen," I said.

The elf king nodded. "We are not in an enviable position. Brant

Rathison will move the engine, but if we go after him, then you may not have enough time to save your family."

I looked down to my watch. It was nearly five p.m. My heart jumped into my throat as I realized that sometimes Tommy took late naps. It was something we had always hated, because it meant he'd be up until late at night, but it was a habit we could never break him of. I turned to the elf king. "I have to go back into the dream world," I said. "I have to find Tommy."

Indyrith sighed. "I will not be able to contact the drakkul you spoke of without you."

"I know, but it would make sense to me that they would attack tonight, through the dream world. I have to go to them."

"Your will is your own, as it always has been," Indyrith said with a nod. "But, before you go, allow me to suggest that while you try and protect them from dreams, allow the teams to take care of them during the day. I never left them unprotected. There are two teams that work in shifts to make sure nothing gets to them in the real world."

"But I am the only one who can protect them from the harbinger wolves."

Indyrith smiled gently. "Then fight well, my friend, and try to be back in enough time to join the fight against Rathison. I will continue planning in your absence. Just as you are obligated to return to your family, I must remain here, and focus my efforts on obtaining the engine."

I nodded and went for the door. I ran to my room, right past everyone else in the hall. Flint and Dan called out after me, but I didn't have the time to wait. Tommy could be asleep even now. I ran into my bedroom and slammed the door just as Indyrith called everyone back into the other room with him.

I jumped onto the cot and thought of home.

No, not home. Susan's mother's house. That's where they'll be. I closed my eyes. This time opening the dream world was much easier. I fell into a dark void. Gray fog swirled up around my body and whisked me across the immeasurable distance in mere seconds. The light opened and grew bigger and bigger as I soared toward the opening. The bright sun lit up the sky with a heat that was stifling at first, but I brushed the feeling aside, knowing that I was traveling as the dream walker. The mountains of the Wasatch Front towered into the clouds as I tore through the sky along their ridges, flying faster than anything in the real world could. I veered toward the west and spied the open front yard at my former mother-in-law's home. I crashed down to the ground and pulled my sword. I looked around to see Carter and Susan sitting upon a blanket in the yard, talking while Susan stroked Tommy's hair. To my relief, his eyes were still open, but even from a few yards away I could see that his lids were growing heavy and his breathing was becoming deeper with each breath.

I looked around, half expecting the harbinger wolves to be waiting in the yard, but there was nothing to be seen. Susan laughed when Tommy's left leg jerked with a spasm and then his eyes closed.

"He's a beautiful boy," Carter said.

Blow it out your shorts, Carter. I walked up to them and knelt in front of Tommy. I was a little confused. I had supposed that he would start to walk around outside of his body like I was doing, but then I realized my error. It wasn't enough to be in the dream world, I had to enter *Tommy's dreams!* I almost started to worry, but I pushed the fear aside, knowing it wouldn't help me keep my boy safe.

"Have you thought anymore about my proposal?" Carter asked.

I stopped and froze. For a moment, I hung on a cliff of hope. It was like Schrödinger's Cat. Until she answered, she was both engaged, and not engaged. I was pulling for the not engaged version, but was more than a little apprehensive to see which *she* would choose.

"Carter..." she began.

I smiled. I knew that tone of voice. She was going to say no.

"Listen, it has been fun catching up with you over the past few weeks but..."

"Susan," Carter said. "I'll always be here for you and Tommy. I can take care of you."

Yeah, until the crap hits the fan, and then you'll run away like the pansy you are.

"Carter, you're a nice guy, and I know you care, but—"

Carter leaned in and kissed her. The urge to punch the slick lawyer rose up in a way that wasn't going to be put down easily, but to my surprise, Susan took care of it for me. She pushed him away and slapped his face.

"I told you I'm not ready for that!" she said loudly. Tommy woke and sat up. I smiled wider, now I didn't even have to get into Tommy's dreams, *and* I got to watch Carter get put in his place.

"We've been going out for weeks, and you called me your boyfriend on the cruise," Carter said as he scooted away from her and rubbed his cheek. "I thought we were moving to the next stage."

"I only said that because I wasn't sure how to explain who you were to the staff on the boat. I'm there on a cruise with a toddler, and they see me spending time with you at meals, I just thought it made it less awkward. I'm sorry, I shouldn't have said that."

"You still love him?" Carter asked.

"How could you ask that?" Susan replied hotly. "Of course I do. I always will. Just the thought that he could come up the driveway any second and see you here with me scares me."

"That isn't love, that's fear," Carter said smugly.

"No, I fear it because I wouldn't want him to think that I have moved on. I haven't, and I don't know that I ever will. Look, I thought it would be okay to hang out as friends, and I needed some support, but I don't have those kind of feelings for you. I never have. You're a good friend, but that's it."

Ha! Take that fancy pants. Now hit the bricks!

"You'll never be able to have a good life with him. He killed his own father. That's no way to raise Tommy."

"I think it's time for you to leave," Susan said. "I don't need any man to raise Tommy. I can do it myself, and Josh didn't kill his father."

"Susan… I'm a lawyer, anyone could see he was guilty. He got off on a technicality."

"Good-bye, Carter," Susan said as she turned and picked up Tommy.

"Are we still on for tomorrow?" Carter asked.

Susan shook her head and grunted. "No, not tomorrow, not next week. Not ever. I needed a friend, that's it. Since you can't be that, then I don't need you around."

"Come on, even your mom—"

"Even my mom what, Carter? How could you possibly finish that sentence without making things worse between us?"

Carter put his hands up and turned to look away. "Sorry," he said quietly. "I'll go."

I was smiling from ear to ear, happier than I had ever been since going to Dallas. My wife still loved me, and better yet, pencil-neck Carter was just shown the door. I followed her into the house and down the hallway to a small bedroom with a window overlooking the back yard. Susan gently laid Tommy down and covered him with a small quilt that she had made for him for his first birthday. Tommy blinked at her a few times and then turned over silently.

"Love you Tommy," Susan said as she stroked his hair.

"Wuv you too," Tommy said.

She bent down and kissed his cheek and then stood up and put her hands on her hips as she looked out the window. I watched as a tear fell down her face.

"Mommy cwying," Tommy said as he pointed to her.

"No baby," Susan said as she wiped the tear away. "Mommy's fine."

"Mommy fine?"

Susan nodded. "Yep. Now you get some rest." Tommy turned to his other side and closed his eyes tight. Susan walked out of the room and flicked off the light. I thought to follow her, but as I looked at Tommy, I realized that he was right back on the verge of falling asleep.

How do I get into that cute little head of yours? I knelt beside the bed and watched my boy as his breathing changed. I stood up again as Tommy began snoring lightly and I still hadn't figured out how to get inside his dreams.

As I rose to my feet, I saw a dark-furred monster outside the window. I drew my sword as it sneered at me and then glanced to my son. The harbinger wolf began laughing and stepped through the wall as easily as I could.

"You don't know how to save him, do you dream walker?" the animal taunted.

"Doesn't matter," I said. "You'll die here!"

"But the other will kill your son while I slay you," the monster retorted. I looked beyond the creature to see the third out in the yard. It stood on its hind legs and smiled at me as it drew a red sword. It then disappeared. "He is inside already, and your son will soon be dead," the harbinger wolf said.

I let out a feral yell and charged the harbinger wolf in front of me. We tumbled through the wall and out into the backyard. The creature tossed me aside easily and then lunged for me. I somersaulted backwards and then came up with a diagonal slice that caught the creature in the shoulder. I knew I had to press the monster as best I could. If I hesitated, then Tommy would run out of time. I came in with a thrust that nailed the monster in the shoulder. It recoiled and slapped my sword away. It then lashed out with a savage kick that sent me flying backward. I bounced along the ground and skidded to a stop.

I looked up and saw a pair of dark-skinned legs towering over me. I followed them up to see the warrior from the council who carried the muzzle-loader. He brought the weapon to bear and fired. The harbinger wolf yelped and then fell to the ground.

"About time you showed up," I said. "How do I help Tommy? He's sleeping."

The warrior yanked me up with an unearthly strength and then threw me back to the ground, only I didn't hit the dirt this time. I fell through a doorway of sorts and landed in a new place altogether.

"Go, save your son, I will hold this one here, brother."

I looked up and saw a doorway to the real world close. All around me were giant stuffed animals. Some I recognized from TV shows and movies that Tommy liked, others looked like toys we had bought for him. I heard a howl to the left and leapt out from behind a massive Toothless toy from How to Train Your Dragon.

My heart leapt in my chest as I spied Tommy, running on his tiny toddler legs. Behind him by some fifty feet was a massive, black-furred harbinger wolf. I rushed in.

The wolf tore through a host of over-sized Toy Story figures and snarled. Tommy tripped, but I got to him before the wolf. I scooped up my boy and jumped into a pile of stuffed toys as the harbinger wolf landed where Tommy had just been.

"Stay here, Tommy, Daddy will stop the bad wolf!"

"Daddy!" Tommy shouted happily.

"So, Daddy has come to hunt the monsters under his child's bed, is that it?" the harbinger wolf snarled.

"I wouldn't be so smug if I were you," I replied. "Weren't there three of you when you first threatened my family?" I looked around with mock confusion and the held up a finger. "And, I think there was an alp too."

"You want to face the nightmares?" the harbinger wolf growled. "I'll make you scream."

The wolf disappeared.

I spun around as Tommy screamed. The wolf was rushing in from behind us. I jumped over my son and landed a kick on the beast's jaw. We tumbled to the checkered floor together and the harbinger wolf clawed and snapped its maw. I deflected the fangs with my sword, but the claws raked my right thigh. I sliced the monster's mouth at the back and then it disappeared once more.

So did the toys.

I rushed to Tommy and snatched him up just as the light winked out and left us in total darkness.

"Can you see me, dream walker?" the harbinger wolf snarled.

I wheeled around and swung my sword, but I hit nothing.

"I'm here!" the wolf roared from the other side. I spun again but missed a second time.

Tommy was wrapping his chubby arms around my neck and crying, making it hard to concentrate on my foe.

Something came toward us, snarling and growling, so I turned and thrusted my sword. I struck something that resisted at first, but then gave way and absorbed the sword. I then heard a gasp that filled me with horror.

Light filled the room once more and Susan stood before me with my sword in her belly.

"NO!" I shouted in horror. "Suzie!"

She looked at me with great, wide eyes filled with terror and betrayal. I set Tommy down and ran to hold her as she stumbled backwards. "J-Josh!" she gasped. "Why?"

"Suzie, no, I didn't know you were here. Please, this can't be real." Her body went limp in my arms and then she broke into a thousand pieces, like a porcelain doll. Each piece skittered across the floor and I realized that I had been had. I jumped to my feet and turned to find Tommy, but then each piece from the shade of my wife burst into flame, erupting in tall columns that blocked my way.

"And now you lose," the harbinger wolf snarled as it closed in on Tommy. It growled low, baring its fangs.

Tommy screamed and filled my heart with dread. The fires grew and pushed me back, licking my skin and searing any part of me that I didn't pull away.

"Daddy!" Tommy cried.

The harbinger wolf laughed.

"No!" I said. I rushed toward the columns of fire and jumped through the first. The heat went up my pants and burned my legs much more than I had anticipated. I hit the ground on the other side of the fist barrier and rolled to put out the flame before jumping to my feet once more and half-sprinting, half-limping to the next wall of flames that was unfurling before me.

"No!" I shouted once more as I rushed toward the flames. I slashed at them with my sword, hoping that my magical weapon would put the flames out, but in the distance I could hear the harbinger wolf laughing at me.

"As the sword is your weapon, so the fire is mine," he said. "You will not live through the next fire."

I staggered through the wall of flame and fell to my knees, coughing and sputtering a mixture of thick smoke and blood. My skin was burned away in several spots on my arms, revealing red, squishy flesh beneath. Flames sprouted on my pants and shirt. I slapped at them and looked through the final barrier of fire to see my boy. My toddler was sitting, surrounded by fires on three sides, with a harbinger wolf stalking up to him from the fourth.

My heart pounded like a drum in my scorched chest. My lungs could barely expand for breath, and my legs were too weak to put me back on my feet. I watched as the harbinger wolf slowly padded on all fours toward my son.

"Watch, dream walker, and know the power of the nightmare," he said as he licked his lips.

My sword vanished from my hands as I lost my focus. I fell forward and barely managed to catch myself with my hands before face-planting on the ground.

Tommy's cries grew louder. I looked up and saw the wolf was now only ten yards away, and coming ever closer. I could see that I was only half the distance away, but my limbs were shaking and turning cold. The wolf was too much for me. This last fire was even wider across than the last, though I could see through the flames enough to see my son, I knew that the moment I tried to cross them, the flames would stretch up and out to prevent my interference.

Tommy then turned and looked at me. "DADDY!" he shrieked. A surge of energy rushed through my body as I saw his eyes. His face was red from crying, and his toddler-sized fists were shaking with fear.

"I'm coming," I mouthed. I pushed up to my feet and ran toward the fire.

The harbinger wolf stopped and looked up at me. "Fool. You are a dead man either way."

"You first!" I shouted as I jumped through the fire. The flames rose up as I had expected. They tore and ripped at my flesh, but I had set my course. I held up my right hand and called my sword to me once more. It appeared with a burst of lightning that dissipated the flames just enough for me to sail out the other side of the barrier.

"Impossible!" the harbinger wolf snarled.

"Surprise mother—" my sword came down point first and ripped through the beast's side as it tried to lunge for my son. My momentum knocked us both to the side. I cocked my left arm back to swing a fist, but as I punched forward, I saw only blackened bones sailing toward the wolf's face. I struck him hard and knocked his head into the ground. The wolf growled angrily and tried to shake me off, but my right hand held fast to my sword, which was buried to the hilt in the monster's flesh. It shook to the side, and I rode it as it thrashed and jumped about. Seeing that my left hand was nothing but bone, I jabbed my index finger into the monster's left eye and pressed until the orb popped.

The wolf howled and fell to the ground, thrashing about once more. My sword came loose, so I yanked on it to open the wound more. Blood coursed out over me and the harbinger wolf howled and raged against me once more. It bit my left arm and ripped the bones free, crushing them to dust.

I was so incensed that I felt no pain anymore. I pulled the sword free and rolled away. The wolf and I got to our feet about the same time and stared hard at each other.

"How is it possible?" the wolf snarled.

"You can bring the fires of hell itself if you like, Tommy is my son, and I will not let you touch him," I spat. The wolf lunged forward once more. I spun around and brought the sword down hard as the hulking mass of fur sailed by. The symbols on my sword glowed brightly, and the blade cut through the harbinger wolf's neck like butter. The monster fell to the ground, and the flames died down.

Tommy was still crying, but he was safe.

"Sorry, my boy," I said breathlessly as I fell to my knees once more. "I'll try to get Indyrith to erase this nightmare from your..." I fell forward before I could finish my sentence. I hit the ground and was about to give in to death when a pair of hands scooped me up.

"Come, brother, it's not your time to die yet."

I looked up and saw the vague outline of the warrior with the rifle.

"Help…Tommy…" I coughed.

"Your son will live, I must see to you."

I don't remember much of what happened next. The warrior shook me a few times to keep me awake, I suppose, for I caught glimpses of a forest as he carried me. Eventually, I opened my eyes and found myself lying under the dogwood tree on my mountain.

The five council members were sitting around me, singing and raising their hands to the sky.

"You are awake," the old man said as I tried to sit up.

I looked down and saw that my body was whole once more. "How did you do this?"

"Repairing the body of dreams is not always easy, but it is possible."

"But I was sure I was dead," I said as I raised up my left hand. *My left hand!* "You fixed my arm."

"You must be more careful," the old man said. "We have used our magic twice now, but we will not be able to do this forever."

"What do you mean?" I asked.

"First, we healed your leg when you fought against the werewolves on the great seas, now we have used another gift to heal you from the harbinger wolf's flames. As there are only five of us on the council that support you, you can only have five gifts. There are only three left."

"Oh," I said. "Well, that might have been good to know before, but honestly I am not sure how either case could have been avoided."

The old man nodded. "I understand, but now we are called to rest. The other three will remain here for you, brother, but we must leave."

"Wait, what do you mean?"

The old man and the warrior with the rifle stood up and turned away. "I will not see you again. Be brave, brother, and fight well. There is still much evil to fight."

"Wait, I thought you said there have to be six of us to form a full council. If you two leave, doesn't that break it?"

The old man nodded. "The council is now weaker. When you have used the rest of our gifts, then you will be left alone. Be careful, brother."

"I don't even know your name," I said.

The old man smiled. "I am your grandfather."

I frowned. "No, my grandpa is named Corbin. I think I would have recognized you if you were my grandpa."

"No, I am several generations before your time. I mean that I am your ancestor. I am Oconostot Moytoy. My daughter, Ani Waya, is the mother of A Li Onai, she was a great dream walker. Go, make us proud. Bring honor to our names, son." With that, he turned and walked toward a mountain off in the distance. I watched as the lush vegetation changed from green to the colors of autumn. The leaves then fell to the ground, leaving barren trees upon the mountain, and Oconostot vanished from view.

The warrior with the rifle bowed to me. I bowed my head in return. He vanished then, without walking away or saying another word. After his departure, a second mountain shed the leaves from its trees and turned barren.

"So, only the three of you remain," I said to the others.

They looked to each other and then back to me. None of them spoke.

"Why did their mountains only lose their leaves on the trees, but this mountain was burned when I came here?" I asked.

Again, they glanced to each other in silence.

"Guys, give me something, please. The man with the gray hair leaned forward and smacked me on the forehead.

The next thing I knew, I was back in the safe house on my cot. I glanced at my watch and saw that it was only six-thirty."

"Are they safe?" Flint asked.

I looked up and saw him, Katya, Dan, Mack, and Indyrith standing at the far side of the room. "Yeah, the harbinger wolves are dead. Susan and Tommy are safe."

"Well, great," Dan said as he clapped his hands together. "You made it back just in time for dinner. Let's go see what Marcus is rustling up for us from the M.R.E. stash, shall we?"

CHAPTER 19

The others all followed after Dan, all except for Indyrith. The elf king remained behind and bade me to stay with him. He asked for an accounting of what had happened, and was more than a little relieved when I assured him that the monsters were in fact dead.

"So, the only threat to your family that remains are the drakkul who seek the engine," Indyrith said.

I nodded. "Yeah," I said.

"Then, I think it's time you show me the memory of when you met the other drakkul who wanted to work with us."

"Why now?" I asked.

The elf king flicked his brow upward for an instant and took in a breath. "Now, with your family safe from all other foes, I can explore your memory with you. It may take us some time to find him."

"How will exploring my memory help us find him now?" I pressed.

"Do you remember the first time I took you inside your memory?"

Then it clicked. "Yes, I was able to interact with the drakkul," I said excitedly. "So now I can go back and talk with him once more."

Indyrith nodded. "And I will go with you. I believe there may be merit to his offer. I have found mentions of feuding drakkul clans in the archives. That, and the fact that their society is built upon a firm foundation of honor and honesty, make me believe that we may have indeed stumbled upon a worthy ally."

"All right, then, let's do this. I scooted to the edge of my cot and waited for the elf to put his hands on either side of my head. Just as with the other times, we were whisked away, but this time we didn't cross distances of miles, but rather into the space of my own mind. We went to the fight with the alp and watched everything together until the scene shifted to the home of the drakkul and the monstrous pterodactyl attacked.

"At the end of this memory, there is a time when I spoke with the drakkul. Perhaps we can get his attention there," I said. The elf king nodded and folded his hands behind his back patiently as we watched the entire memory unfold.

I waited until the point when Drendarin extended his hand to shake mine and seal the alliance. Then I walked forward. I knew that the old me was only going to look at the hand for a few moments before suddenly ending the dream. I reached out and grabbed Drendarin's hand. Drendarin felt the connection and then looked up and smiled.

I nodded to him. "Come now, and meet me. I am ready to speak with you."

Then the memory ended and everything went black.

"Do you think he heard me?" I asked.

Indyrith smiled. "I would think so. Come, let us return to the real world and see if he contacts us through a portal."

We ended the session and waited in the bedroom for a few minutes. When Drendarin didn't come, I suggested that I try to contact him again through the dream world in real time, rather than reaching through the memory to affect the past.

"I will go and watch with Rolf. Should a portal open and Drendarin wish to speak, it would be a disaster if Rolf slew him first."

I laughed a bit at that, but Indyrith didn't share in my mirth. The elf king frowned and arched a brow. After he left, I worked on finding the state between sleeping and consciousness. I guess I shouldn't have been surprised, but I was unable to keep the delicate balance. Instead, I fell over on my cot and dropped into a deep sleep. I had a couple of dreams then. The first two I didn't remember or even notice. My body had been so tired from all of the activity lately that I was sleeping more soundly than I could recall at any other point in my life.

Then, during a particularly fun dream where I was flying upon the back of a great bird, I looked down and saw a familiar face on a hillock. Drendarin was there, and suddenly I realized where I was. The bird vanished and I floated down to Drendarin.

"I had hoped you would reconsider," Drendarin said.

I nodded and then looked the lizard-man straight in the eyes. "Tell me about Moscow."

Drendarin frowned and swished his tail nervously behind him. "That was not my doing. I had no knowledge that they were going to strike, but this serves only to strengthen my argument. You see now that they do not even respect the laws set forth by those who separated the seven realms. They enter your world and plunder and murder so that they can get gain. They have no honor. They could never be fit to rule."

"How would you dispose of the engine?" I asked. "We have some resources here, but some of the people we could bring to the fight will likely want to keep it as badly as this other clan of drakkul does."

"Do you trust me?" Drendarin asked.

I shook my head. "Not entirely, but Indyrith was intrigued when I told him about you, and I think I believe you about Moscow."

"What can I do to convince you more?" Drendarin asked.

"You can tell me what you have that I need. You said you could offer me something that would help in the fight. What was it?"

Drendarin smiled. He held out a sword. "Take this," he said eagerly.

"A sword? I already have one, and it glows with magic symbols and everything. You're gonna have to do better than that."

Drendarin laughed. "The sword I offer you is very precious. It is made of mithril, the same metal that prevents you from dream walking into Rathison's mansion."

"And this will let me pass through the door if I hold it or something?" I asked.

Drendarin shook his head. "No, but you know how werewolves react to silver, yes?" Drendarin asked.

I nodded.

"This sword will be like a blade of fire to the gargoyles. Just the slightest cut from this will incapacitate or kill even the largest of the monsters. Slay a good number of them, and the swarm will disperse and abandon the hall."

"Are you certain?" I asked.

"Gargoyles are good guardians for vampires, but they are not loyal servants. Wreak havoc with this sword, and they will flee. I should know. You see, before my clan became tinkerers and inventors, we were the most successful vampire hunters on my home world. We have eradicated the foul creatures from our lands entirely. This weapon was forged for that sole purpose. It is known as the Gargoyle's Bane. Also, what you may not know, is that whatever you cut off of a vampire with this blade, will not grow back. Whether you take a hand, a foot…"

"Or a head?" I jumped in.

"Exactly. It puts you on more even footing with the foul things."

"That's all well and good, but how do we get into the door?"

"For that, you will have to rely on human ingenuity. I assume a few of your bombs should open it up nicely. If I were you, I would be more concerned about the vampires. Kill the gargoyles and chase them away first, then go for the door while the rest of your warriors try to hold off the vampires. Find the engine, and then summon me through the dream world. Once I have your signal, I will come through in a portal and destroy the machine."

"Actually, we can skip the gargoyles. I won't be in the dream world for this fight."

Drendarin smiled and let out a sly hiss. "The gargoyles will smell you coming. They may appear as stone in the real world, but when someone like you comes to them, they will come to life whether in the real world or the realm of dreams."

"I see," I said. "And how will you use a portal if the room is encased in mithril?" I pressed.

"Once you have blasted the door and opened the room, it will be like taking the lid off of a jar. The mithril only keeps portals out if it is sealed. Leave a hole, and I can come to you."

"And so can the other clan, then, am I right?"

Drendarin's smile faded. "Yes, and that is why you must contact me as soon as the way is clear." He reached under his shirt and brought up a necklace with a single fang on it. "Take this, it is my first tooth. When you want to contact me, think on this item, and I will hear your call in the dream world."

"Your first tooth, like a baby tooth?" I said as I took the necklace and looked at the small fang.

"Each of us drakkul are born with a single fang. It grows in the middle of our jaws until the third year of our lives, when it falls away and our full sets come in. Our first tooth is always kept close, as it symbolizes rebirth, and helps us heal, or so the tradition says."

I nodded. "All right, then I will take your sword and your tooth, but how do I get them into the real world from here?"

"You already have," Drendarin stated. "One more thing. I have instructions for you." Drendarin pulled a folded paper from a pocket and held it out to me. "We once had to deal with harbinger wolves that infested our world. Eventually, one of our clans discovered how to make them stop. I believe if you follow the instructions I have outlined for you here, then you can rid your world of the harbinger wolves."

"All of them?" I asked skeptically.

Drendarin smiled. "It worked for us. There is a particular item you will need, but I think you will see that it is not beyond your grasp."

I unfolded the paper and read the few lines on it. It was so simple, and yet I would not have thought of it. "I will try this," I said.

Drendarin nodded and then sighed. "I must go and prepare for the battle that is to come. I must take care that no one suspects my true intentions. Fare well, my new friend."

Drendarin vanished from the dream.

I sighed and looked at the items in my hand. "A magic necklace and a mithril sword... sure, why not?"

Waking up after that was easy. I blinked a few times and found myself lying on the cot. What I hadn't expected, was to be lying next to the sword that Drendarin had given me in the dream. In my right hand was the necklace with the fang as well.

"All right, then," I said to myself. I turned and stood up just as Dan opened the door to my room and walked in.

"Rise and shine—" Dan stopped and looked at the sword in my hand. "You're up," he said. "Where'd you get that sword?"

"The drakkul gave it to me last night, along with this necklace."

"You let him in here, and didn't have any of us—"

I shook my head. "No, I spoke with him in the dream world."

"So now you can pull objects out of dreams?"

I shrugged and nodded. "Looks like it."

"Remind me when this is over to have you dream up a couple million dollars so I can retire, okay?"

I laughed. "Is Indyrith nearby? I want him to look at this sword."

"Yeah, he's talking with the three Vikings. The door's locked, so you'll have to wait your turn, but we don't leave for another half hour, so you should be good."

"Going to Rathison's mansion?" I asked.

Dan nodded. "Flint called it in to Briggs. It took most of the night to convince the idiot. Even an agent as trigger happy as Briggs doesn't want to be caught with the kind of paperwork that would come with storming Rathison's place in error."

"But he's coming?"

Dan sighed. "Yeah, along with some heavy crews. He'll handle the quarantine, and then we're gonna ride in there just like Rolf wants, guns blazing, swords gleaming, the whole nine."

"Then I should go and talk with Indyrith now," I said as I looked down to the sword. "Apparently this is supposed to be a great anti-gargoyle weapon."

"That little toothpick?" Dan scoffed. "You take what you like, but I'm gonna be sitting behind a fifty cal with incendiary rounds. It's a special mix I've been working on for a while now. It will be fun to try it out. Gargoyles, stone, vampires, everything should go down once I get that beast humming."

"I wasn't aware you could use incendiary rounds in a fifty cal," I said.

"I have several tricks up my sleeve. You should see my Tomb Breacher. It's a modified AA-12." Dan quieted down and then offered a sheepish smile. "Sorry, I get excited about my creations. I have to go prep the others. Be ready to leave in thirty minutes.

I went down the hall and turned left at the first tunnel branching off.

Indyrith was three doors down and on the right. I knocked lightly, hoping I might be able to interrupt whatever was going on inside with the three Vikings. Indyrith's daughter opened the door and smiled at me.

"We have been waiting for you, Joshua Mills." She stepped back and opened the door. I walked inside and saw the three Vikings painting their shields and weapons with a fresh coat to brighten their appearance.

"Ah, Joshua Mills, how did you sleep?"

I raised the sword from Drendarin. "I wanted to show this to you," I said. "Drendarin gave it to me and said it was made of mithril."

Indyrith rose from his position sitting cross-legged on the floor and crossed the distance between us in three steps. He plucked the weapon from my hand and pulled it free from the scabbard. "The drakkul told the truth, this sword is made of mithril. I have been reading and studying through the night. I was going to say that we would need such a weapon to ward off the gargoyles."

I looked around the room and frowned. "I'm sorry, is there a secret library somewhere? I don't see any books."

Indyrith pulled a small device from the folds of his robes. "I may be an elf, but I live in the modern age. I can carry thousands of books in this device. It's a marvelous time to be alive, is it not?"

I smiled and laughed at the sight of the e-reader. "Yeah, I guess that makes sense. I thought you were going to say something crazy like Nick the Sasquatch is telepathic and you read the books through his eyes or something."

"One does not always need to look far to find magic," Indyrith said as he placed the device back into his pocket. "Now, what is in your other hand?"

I showed him the necklace. "Drendarin said that once I blast through the doors that have the mithril plating, I should contact him and he will use a portal to come and destroy the device."

Indyrith nodded. "Do you trust him now?" the elf king asked.

I shrugged. "I'm not entirely sure, but I think he is sincere."

"Well, that will have to do," Indyrith replied. "Come, join us. Rolf is preparing for the battle."

"No, I didn't want to intrude, I just wanted to see if Drendarin was telling the truth about the sword."

"Come, sit!" Rolf said. I looked beyond Indyrith to see the large Viking staring up at me. "You fight like one of us."

Indyrith nodded and then stepped aside, gesturing for me to go and sit with Rolf.

I went to him and sat as he polished the side of an axe.

"It will be a worthy battle, with much honor to win," Rolf said. "Vampires are some of the most foul creatures; they offend Odin. The All-father will grant us victory over them." Rolf laid his axe on the floor to his left and pulled a sturdy sword. "Come, we will pray to Odin."

"I do not share your belief in Odin," I said as politely as I could.

"HA! No one is perfect," Rolf said as he slapped me on my back. Arne and Bjorn joined in. "Tell me, Christian, does your God grant you strength?"

I nodded. "I believe that he does."

"Then we are not so different," Rolf said. "You fight with a fire in your heart, yet you acknowledge that strength comes from virtue as a blessing and favor." Rolf's smile disappeared and he raised his sword to study the edge closely. "Where we differ is in the length of our lives.

Our kin are all passed to the halls of Valhalla, yet we are denied the opportunity to see them. We remain below, fighting the beasts and monsters that plague this world. We fight, as Odin wills it, for as long as Thor shall give us strength. You shall one day grow gray of hair and weak of body. You shall have your rest, and we three shall remain here, standing watch at the gate. We are not permitted to die." Rolf set his sword down and looked at me with fierce eyes. "I do not know by what magic you walk in the realm of dreams and nightmares, but I know that I admire you as a brother, Christian."

"As do I," Arne said.

"And I, added Bjorn.

"We three will be honored to fight beside you, Joshua Mills."

Given what I had seen Rolf do to the drakkul champion back in the forests of western Washington, I took that as a tremendous compliment. I offered a nod and a half-smile while fumbling for the right words to say. All that came out in the end was a simplistic "thank you" but it got the point across and Rolf didn't seem bothered by my less than eloquent expression.

The three Vikings placed their weapons in front of themselves and moved from sitting to kneeling. Arne looked upward, while Rolf and Bjorn focused on their weapons.

"Lo, there do I see my Father. Lo, there do I see my mother. Lo, there do I see my brothers and my sisters. Lo, there do I see my people back to the beginning," Arne said solemnly. "Lo they do call me. They bid me take my place among them in the halls of Valhalla, where the brave shall live forever."

Arne then bowed his head and Bjorn looked upward.

"Lo, here I see my enemy. Lo, here do I see his father. Lo, here do I see his mother. Lo, here do I see their warriors and their sorcerers. Lo, they are weeping and crying to their kin. They cry out for my blood, and for my life, but I shall not give it to them." When Bjorn finished speaking, he bowed his head and Rolf looked upward as the three of them took their swords in hand.

"Lo, I do feel my sword. Lo, I do feel the heat of battle. Lo, I do feel the cold fingers of death. Lo, I do feel the strength of mighty Thor. My sword shall answer the threat, and my foes shall be laid low, or I shall live in Valhalla, where the brave feast forever."

The three Vikings then stood and finished readying their weapons. Arne and Bjorn turned and walked toward the door. Rolf looked down to me and smiled. "It is an old prayer of our people, though most do not know the second or third parts."

"It was stirring," I said honestly as I got up to my feet.

Rolf placed a hand on my shoulder and his eyes narrowed ever so slightly on my own. "Come what may, this will be a day to remember, one worthy of song."

I nodded.

"You should take this," Rolf said as he pulled a long knife from his belt. "I have two of them. Wear it on your waist and pull it in a time of need. It has always kept me safe."

"Wow, I'm not sure what to say," I said as I turned the blade over in my hand.

"The handle is carved from the antler of an elk, and the blade was forged by my father."

"Thank you, Rolf."

The large warrior smiled and nodded once more. He then turned and followed Arne and Bjorn to the hallway. Indyrith approached and looked down at my sword once more. "I am envious," he said. "I have not seen such a weapon in person for many years. If I did not think it was better that you have it, I would ask to use it myself."

"You could use it if you wish," I said. "I'll feel a lot safer than before with Katya and Dan bringing in the heat, and I will have my own sword."

Indyrith shook his head. "No, it is better that you keep it. I cannot walk in the dream world as you can. Should any of the gargoyles be lurking there, I would want you to have the equipment you need."

The door opened quickly and Katya stuck her head in. "Time to go."

Outside the safe house there were two large vans prepared. Indyrith and the three Vikings went in the second van along with some of the other team members that had survived the ambush in California. I went with Flint, Dan, Katya, Marcus, and a driver by the name of Lucas. Marcus rode shotgun, while Flint helped Dan work a mess of rigging that held a very large machine gun on it. As I squeezed into the back with Katya, who was busy checking her magazines for the obscenely large rifle standing next to her, I saw that the roof of the van had been cut out during the night to allow for Dan and Flint to raise the machine gun up and fire at enemies.

That was when it hit me.

This was going to be a big fight.

The engines roared to life and then we sped out and away from the safety of the underground bunker. After a couple hours of driving, we crossed into California once more. We took a slight detour off of I-15 to stop in Mojave National Preserve just long enough to meet up with Briggs and the four black SUVs he had along with him. When we got back on the road, there were two SUVs in front, and two in back. I would have expected Briggs to ride in the last car, but he proved more courageous than I had given him credit for and was in the lead vehicle.

We drove straight and then hooked south around Barstow, taking the 247 down to Yucca Valley. Then we cut across on highway 62 until we hit I-10. We followed that to Indio and then went south on highway 86. I only remember the signs because compared to the beauty of the Olympic Peninsula, there wasn't much to look at on this drive. It likely didn't help that the entire drive felt as though I was walking into something far too large for me to handle. Highway 86 took us down to Salton Sea where I finally had something worth looking at.

We pulled off in some small town and Briggs called Flint up to his car. Flint cursed, but did as he was asked and threw the door of the van open. A couple of the guys took the opportunity to find a roadside bush to take care of some business, and then we waited until Flint came back.

The ex-special forces operative had a foul look on his face, and told Dan to mind his own business when asked what had happened. Flint turned on a hand-held radio and then tossed it on the floor at his feet. The vehicles started up again and we drove eastward on a small road. I think Flint was trying to go unnoticed, but I saw him pull out the bullet with the two red marks and kiss it just before loading it into the top of a magazine that had no other bullets in it. I thought about saying something to Katya or Dan, but then I remembered how much of a douche bag Briggs always was. The memory of the silencer pointed at my face in a crappy hotel room in Texas gave me a few moments to pause and think about which of the two men I would rather side with. Thinking about Flint's family solidified my decision. I kept my mouth shut. Briggs was on his own.

The caravan slowed considerably as we went over unmarked gravel roads winding through the mountains. I stared out the window, bouncing in my seat and wondering why any billionaire would ever bother building his mansion in such a remote spot.

Then I thought of the vampires and sighed. *Where else would a vampire family live if they wanted privacy?*

We drove for a couple hours, making our way through the unpopulated hillsides and mountains and then finally came out around a bend to find a paved road. The blacktop was smooth and smelled of fresh tar. Ahead of the lead car, I saw a large stone wall with an iron rod gate over the road. A guard shack stood off to the side. A pair of dragon statues sat on either side of the massive gates. I gripped the mithril sword, half expecting the statues to come alive. Thankfully, they didn't.

Drendarin's sword might be great against gargoyles, but I wasn't sure what would work against a dragon, and I frankly didn't care to find out.

A guard came out with a clipboard in hand. He motioned for Briggs' SUV to stop.

"Buckle up," Dan said. "This is where things get bumpy."

I watched as the second SUV broke out to the left. The side door opened and then some sort of mechanism extended out the side of the vehicle and an agent with a minigun let loose on the guard.

"Wait, what if he's just a normal guard?" I shouted.

"Section Four operates a little differently than we do," Dan said.

"That's why I generally avoid calling them in to work with us," Flint put in.

Briggs' SUV sped up and a man in riot gear stood out of the sun roof. He pulled out something that looked like a bazooka and then there was a flash and a trail of smoke. Two seconds later the gate exploded to pieces. The caravan sped through the demolished barrier.

I turned around to see the last vehicle stop long enough to let two men out. They ran to the guard shack. One went inside while the other took up a position outside the door and held his weapon at the ready.

"What are they doing?" I asked.

"Hacking into Rathison's network," Dan said. "They're probably not as fast as Mack, but they'll get the job done."

Come to think of it, I hadn't seen Mack at all before we left. I was about to ask where he was, but Briggs' started shouting over the radio at Flint's feet.

"Tangos at one o'clock!"

I watched as the second SUV veered out to the right. The man dangling from the extended seat went to work with his minigun. There was another guard shack. This time, they came out with rifles instead of clipboards.

"Going hot!" Dan shouted.

A couple of bullets hit the front of the van, but I was the only one startled by it. The minigunner made quick work of the handful of guards that came out. Then the agent in the lead car with the RPG hit the building.

The caravan sped up. I could see the pools and gardens zipping by us as we made our way toward the mansion. My stomach twisted in knots and I nearly retched on the floor of the van. Every fight up until now had been so different. I was ambushed in Dallas. I was attacked in my dreams. The only times I led assaults were the cruise ship and then another time in the dream world to stop the harbinger wolves, but even though I initiated the fights, they were in defense of my family. Even when I had my memory wiped and confronted the men on the street corner that had roughed up the beggar woman I was defending someone else.

This was the first time I was starting a fight without it being a purely defensive action. I started to feel sick as I wondered how many innocent people might be in the mansion right now. What about Stanley, did he deserve a bullet from Briggs? And the guard out front with the clipboard, he could have been a normal rent-a-cop.

I dropped my head and started to struggle for breath.

Katya was there in an instant. She slapped me across the face and grabbed the front of my shirt. "War is not pretty," she snapped. "Do not forget those you fight for! The engine cannot be allowed to launch."

"The guards," I said. "They were just normal people."

Katya shook me. "Today we are a club, not a scalpel. We hit hard, kill everything that stands in our way. You stop to think, you die. You die, we fail. We fail, the world dies."

I looked up to her hard eyes as the van veered suddenly to the left.

"Here they come!" Dan shouted. "Flint, get me up!"

"The gargoyles smell you," Katya said. "Tell me, do they smell your fear, or do they smell their own deaths?"

I looked up and saw wings darkening the skies above us as Flint and Dan worked the rigging to raise the fifty cal machine gun. I felt the sword in my hand and I knew that Katya was right. Looking up at the swarm coming toward us, there was no other way. We had to hit hard and fast. If we stopped to show mercy to anyone, then we would lose, overwhelmed by the sheer number of creatures that served Rathison.

"Holy frickin sh—" a voice came over the radio just before a massive gargoyle dove and slammed into the minigunner in front of us, ripping him and the entire rig out of the SUV. A second monster crashed down into the roof of the vehicle and brought it to an immediate halt as glass and metal shout outward.

I decided in that moment that everyone at Rathison's mansion was guilty.

"For Hank!" Marcus said as he popped something into the CD player up front.

I'll tell you this. Most people would choose a million different things to play while charging into battle. Heavy metal would seem the obvious choice. Maybe even something angry from DMX if you wanted more of a rap vibe, but nobody on God's green earth would turn on Mama Mia. Yet, as Dan and Flint finished loading the monstrous machine gun and let loose with a barrage of deafening bullets that lit up the sky, it somehow felt right to blast ABBA as loud as the van could. I could almost see Hank singing along as he rode with us in spirit. I bet he would have enjoyed watching the fiery red shots explode on impact, blowing the gargoyles apart and scattering them in the sky.

"Come get some!" Dan shouted out as Flint kept the gun fed with a steady stream of bullets.

"Dream world," I said.

"What?" Katya asked.

I took in a deep breath. We would be at the mansion soon, but if I could join the fight on the dream world side, then I could engage the gargoyles and put the mithril blade to the test. I closed my eyes and focused my thoughts. Then, instead of trying to create a dream, I envisioned myself standing and stepping out of my physical body. I felt a rush of cold air and looked down. Katya was poking my body in the chest and talking to me, but I was not in my body. I was in the dream world.

It was time to put the gargoyles down.

I flew up through the ceiling of the van and shouted.

The swarm of monsters turned as one, like bees defending their hive. I charged through the air, sword at the ready. Drums pounded in my head as the first gargoyle sailed toward me, and I knew that I was about to do something marvelous.

The monster roared and stretched forth its massive hands, tipped with deadly claws. I spun away and lashed out with the mithril blade. The gargoyle's hands came off at the wrists as if I was cutting a pair of threads, and then a fire burst out from the open wounds and the gargoyle fell to the ground, hissing and screaming until it crashed into the dirt below, nearly crushing the fifth car in the caravan.

A second gargoyle rushed in. I dodged by, ascending upwards, and drew my blade across its left wing. The gash was small, but it too burst into flame and the gargoyle fell from the sky.

I laughed and went to work hacking and slashing at any gargoyle foolish enough to come close. I killed a third, then a fourth, and then a fifth and sixth in the span of a few seconds. I flew into the heart of the swarm, unaffected by the raucous incendiary rounds Dan fired into the air as I went on the offensive, driving the gargoyles from before me. One of the creatures managed to scratch my left calf, but I paid the wound no mind, knowing that I was in the dream world and that it wasn't a mortal wound. I cut the head off of one gargoyle, and then spun around to slash another's chest. Then, there was a terrible scream that rent the air. The gargoyles split from the battle, taking off in all directions.

Dan's blazing fifty cal continued to chase them, as did gunfire from the other vehicles, but they were no longer a threat.

I flew back down and sat into my body just as the van pulled up on the fountain in the driveway.

Katya looked at me curiously as I opened my eyes and smiled at her.

"The drakkul's sword worked," I said with a wink.

"You were just…" Katya pointed to the sky and I nodded.

The van screeched to a halt and doors flew open. Dan continued to unload the fifty cal at the sky until the belt ran dry, and then he grabbed a pair of MP5s and jumped out. Katya ran out to the side about forty feet and then scanned the windows. Before I had even joined with Dan, she was firing at the building.

"Windows, two o'clock high," Flint shouted.

The Section Four agent with the RPG fired up and destroyed a good portion of the mansion. Briggs ordered a team up to the door. Six men from the SUV behind our van sprinted up to the front doors.

Then all hell broke loose.

The front doors exploded open with fire and smoke spewing out just as Briggs' team got into place.

Before the smoke even cleared a horde of monstrous things that looked like giant mastiffs with burned skin lunged out. They tore through the remaining three agents that survived the explosion and then started down the steps.

Katya's rifle clapped like thunder, catching one of the dogs in the head and stopping it cold.

Briggs pulled out an AK-47 and blasted into one of the monsters, but the creature seemed unfazed.

That's when I heard the shouting and hollering from behind.

The three Vikings charged in. One threw a spear and caught one of the nasty dogs in the eye. Another threw an axe and struck the same monster in the skull. The dog fell and skidded to a stop just as Rolf rushed in and jammed his spear into the thing's snarling mouth and down its throat. Gunfire erupted all around and the fight was in full swing now. I ran forward with my mithril blade and joined with Rolf. Shoulder to shoulder we cut and hacked our way through the burned dogs. Blood and smoke spewed out from each wound we gave them as we pressed forward. Bjorn lifted his mighty axe and cut through the spine of one dog as it lunged at Arne. Arne used his shield to rebuff another animal and then kicked its lower jaw so hard that its bone shattered and it fell to the side. Down came Arne's sword into the creature's chest and it convulsed, scratching at his shield with its claws until its life expired.

"Come on, Mills!" Dan shouted. I turned to see Flint working a hand-held minigun and my team was forming a wedge of sorts.

"Go on, Christian," Rolf said. "We'll be at your back!"

We worked our way up the stairs. The three Vikings kept me safe from the monstrous dogs trying to circle around while Flint cleared the front.

Briggs and his men had formed a wedge of their own as well. We all went up and into the mansion.

"Which way?" Dan shouted.

"Straight!" I replied. "To the elevator."

Dan patted Flint on the shoulder twice and the mini-gun kept whirring as more dogs poured into the entryway from the grand staircase and the hallways. Blood and limbs flew into the walls as Flint swept the monsters away from before him.

A fiery explosion threw several of the dogs into the air and I looked over to see Briggs holding his own against a mess of the beasts. He stomped one in the face as he poured a magazine into its body, and then he used his left hand to fling another grenade.

BOOM!

Just like that, the dogs were dead. Briggs' agents kept firing at anything that twitched or moved. We got to the back wall where the elevator was and then Marcus ran up and slapped a strange contraption into the door and forced it open.

I caught the slightest glimpse of a pale-faced man in the elevator and then the lights went out and there was a snarl followed by Marcus screaming. There was a wet squish and then Marcus went silent. I heard the whir of a machine and then Flint's minigun exploded into the darkness. Yellow and orange flashes streaked forward and something screamed.

A red flare shot out overhead and Briggs put his men to work setting green glow sticks that were as powerful as flashlights. A few of the agents clicked on headlamps and tactical lights mounted to their weapons as well. Soon I saw what was coming.

Vampires.

The one that had slain Marcus was cut in half by Flint's minigun, but there were more of the cursed things. They were crawling along the walls and ceiling, and coming at us fast. One leapt out from the hall on the right, but Katya pushed me aside, raised her massive rifle, and blew a hole in the monster's chest big enough to let a watermelon pass through.

It sneered at her and started advancing, but Dan whipped one of his MP5s up and riveted the vampire to the wall with an entire magazine. I jumped in then and swung for the vampire's neck with my mithril blade. Off came the head, and the mutilated body fell to the floor.

"Down!" Briggs shouted at the top of his lungs. I turned and saw three agents pointing massive weapons up at the vampires on the ceilings. An instant later there was a giant *WHOOSH!* The air seemed to get sucked away as flames poured upward and engulfed the vampires. There was a chorus of screaming and wailing and the creatures backed off.

"Enough Briggs! You tryin to bring the whole place down on top of us?" Flint shouted.

Dan turned to me. "Get to the elevator. We'll be right behind you. Go!"

I didn't think. I ran. Rolf, Arne, and Bjorn went with me as Dan, Katya, and Flint kept firing at the vampires closing in from all sides.

"Grab Marcus' bag," Flint shouted as I sprinted by. I grabbed the green duffle bag and then leapt into the elevator. Rolf and the others made it into the little box and I pressed the button that would take us to the appropriate subfloor. The doors closed, and then the elevator started moving. Gunfire and explosions sounded from above, shaking the whole house and the elevator as well.

"They'll be right behind us, right?" I said as I looked up.

Rolf looked to Arne and grunted. "I fear Odin has not heard our prayers this time."

CHAPTER 20

The elevator moved far too slowly for my comfort. Gunfire echoed from above and the cables squealed and shook with each explosion. I remembered how far down we had to go to reach the hallway with the red door. We weren't even half way there yet. The red numbers at the top of our shaking death box kept counting off the floors, but I swear it felt as though we were crawling to a halt.

"I could cut the cables," Bjorn suggested.

"No!" I said quickly. "We'd fall to our deaths."

"At least our deaths would be quick," Arne muttered.

"Patience, brothers," Rolf said as he took inventory of the many weapons dangling from various belts and straps on his body. "We have not come here to die. Not today. Not until the engine is destroyed."

The elevator stopped and a bell rang out. *DING!*

Each of us took a step away from the door and readied our weapons.

The doors opened slowly to reveal an empty, dark hallway.

Nothing was there.

"I'll hit the button," I said. I reached for the button to close the doors once more, but just as my hand came within an inch of the panel, a dark, slimy tentacle reached in and wrapped around my wrist. It pulled me toward the hallway. Rolf was there in a flash. Steel cut through the gooey tentacle, slopping slime and black blood all over the elevator floor while the severed bit clung to my wrist and dug in with sharp suckers. I cried out as a terrible stinging erupted in my arm.

Two more tentacles shot into the elevator. Arne stabbed one with a spear and Bjorn severed the other with his axe. There was a great hissing sound coming from the dark hallway, followed by a gurgling scrape along the marble floor. Whatever was out there was coming closer.

I set the mithril blade down and reached for the knife that Rolf had given me. I used the blade to pry the constricting tentacle from my

238

wrist and then I bent down to dig in Marcus' bag. I wasn't sure what all of the different devices were. I saw yellow and red wires, rectangular blocks of what appeared to be C4, and several different canisters and grenades. Not wanting to blow up more than I needed, I reached through the explosives and pulled a pair of emergency flares out of the bottom. I opened the top and then lit the stick. A brilliant red flame roared to life.

As another set of tentacles came in, the three Vikings hacked and slashed, throwing slime and goo all over the floor and walls. What was worse, the severed bits writhed on the ground like leeches, hungry for our flesh and stretching out to seize us. I tossed the burning flare into the hallway, illuminating the darkness and allowing us to see our foe.

A great, jelly-like glob of blue and black ooze swelled in the hall and slid away from the flare until the stick spun to a halt and hit the wall. I then noticed that the creature was extremely careful to stay away from the flame as it surged back toward us. I struck the next flare and pointed the flame down at one of the still writhing tentacle pieces. The limb curled away in protest as I quickly burned a hole through it. I stepped toward the opening and took a more careful aim with my next throw. The flare whooshed through the air and slapped into the side of the goo-monster.

It hissed and moved away, but the flare was stuck to it. Smoke and steam erupted out the top and there was a sound somewhat like a whoopee-cushion as the goo seemed to deflate and fall flat to the floor.

I turned and pressed the button to resume our descent.

"Interesting creature," Arne said as he wiped some of the goo from his weapon.

"This place is filled with the creatures of hell," Rolf noted. He then looked down and pointed at my wrist. "How is your arm?"

I raised my wrist and saw a network of red and purple welts running down the top of my hand and around to my palm. "It stings," I said. "Maybe it was like a large jell fish or something." I had heard once that peeing on a jellyfish sting was beneficial, but I was not about to pee on my own hand in front of three immortal Vikings. I put the pain out of my mind, figuring it would subside eventually.

We passed three floors and then there was a terrible tremor that shook us all so that we fell to our knees in the elevator. Something exploded high above us, and then I got that feeling you get when a roller coaster goes up and down really quickly. I would have enjoyed the sensation if not for the fact that it meant the cables to our elevator had been severed and we were still far too high up to freefall without certain death being the outcome.

We sailed downward at an alarming speed. I could hear metal scraping and screeching outside the elevator, but we didn't seem to be slowing. Then, we slammed to a halt. I fell backward into the wall, but was mostly unharmed. Rolf hit the floor, but absorbed the impact. Arne fell on top of him, which cushioned his blow, and Bjorn had propped his long axe up on top of the hand rails on either side, and so kept his balance. The rest of us clambered back to our feet and went to work prying the door open. Unfortunately, we hadn't landed directly in front of any floor, and were greeted only by the wall.

I strapped Marcus' duffle bag to my back and after getting a boost from Rolf, climbed up to undo the access panel at the top of the elevator. It was dark in the shaft, but there were a few emergency lights flashing that offered just enough light for me to see how far up we needed to go. Luckily, we had come to rest just a few feet below an opening, so it didn't appear to be a difficult transition. I reached down and pulled Rolf upward. Once he was up he went to work prying the doors open while I helped Arne and Bjorn climb out of the elevator. We then clambered up into an open hallway and stopped to take stock of where we were.

"How much farther?" Rolf asked as he pointed to the number panel near the open doors.

"I think we're still quite a ways up," I said with a sigh. "Another six floors if I remember correctly."

The Vikings checked their equipment while I dug out another couple of flares just in case the lights went out again. We moved out around to the left and searched for the stairwell access. Lights flickered in the hall and doors stood closed on either side. I looked back to Rolf and shrugged.

"Do we just search for stairs, or do we need to clear the rooms too?" I asked. The last thing I wanted to do was walk half way down a hall only to get swarmed by vampires coming out of every door.

Bjorn stepped up to the first door on the left and then glanced back to Rolf. Rolf gave a nod and the massive Viking kicked the door in. We all filed in after him, ready to put down anything that moved. What we saw inside made my stomach churn.

There was a long couch along one wall, and a stone slab directly in front of it with old blood stains darkening the gray surface. Near the back of the room sat a man behind bars. He looked up at us with hollow eyes. He didn't make a sound, he just pulled his long, scraggily hair back from his neck and then turned his head as if offering us a vampire's meal.

"Kill him," Rolf said.

"Wait, doesn't a vampire have to choose to turn someone?" I said. "I mean, I read in books that they can feed on people without transferring their... vampire-ness." Admittedly, I didn't finish that statement very eloquently, but I got the point across.

"If you get to them early enough that's true in some cases, however, this man is obviously a long term feeder. He's been exposed for far too long. There are dangers other than just the victim turning into a vampire. He could have all sorts of diseases that vampires carry as hosts and pass on to their victims. Besides, you could see it in his eyes. Odin's fire has left this man a long time ago."

Arne walked forward and deftly thrusted his spear into the man's heart. The man made no sound. He didn't fight back. His body simply went limp and he fell to the floor.

"Trust me, we did him a favor, there's no coming back from that," Rolf said as he slapped my shoulder. We went through the rest of the hall, checking a few more rooms as we went. To my horror, we discovered that each room held a similar cell. Some had one person inside, others as many as four or five, but the scenario was always the same. The doors would open and the victims would offer their necks willingly.

In the interest of time, Arne stayed behind to end each prisoner's suffering while the rest of us made a more direct line for the end of the hall where the stairs were located.

"How can they take so many people and no one notices?" I asked.

Rolf shook his head. "Some of them are stolen from people who look for them afterwards. Others are taken from people who never noticed they existed in the first place. It is a dark evil that festers in this home."

We pushed into the stairwell and bumped into a pair of tall, gaunt men. We all stopped and stared at each other for a moment, and then the vampires hissed and made to lunge at us, but Rolf and I were quicker. I plunged my mithril blade deep into the first vampire's chest and Rolf lopped off the second vampire's head. Had I only been using a regular sword, I doubt I would have survived, but as my blade burned the vampire, the creature was unable to react before Bjorn stepped in, held up a wooden stake over the vampire's chest, and then pounded it in with the bottom of his right fist. The vampire hissed and then fell backward down the stairs.

"Thanks," I said.

Bjorn sniffed and grabbed another wooden stake from his belt. With his right hand, he pulled out a warhammer and then he took the lead. Rolf put me in the middle and glanced at my duffle bag.

"We'll get you to the door, and then it's up to you to finish this."

I nodded and we redoubled our pace running down the steps as quickly as we could without tripping. We made it two floors down before one of the access doors opened and another vampire came rushing at us. Bjorn ducked under the swipe of a sword and then came in hard, planting his shoulder square in the vampire's stomach and driving the creature back into the wall. The vampire hissed and raised his arm to strike down, but I was there first. I thrusted my sword into the vampire's right bicep and kept him from bringing his sword down on Bjorn. The large Viking then quickly set the wooden stake with one hand and drove it in hard a second later with his hammer. The vampire cried out in pain and then gasped his final breath before falling to the ground. Rolf took the creature's head for good measure as we continued on our way.

That was when the door on the floor below opened and out came three more vampires, only the first one had a pistol, and began taking shots at us. We ducked into the open hallway behind us. Bjorn threw his hammer into the stairwell as one vampire came up over the railing. The monster caught the spike on the back of the hammer in the face and fell from the railing. Bjorn then pulled his mighty axe and stepped just inside the door to wait for the next one to come.

A shower of sparks exploded from the wall and ceiling as the first vampire kept raining bullets after us.

"Don't you have one of those fancy boomsticks?" Rolf asked me.

I shook my head and raised my mithril blade. "I was prepped more for this," I said.

Out of nowhere we heard Arne shouting a warcry that stirred our very souls. I looked out to see Arne leaping downward from the floor above us, his shield out in front as the vampire turned to fire at him, and his spear out over the side. I was stunned by the sight, but Bjorn and Rolf were quick to rejoin the fight. Bjorn buried his axe deep in the gun-wielding vampire's back as Arne came down and ran his spear through the vampire's chest. Rolf spun around the mess to strike down the other vampire that had been following the first up the stairs. Black blood painted the walls, but miraculously none of the Vikings were given so much as a scratch. I stared in disbelief as Arne stood up and checked his bullet-riddled shield.

"Are you hit?" I asked him.

Arne smiled and shook his head. "Today is not my day."

A blur of black and gray movement came down from somewhere above us and pinned Arne into the wall.

"Arne!" Bjorn shouted.

It was too late. The valiant warrior fell to the floor, his throat ripped out by a tall, slender vampire. Bjorn cut off the vampire's right arm, and Rolf stabbed through the vampire's chest, but even as they hacked the monster to pieces, there was nothing to be done for Arne.

A chorus of snarls and wicked laughter came from above. I looked up and saw a group of at least twenty vampires making their way down the stairs. Some were jumping between the flights, others were climbing down the walls and over the rails. We had just a few seconds until they were upon us.

"Rolf, there was a glass box with a hose inside back in the hallway, can you go and grab it?" I asked.

Rolf looked at me curiously, but I didn't have time to explain. I grabbed the duffle bag and started fishing around for something I could conceivably use with minimal prep time. Bjorn decided that he would do as I asked and rushed back into the hall. I heard shattering glass and then the sound of the thick hose fabric rubbing against the side of the metal box and sliding along the floor as he brought it out.

"Here, dream walker," Bjorn said.

"Tie it around us, we're going to jump the last few floors," I said.

Rolf looked over the edge and then back up to the vampires coming for us. It must have clicked for him then, because he quickly joined Bjorn. The two measured the hose and then Bjorn hacked off what we needed. They tied one end to the railing and then looped the other around the three of us. I found what I was looking for by then and smiled.

"All right, let's jump!" I said. I left a small brick of pre-wired C4 on the floor where we had been and then took the remote detonator with me as we all clambered over the rail and dropped down.

The vampires hissed and sneered as they came ever closer. Time seemed to slow as we gave in to the arms of gravity and trusted our lives to how well Bjorn had tied the hose around us. I watched as we fell, waiting for the pursuing vampires to get close enough to make the trap effective.

What I hadn't thought about until we were most of the way down was the fact that the C4 was likely going to obliterate the railing, and the top of the hose. Whatever support we were counting on to catch us, was going to be gone by the time we needed it. My fingers hesitated as the vampires swarmed over and around the landing we had leapt from. I could already calculate by the vampires' speed that they would reach us before we made it to the bottom unless I hit the trigger, but there was no way of knowing *if* we would survive without the safety of our make-shift rope.

One of the vampires picked up the C4 and moved to pull the wires out. Instinct kicked in. It was now or never. There was no more time for doubts.

I pressed the button and heard the click.

A blinding flash like nothing I had ever seen before erupted overhead. The vampires were vaporized in an instant. We fell for another couple of seconds that seemed to stretch on forever, and then finally we crashed down in a heap. We grunted and groaned. I heard snapping bones and lost my breath upon impact. Before I really knew what was happening, bits of vampire and cement were raining down all around us. I tried to move, but the hose held me tight to the other two. A piece of some vampire's hand slapped me in the face, and then there was the heat wave from the explosion. It felt like I had stepped into a kiln for a few moments, and then everything was quiet as smaller particulate continued to fall over us.

Rolf managed to undo the hose and free us. He reached over and picked me up, helping me finally catch my breath. That was when I noticed that Bjorn had been on the bottom. His left leg was broken in at least two places below the knee, and twisted horribly up under him. To make it worse, the jagged edge of his broken femur protruded through the side of his right leg. There was no way he was going to make it. Rolf turned the bear of a man over onto his back. Bjorn's nose was broken and crooked, a couple of his front teeth were missing, and there was a large gash in his forehead.

"Bjorn, I'm sorry," I said.

Bjorn shook his head. "We never could have outrun them," he said. "It was the right decision." He shakily raised a right arm and pointed to the duffle bag. "Give me one more, and I shall keep watch from here. If any more come, then I will turn them to dust."

"Die well," Rolf said as he placed Bjorn's axe in his left hand.

Bjorn nodded. I handed the broken warrior a block of C4 and a second detonator.

"It was an honor to know you," I said.

Bjorn smiled. "May Odin give you knowledge on your path, may Thor grant you strength and courage on your way, and may Loki give you laughter as you go."

"Godspeed, my friend," I replied with a nod.

Rolf and I turned to the door behind us and made our way into the long, bare concrete hall. The familiar metal conduit was running along the corner, but it only lit a few of the lights. The portion that I had ripped out while in the dream world remained unfixed. Sparks spat out of the ragged end, hissing and popping every few seconds. We were careful to step around it as we continued toward the red door.

We were met with no resistance here. Either everything was dead, or we had finally managed to scare them off.

I tried the handle of the red door only to find it locked. I knelt and looked into the duffle bag. Unsure of how much to use, I grabbed the last four bricks of C4. I placed one on each hinge, and then the last one I put on the handle, figuring that would destroy all of the strongest points and let us in.

"This will destroy mithril?" Rolf asked.

I shrugged. "This is what Marcus brought, so I'm hoping it's enough."

"Maybe use more, just to be sure," Rolf said. He reached in and grabbed a few grenades and was about to pull the pins, but I stopped him. "What? I have seen others use this. They pull pin and then it explodes."

"If you put those here, we won't have enough time to run away," I said. "Just, put them back in the bag."

Rolf frowned and angrily dropped the grenades. My heart jumped into my throat for a split second as I half-expected one of them to go off with how rough he was handling them. A moment later, realizing that I was still alive, I gestured for him to follow me back to the elevator shaft. We pried open the doors and looked up.

"Will it fall down?" Rolf asked.

"I'm not sure, but we have to get out of the way of the blast." I measured the cut out in the hallway and saw that we had four feet of wall we could back up against and hope the blast wave shot down the hall past us. We were about sixty yards from the door, but I had no idea if that was the right distance for safety. Still, Rolf could be right. The blast could very well shake the elevator loose once more, and then we would be pancakes. We were in trouble regardless of how we proceeded.

I couldn't make up my mind which was the safer option.

Rolf grabbed me by the shirt and pinned me to the wall in the corner by the open elevator shaft doors, and then he made the decision for me. His hand squeezed mine, and the most thunderous explosion shook everything around us. A flash of fire was followed by smoking hunks of debris. My head was spinning from the sheer volume of the blast. My ears rang loud and sharp, and I wasn't sure I'd ever be able to hear again. Rolf must have been hurting too, for he was bleeding from his right ear. I was fairly certain his eardrum had ruptured, but he just slapped my chest and led the way toward the door.

I grabbed the single flashlight in the duffle bag and used it to light our way, as the explosion had knocked out all of the lights around the door. I smiled when I saw the opening. The way to the engine was clear now. All we had to do was find it.

We stumbled down the hallway, our balance apparently affected by the explosion and its after effects. To be honest, I was just happy we lived through it. When we crossed the threshold of the red door, I noticed the air changed and became much cooler. I drew my sword and used the bandolier strap inside the duffle bag to carry the grenades so I wouldn't have to lug the drab green sack around everywhere I went.

Rolf readied his weapon and sniffed the air.

I pointed to the hallway where I had seen Mateo dragged into and slain. We walked through a corridor that reminded me of an old nuclear missile bunker. Not that I had seen one outside of video games, but it looked fairly similar. Steel walls, consoles with numerous buttons, and glass panels that looked into a silo. Only thing was, there was no rocket or missile inside. Instead, there was a cube. It measured thirty feet across, high, and wide. It was really nothing special to look at, frankly. Certainly not what I had expected to say the least. The surfaces were smooth, polished to a shine, and there appeared to be no door or opening of any kind.

"Is that it?" Rolf asked.

BOOM!

Rolf's body slammed into mine and the grand, unbeaten gatekeeper groaned.

"I knew you would come again," Brant Rathison said as he stepped in from behind us. He opened the massive rifle he was holding by separating the barrel and the stock. "Magnificent weapon, this," Rathison said. "I find it even keeps some of my more, sinister relatives in line when I pull it out."

I looked down to Rolf and saw the life slipping from his angry eyes. "Sword," Rolf whispered.

I slid down to gently lay the warrior on the ground. There was a massive hole in the right side of his chest. There was no way he would live. I reached over and grabbed the sword he had been holding before the shot and placed it in his hand.

"Thank you, Christian," he said with a weak smile. "I will go now, to the halls of my fathers, and we will watch you from above."

"No, not you too!" I started to cry. "You have to stay. I can't do this without you. Rolf!"

"Pity," Rathison said. "I expected more from the fabled three Vikings." I looked up just as Rathison shoved a massive cartridge into the rifle and clicked it shut. "You're an interesting one though. I saw you when you tried to sneak into my home the first time. I guess you didn't realize that my vampire parentage gave me the ability to see you just fine. I had actually seen you upstairs in the parlor, and that was why I led you down here. I had hoped the gargoyles would finish you, but you have proven to be extremely resourceful. Then again, perhaps it was just blind luck eh? Otherwise you wouldn't have let the trekawak grab your arm." Rathison motioned with his chin at the welts on my wrist. I looked down and noticed they had become much darker. "You've been poisoned, you see, but then again I would wager you have already noticed that. Perhaps you have hesitated lately when you should have acted, or found it hard to decide what to do? That's how

247

it starts. The poison melts your brain, turns you into a meal for the trekawak. So you see, I'm doing you a favor now. You're already dead, but the poison will kill you slow. I offer a quick release. It's more honorable for a warrior, don't you agree?"

"Do you ever shut up?" I spat. "Either pull the trigger or get out of my way."

Rathison smirked. "You came close, I'll give you that, but this is where it all ends." Rathison raised the rifle to take aim.

There was no way for me to escape.

Unless...

I gripped Drendarin's necklace in my hand and closed my eyes.

What happened in the next two seconds changed the course of human history forever.

I dropped back, and then I slipped into the dream world, sitting forward as my physical body fell behind me. As before, the mithril blade came with me into the dream world. Being much faster in this form than in the physical world, I willed myself toward Rathison. The confident billionaire's smile vanished as he caught sight of my dream world form rushing toward him. The muzzle of the rifle shifted just an inch to the side as Rathison nervously pulled the trigger. An instant later I ran the mithril blade through his heart.

The billionaire stumbled backward as the bullet erupted out of the rifle. I watched him fall, delighted in my triumph, and then some force knocked into my left shoulder and threw me to the ground. I cried out in terrible agony as it felt like fire was ripping me apart. My arm went numb and cold, and then it fell off from my body. Panicked, I looked back to where my physical body was sitting. Only then did I realize that the bullet from Rathison's rifle had torn off my limb. Blood was pouring out of my physical body, and I could feel my strength leaking away. I gripped Drendarin's necklace and then stood and with all the strength and focus I had left in my dream world form, I crashed my right fist through the glass panel separating me from the terrible cube sitting in the silo.

A flash of blue light blinded me and then Drendarin stepped through. He was unarmed, but carried a strange device that looked like a box with wires coming out of it. He looked down at me. I pointed weakly to the broken window, and Drendarin knew what to do. He took two grenades from the bandolier on my physical body and reached through the broken glass and secured the grenades to the outside. When his arm came back in, his hand was full of pins. The drakkul darted away and took cover. The grenades erupted in a cacophony of sound that reverberated up through the silo and widened the hole I had made.

"There is nothing I can do for your body, my friend," Drendarin said. "But, with this victory, I shall unite the other clans under my rule, and I will stop the drakkul from coming to your world for as long as I live." He bent down to my dream world form and I saw a single tear falling down his green skin. "A friendship between two individuals, sealed by your sacrifice, shall create peace between our peoples."

I weakly offered a smile and watched as Drendarin disappeared through the hole. A few moments later I heard several beeps and clicks. Then the fires of massive engines burst into life and I saw the cube fly upward through the silo. Drendarin was riding upon its side, with his strange device that he had brought through the portal strapped to his back. Daylight streamed in from above as the doors to the silo opened and let the cube escape upwards. I could only hope that Indyrith and I had not misplaced our hope. If, after all this, Drendarin used the engine to unite the seven realms, then I swore I was going to haunt that lizard-man for the rest of his miserable life.

My fears were put to rest soon, however, when I heard a massive explosion echoing down through the silo and into the hallway where I lay dying. Drendarin had destroyed the engine, and we had won.

I pushed up to my knees and stared at my physical body. The thought of sitting back inside of it was more than a little daunting. At least in the dream world, I could dampen the pain I felt. If I were to retake my physical body, then I would be at the mercy of all the nerves that were so loudly screaming out about losing my left arm and a sizable chunk of my shoulder socket.

I thought of the dogwood tree, back on my mountain. I hoped the other council members would be pleased with me. I had done the best I could. I closed my eyes and fell forward to the ground. As the life ebbed from my physical body, I could feel my focus turning into nothingness. I rolled onto my back, wondering whether I would see that bright light talked about by so many, or whether I would simply fade away, and join the vast expanse of nothingness that seemed so close to me now.

The silence was deafening as I stared up at the ceiling.

I was almost lost to despair, and then I heard the distant sound of drums.

CHAPTER 21

The two warriors who dressed alike came to my side. They spoke to each other in their language while looking down at me and my broken physical body. One prayed over me, and the other prayed over Rolf. I watched from my dream world form as a bright white and gold light encircled my physical body, and Rolf's as well. Then, in a blur of light and warmth, I opened my eyes to find myself back inside my body, completely whole.

"I'm alive!" I shouted.

Rolf sat up next to me and shot me a glaring eye. "Bloody hell, will the gods never let me rest?!"

I laughed and helped the Viking up to his feet. "It seems you still have work to do," I said.

"I have half a mind to tell Thor to get his thunderous self down here and do it himself," Rolf spat.

"Brothers!" a familiar voice called out from around the corner. "You won't believe what happened! A valkyrie came to me, and healed my wounds."

"Bjorn!" Rolf shouted. "Praise Odin!" Rolf rushed in and embraced Bjorn.

"When I first saw it coming to me, I almost pushed the button, but I'm sure glad I didn't!" Bjorn held out the brick of C4 I had given him. "Here, Christian, you take it."

I smiled and took the explosive from him. "What did the valkyrie look like?" I asked.

Bjorn frowned. "I couldn't see very well, on account of my eye being swollen shut and dim, but I know she had darker skin and long, braided gray hair."

"Not hair of gold?" Rolf asked skeptically.

Bjorn shrugged. "No, the hair was gray, but she was still beautiful. Her hand was warm and gentle, and she made me whole again!"

I bit my lip, knowing that it was no valkyrie he had seen, but the fifth and final member of the council. They had each spent their last gifts to bring us back from death. While I was on the one hand ecstatic about the additional chance at life I had been given, I couldn't help but realize that now there would be no more help from the council. All five had given their gifts. If ever there was another challenge to face, I would be on my own.

The three of us spent the next several hours climbing up through the wreckage that had once been a massive, sprawling mansion. When we finally reached the top floor, we emerged in a far wing of the building and had to work our way through burned structures, cracked beams, and ruined marble pillars. As we passed through a room that contained many swords and axes on display, I noticed that there was a black safe toppled over onto the marble floor, with the door hanging open and cash sticking out.

Now, I had never been one to steal, but under the circumstances, I considered it only fair that I should be compensated with whatever the billionaire might have left around. Besides, I knew that Section Four was likely going to seize all his assets anyway, assuming any of Briggs' men survived the ordeal.

I went to the safe and picked up several stacks of what looked like hundred dollar bills wrapped in mustard yellow bands. I stuffed them into my pocket and continued winding my way through the mansion. When we got to the entryway, my heart sank. The destruction was so massive. It was hard to tell if anyone had survived. There were remnants of the cursed dog beasts, vampires, and more than a few of Briggs' agents. We picked our way through the corpses, looking for Dan, Flint, and Katya. We found Marcus' body where it had been left. Bjorn pulled his axe and moved to Marcus' corpse.

"Hey, what are you doing?" I asked.

Rolf put a hand on my shoulder, the same one that only a short time ago had been blown off by Rathison's elephant gun, and said, "We have been at this long enough to know that sometimes they only pretend to kill our friends. Vampires can inflict their curse on you with a single bite, and it takes no longer to transfer than the venom from a viper. Cutting his head off now, although disrespectful, is the only way to make sure he does not come back later to attack us. An ally turned vampire would be extremely deadly, as they would know all of our hideouts."

Bjorn raised his axe and I closed my eyes while turning away until it was over.

"And Mack thinks this is the best job in the world," I grumbled.

Rolf squeezed my shoulder and continued walking. "It is not, perhaps, as glamorous as some, but tell me how many friends you have who have saved the world?"

"Yeah, I guess that's true," I said. As we crossed along the carnage, I heard a familiar tune playing outside. I had to smile. ABBA was blaring loud and true. "Let's take a look outside," I said.

Rolf and Bjorn nodded and followed after me. I stepped out onto the scorched stairs leading to the driveway and smiled wide. The van was sitting right where it had been. Indyrith and his daughter were meditating. Dan, Flint, and Katya were sitting in the open cargo door and passing a canteen around. All of them had lived.

"He lives!" Dan said as he threw his arms out.

We marched down the stairs like the triumphant heroes we were and shared embraces with our teammates. There was much rejoicing, and a few tears of happiness from Flint of all people. Indyrith and his daughter broke their meditation and came to congratulate us as well. They asked about Arne, and Rolf proudly puffed his chest and told them about how valiantly Arne had fought with the strength and grace of an eagle, fighting off whole groups of vampires.

He may have embellished the retelling a bit, but I sure wasn't about to correct him.

"And Briggs?" I asked, looking at Flint.

Flint smirked and rubbed his thumb over the grip of his 1911. "The mean ones always survive," he said. He thumbed out toward the south. "He and what's left of his team are inspecting the silo and trying to figure out how to clean this mess up before it hits the local news."

"And what of Drendarin?" Indyrith asked, cutting in.

"He followed through with his word. He was the one who launched and destroyed the engine."

Indyrith smiled. "Then our work is done. We should go home."

"Not yet," Briggs shouted. We all turned to see the man, spattered with dark blood across the front of his uniform and face. "I want to know how that engine was launched, and I want to know which one of you d-bags blew it up!" He stormed up toward me and pointed at my face. "Was it you, you little twerp?"

Rolf stepped in Briggs' way and laid the man out on the ground with a single punch. Briggs shook his head and spit out a bit of fresh, bright blood and then pushed back up to his feet.

"You want to try that again?" Briggs snarled.

Rolf obliged and put the Section Four enforcer down on his backside once again. Dan and Flint had to turn away to stifle their laughter, but I had seen enough for one day. I put my hand on Rolf's shoulder and then moved over to extend a hand to Briggs. The agent looked at it, and then up to my eyes. I could tell he was thinking about whether he should actually take it, but he eventually let me help him up.

"The engine wasn't operational," I lied. "When we made it down to where it was, Rathison was there. He had already started the launch sequence. We tried to stop him, but it was too late. Fortunately for us, the engine wasn't ready yet. The specs that my dad stole from Twin Turbo a couple decades ago had a fatal flaw, and the engine ruptured. Nothing we could do about it."

"And how do I know you aren't lying?" Briggs shouted.

I shrugged. "You don't. But, if you want to check out the story, just go down to the lowest subfloor. You'll find Rathison dead at the controls. That should confirm my story." I paused for effect. "Of course, I can't guarantee there aren't any additional vampires down there, and both the stairs and elevator are out of commission."

Briggs shook his head and then turned to Rolf. "You, Viking, you won't lie to me, it's dishonorable. Is this man telling the truth?"

Rolf folded his arms. "I have never found fault with anything the Christian says."

Briggs clenched his fist and cursed under his breath. "You all better just get outta here before I change my mind and lock the lot of you up." He spun around and made a circle motion in the air with his finger. Three agents in busted up riot gear responded by starting to jog back toward him.

"Before we go," Flint started. I felt a knot form in my stomach as Briggs turned to face Flint. Flint reached down and I thought for sure he was going to pull the 1911 up and end the man right there. Instead, he unbuttoned a pouch and pulled out the magazine with the special bullet. He pulled it from the magazine and then offered it to Briggs. "A little present for you."

"What the hell would I want that for?" Briggs said sourly.

"So you can remember that all debts will eventually be paid," Flint said.

"And this means what?" Briggs said as he took the bullet.

"It's from my wife and daughter."

For once, I saw fear flash across Briggs' face. His lower lip quivered ever so slightly, and then he quickly shoved it into his pocket. "That was…" his words failed him and he shook his head.

Flint turned and headed for the van. "All right, where we gonna eat? I'm starving."

*****

It was a long journey back to our underground home in western Washington. Nick was so happy to see everyone that he prepared a feast. Roast pig, pheasant, duck, grilled salmon, and more bread and fruit than any of us could have eaten in a week. I was skeptical at first, but after a couple of bites I was completely convinced that Nick was the best chef in the world. That's right, a Sasquatch is the best chef. And to think, people always portray them as little more than big gorillas that lope around the forest. It was great to be back, although it did also accentuate the fact that we had lost Hank and Marcus. Katya and Dan saw to packing up their things. Equipment that belonged to the team was put into a store room for later redistribution. Personal effects were put into boxes and mailed out to family, along with canned letters appropriate for each recipient. It seemed a bit distant, but I couldn't blame them. I had to think of all the people that had likely lost their lives during Indyrith's time here. I imagine I would have eventually come up with a similar system.

After things settled down a bit, I tried to look into the ambush in California. I was more than a little shocked to see that the news had reported a residential gas leak and explosion. Seemed a bit far-fetched that none of the neighbors had come forward to talk about what they had seen or heard, but I guess sometimes the best option, even for Section Four, is to help with memory wiping. It was comforting to know that they didn't just let Briggs run around and put people down when big incidents occurred. Though, thinking back on how he seemed to enjoy himself in that dingy motel room in Texas, I bet Briggs wouldn't have a problem with sweeping a whole neighborhood.

The story behind Rathison's mansion was far more plausible. The official story was that somehow the rocket he was designing had malfunctioned and launched early, causing widespread fires and damage to the building and grounds. Officially, no bodies were recovered at the scene after the Forest Service was called in to put out the fires before they spread outward to surrounding forests.

A billionaire dead. Apocalypse averted. Family safe.

Finally, everything I had gone through in Dallas seemed worth it. I'm not saying I would jump back into the same alley if I had a time machine… but it was worth it.

As for the harbinger wolves, well, Indyrith had recovered the red sword of oaths from the cruise ship. He held onto it until after we had averted the disaster with the trans-dimensional unification engine so I wouldn't be distracted. Then, he gave it to me.

I looked at it, sitting in my room with the door closed. I knew what it was for. If Drendarin's necklace could connect me with that particular drakkul, then this sword would connect me with the family that it belonged to.

I closed my eyes and felt the familiar rush of air around my body.

When I opened my eyes, I was in the dream world, but more than that, I was in a massive cave lit by several bonfires and torches. A host of harbinger wolves were gathered together, dancing around the fire and feasting upon raw flesh strewn about along long slabs of stone that had been carved to serve as tables.

At the far end of the cavern I saw a harbinger wolf bigger than any other I had seen to that point. His fur was black, and his muscles looked like the kind of bulging mounds you would see in comic books. He sat upon a throne of bones and watched as the others danced and ate. He was the alpha. Their king.

I waited for several hours until the large beast took two of the females back to his room. Once they settled in for the night, lying upon a bed of hides that would make a Safari hunter green with envy, I entered the room.

As a child, I may have been the one they hunted, but now I was grown. It was my turn to do the hunting. I focused my mind until I was able to make the connection with the alpha. Then, I slipped into his dreams. I watched at first, soaking in what the alpha had for a pleasant dream. There were fields with endless game. Harbinger wolves roamed freely, hunting and eating their fill. Young wolf pups played in the tall grasses and chomped on long-stemmed daisies. The king sat upon a mound of stones and laughed as some of the younger harbinger wolves tumbled into a nearby stream and then turned to trying to catch fish in their mouths.

Indyrith had prepared me for this, saying that once I got into the minds of my enemies, I would see that their inner desires matched my own. The only real difference was what they were willing to do to accomplish their desires. I understood what he meant when he said it, but seeing this monster dreaming about having what essentially amounted to a large family picnic was intriguing.

Still, I had not come to enjoy the view. I had come to give the king nightmares.

I walked in from the grass and swung my sword, not the mithril blade that Drendarin had given to me, that was hanging in Indyrith's room. I was back to using the sword I had conjured up for myself, the same one that the old Cherokee man had engraved with sacred symbols. In order to ensure the safety of my world, I was now going to use it to put fear into the hearts of every harbinger wolf. They were going to shrink at the mention of my name from this night forward.

I walked up to the first harbinger wolf and cut off its head. A chorus of screams and snarls rose up all around. The pups yipped and ran in all directions. The males snarled and charged. This time I had no fear for my safety, for there was only one harbinger wolf here who could really fight back, and he was currently asleep, trapped in his own dream. I cut down seven more harbinger wolves before turning to walk toward the alpha. On my way, I snatched up one of the pups and held it upside-down by its rear left leg. I put the tip of my blade to its throat. It looked at me with terrible fear in its eyes and I almost shrank away from my plan. I had to force myself to remember that none of these images were real. I could slay or mutilate any harbinger wolf in the dream except for the alpha himself and no real harm would come to any living soul. They were just part of the alpha's dream.

I steeled my gaze on the alpha and set my jaw, displaying far more confidence and hatred than I truly felt.

"What do you want? Who are you?" the alpha said in a voice that trembled with each word.

"Do you know my name?" I asked.

The alpha eyed me up and down for a moment. Anger threatened to rise in the monster's eyes, but then the realization of who stood before him dawned on him, and his anger was entirely replaced by fear. His eyes flashed wide and his lower jaw quivered. "You are the dream walker," the alpha said with a nod.

"Then you know what I am capable of, don't you?" I pressed the tip of my sword to the pup's chest. It yipped and struggled. The alpha jumped up.

"No, please! I'll do anything you want."

I nodded. "I want your name," I said.

"I am Kuwam, the Alpha," the king said.

"Kuwam, I have two options for you to choose from," I said. I let my sword disappear and I pulled the bright red sword of oaths into the nightmare. The alpha's eyes locked onto the blade. "You recognize this?"

Kuwam nodded. "My sons made an oath with that sword."

"And when they tried to hunt me and my family, I killed them," I finished.

Kuwam snarled. "I could fight you here!"

I roared, giving my best impression of a lion. The fact that I was in the dream world helped me amplify the effect. The lush fields burned around us, turning to gray, dull ash in a matter of seconds. Many of the harbinger wolves perished in the fires, leaving only the alpha, me, and the pups. All of the younglings, except the one I held, gathered around the alpha's feet.

"I think you will find that a quick battle, and you will not be the victor," I said.

"What are your options?" Kuwam asked.

"The first is to take this sword and make a blood oath that you and your descendants will never come to my world again. You will not haunt the dreams of my world. You will not sneak into my world. You will not harm another person on my world."

"No, such an oath is too much!" Kuwam said.

I tossed the red sword toward him. It spun gracefully and stuck in the dirt before him.

"The second option is that I visit your world every night. I will stalk your pups in the shadows. I will slay your females in the night. I will cut down your warriors in their nightmares, and I will start with you, right here, and right now."

"No," Kuwam said. "You are not like us. You are a human. You wouldn't wage such a war. No dream walker has ever been so heartless."

I smiled and let the dangling pup go. My sword appeared in my hand once more. I took in a breath and blew the pups far, far away. I guess even knowing they aren't real I couldn't bring myself to hurt the young, but now there was only me and the alpha. This I could easily do.

"Your sons attacked my family. They scared them. They tried to kill them. You think I am too soft to do what I have said, but you misjudge. I know that the only way to beat monsters like you is to become as depraved and mad as you are. Trust me, if you doubt my resolve, then you should forget about the fact that I am a dream walker, and just remember that I am a husband, and a father. You could not fathom what I will do to keep my family safe from ever seeing your kind. You have plagued me since I was four years old. Now, it is I who will scourge you. Your reign of terror is over. Now choose, will you make the oath, or do I cut you all down like the miserable mongrels you are?"

Kuwam's hand trembled. He reached out for his red sword and picked it up. For a moment, I thought he was set on fighting, but at last he knelt on the ground and bowed his head.

"So long as you let us live, I will make the oath, dream walker."

I nodded. "So long as you make the oath, you have my word that I will not attack your people, but if any of you come to my world again, I will come back to exact my vengeance."

Kuwam snarled and then nodded. "I make an oath: Upon my sword I swear that neither I, nor any of my kin, nor any of my subjects, shall come to your world, either in dreams, or through the portals. I swear to uphold the peace, upon my life, and that of all my kin."

I smiled and then left the dream, turning and walking away as easily as if there were a door between that place and my room back in Washington.

When I opened my physical eyes, the red sword was gone.

I walked to meet Indyrith in the main hall.

"It's done," I said. "Drendarin's instructions worked."

"Well, that should make Rolf's job a bit easier," Indyrith replied with a bow of his head. "You have become quite powerful, Joshua Mills."

"Well, the better to help the little people with, am I right?"

Indyrith nodded. "What will you do now?"

I smiled and patted an envelope that was in my pants pocket. "Actually, I thought I might take a flight."

"When will you come back?" Indyrith asked.

"Soon, I think. There's just something I need to do."

*****

I took a flight from Sea-Tac airport to Salt Lake International the next day. I rented a car and drove to my mother-in-law's house. I found Susan and Tommy playing in the front yard, splashing in a small plastic pool. I stopped at the edge of the driveway and just watched them for a few moments. Her smile was the most beautiful thing I had seen in so long, I almost turned around to run away, but the longer I watched, the more it felt right. I exited the car and started walking toward them.

"Daddy!" Tommy shouted. He wiggled away from his mother and did his funny little toddler run through the grass. I picked him up and squished him in a big hug as water drenched the front of me from his swimsuit. His little hands grabbed each of my cheeks and pulled my head to the side so he could give me a big, smacking kiss on the cheek.

"I love you, little man," I said.

"I'm not a man!" Tommy said. "I'm a boy!"

I smiled wider, just happy to be holding him once again.

"Hello Josh," Susan said as she walked up to me. She was standing there with her arms folded across her chest. Her face was a mix of emotions that I couldn't quite read. "It's been weeks since they let you out, and I haven't heard from you at all."

"I tried to call," I said. "Did Jill tell you?"

"No." Susan said flatly.

"I've missed you," I said. Tears filled her eyes and her arms opened up. We each took a step forward and grabbed each other in a tight embrace. "I love you, Suzie."

"I love you too, Josh," she said. She then pushed me away gently and wiped tears from her eyes. "Look, I know we both thought it was best to divorce while you were on trial..."

My heart skipped and I smiled wide. Finally, I was about to win my family back.

She shook her head and folded her arms again. She looked down at Tommy. "Go back in the pool, we'll be right there," she said.

"Okay mommy," Tommy said as he toddled away. "Watch me jump!"

"Okay," she said. We watched as Tommy flopped into the pool and splashed a good amount of water out.

"He's so beautiful," I said. "Like his mother."

"Josh, I still think we need time apart."

What?

"I thought that if they released you, we could make things work, but it's been hard for me here. People still talk…"

"Let them talk," I said. "I didn't do anything wrong. You know me, Suzie. I didn't hurt my dad. I mean, as a kid I would have loved to slug the punk across the face, but I didn't touch him. We went to dinner, we left, and we got jumped in the alleyway, that's all."

"I know," she said.

"Then what is it?"

"It isn't about me, and it isn't even you," she said. "It's Tommy. How will people treat him if we get back together? How will kids at school treat him? How will future employers treat the son of a man accused of murdering his own father?"

"Screw 'em," I said quickly. "Let's go somewhere else. We can move."

"It was national news," Susan said. "Where will we go so that someone doesn't recognize you?"

I looked at Tommy and sighed. My hopes were crushed. "So, what are you saying exactly?"

"I'm just saying that I need more time. Let me see how things go here. His grandma is here, so are his aunts and uncles. I don't want Tommy to lose all of them while we go in hiding."

"I…" I didn't know what to say. "If you change your mind, I will always wait for you, Suzie."

Susan wiped tears from her eyes and nodded. "Look, don't worry about alimony or anything. I know it will be hard for you to find work now. We'll be all right. Send extra if you have it, but don't stretch." I stepped in and kissed her long and hard. She returned the kiss and wrapped her hands around my neck. As I stepped back, I gave her one more soft kiss and then reached into my pocket.

"Actually, I found good work," I said. I handed her the envelope. "How about, we just agree to wait six months. I'll call you then, and we'll see how things are."

"Okay," Susan said.

"I'm only a phone call away though. From now on, if you or Tommy need anything, I'll come running." I pointed to the envelope. "That should cover things from the time I left for Dallas up until now. I'll be sending checks regularly too. Even if in six months you think it's still too hard to make it work, I'll always be there for you both. No matter what. I love you."

"I love you too, Josh."

I turned and left then. Got back in the car and drove away. I was on my way to the airport, but then I saw Carter's BMW parked outside the local gym and I had to stop.

I should have known better than to book my ticket for a Tuesday.

Anyway, I parked next to his car. I couldn't help myself. I keyed the crap out of it, and I let the air out of his tires. If I had stopped there, I probably would have gotten away with it all, and then I wouldn't be sitting here writing this really, really long statement, but, I didn't stop there. I took off my shoes and wadded up my socks and stuffed them up the tailpipe. Carter came out, saw me messing with his car, and started shouting and cursing at me. I stood up and he ran back into the gym, pulling out his phone on the way inside.

A patrol car just happened to be across the street at the gas station, so there wasn't any time for me to get out of there. That's it. That's the truth, the whole truth. So help me God.

CHAPTER 22

I sit back in the uncomfortable chair and watch as the older detective reads through my statement. He laughs at several points, and mumbles as he shows other parts to his partner. I'll give him credit for reading several pages before slapping the papers down on the table and rubbing the sides of his nose.

"You expect me to believe any of this garbage?" he asks.

I shrug and wiggle my wrists in the cuffs. "I'll make a deal with you," I begin. "I can visit you in your dreams tonight if you doubt me. You see me in your dreams, you let me go, no questions asked."

"This is ridiculous," the shaggy haired partner says. "He's just trying to go for the insanity angle this time. He knows if he's caught harassing his ex-wife's boyfriend that we'll be all over him. I'm not playing his game."

"Carter is not her boyfriend," I say. "If you had read the whole statement, you would have seen that they had a whole discussion about that."

"Oh why me?" the gray haired detective asks. "It's Tuesday, why do we have to catch the weird ones on Tuesday?"

"See?!" I say excitedly. "Tuesdays suck!"

"No!" the shaggy-haired detective says as he slaps the table. "Your story sucks. I get it, you're pissed cause your wife left you after you murdered your dad and you want to scare off her boyfriend, but you can't do stuff like this. Jill already called us too, that's why the patrol car was so close. It's not like the officer was at the gas station or something."

"Actually…" I start to refute him, but then decide not to bother.

"So what happens now?" the senior detective asks. "Some big agent in a dark suit named Briggs comes in and tells us to let you go, is that it?"

I shrug.

"I'll give him five minutes," the shaggy-haired detective says.

"Five minutes, and then I'm locking your sorry, pathetic carcass in a cell, and I'm gonna throw away the key. We have enough to hold you for—"

The door opens and a uniformed officer leans in. "Sorry to interrupt," he says.

"What is it, Davis?" the shaggy-haired detective asks.

"I've got a couple of federal agents out here and they say that…"

"That'll do," a familiar voice calls out. Briggs walks in with his dark, off-the-rack suit and smiles. "Hello, Mills, nice to see you again."

"Who in the heck are you?" the senior detective demands.

"The name's Briggs." He reaches into his jacket and pulls a badge out for the others to see.

A second agent walks in and pulls his badge as well. "Why are you holding this man?" he demands.

"Well he…"

Briggs doesn't bother waiting for the explanation. He slaps a paper into the shaggy-haired detective's chest. "You'll see that is signed by the governor."

"I'll get this verified," the shaggy-haired detective says.

Briggs shrugs and frowns. "Sure, be my guest." He reaches out and unlocks my cuffs while the detectives both step out and pull out a cell phone.

"Sorry," I whisper.

Briggs sniggers and shakes his head. "Don't think I'm gonna do this every time you get into trouble."

"So why you doing it now?" I ask.

Briggs reaches into his pocket and pulls out a bullet with two red marks on it. "I failed a family once. If I can, I'll try to help you get yours back, but you can't go running around keying cars. Got it?"

I smile wide and nod. "Won't happen again," I promise.

"And, just so you know, Flint told me about you cold-cocking this Carter guy on the cruise ship. No more of that either. Just because he can't remember doesn't make it okay."

"This coming from the guy who was going to shoot me in a motel room?"

Briggs looks up and winks as he slaps me on the cheek just a bit harder than a playful pat should have been. "That was different."

The detectives come back into the room with sullen looks on their faces.

"The paper is valid," they say in unison.

"Nice doing business with you boys." Briggs gestures to the other agent. "Johnson, can you escort Mr. Mills to the car? I need to speak with these two for a few minutes."

Johnson nods.

I hurry and exit the cell. After a few steps, I look back over my shoulder as the door to the room closes. "He's gonna wipe their memories, isn't he?" I ask.

Johnson chuckles and shakes his head. "No, just a gag order this time. They didn't see enough to warrant the expense of a memory wipe."

"Well, if you change your mind," I begin, "I happen to know an elf who's really good at it. He'll probably do it for free."

About the Author

Sam is the author of several fantasy series, including The Haymaker Adventures, The Dragon's Champion, The Sorceress of Aspenwood, and the Netherworld Gate trilogy as well as other stand-alone novels. He enjoys competing in powerlifting meets, collecting swords, and spending as much time as he can wrestling with his sons and cuddling with his wife.

You can follow Sam on his blog, Twitter, or Facebook accounts:
Blog: www.Talesfromterramyr.com
Twitter @Author_SamFerg
Facebook: https://www.facebook.com/TalesfromTerramyr/
Amazon Author Page: https://www.amazon.com/Sam-Ferguson/e/B00FO68DH2/ref=sr_tc_2_0?qid=1503105308&sr=1-2-ent